THE LOVER OF THE GRAVE

THE LOVER
OF THE GRAVE

Andrew Taylor

St. Martin's Press ♨ New York

Library of Congress Cataloging-in-Publication Data

Taylor, Andrew.
    The lover of the grave / Andrew Taylor.
        p.   cm.
    ISBN 0-312-15573-5
    I. Title.
PR6070.A79L68   1997
823'.914—dc21   97-12328
                                            CIP

First published in Great Britain by Hodder & Stoughton,
a division of Hodder Headline PLC

First U.S. Edition: August 1997

10 9 8 7 6 5 4 3 2 1

For A.J.T.

AUTHOR'S NOTE

The title comes from poem xvi in *A Shropshire Lad* by A. E. Housman. All chapter epigraphs are taken, with permission, from the *Lydmouth Gazette*.

THE PRINCIPAL CHARACTERS

JILL FRANCIS – a journalist on the *Lydmouth Gazette*
RICHARD THORNHILL – Detective Inspector
EDITH THORNHILL – his wife; DAVID and ELIZABETH their children
BRIAN KIRBY – Detective Sergeant
P. C. PORTER –Lydmouth Division, Uniform Branch
CHARLOTTE WEMYSS-BROWN – owner of the *Lydmouth Gazette*
MARY SUTTON – detective novelist; wife of the vicar of St John's
FRINTON – manager of the Bull Hotel
MR QUALE – factotum at the Bull Hotel
JOAN DAVIES – a chambermaid at the Bull Hotel
MR and MRS WEALD – guests at the Bull Hotel
LAWRENCE JORDAN – an actor
BERNARD SANDLEIGH – Headmaster of Ashbridge School
VERA SANDLEIGH – his wife
DOROTHY, JUNE and PETER SANDLEIGH – their children
WALTON – a sixth former at Ashbridge School
HUBERT PAXFORD – the groundsman at Ashbridge School
NEVILLE ROCKFIELD – a master at Ashbridge School
KATHLEEN ROCKFIELD – his wife
MERVYN CARRICK – a master at Ashbridge School
LES CARRICK – his brother; of Moat Farm
DILYS CARRICK – wife of Les Carrick
UMBERTO NERINI – a farm labourer
FRED SWAYNE – Police Sergeant, of Ashbridge
MEG SWAYNE – his aunt; landlady of the Beaufort Arms, Ashbridge

THE LOVER OF THE GRAVE

ONE

The Hanging Tree of Ashbridge

County Historical Curiosities No 8

The oak, now a hollow ruin of its former self, is believed to be at least four hundred years old. It acquired its sinister sobriquet because at one time the corpses of executed malefactors were hanged in chains from its boughs as a dreadful example to those who might be tempted to stray from the law of the land.

This practice was known locally as 'keeping sheep by moonlight', an expression which may have been confined to parts of the Anglo-Welsh Marches. The *Oxford Dictionary of Proverbs* cites only one other example – a footnote in A. E. Housman's *A Shropshire Lad*.

The *Lydmouth Gazette*, 6th January

1

Richard Thornhill first saw the crocuses on a dark February evening. He was in his little office at police headquarters, packing up to go home and wondering what he would find when he got there. It was bitterly cold despite the fact that the gas fire was on and the window was shut.

He heard a tap on the door and Sergeant Fowles marched in with the bowl of crocuses.

'They're for you, sir.'

'Are you sure?'

'A gentleman left it downstairs. Said you won it.'

Thornhill stared at Fowles, who as usual looked grave and preoccupied, as if playing a pivotal role in the great drama of life – a drama which, but for his efforts, might at any moment tip over into tragedy. A memory stirred. Victor Youlgreave, one of the churchwardens, had buttonholed Thornhill in the library a few weeks earlier and persuaded him to buy five raffle tickets for a draw in aid of the Repairs Appeal at St John's.

'Sixth prize.' Fowles set down the bowl on Thornhill's desk, adjusted it so that it was centrally placed between the corners of the blotter, and backed away. 'There'll be a full list of winners in the *Gazette*. Congratulations, sir.'

The door closed behind the sergeant. Thornhill put on his hat and overcoat and turned off the gas fire. He returned to the desk and stared down at the glazed bowl, which had been painted a shade of white that reminded him of the tiling in public urinals. The crocuses were dark green stakes tipped with purple. They made him think of funerals.

Best take them home for Edith, who liked such things. She might see them as a peace offering. Not that he and Edith were at war, of course. There was no need for olive branches.

He scooped up his briefcase in one hand and lifted the bowl with the other. By the door, he hesitated, realising he would need a third hand to open it. The hesitation was fatal. As he turned to put down the bowl, the phone on his desk began to ring. Again he hesitated, swinging as so often between duty and inclination. As so often, the former won. Too often? He put down the bowl and picked up the handset.

'Call for you, sir.' It was the clerk on the switchboard. 'Wasn't sure if you'd gone.'

'I was just leaving. Can't Sergeant Kirby take it?'

'The caller asked for you personally, sir. Very insistent, she was.'

She? 'Who is it?'

2

'Mrs Wemyss-Brown.'

Disappointment touched him. *Wrong she. Wrong damn everything.* 'And did she say what she wants?'

'I did ask.' The clerk's voice was defensive. 'She said her business was with you.'

The clerk sounded plaintive as well as defensive – typical reactions in those who had dealings with Charlotte Wemyss-Brown. Thornhill was tempted to send a message to the effect that he would telephone her in the morning if Sergeant Kirby could not help. But by doing so he would expose the unfortunate clerk to the rough side of Mrs Wemyss-Brown's tongue. He would also run the risk of offending the lady himself. One thing he had learnt since coming to Lydmouth was that one didn't offend Mrs Wemyss-Brown without good reason.

A moment later she was on the line. 'Inspector Thornhill! Good afternoon!'

He moved the earpiece away from his ear. 'Good evening, Mrs Wemyss-Brown. What can we—'

'The lavatories, Inspector. This simply can't go on. What do you propose to do?'

'I'm sorry, I don't follow you.'

'Surely you have the matter in hand? I had a long discussion about it with your desk sergeant only last week. Not more than ten days ago.'

'Ah. That must be it. No doubt Uniform Branch are dealing with it.'

'Nonsense.'

'I beg your pardon?'

'It's not something for a bobby on a bicycle, Inspector. This is a criminal matter. Criminal damage, certainly. As for the other charges, well, we must leave that to the experts. Harassment? Indecency? There must be something appropriate. But that's a mere detail. The point is, this must stop.'

While she was speaking, Thornhill put down his briefcase and sat down, still in his hat and coat, behind his desk. He drew a notepad towards him.

'Perhaps you'd like to explain?'

'Again?' She inserted a brief silence, heavy with implicit criticism. 'You may not be aware that I am Chairman of the Jubilee Park Committee.' Another pause, short and sour. 'You do know it?'

Thornhill agreed that he did. The park lay at the top of Victoria Road. As Mrs Wemyss-Brown almost certainly knew, the Thornhills' house was at the lower end of the same road.

'There are public conveniences at Jubilee Park,' Mrs Wemyss-Brown went on, her voice slow and patient as if addressing a class of well-intentioned but backward infants. 'For men and for women. They were built by the town council but we still own the land. The maintenance has sometimes been a bone of contention between us.' She lowered her voice. 'The cubicles in the men's section of the convenience back onto the ladies' cubicles. Someone has bored a hole in the partition wall.'

'Easily blocked, I imagine.' Thornhill's stomach rumbled. He looked at his watch. It was a long time since lunch.

'It has been blocked, Mr Thornhill, Inspector. It was done this morning. And afterwards the committee and I paid a visit of inspection. I happened to look upwards.' Charlotte Wemyss-Brown paused once more, this time for dramatic effect. 'I saw holes.'

'In the ceiling?'

'Just so. One over each cubicle. About half an inch in diameter.'

'The block has a pitched roof, hasn't it? But there can't be much room for a loft, surely?'

'The loft is no more than four or five foot high at the ridge. The hatch which gives access to it is above one of the cubicles.'

'Would you need a ladder to get up there?'

'A ladder would certainly make it much easier. But I think a reasonably agile man might manage without if he stood on the lavatory pan, pushed open the hatch and hauled himself up. I stood on the lavatory myself, you know, and I could touch the hatch with my fingertips.'

Thornhill's first reaction was admiration for Mrs Wemyss-Brown's practical intelligence. But admiration was rapidly overwhelmed by a vivid image of the scene in the ladies' lavatory. Charlotte Wemyss-Brown was not a tall woman, but she was large in other directions. As he visualised her plump and sleekly corseted figure standing on tiptoe with arms aloft and fingertips outstretched, he thought of an elephant he had seen in a circus before the war – attired in a short, pink skirt and standing on its hind legs on a barrel.

'Well?' she prompted. 'What do you propose to do?'

'I shall need to discuss it first with my colleagues. In the meantime, if I were you I'd lock the lavatories.'

'We already have. And at least two members of the public have complained.'

'I'll make sure someone examines them tomorrow.' A job for a uniformed officer; a job sure to arouse hilarity.

'If I don't hear from you or another officer by midday tomorrow, I shall telephone you again. This is really quite disgusting, you know. A pervert preying on defenceless women. It would never have happened before the war. I just don't know what this country's coming to.' Mrs Wemyss-Brown was suddenly brisk. 'Give my regards to Mrs Thornhill. Good evening, Mr Thornhill.'

She put down the phone before he could reply, leaving him partly irritated and partly amused. Something would have to be done about the Peeping Tom, of course: Mrs Wemyss-Brown was right – it wasn't a pleasant business. But it wasn't a job for the CID, either, or not yet.

Once more his stomach rumbled. Thornhill picked up his briefcase and, balancing the crocuses on the crook of his arm, turned off the light and left the office. He clattered down the wide stairs to the reception area. He heard footsteps running along the landing above.

'Message for you, sir.'

He looked up. His sergeant, Brian Kirby, was hanging over the banisters.

'I'm trying to go home,' Thornhill complained. 'It's not Mrs Wemyss-Brown again, is it? If it is, I'm gone.'

Kirby grinned down at him. 'It's Mr Frinton. You know? The new manager at the Bull. Wants you to step round and see him right away.'

'Why?'

'He's got a VIP guest who's having problems.'

'Who? And what problems?'

'Didn't want to tell *me*.' Kirby joined him on the stairs and added in a lower voice, 'Mr Frinton's in quite a state, sir. He wanted Mr Williamson, but he's on sick leave of course.' Kirby cleared his throat, stared at the flaking yellow paint of the ceiling and murmured, 'You know Frinton's on the square?'

Thornhill sighed. The prospect of supper receded still further. Superintendent Williamson was a mason, too, and Williamson would not be on sick leave for ever. Thornhill knew nothing else about Frinton, apart from a rumour that he was finding it difficult to drag the Bull Hotel into the second half of the twentieth century. 'All right, Brian. I'll look in before I go home.'

He left the bowl of crocuses in the care of Sergeant Fowles at the desk. When he opened the front door, the cold caught his throat. He tightened the knot of his scarf and fastened the top button of his overcoat with fingers that were suddenly clumsy. He walked cautiously down the steps and along the High Street towards the Bull Hotel. Dirty snow was piled up along the kerbs. One or two cars passed but the street was already empty of passers-by. Thornhill's heels rang on the pavement. There had been no fresh snow during the day, thank God, but the pavement was icy in places and the northeast wind made it feel even colder than it really was. He glanced upwards, trying to see beyond the glow of the streetlamps to the sky above; he sensed rather than saw the thick cloud cover and wondered if there would be more snow tonight. It was February, but the long winter showed no sign of losing its hold.

He turned into the portico of the Bull and went through the double doors to the long hall beyond. Old Quale slid out from behind the reception counter, his eyes bright in his dry, lined face.

'Mr Thornhill, sir. They're waiting for you in Mr Frinton's office. You know where it is?'

Thornhill nodded, unbuttoning his overcoat, grateful for the warmth of the hotel.

The old man sidled closer, bringing Thornhill within range of his distinctive aroma. 'Who'd have thought it, eh?' he muttered. 'I know we get all sorts here, but this is something else.'

Again Thornhill nodded, preferring not to betray ignorance.

'All very hush-hush,' Quale went on. 'But I don't need to tell you that.'

Thornhill went upstairs and tapped on the door of the manager's office. He heard voices within, a wordless mumble. A thin, middle-aged chambermaid scurried past him with her face averted and a small pile of bed linen in her hands. She stopped outside the door further along the landing. As she was unlocking it, the office door opened a few inches, and a large, porcine man slipped through the gap, shutting the door behind him.

'You must be Thornhill. Good man.' He took Thornhill by the elbow in a grip that was almost firm enough to be painful and steered him down the landing, away from both the chambermaid and the stairs. 'I'd better put you in the picture. Something rather delicate has come up.' He nodded towards the office. 'I've got Lawrence Jordan in there, believe it or not.'

'Who?'

Frinton stared at Thornhill, his eyes dull, bulging and brown. 'The film star. Don't you ever go to the flicks?'

'Of course I know him. Know *of* him. It's just—'

'Precisely.' The big face split into a broad, practised smile, revealing a set of sparkling dentures. 'Not the sort of chap

7

you expect to see in Lydmouth. Just turned up out of the blue this afternoon. The thing is, he's travelling incognito – false name, the lot.'

'Why?'

'Apparently he is liable to get mobbed if the ladies find him unprotected. Extraordinary, eh? But it seems that someone *has* found him. He was in his room about an hour ago, lights out, forty winks before dinner. Half-awake, half-asleep. Then someone tried to get in. Room faces the back. Whoever it was must have been standing on the fire escape. Jordan opened his eyes – saw a face pressed against the glass. And then the intruder tried to lift the sash. So Jordan gives a yell, leaps up, still half-asleep, and runs for the door. By the time he got back with Quale and me there was nobody there.'

'Do you think he might have dreamt it?'

'That's not the point, Inspector. It's what Jordan *believes* that counts. And if he talks about it . . . Damn it, quite frankly it's the sort of publicity we can do without. Especially at present. All rather tricky.'

Thornhill frowned. 'It sounds as if you want me to calm him down.'

'In a manner of speaking. Knew I could rely on you. Ray Williamson's mentioned your name. You'd better come and meet Mr Jordan.'

'When's he leaving, sir?'

'He's not sure, unfortunately. He plans to visit friends in the area.'

Frinton led the way back to the office. A man was sitting very close to the fire, nursing a glass of whisky. He leapt to his feet as Thornhill and Frinton came in. Thornhill felt a slight shock as reality meshed with its celluloid image. Lawrence Jordan was taller than Thornhill had expected, a fair-haired man with fine, regular features. His vivid blue eyes could not keep still: they darted from Thornhill to Frinton, from Frinton to the door. He wore a new and beautifully cut sports jacket and twill trousers.

A few drops of whisky had fallen on the trousers but he appeared not to have noticed. Frinton performed the introductions.

'Sorry to be such a nuisance,' Jordan said as he shook Thornhill's hand.

Frinton unleashed his smile. 'That's what the police are here for, Mr Jordan. Now why don't we go across to your room? Then you can show the Inspector exactly what happened, and where.'

'I can't stay there, you know. Out of the question.'

'Don't worry about that, sir,' Frinton said. 'They're getting another room ready for you now. Unless you'd prefer to go elsewhere?'

Jordan shook his head. 'No, I can't face it.'

Frinton took them across the landing to a large bed-sitting room. Jordan had brought a large quantity of gleaming leather luggage in assorted sizes, a porter's nightmare. Prominently stamped on each item were the initials LQJ. The bed had not been turned down but the coverlet was rumpled, as if someone had lain there, and the eiderdown had fallen on the floor. A gas fire was burning, and at the other end of the room a two-bar electric fire was on. Nevertheless Jordan shivered.

Frinton hovered in the doorway. 'I'll make sure they put a couple of hot-water bottles in your new bed when they make it, Mr Jordan. One or two other little jobs . . . I'll leave you to it, eh?' Then he was gone, closing the door behind him.

As if the manager's departure were the signal he had been waiting for, Jordan began to speak in an urgent undertone: 'I'd drawn the curtains but they didn't meet at the bottom. There was a gap of about six inches.'

There was no gap now. Thornhill crossed the room to the window and pulled back one of the curtains. Immediately to his left a fire escape ran diagonally down the side of the building from the upper storeys. Below him was the hotel yard, fitfully illuminated by a handful of lights. Thornhill stared across slate roofs, ghostly in the streetlamps, towards the tower of St John's Church.

'This must seem very stupid to you, Inspector.' Jordan had followed him across the room and was now standing unexpectedly close to him. He swallowed. 'But it can be quite terrifying sometimes. Being famous, I mean. Everyone wants a part of you. Even if they have to tear you apart to get it. Literally.' He turned away. 'I'm sorry. You don't want to hear my problems.'

'When did you arrive, sir?'

'About half-past three. I drove down from town.'

'Who knew you were coming?'

'No one. I didn't know myself until yesterday evening. I live in Los Angeles now. I came back to England last week for a little holiday. See friends, you know, buy one or two things. I was staying at the Savoy, and yesterday town suddenly seemed awfully claustrophobic so I thought, why not just take the car and drive where the fancy took me? See some real country again. Drop in on a few friends.'

'You have friends in Lydmouth, sir?'

'In Ashbridge, actually. Up in the Forest. I thought I'd phone them tomorrow, once I've had time to grow accustomed to being here.'

'Do you mean that even they don't know you're here?'

'That's right.'

'You registered under another name, I understand?'

'Yes – Markham; my mother's name.'

A pretty pointless exercise that had been, Thornhill thought, with all the monogrammed luggage.

'I wore glasses, too.' Jordan fished out a pair of horn-rimmed glasses from his jacket pocket. 'In any case, I rather assumed people would be less likely to recognise me outside London. Still, I suppose someone must have done.'

'Have you been out of the hotel since you arrived?'

'Only to buy a paper and some cigarettes. And I walked down to the river. Needed to stretch my legs.'

'Plenty of time for someone to have seen you.'

Jordan pulled out a gold case and offered Thornhill a cigarette.

'Ironic, really. I asked for a room at the back because I thought it would be quieter.' He shivered and added in a voice that was half-amused, half-puzzled, 'I'd forgotten how bloody uncomfortable provincial hotels can be in this country.'

'Are you sure the intruder actually tried to raise the window?'

Jordan shrugged. 'I was half-asleep. That's what it sounded like to me. I saw the woman's face against the glass. But it was just a blur. There was very little light.'

'You're sure it was a woman?'

'It usually is.' Jordan smiled ruefully, and Thornhill found himself wanting to smile back.

'The other possibility is that it was a common-or-garden thief, sir.'

'What do you advise?'

'That depends, sir.' Thornhill glanced at Jordan's perfect face, wondering what it must be like to be so rich, so well known and so scared.

'We could have a look at the fire escape and the outside of the window. There might be usable fingerprints. We even could send an officer round to keep an eye on you. The trouble is, all that would attract a good deal of attention.'

'A gift for the newspapers.'

'It's up to you, of course.'

'What's the alternative?'

'If you want to stay here, we could go over your new room together – make sure it's secure. You would want to lock your door, of course. The chances are that whoever you saw won't be back. You must have terrified them, leaping up like that. They can't know that you didn't see their face clearly.'

'I hadn't looked at it from that angle.' Jordan tapped ash from his cigarette in the hearth and warmed his hands at the gas fire. 'It's a filthy night. I think I'll take your advice and stay. I do appreciate all this, by the way – it must be a frightful bore. I expect I'm keeping you from something far more important.'

As if on cue, Thornhill's stomach rumbled. He moved towards the door, hoping that his footsteps and perhaps a creaking floorboard would cover the sound. 'That's what we're here for, sir.'

'I don't suppose you'd care for a drink before you go?'

'I'd better not.'

'Not on duty?'

Thornhill smiled but did not disabuse him.

There was a tap on the door. When Thornhill opened it, he found Quale's face a few inches from his own. He wondered how long Quale had been listening.

'Sorry to interrupt, sir, but Mr Frinton sent me up to move Mr—' There was a short but pregnant pause, one of Quale's specialities '—Markham's luggage into his new room. Shall I do it now?'

Jordan had come up behind Thornhill. 'Why not? No time like the present.'

Quale came into the room and picked up two of the cases, which were still fastened. His eyes were everywhere.

'I'm sure you're right, Inspector,' Jordan murmured. 'It's easy to overreact.'

Quale ferried the luggage from Jordan's old room to the new one at the front of the hotel. The sad-faced chambermaid had just finished making up the bed. She glanced at Thornhill in a way that made it clear to him that she knew what he did for a living.

Jordan went straight to the window and looked down at the street below. Thornhill joined him. There was a sheer drop to the pavement. There was also a streetlight within a few yards. Thornhill made a show of checking the locks on the window and the door. Meanwhile Quale distributed the luggage with courtly inefficiency around the room. Jordan tipped him, and Quale bowed himself out.

Soon afterwards, Jordan announced his intention of changing for dinner and going downstairs for a drink in the bar beforehand.

Thornhill took this as a signal that he too could go. Jordan held out his hand and thanked him again.

Thornhill walked slowly down the curving stairs. A plump, dark-haired woman was going up as he was going down. She bowed and smiled, taking him for another guest. Thornhill felt reassured. The thought that almost everyone knew that he was a policeman made him uncomfortable, which was one of the problems associated with living in a town the size of Lydmouth.

Quale was back behind the reception counter. As Thornhill rounded the curve of the stairs, he heard the old man say, 'Good evening, Miss Francis.'

For a brief but humiliating instant, Thornhill was tempted to retreat upstairs until she had gone.

'Good evening, Quale,' he heard Jill say. He couldn't help thinking of her as Jill.

He continued down the stairs, clearing his throat. Quale glanced up and saw him.

'They say we'll have snow tonight, miss,' he said.

Jill looked up. 'Good evening,' she said to Thornhill.

'Good evening.' He was close enough to smell her perfume now. He stared towards the door, knowing that at all costs it was important to avoid looking at her.

Quale leant across the counter. 'Not going far tonight, I hope, sir?'

'No. Goodnight.' He managed to address the last word to the space between Quale and Jill Francis. He walked steadily towards the door, conscious that at least one pair of eyes would be watching him.

'Take care on the ice, sir,' Quale called after him.

It was not until Thornhill was outside, striding along the pavement with his hat pulled low and his hands deep in the pockets of his overcoat, that he wondered what Jill was doing at the Bull on a night like this. He put on speed, hurrying towards police headquarters. He was afraid that if he lingered he might be tempted to turn round.

2

After leaving the Bull Thornhill collected the crocuses and the Austin from police headquarters. He put the flowers on the front passenger seat of the car and drove up to the High Street.

He was glad he had gone to the Bull. A storm in a teacup, of course, but the wasted time was a small price to pay for keeping Frinton, Jordan and Williamson happy. Life was too short, and Lydmouth too small, to make enemies unnecessarily. And he had seen Jill Francis.

As he was thinking of her, a boy appeared from nowhere and ran across the zebra crossing outside Butters, the men's outfitters. Thornhill braked sharply. The car went into a skid — not a serious one, either for the car or the boy, but the temporary loss of control made Thornhill's stomach lurch. Hard braking made the bowl of crocuses tumble onto its side. Fragments of moist earth spilled over the leather. Thornhill swore under his breath. It was as if providence had decided to rap him over the knuckles for thinking of Jill.

It was almost eight-thirty when he reached home. He parked outside the house and cleared up the mess in the car as best he could in the near-darkness; the courtesy light was almost worse than having no light at all. When he let himself into the house, he discovered that he had got earth stains on his new gloves, which were pale grey leather. Nor had the crocuses been improved by their adventure.

The children were still not in bed. He guessed they were with Edith in the kitchen, the warmest room — in fact the only warm room — in the house, because the hot-water boiler threw out constant heat. Elizabeth was crying fretfully, the sort of tears for which the only answer is sleep. As Thornhill was hanging up his overcoat, the kitchen door opened and his son launched himself down the hall.

David was in his pyjamas and dressing-gown. He flung himself at Thornhill. 'I want you to do the story, not Mummy.'

'We'll see,' said Thornhill, automatically avoiding commitment. 'Anyway, haven't you already had it?'

'Elizabeth fell over in the playground today,' David said as they went into the kitchen. 'It bleeded and bleeded. She had to have a plaster.'

Elizabeth was sitting on Edith's lap in the Windsor chair by the boiler. Her wails intensified: grief turned to rage, directed at her brother. 'I wanted to tell Daddy. It's not fair. I hate you.'

David began to dance round the table singing 'I don't care' over and over again, in a voice designed to annoy his little sister even further. Thornhill put down the bowl on the table and bent and kissed the two fair heads, Edith's and Elizabeth's.

'Where did you get those?' Edith asked, looking at the crocuses, her forehead wrinkling.

'I won them in a raffle. Something to do with the church. I thought you might like them.'

'We've already got a bowl of crocuses. In the sitting room – haven't you noticed? Anyway, that one looks rather a mess.'

'David, do be quiet,' Thornhill shouted. He turned back to Edith. 'It tipped over.'

'You're very late.'

'I'm sorry. Something came up just at the last moment.'

Edith rocked Elizabeth to and fro, and the child's crying began to diminish in volume and intensity. 'Sylvia rang. Mother's not well.'

'I'm sorry.' Thornhill said again. He had never liked Sylvia, who was Edith's elder sister; their widowed mother lived with her and her husband. 'What is it now?'

'Bronchitis. They're afraid it may turn to pneumonia.'

Thornhill doubted it. His mother-in-law's principal interest in life was the state of her own health; but despite numerous crises it never seemed seriously to worsen.

'I think I'd better go and see her on Sunday,' Edith went on. 'Could you come?'

15

'All being well.' He tried not to sound as unenthusiastic as he felt.

'As long as something else doesn't come up at the last moment.' She sniffed. 'Usually you phone if you're going to be late.'

'I'm sorry.' Thornhill said for the third time. He knew that she would be upset and angry if he told her the truth – that he had simply forgotten – so he changed the subject. 'But as a result I met someone rather interesting.'

'Someone we know?'

'Know of. He's quite a celebrity, actually.'

'Who?'

'Lawrence Jordan.'

For a moment, surprise wiped all expression from her face. '*The* Lawrence Jordan?'

'He's staying at the Bull.'

'I thought he lived in America now. What's he doing in Lydmouth of all places?'

'Visiting friends in the area, I gather.'

'Who is?' David demanded, sensing competition.

'None of your business, David Thornhill. It's long past your bedtime.'

Sometimes Thornhill thought that Edith kept the children up late only in order to avoid having to talk to him. Not tonight, though – Lawrence Jordan had seen to that. She ruthlessly ignored their pleas for another drink, a story, a piece of bread. She brushed their teeth, listened to an abbreviated version of their prayers and packed them off to bed. Afterwards she made Welsh rarebit for Thornhill. While he ate it, she questioned him minutely about what had happened.

'I'm not surprised,' she said when she heard about Jordan's intruder. 'There was a piece in the paper about the New York première of *Broken Night*. He was almost mobbed by a crowd of women when he came out.'

'That was New York.'

'But Lawrence Jordan's Lawrence Jordan wherever he is. When

Broken Night was on at the Rex, there wasn't a dry eye in the place. Do you remember we saw him in *The Dark Sea?* It was during the war, before we were even married. Do you remember? Even you liked that. But what's he really like?'

'I must admit, he seemed very pleasant.'

'You should have taken him up on the drink,' Edith said, her voice almost angry.

Thornhill lined up his knife and fork neatly on the plate and reached for an apple. 'I was already late. I didn't want to be even later.'

'Do you think you might see him again?'

'I hope not.'

'I need to go shopping tomorrow,' Edith murmured, as if to herself, 'I wonder . . .'

'You won't tell anyone? He's trying to remain incognito.'

Edith looked at him. He had the disconcerting impression that she looked through him and saw someone else beyond. 'I won't mention it. But if that man Quale knows that Jordan's here, then he's not going to be incognito for very long. They say he's always feeding stories to the *Gazette.*'

Thornhill stared back at Edith. He too saw someone else. He should have made that connection an hour earlier as he was leaving the Bull Hotel. He had been distracted by his own stupidity, by the antics of his own feelings. Any fool should have realised why Jill Francis had come to the Bull. After all, she was the chief reporter on the *Lydmouth Gazette.*

3

It had been surprisingly easy. Lawrence Jordan did most of the work himself. The glasses had heavy frames which changed the shape of his face. Nevertheless he was instantly recognisable to those who were expecting him and probably to many who were not. That profile was unmistakable.

When he came into the bar, he hesitated in the doorway, his gaze panning round the room. He lingered for an instant on an attractive, well-fleshed woman. She was in her forties, with black hair, probably dyed, and was having a drink with a man whose inattentiveness suggested that he was her husband.

The restless eyes moved on. Most of the other people in the bar were middle-aged men, sitting in twos and threes, studiously avoiding eye contact with anyone they did not know.

Then Jordan saw Jill. She was sitting by herself at a table in the corner. One of the barmen had just brought her a dry Martini. He looked away almost instantly but she sensed that she had caught his interest.

She watched surreptitiously as he settled himself at a table not far from hers and ordered whisky and soda. Despite those ridiculous glasses, he looked almost unbelievably dashing in a dinner jacket. She was glad he had come at last. While she was waiting, she had been thinking about Richard Thornhill and wishing he had not seen her talking to Quale in the hall. It made her feel morally – well, not exactly shabby – merely a little threadbare in places. Not that what she was doing was in any way wrong, of course. She was employing a perfectly legitimate tactic in the course of earning her living.

There was a wariness about Jordan, she thought, a sense that he half-wanted recognition and half-feared it. He had already attracted the attention of the plump woman, who was darting glances at him over the rim of her glass, secure in the knowledge that her husband was deeply involved in the *Lydmouth Gazette*.

Jordan's technique was practised but unsubtle. Jill had just found herself a cigarette and was looking for her matches. He sprang up with a lighter and lit the cigarette with a flourish. In doing so he contrived to jog her drink, spilling a little of it onto the table.

'I'm so sorry.' The famous voice made her think of golden honey dripping from a spoon. 'Stupid of me. Look, you must let me get you another.'

'It's perfectly all right. I—'

'I insist.'

It was too late. The barman clearly knew the identity of this guest and was prepared to cooperate with an enthusiasm which verged on the indecent. He was already weaving his way among the tables towards them, ignoring the signalling hand of the plump woman's husband. Either he expected a Hollywood-size tip or pandering to the whims of the famous was its own reward.

'Always was terribly clumsy.' Jordan leant on the back of a chair, as graceful as a black cat with a white bib.

'A cloth, sir?' said the barman, rising magnificently to the occasion. 'Another dry Martini for madam?'

When the barman brought the drink, his assistant, a swarthy youth with a forest of black hair on the backs of his hands, followed behind and unobtrusively drew out a chair at Jill's table for Jordan.

Meanwhile Jordan was talking to Jill, describing an example of his clumsiness as a child, asking whether Lydmouth Castle, a picture of which hung in the hall outside the bar, was open to the public. The performance was seamless: at no point was there an opportunity for Jill to intervene and make it clear, without crass rudeness, that she did not want to share her table with this man. Not that she would have done, of course, even if the opportunity had presented itself.

When the tip-off from Quale had arrived, her first reaction had been to think that the old man must have made a mistake. People like Lawrence Jordan, however British they sounded, didn't belong in this country any more, let alone in Lydmouth. They inhabited a fairytale world on the other side of the silver screen, a place of excess where virtues and vices grew to huge and often twisted shapes. You no more expected to meet one of them in the flesh than you expected to meet a unicorn.

Jordan talked easily about safe, neutral topics – the weather, the political news, a Christopher Fry play he had recently seen in London. At some point he moved smoothly from the general to

19

the particular, and began delicately to investigate Jill. She knew that he would have already noticed the absence of a wedding ring; he was the sort of man who automatically looks at the third finger of a woman's left hand. Soon she was forced to concede that she lived alone in Lydmouth, and that she was a journalist on the *Gazette*. She saw the alarm in his eyes. Frankness was her best policy.

'Someone telephoned and said you were here.'

'Well, I'm damned.' Jordan leant back in his chair, tapping a cigarette against his cigarette case. 'And I thought I was striking up an acquaintance with *you*.' He smiled at her, and she felt his charm like heat from a stove. 'Serves me right, doesn't it? I'm trying to avoid publicity, actually.'

Jill doubted it. She said, 'We needn't print anything until you've left.'

He removed his glasses and stared at her, squinting through the smoke. 'It's not just me, you see. I wouldn't want to have my friends embarrassed. It's their privacy I'm thinking about.'

'If you did agree to be interviewed, the content would be up to you.'

'You'd let me see it before you print it? And make changes, if I wanted to?'

Jill nodded. It was a concession she was reluctant to make but with luck it would be worth it.

'Then why don't we talk over dinner?' he suggested.

Jill thought of the tin of tomato soup waiting for her at home. 'That would be lovely.'

4

Despite the new manager's attempts to improve matters, dining at the Bull was not one of the great gastronomic pleasures of life. The food still tended to be unimaginative and overcooked.

Like much of the food and many of the diners, the big dining room had seen better days – though not recently; Jill suspected that the decor was fundamentally unchanged since the 1890s. Service was generally slow and inefficient unless Forbin, the head waiter, decided to take a fancy to you, in which case the service was a little faster and much more obsequious.

Jill watched with some amusement as Jordan turned the charm on Forbin, who had evidently been forewarned by Quale and was all too ready to be charmed. The two men explored the dustier recesses of the wine list. Forbin allowed himself to be coaxed into producing a bottle of prewar claret, a Pauillac from Château Croizet-Bages. During the meal Jordan kept refilling Jill's glass. She wondered if he were trying to make her tipsy: if so, he had almost succeeded.

He did most of the talking at first. Jill hardly needed to ask the questions. In its way it was a skilled performance: he managed to create the illusion that he had never talked so fluently and amusingly to anyone before, never told these anecdotes, never made these charmingly self-deprecatory admissions. Jill scribbled hieroglyphics on her shorthand pad. Jordan was doing her a good turn, she knew. He had no need to talk to a journalist on a provincial paper. Yet for her, this interview meant money in the bank. It wouldn't be difficult to sell an interview with Lawrence Jordan. He belonged in Hollywood, London and the South of France. The very fact that he was in Lydmouth would give the material a fresh slant and make it saleable. And this was a time when the extra money would come in very useful.

Jordan had grown up in Surrey. His father, now deceased, he described vaguely as a businessman. Jordan had gone to a minor public school, where, by his own account, he had a completely undistinguished career apart from his performances in the school dramatic society. He left school in 1936 and wheedled his way into a repertory company.

'If you can survive that as an actor, you can survive anything. It's one way to discover if you really have a vocation as an actor.'

With a skill born of good timing and much practice, he told

stories of poky little theatres in soot-stained northern towns, of sparsely attended matinées, where the audience either dozed or jeered. Actors dried up in mid-speech, curtains refused to fall, lights failed, landladies exacted draconian penalties for using the bathroom at proscribed times, and the company was riven by titanic feuds triggered by a missing pot of face-cream or the position of a name in the programme.

'Under-rehearsed, underfed and underpaid – still, we were young. I wouldn't have missed it for worlds.'

Jordan's real break had come with the war. He had been given a small part in a propaganda film about fighter pilots. His career steadily gathered momentum. Towards the end of the war he had a starring role in *The Dark Sea*.

'It changed my life, to be honest. I was enormously lucky.'

'I remember when I saw it,' Jill said. 'Just after D-Day. The audience started cheering at the end.'

It had been one of those films that catch perfectly the mood of the moment. Jordan had played a young naval lieutenant who was in love with an American girl. A subplot involved spies and a submarine flotilla. The film's success in America led to Jordan moving to Hollywood, where he had been ever since. In films like *The Oldest Friend* and *Broken Night* he had played peacetime equivalents of his wartime roles – the sensitive English gentleman, brave, courteous and usually doomed to love not wisely but too well.

Jordan was reluctant to talk about his own romantic history, which was reputed to be varied and colourful. Though he had never married, his name had been linked to those of several actresses and he had figured in one prominent Hollywood divorce case.

When the subject loomed, Jordan adroitly turned the interview on its head and began asking questions about Jill. He soon established that she was not a native of Lydmouth, and that she had worked for many years in London. Part of his charm, Jill decided, was his ability to give the impression that he was genuinely interested in other people's lives. He whistled silently when she told him the name of the magazine where she used to work.

'I thought I knew your name. You used to do those gossip pieces about Westminster, didn't you? What brought you down to this part of the world?'

As he spoke, he offered Jill a cigarette. She accepted, aware that she was smoking too much at present, but also aware that she needed a few seconds to frame her reply. 'I felt like a change, I suppose. The Wemyss-Browns – they own the *Gazette* – they're old friends. They offered me a job. In many ways a good provincial paper is much more fun, too. The work's more varied.'

'All of human life, eh?' He smiled at her, expertly creating that seductive illusion of intimacy. 'Obviously you're a free spirit.' He spoke lightly, but it was easy for Jill to take the words as a compliment – just, she suspected, as he had intended.

They took their coffee into the lounge. Jordan's entry into the room caused a flurry of excitement among the other guests. After one cup, he suggested that they adjourn upstairs, where he had a bottle of exceptionally fine brandy.

'I think I should go home now,' Jill said. 'I have to be up early in the morning.'

'When will you write up the interview?'

'In the afternoon, if I have time.'

'Why not telephone me tomorrow afternoon? I'd like to know how you're getting on. You can leave a message if I'm out.'

His words said one thing, his face said another. *I want to see you again. Soon.*

'I'll just fetch my coat, and I'll see you home.'

'There's no need. It's only a few yards.'

'I insist.'

She smiled at him. 'So do I.' Walking in the darkness with Lawrence Jordan would be fraught with danger and she wasn't sure she could prevent herself from asking him in.

'But I'd *like* to.' He sounded like a spoilt child deprived of an expected and well-deserved treat.

'This isn't London,' Jill said firmly. 'And I wouldn't dream of dragging you out on a night like this just to walk round the corner and back.'

Jordan gave way in the end, leaving Jill with an agreeable sense of power. He was not used to women refusing him. Under the benignly lascivious eyes of Quale, he saw her out of the hotel.

'You will phone, won't you? Promise?'

'I promise,' Jill said, feeling like a character in one of Jordan's films. 'Goodnight, Mr Jordan.' She held out her hand. 'And thank you for dinner.'

'My friends call me Larry. I wish you would.' He retained his grip on her hand, forcing her to linger with him, forcing her to answer.

'Very well.' She tried to keep her voice light and amused. 'Goodnight, Larry.'

'Goodnight, Jill.'

As he spoke he fractionally lowered the pitch of his voice. A deliciously enjoyable shiver ran down her spine. Her body was treacherous.

At last she pulled her hand away and broke away from him. She turned right, facing into the wind, and her eyes began to water. It was a relief when she heard the door close behind her. *Safe now, safe from the perfect profile, the strange blue eyes and the charm like an offensive weapon.*

Cold and vindictive, the wind tried to blow off her hat, to pull apart the collar of her coat, to thrust chilly fingers round her neck. She staggered across the mouth of Bull Lane and continued down the High Street. She was glad there was no one to see her. She suspected that the wine and the weather combined to make her look undignified. At least it wasn't snowing yet. She tried not to think of the warmth of the hotel – and the warmth of the man – behind her. There was something terribly demoralising about sexual attraction. *We are all animals. No wonder Cupid was blind.* She blocked Larry Jordan from her thoughts and in the space he had occupied she suddenly saw the face of another man, Richard Thornhill. She told herself not to be so tiresome. *Too much wine.*

It was then that she heard the footsteps. At first they were regular – six or seven paces; then they faltered and almost immediately stopped. There was nothing odd in hearing footsteps. There was no reason why someone else should not be out late in the evening. But the way the footsteps had faltered and then stopped created an impression of stealth.

Jill glanced back over her shoulder. The street behind her was empty. The streetlights stood like two files of soldiers on either side of a roadway sparkling with frost. Nothing moved.

Someone had turned into Bull Lane? Stopped to light a cigarette? Gone into the public lavatory or the Bull?

She walked on. Just before she turned left into Church Street, she thought she heard the footsteps again. She quickened her pace as she rounded the corner. It was darker here. A car passed slowly down the High Street. As the sound of its engine died away, the footsteps became audible once more: they were moving more quickly than before, out of sight somewhere in the High Street.

A moment later Jill reached the freshly painted door of Church Cottage. She opened her handbag and tried to find her key. Usually she enjoyed this moment, for the experience of having her own front door which she could shut against the world was still sufficiently novel. But now she found herself muttering, 'Where's the bloody key?' At last her gloved fingers closed around it.

The footsteps were louder now. In a moment they would reach the corner of Church Street. Jill was tempted to run on down the street to the vicarage next door and knock up the Suttons. But they might already be in bed. Besides, she would feel such a fool: *I heard footsteps, I was scared. For heaven's sake, I'm a grown woman.*

The key turned in the lock. Jill twisted the door handle and almost fell into her own hall. Immediately she closed the door, shot home both the bolts and turned the key on the inside. She switched on the light and the hall and stairs came to life. She stood there for a moment, leaning against the door and listening for sounds of movement outside and inside her house.

The house was chilly and it smelt of polish and new paint. Jill went into the low kitchen at the back, filled the kettle, lit the gas and put the kettle on to boil. She felt calmer now, able to laugh at her fears. What with one thing and another, it had been an unsettling evening. But now she was safe at home, and safe with her own company.

A noise at the window made her start. She snatched the bread knife from the draining board and glanced across the room. A quivering shape about the size of a rugby ball was visible on the other side of the glass, its form blurring into the darkness behind. For a moment, Jill was convinced that a masked man was kneeling in her garden, his head on a level with the windowsill. Then she realised the truth: it was Alice.

Jill unbolted the back door and the cat sneaked through the gap. While the Suttons were having Church Cottage repaired and redecorated for Jill, Alice had lived at the vicarage. Jill had moved into the cottage ten days earlier and had been secretly piqued by Alice's failure to recognise this was now her home.

The way to Alice's heart lay through her stomach. Jill went into the larder and filled the cat's bowl with scraps from the butcher. Alice followed her and wreathed her soft, elegant body around Jill's ankles, depositing cat hairs on Jill's stockings.

She left Alice in the kitchen, gobbling what was almost certainly her second supper of the evening. In the hall Jill was struck once again by the cool silence of the rest of the house. For an instant she glimpsed the terrifying possibility that there might be someone waiting for her upstairs. She pushed it out of sight.

Humming to herself, to show that she was not frightened and to fill some of the silence with a sound, she went upstairs to take off her hat. The cottage had two bedrooms, both at the front of the house and each with a dormer window looking across the road to the churchyard. Jill went into the larger of the two rooms, switched on the light and opened her wardrobe door. As she took off her hat, she glimpsed herself in the long mirror on the inside of the door. Pale cheeks, pink nose, an unsmiling mouth. *Do I really look like that? What did Larry Jordan think of me?* Even saying the name 'Larry' made her feel a little breathless.

She turned away from the mirror, unwilling to see what it might show her. Her eye was caught by the black rectangle of the window. Suddenly she felt vulnerable, her privacy exposed. She skirted the end of the bed and began to draw the curtains. It was not entirely dark – there was a streetlamp on the corner by the almshouses over the road. But the churchyard was large and full of shadows, including deeper, thicker ones which were not really shadows but yew trees. To her right reared up the black mass of St John's. As far as she could see, the street was empty.

Jill was actually drawing the curtains when it happened. There were two yews near the east end of the church, pools of darkness. A shadow detached itself from the further tree and crossed a few yards that separated it from the nearer one.

With a jerk, she tugged the curtains closed, pulling them so violently that there was a ripping sound as stitches gave way. She went quickly out of the room, turning off both the bedroom light and the landing light. She took a deep breath and opened the door of the other bedroom.

This room, reserved for guests who were yet to come, was still full of packing cases. She crossed the room to the uncurtained window, avoiding the obstacles by the faint light from the streetlamp. At the window she knelt on the floor and peered cautiously outside. Nothing moved in the churchyard. The shadows were still.

Jill waited for a moment. Had she imagined it? Or was it simply someone taking a short cut home? She shivered, as she had when Larry Jordan had said goodbye; but this time there was no pleasure at all in it. She was about to turn away from the window when the first flakes of snow began to drift down from the sky.

TWO

Bad Weather Continues

Motorists making their way into Lydmouth this morning had one of their most hazardous journeys of the winter. Overnight snow and rain led to this morning's dangerous conditions.

At Lydmouth yesterday evening, ice on the River Lyd was so strong that it bore the weight of a motor cycle.

Some minor roads are still closed in regions of high ground. There are many reports of lost sheep. The Ashbridge area has been particularly badly hit . . .

The *Lydmouth Gazette*, 7th February

1

Bad news travels fast. The phone rang just after seven o'clock on Thursday morning, wrenching Richard Thornhill out of a shamefully erotic dream. Beside him, Edith stirred and then snuggled deeper into the bed.

He clambered out of bed, wincing as icy air touched warm skin, seized his dressing-gown and staggered down the stairs, hoping the bell had not woken the children. It was Brian Kirby.

'Sorry to disturb you, sir, but we've got what sounds like a suicide.'

'Where?'

'A mile or two this side of Ashbridge. Just had a call from Fred Swayne. Apparently the body's hanging from a tree.'

'Who is it?'

'Not sure yet. Swayne's gone over there.'

With one hand, Thornhill tried to cover himself more effectively with the dressing-gown. He knew by the quality of the light on the other side of the curtains, which was brighter than it would normally have been at this time in February, that the promised snow had fallen. 'Who found it?'

'A postman on his way into work.'

'I thought postmen knew everyone.'

'This one's new to the area – Yorkshireman, Swayne says, married a local girl.'

'Is he still there?'

'No. Gone to pieces. Mrs Swayne's feeding him tea and toast.'

Thornhill shivered, yawned and rubbed the sleep from his eyes.

'Just our luck,' Kirby was saying. 'They say the snow's worse in the hills. It would have to be Ashbridge.'

Ashbridge was a large village at the eastern end of Thornhill's division, some ten miles distant from Lydmouth itself.

'Give me twenty minutes.'

At that moment Elizabeth began to call. 'Daddy. Daddy.'

Thornhill went in to her. Only her pink, determined face was visible under the mound of bedclothes. He kissed her and told her to go to her mother.

By the time Kirby rang the front-door bell, Thornhill had washed, shaved and dressed. He had also managed to drink half a cup of tea. Edith was up now, wearing an old army greatcoat over her dressing-gown. When he left, she was in the back kitchen stirring a saucepan of porridge. She did not look up when he kissed her cheek.

'I'll try to let you know when to expect me.'

'All right.'

'Goodbye, then,' Thornhill said, more brusquely than he intended.

He patted her shoulder and went out to Kirby. Victoria Road glowed luminously in the steadily increasing morning light. Sounds were muffled by the snow, which as yet had hardly been disturbed. The wind had dropped and the air felt crisp and cold. The world looked clean and empty, ready for a new beginning. He climbed into the back of the police Wolseley. Kirby, who had been on duty overnight but still managed to look fresh, gave him a quick smile. The driver, a young constable named Porter, let out the clutch and drove down to the junction at the end of Victoria Road.

'Not quite as bad as it looks,' Kirby said. 'Just an inch or two down here. Even up in Ashbridge traffic's moving OK.'

They travelled the length of the High Street, which was just beginning to come to life, and turned right through the Templefields area of town.

'So where's this tree?'

'In the middle of nowhere – beside a lane. The postman has to cycle that way into Ashbridge.'

After the railway station they crossed the frozen river by what the locals had called the New Bridge for the past seventy years. Soon the road began to climb, winding to and fro, higher and higher, following the contours of a steep, wooded hill. To the left there were fewer trees. Sometimes, between leafless branches, Thornhill caught a glimpse of Lydmouth far below, a black-and-white town, shimmering and unearthly.

'One thing I ought to mention, sir.' Kirby fiddled with an unlit cigarette. 'According to Swayne, our friend's trousers were somewhere round his ankles.'

Thornhill raised his eyebrows. 'One of those?'

'Could be. There was one like that when I was up in the Smoke. Middle-aged geezer in a bedsitter in Kilburn. He was starkers, except for three woman's stockings – one for each leg and one round his neck. He'd rigged up this knot that was meant to come apart. Trouble was, it didn't.' Kirby stared at the cigarette from which flakes of tobacco were beginning to fall like a scattering of blond snow. He brushed them off his coat. 'You wouldn't have thought it. Very respectable. A solicitor's clerk or some such.'

Porter took the next bend a little too fast. The rear wheels went into a skid. For an instant, the car was out of control.

'Slow down,' Thornhill snapped. 'We're not in a hurry.'

Or not now, if Kirby was right. He watched the tips of Porter's ears turning pink and noticed how the colour exactly matched the boil developing on the back of the constable's neck, where the stiff collar rubbed against the skin.

'Death by misadventure, of course,' Kirby went on. 'I mean, they tried to hush it up, but what can you do? His landlady found him and she was a gossip. The worst thing was the man's old mother. Eighty-six and sharp as a knife. I was the one who had to tell her.'

That was always the worst part: telling the wife, telling the mother, telling the daughter, even. There was always someone who had to be told.

'I don't know,' Thornhill said. 'You'd think if he wanted to play games, he'd want to play them inside. Especially last night.'

Kirby lit the cigarette at last. Thornhill turned away and stared out of the window. The winding road was still climbing into the hills, between high banks topped with trees. Lydmouth had vanished. Overhead the sky was grey. Leaves and twigs took on strange shapes, tangled, monochromatic sculptures made of frost, snow and ice.

They met few vehicles coming in the other direction. Luckily the surface had been gritted the previous evening. The road had had more than its fair share of accidents, and was always gritted at the first sign of snow or frost. Inside the car it was too warm, and the cigarette smoke was making his eyes smart. Thornhill closed his eyes.

If the man they were going to see had been some sort of sexual pervert, who was he to judge? The imagination could push you in strange directions, especially if your desires weren't being satisfied in more orthodox ways. He thought of Edith, increasingly unresponsive since the birth of Elizabeth, and particularly so since their move to Lydmouth. For an instant, he saw Jill Francis's face, bright and perfect in every detail, on the dark screen of his mind. Outraged with himself, he pushed the image away and glanced guiltily at Kirby, as though his thoughts were visible on his face.

'There was no need for you to come, Brian. You're off duty.'

'I thought I'd see it through, sir.' Kirby fiddled with the crease in his trousers. 'Having taken the call, you see.'

The car slowed. Porter pulled up by the mouth of a lane.

'I don't know what it will be like down there, sir,' he said over his shoulder.

'Try it and see. Slowly.'

The car edged into the lane. Virgin snow stretched away downwards. On either side were high hedges and banked snow. After a few yards Thornhill felt the wheels slipping.

'Stop,' he said. 'How far are we from this tree?'

Porter glanced down at the Ordnance Survey map on the seat beside him. 'Maybe a hundred yards, sir.'

'We'd better walk. You stay with the car.'

If one thing could make this morning drearier than it already was, it would be getting stuck in a snowdrift in the depths of the country. Thornhill waited in the back of the car, a privilege of rank, while Kirby fetched the wellingtons from the boot. He and Kirby changed out of their shoes. Thornhill finished first and stood in the lane, stamping his feet in an attempt to warm them up, and pulling on his gloves. He stared down at the snow, smooth as a freshly laundered sheet.

'How did the postman get to Ashbridge? What route did he take?'

Porter, who was standing by the car, pored over the map, breathing heavily. Kirby leant across him and pointed.

'Looks like there's a sort of track which goes there direct from where the tree is, sir.' Kirby pulled the map away from Porter and thrust it under Thornhill's face. His forefinger stabbed at the map. 'Coming up here and then up the main road would be like doing two sides of a triangle.'

'You wouldn't get a car down there, look,' said Porter, a local man suddenly authoritative with specialised knowledge. 'And in places it's not wide enough for a tractor. But you could ride a bike for some of the way at least, or better still a horse.'

Thornhill nodded, making a mental note that the lad knew the area and might have his uses later. 'We'll take the map with us. Send Dr Bayswater along when he arrives.'

He and Kirby plodded down the lane, their heads bowed, their boots sending up plumes of soft snow. Neither spoke. It was colder up here than down in Lydmouth. On either side of them were hedges, beyond which they glimpsed small, sloping fields – hummocky, studded with rocks and empty of life. It was as if, Thornhill thought, the weather had devastated the landscape like an atom bomb.

They swung round to the left and found themselves walking suddenly down a steep slope. Kirby skidded, almost falling. The lane dropped down to meet at right angles a track running in a groove between the land on either side of it. On the far side of the track and immediately in front of the two men was the outline of an oak, its boughs dark against the sky. After crossing the track, the lane which Thornhill and Kirby had followed from the main road continued down the slope of the hillside.

As they drew nearer, Thornhill realised that the tree was a ruin, its trunk and branches encrusted with holly and ivy. Its roots were on the same level as the track. Its lower branches almost touched the higher ground behind the track. The dead man was hanging from one of these lower branches, his body dangling down into the track. At the base of the tree, on the other side from the body, was a small pond covered with a sheet of ice.

Thornhill glanced to left and to right. In most places the track was a good six feet below the fields and sometimes more.

Overgrown hedges and the branches of overhanging trees had given it protection from the weather, so there was much less snow on its surface than elsewhere. He saw Sergeant Swayne standing in the lee of a hawthorn, a good thirty yards away from the tree. The man was built like a Viking, with coarse yellow hair and a broad, florid face. Thornhill had met him once or twice, but had never worked directly with him. He was smoking, and the top of a thermos flask poked out of the pocket of his greatcoat. The sergeant threw away the cigarette, leaving a blue arc of smoke suspended in the still air, and began to move towards the new arrivals.

Finally Thornhill looked more closely at the body. He knew from experience the importance of first impressions; and he also knew that what he saw now would stay with him, waking and sleeping, for weeks and months afterwards.

The feet of the corpse trailed against the sloping bank immediately behind the oak tree. The man was small and thin, and something in his shape reminded Thornhill powerfully if irrationally of a whippet he had known as a child. He was wearing a sheepskin jacket that came down to his thighs; the jacket was open, revealing a tie with red and black stripes and a tweed jacket. The trousers were bunched down between the knees and the ankles. On the ground lay a flat cap.

There was a powdering of snow on the bare head and on the shoulders. Frost clung to the clothes. The legs were hairy, and appeared more so than they had usually done in life because the cold had made the hairs erect. The body glistened, as though gift-wrapped in aspic. Thornhill forced himself to look upwards: to look at the face.

'Do you know him?' he said to Swayne without removing his eyes from the rigid, distorted mask.

'Local farmer, sir.' Swayne waved his arm, pointing further down the hill. 'Name's Les Carrick. Lives just down there, place called Moat Farm.'

'Any family?'

'Just the wife, Dilys. There's a brother, too, but he doesn't live at the farm. And there's something else, sir. The postman, Mr Bratchley who found the body: he says he saw a man walking across that field.' Swayne pointed towards the field which had been on the left of Thornhill and Kirby as they came down the lane. 'Couldn't see much, he said – big chap, no hat. Wearing a battledress top, he thought.' Swayne hesitated – not to weigh his words, Thornhill guessed, but to create unneeded suspense. 'The thing is, he looked as if he was coming from the crossroads. And, sure enough, when I looked for his footprints in the snow, there they were. Big feet – size eleven, maybe. He'd come up the lane from Moat Farm.' Swayne sucked in air, inflating his chest. 'He must have seen the body, look. So why didn't he raise the alarm?'

'Might he have been going to do that?' Thornhill asked.

'There are several houses he could have gone to easily enough. Anyway, if he was going to raise the alarm, why walk across the field? He could walk a lot more quickly up that track, or if he went up to the main road he'd have been able to hitch a lift.'

Thornhill nodded, accepting the strength of the argument while disliking the sergeant's manner.

Swayne puffed out his cheeks and let his breath out. 'Now obviously Les Carrick's been up there for a good few hours. No trace of *his* tracks or anyone else's. So that means he must have got here before the snow. So we're talking about before one o'clock, at least. I had to get up last night,' Swayne added parenthetically. 'Call of nature. I happened to open the curtains and look outside before I got back into bed. It wasn't snowing then. So, if you ask me—'

'*If* I ask you, Sergeant,' Thornhill said quietly, 'I shall expect clear, concise answers. But there's no need to answer until I ask the questions.'

In the silence, Thornhill turned away. He looked down the lane, at the single set of evenly spaced footprints coming up the hill to the crossroads. He turned to Kirby, who had already pulled the map out of the pocket of his coat.

'Moat Farm, sir,' Kirby said. 'Then it's a mixture of woodland and fields right the way down to the Lyd.'

There was no guarantee, Thornhill thought, that someone else had not used the track rather than the lane. The track's surface was a mixture of mud, stones, rock, frozen slush, ice and a few patches of new snow. Tracing fresh footprints in that mixture would be difficult if not impossible. And of course anyone who had passed by before the snow stopped falling might have left no trace.

'How is the postman taking it?' he asked Swayne.

'Badly. Shocked.' The big sergeant squeezed his lips together as though to prevent more words slipping out.

It was natural enough to be shocked, Thornhill knew. One consequence of another's violent death was to bring home the fragility of all human life.

Swayne said, 'He kept saying he should have listened to his wife.'

'Why?' Kirby said.

'She didn't want him to use this path to Ashbridge. Especially in the dark.'

'How come? Must be much shorter than going up to the main road.'

'Because of the tree, of course.' Swayne looked smugly at Kirby, perhaps glad to have an opportunity to vent his irritation with Thornhill on someone less able to hit back. 'That's not just any old tree, you know. It's the Hanging Tree.'

2

There was nothing for it but to walk. According to the map, Moat Farm was half a mile away on the other side of a belt of trees, a broad, dark smudge against the snow. Thornhill and Kirby tramped down the lane, every step twice as much effort as it usually was. They left Swayne with the body to await the arrival of Dr Bayswater and the scene-of-the-crime officers.

They did not talk. The only sound was the muffled plodding of their footsteps through the snow. Thornhill was chiefly occupied in rehearsing what he would say. 'I'm sorry, madam, there's been an accident.' Whatever formula he used, it would be inadequate and insensitive. And in a case like this there was no shred of comfort, now or later. A man had died, by his own hand, by someone else's, or by accident – and if the latter, perhaps in the act of degrading himself in a manner that also degraded those he left behind. For most of the time people contrived not to notice the grotesque unfairness of life, but a death like Carrick's ripped aside that kindly self-deception and showed the survivors what lay underneath.

In another part of his mind, Thornhill allowed irritation with Swayne to fester. He also noticed how cold his feet were becoming. Finally, he wondered whether Jill Francis had met Lawrence Jordan last night and what she looked like at breakfast.

The lane skirted the belt of trees and brought them round to the farm buildings. The house lay sideways to the road, a two-storey building, one room deep, with a scullery attached at right angles; it was little more than a large cottage. It backed onto a yard whose remaining sides were lined with a sty, a small barn, a cowshed and stabling. The place did not look prosperous, but Thornhill knew enough from his own childhood in the Fens to understand that many farmers did not flaunt their wealth, preferring to store it away in darkness in the bank or under a mattress. He also noticed that the gate to the yard looked dilapidated but it swung open on hinges that had recently been greased.

Before he and Kirby had entered the yard, two border collies sprinted out of the barn, their bellies low to the ground and their ears laid back along their skulls. Thornhill and Kirby prudently retreated, closing the gate behind them. The dogs snarled and barked. The back door of the farmhouse opened with a creak loud enough to be heard above the barking. A woman appeared in the doorway, her hands white with flour up to her wrists. In her right hand she held a large rolling pin.

'Yes? What is it?'

She was in her late twenties or early thirties, sturdily built, with a square face and full lips. The dogs quietened when they heard her voice but took up position between her and the strangers, ready to attack.

'Mrs Carrick?'

'Yes. What do you want?'

'We're police officers. May we come in?'

Her face expressionless, Mrs Carrick came across the yard towards them. She did not open the gate but leant on it, keeping it between her and Thornhill and Kirby. The voice was Welsh, rising and falling.

'What's happened?'

'I'm afraid there's been an accident,' Thornhill heard himself saying.

The hostility vanished from her face, to be replaced by shock. 'What's happened? Who?'

'It's your husband.'

She frowned.

'I'm terribly sorry, Mrs Carrick. I'm afraid he's dead.'

To Thornhill's consternation she threw back her head and laughed, the sound wrenched out of her. Then, before the hysteria had time to take a grip, she stopped and backed away from the gate. 'Are you having me on? Who are you?'

The dogs snarled softly.

'I assure you we're police officers, madam,' said Thornhill, hoping he did not sound as bewildered as he felt. 'There seems to be—'

'Les!' Mrs Carrick shouted, revealing a voice of considerable power. 'Les!'

She turned her back on Thornhill and Kirby and strode towards one of the sheds. Before she reached it, the door slid back and a small man with a dark, unshaven face came out, wiping oily hands on a rag.

'What is it, Dilys? I'm busy.' At that moment he caught sight of Thornhill and Kirby. 'Who are they?'

'Policemen. So they say.'

'Have they come about Bert?'

She seemed not to hear. 'They've just tried to tell me you're dead.'

'Don't be so bloody stupid.' Carrick walked across the yard. He wore wellingtons, corduroys, several jackets and a woollen hat pulled down over his small skull. 'You've got some explaining to do, mister.' He looked a good ten years older than his wife. 'You can start by proving who you are.'

Thornhill took out his wallet and showed his warrant card. Carrick made a show of examining it.

'And how am I to know this isn't forged?'

'You can ask Sergeant Swayne if you like,' Thornhill snapped. 'He's up at the crossroads.' Irritation made him more direct than he would usually have been. 'There's a dead man up there. That's why we're here.'

'You trying to tell me it's Bert?'

'Who?'

'Our wop.'

'He's an Italian who works here,' Dilys explained, edging forwards. 'Umberto Nerini.'

It was a diversion, but a sufficiently promising one for Thornhill to want to pursue it. 'So what's Bert done?'

'It's what he hasn't done that's the problem,' Les said. 'He's just buggered off.'

'Where does he live?'

It was Dilys who answered. 'Here. He's got a room over the stables.' She was standing very still, her arms folded underneath her substantial breasts. 'He was OK last night. His bed's been slept in.'

'Prisoner-of-war, was he? One of the ones that stayed?'

She nodded. 'Bert's all right.'

'Do you know what he might be wearing?'

'Army surplus stuff, probably.' Her eyes were full of alarm. 'Khaki jacket. He's a big bloke, black hair. Listen, it's – it's not him that's dead, is it?'

'I don't think so.' The man the postman had seen walking across the field sounded like Nerini. Thornhill looked at Les. 'Sergeant Swayne identified the body as yours. Any idea why?'

Les's face, sallow to begin with, bleached still further. The aggression vanished. One of the dogs nuzzled his hand.

'You haven't answered my question, Mr Carrick. Why did Sergeant Swayne think the body was yours?'

Les stared at Thornhill. His face was like a sheet of grubby paper through which a bored child had stuck ragged holes for eyes, mouth and nostrils. Suddenly he spun round and ran clumsily towards the barn from which he'd come, with the dogs close behind him.

'Les has got a brother.' Dilys touched her mouth with her fingers, almost as though she were trying to conceal a smile. She turned to follow her husband with her eyes, and Thornhill could no longer see her face. 'He's a schoolmaster up in Ashbridge. They're twins, him and Les. Not quite identical, but still very alike. Les thinks it's Mervyn out there.'

3

Most men hate being made fools of, and those who are professionally obliged to be both right and in the right, such as judges and policemen, hate it more than most. Thornhill was not in the best of moods as he drove up to Ashbridge. It was a reminder that one should take nothing for granted, nothing at all.

To be fair, Swayne's mistake had been natural enough. Les Carrick was on his patch, and Les Carrick lived at a farm a few hundred yards away from the Hanging Tree; and on the Hanging Tree was the body of a man who looked like Les Carrick; after strangulation and a night out with temperatures below zero no one looked quite as they usually did. Still, the original mistake had been Swayne's. Nor had Thornhill liked the sergeant's subsequent attitude: a sulky reluctance to admit that he was in any way to blame.

By now it was mid-morning. The weather was dry and slightly warmer than it had been a few hours earlier. Thornhill was alone in the car with the driver, young Porter. He had left his sergeant in charge of the familiar routine around the Hanging Tree: Kirby could handle that sort of job just as well as himself. They had already managed to bring two Land Rovers and a trailer down to the crossroads. The scene-of-the-crime officers were there; the area had been cordoned off; uniformed men were searching the surrounding fields; Dr Bayswater had done his preliminary examination and the body could now be brought down. Later that day they would have to talk to the postman and to return back to Moat Farm to see Les and Dilys Carrick. But before that Thornhill needed to pay a visit to the place where the dead man had lived and worked.

'Do you know where to find Ashbridge School?' Thornhill asked Porter.

'Oh yes, sir. Everyone knows the school.'

They drove slowly up the winding road. Apart from one bus and two military lorries they met no traffic. Ashbridge was the nearest boarding school to Lydmouth, a minor public school whose activities were reported at what Thornhill considered to be disproportionate length in the *Gazette*.

Ashbridge itself was a sprawling village on the edge of the Forest. In the centre, the road forked on either side of the stump of a mediaeval preaching cross. Porter turned left. A moment later, the Wolseley swung through a pair of open gates into the school drive.

There was a lodge cottage beside the gateway, and on a patch of ground beside it a tall, thin man was washing a large grey car, a prewar Hudson saloon with red leather upholstery. He glanced up, saw the police car and quickly turned back to his work.

'Pull up,' Thornhill said.

He got out of the car and walked a few paces back down the drive. The Hudson was a beautiful vehicle, probably with a 20-horse-power engine to match its size and the weight. It must have been ten or fifteen years old but it looked almost new. The man continued polishing the radiator with a chamois leather. He was wrapped in several layers of clothes, and his bare hands were raw and red with the cold. Not a pleasant job in weather like this, Thornhill thought, or even a very sensible one; it would soon be filthy again.

'Good morning.' Thornhill stopped a few yards away from the car. 'Could you tell me where to find the Headmaster?'

At last the man looked up. Thornhill saw his face and, before he could prevent himself, he took a step backwards. *A face? Half a face? Dear God.*

Its right-hand side was relatively normal – long, bony, covered with raw skin which was pink from exposure to the cold. The eye was pale blue, the white bloodshot, watering in the wind. But on the other side of the long nose was a shambles which bore little resemblance to anything human. There were patches of pink, shiny skin, grafts which had not taken well. The eye socket was concealed by a patch, which had slipped askew, providing a glimpse of the cavity beneath. The ear was puffy and misshapen.

'My name's Inspector Thornhill.'

The man cowered back against the car. *Poor devil: nerves all to pieces.* Thornhill forced himself not to look away from the single eye and the devastation beside it.

'Could you tell me where to find the Headmaster?'

The man pointed up the driveway with the chamois leather. 'On your left, sir, just before the main school.' The voice was local, Lydmouth rather than Forest. 'First door you

43

come to is his house. It's marked. The secretary'll know where he is.'

Thornhill thanked him. The man had already turned back to his work, averting the damaged side of his face. Thornhill went back to the Wolseley.

'Jesus Christ,' said Porter, letting out the clutch with a jerk. 'Sorry, sir.'

They drove up the drive and stopped outside a huddle of buildings, most of which looked as if they had been built towards the end of the last century. They were faced with the local stone, a muddy-pinky colour, and roofed in slate. The architect had obviously hoped that they would look several hundred years older than they were, but his hopes had not been crowned with success. Over the years, additions had sprouted in various directions, some attached to the main block, and others not. The Headmaster's House was a separate wing linked to the largest of the other buildings by a single-storey annexe.

Thornhill climbed the steps into the porch and rang the polished brass doorbell. The door was answered by a uniformed maid. When Thornhill introduced himself and asked for the Headmaster, she conducted him down a long hall, tall, thin and dark, but shiny with polish. Somewhere a clock ticked. Thornhill thought he heard movement overhead and glanced upwards in time to glimpse a flash of pale material on the other side of the banisters; a board creaked on the landing.

The maid tapped on a door at the end and opened it. 'It's the police,' she announced in a breathless voice. 'Inspector Thornhill.' She stood aside to allow him to pass through.

He found himself in a large anteroom, part of the single-storey annexe, with windows overlooking the drive; he could see the bonnet of the Wolseley, against which Porter was leaning, cigarette in hand. At the far end of the room a middle-aged woman in a tweed suit sat behind a desk. An open fire burned in the nearby grate. The woman stood up, came round the desk and moved towards him, her hand twitching as though uncertain whether or not to hold it out to him.

'I'm Mrs Johnson, Inspector, the Headmaster's secretary. How can I help you?'

'I'd like to see the Headmaster.'

'He's teaching, I'm afraid. He will be free in twenty minutes. Would you like to wait?'

'I'm afraid I can't. I'd be grateful if you'd fetch him for me.'

The woman toyed with a silver chain that hung round her neck. 'It really is urgent, then? Usually the Headmaster—'

'Yes, Mrs Johnson, it is urgent.'

She held his gaze for a moment. Her shoulders twitched, a barely perceptible shrug. 'Very well, then. I'll send the typist. May I ask what the call is about?'

'I'd prefer to discuss it with the Headmaster. What's his name?'

Mrs Johnson's eyes widened. Thornhill realised that he had managed to shock her.

'Mr Sandleigh. Mr Bernard Sandleigh.'

'Thank you.'

Mrs Johnson opened one of the doors leading into the anteroom and held a whispered discussion with someone in the room beyond. When Mrs Johnson turned back to Thornhill, she had evidently decided that he deserved to be treated more like a prospective parent than the village bobby. She took his hat and coat and offered him first a chair and then a cigarette.

He stood warming his hands by the fire and allowed the silence between them to lengthen. Like many policemen, Thornhill knew the power of silence. At last Mrs Johnson burst into speech, remarking that the weather was inclement for the time of year. Thornhill agreed and the conversation died. Thornhill kept an eye on the clock on the mantelpiece, as first one minute slipped past and then another.

They heard the Headmaster before they saw him. There were footsteps, fast and firm, on the other side of the half-open door that led to the school. The door swung open. Bernard Sandleigh filled the doorway. He was a big man built like a second-row rugby forward who no longer took much exercise. His black hair was thick, glossy with oil, swept back from a widow's peak. He wore a dark suit with a gown which had slipped over his right shoulder and on that side trailed almost to the ground, like a great crow with a trailing wing.

'Inspector.' He surged towards Thornhill, his hand out-stretched. 'Come into my study. Would you like some coffee?'

The two men shook hands. Thornhill declined the coffee. Sandleigh opened the door to a large room with tall windows looking over snow-covered lawns towards woodland, a broad swathe of dark green speckled with white, sloping down in the direction of the river. On a clear day, Thornhill thought, the view to the west must stretch deep into Wales.

'Take a pew, Inspector.' Sandleigh sat down behind the desk, his back to the windows, and went through the ritual of offering Thornhill another cigarette he didn't want.

'Now, how can I help you?'

'I understand you have a Mr Mervyn Carrick on your staff.'

'That is correct.' Sandleigh's eyes were wary but that was only to be expected. No headmaster wanted his school to attract the attention of the police, especially a school like this one whose continued prosperity depended on a ready supply of fee-paying parents.

'I'm afraid there's been an accident.'

'Oh dear.' Sandleigh leant forward across the desk, placing his hands together as if about to pray. 'I noticed that Carrick wasn't in chapel this morning. Most unlike him.'

Thornhill told him what had happened: merely the bare facts that Mervyn Carrick had been found dead, hanging from a tree near his brother's farm; and that his brother had been notified and had made the preliminary identification of the body.

'But I don't understand,' Sandleigh said. 'What was he doing out there? I saw him here myself yesterday evening.

We were both at a meeting of the Classical Society in the school library.'

'And when did that finish, sir?'

'Let me see.' Sandleigh picked up a pipe and began to play with it. 'A little after ten, I fancy.'

'What happened afterwards?'

'I can only speak for myself, Inspector. I came back here, I wrote one or two letters and had a cup of tea with my wife. We must have gone to bed at about half-past eleven, I suppose.'

'And Mr Carrick? How did he seem yesterday evening?'

Sandleigh considered the question for a moment. 'In his normal good spirits. I remember that he asked one or two questions after the talk. We had quite a lively discussion.'

'And then?'

'I really didn't notice. I imagine he went back to his rooms. Most of our boarding houses are separate establishments in the grounds, you see. Carrick has – had – rooms in Burton's House. He was house tutor there.' Sandleigh added, sensing an explanation was necessary, 'A house tutor is a sort of deputy housemaster, as it were. He's responsible when the housemaster is not there or is off duty. I imagine you will want to talk to Burton. He may have seen Carrick yesterday evening, though it's by no means certain. He and his wife live in a different part of the house, you see.' Frowning, Sandleigh began to fill his pipe from a leather pouch. 'Actually, Carrick was technically on duty after ten o'clock. Mrs Burton isn't well and needs help in the night, so he and Burton came to an arrangement.'

Thornhill glanced surreptitiously at his watch. 'The tree where he was found is a good two miles away. How do you think he might have got there?'

'Carrick didn't drive, you know. I don't think he even had a bicycle. I suppose he could have walked. But as you say, it's a fair step. And he was on duty. Besides, it was the sort of evening when one wants to stay as close to a fire as possible.'

Thornhill changed direction. 'You say that you noticed his absence this morning.'

'Yes – and so had Burton. We thought perhaps he might have overslept. It does happen, you know. Not very often, but sometimes even the best of us fail to set our alarm clock.' Sandleigh smiled in a way that suggested he included himself among the best of us. 'Burton was going to look in on him after chapel. I imagine if you hadn't arrived, I would have had him wanting a word with me later on.' He hesitated, glancing at Thornhill. 'I suppose you can't tell me what actually happened. Was it suicide?'

'I'm afraid it's too early for us to know, sir.'

'I don't want to appear unnecessarily curious, Inspector. But I have to think first and foremost of the good of the school. An unfortunate event like this can have unfortunate repercussions.' Sandleigh put the pipe in his mouth and struck a match. 'Oh dear, yes,' he went on between clenched teeth. 'Most unfortunate.'

'Had Mr Carrick been here long?'

'Since just before the end of the war – before my time, in fact. We came in 'forty-eight.'

'A good teacher?'

'Oh yes – though I dare say he wouldn't have been taken on if it hadn't been for the war – on paper, his qualifications weren't outstanding; a third from one of the Welsh university colleges, I seem to remember. Before he came to us he'd taught at a grammar school in Birmingham.'

'He wasn't called up?'

'There were medical reasons, I believe. A weak heart, perhaps. Something of that nature. I'm sure we can check – it'll be in his file. The thing is, a chap like Carrick showed how misleading qualifications can be, or their lack. He was a first-class man. Very sound teacher, and a fine administrator.' Sandleigh puffed vigorously on his pipe. 'In fact I had decided to promote him.'

A thought occurred to Thornhill, prompted by Swayne's

mistake about identifying the body. 'Do you have a photograph of Mr Carrick, sir?'

'We have school ones, of course.' Sandleigh stood up and walked to the door. He was surprisingly light on his feet for such a big and apparently clumsy man. He opened the door. 'Mrs Johnson? Could you find us a recent photograph of Mr Carrick, please? The larger and clearer the better.' He shut the door and said to Thornhill in a much quieter voice, 'The sooner I tell the school something, the better. In a closed community like this, news tends to travel fast, and so does speculation. I really would be very grateful if you could keep me informed.'

A moment later there was a tap on the door and Mrs Johnson came in with a mounted photograph in her hand.

'This is the most recent one I could find, Headmaster,' she said, holding it out to Sandleigh and avoiding Thornhill's eyes. 'Is there anything else?'

'Not at present, thank you.' Sandleigh waited until the door closed behind her before he gave the photograph to Thornhill. 'The Colts cricket team. It was taken last summer. Carrick coached them.'

Thornhill got up and took the print across to the window where the light was better. The photograph was slightly out of focus and part of Mervyn Carrick's face was in shadow. There was enough to see that he had been small, dark and wiry – very similar to his brother Les – and that he wore glasses with dark, heavy frames.

'May I keep this for a while, sir?'

'By all means. I imagine his brother is the person to ask if you want a larger or more up-to-date photograph.'

Thornhill nodded and moved towards the door. 'I'd like to see Mr Carrick's rooms now, if I may. And also to meet Mr Burton.'

'Easier said than done. I'm afraid the Burtons are in Lydmouth this morning. Mrs Burton is having some tests at the hospital. But I can take you down to the house myself.'

Sandleigh held open the door. He followed Thornhill into the anteroom, where he told Mrs Johnson where they were going.

'Shall I cancel your appointments for the rest of the morning, Headmaster?'

Sandleigh looked at Thornhill and raised his eyebrows. 'What do you think?'

'I shouldn't need to trouble you for too much longer this morning, sir. There may be further questions later.'

'Shall we say an hour?' Sandleigh said to Mrs Johnson. He turned back to Thornhill. 'Would you mind if I tell my wife what's happening on our way? She will have seen your car out there, and she'll be wondering.'

Thornhill and Sandleigh walked down the long, dark hall. They found Mrs Sandleigh writing letters by the fire in what was evidently used as a morning room. She was a slim, fair-haired woman with large grey eyes, slightly bloodshot. Thornhill wondered if she had been the person on the landing when the maid let him into the house. Like her husband, she stooped; it was as if her head were a little too heavy for her neck to carry. There were photographs on the bureau and on the mantelpiece – of the Sandleighs' wedding, of two girls and a boy taken at various ages, singly and together, presumably their children. Sandleigh explained briefly what had happened.

'How terribly sad,' she said in a thin, high voice. 'And won't it cause problems for the school?'

'We'll manage, dear.' Sandleigh patted her shoulder, and she turned her face up to his and simultaneously touched his hand with her own, an unguarded and unforced demonstration of intimacy, of the kind which is taken for granted by both parties.

'Mr Thornhill and I will be at Burton's. I shouldn't be long.'

The two men put on their outdoor clothes and went outside. Thornhill told Porter what was happening. As he was speaking to him, a cream-coloured Rolls-Royce glided up the drive. Thornhill was astonished to see Lawrence Jordan behind the wheel.

Sandleigh, who had been lingering in the porch of his house, pulling on his gloves, muttered something under his breath and came out to meet the visitor. The Rolls stopped beside the police car. Jordan rolled down his window and waved at Thornhill.

'My dear Inspector – what a surprise!'

'For both of us, Mr Jordan.'

'I told you I wanted to visit friends in the area.' He got out of the car and smoothed down the folds of his neat check overcoat. 'But what brings you here?'

'Mr Jordan,' Sandleigh said before Thornhill could answer. 'Good morning.'

'Sandleigh, my dear fellow.' He thrust out his hand. 'How's Vera?'

The Headmaster shook hands with Jordan, saying stiffly, 'I'm afraid you've caught us at rather a difficult time.'

'I *knew* I should have phoned. And I realise it's in the middle of term, not a good time to call on a schoolmaster and his wife. But I thought it would be fun just to turn up.' Jordan hesitated. 'Didn't want anyone to feel they had to make a fuss.'

Sandleigh showed no sign of wanting to do that. 'I wonder if you'd mind if I—'

He broke off as the front door opened again. Both men turned as Mrs Sandleigh came through the porch. She darted across the slushy gravel, slipped her left hand through her husband's arm and held out her other hand to Jordan.

'Larry – what a surprise.'

'A nice one, too, I hope.' Jordan sounded slightly pettish. 'How lovely to see you, Vera.' He took her hand but, instead of shaking it, bent gracefully forward and kissed her cheek. 'Now I know you must both be frantically busy, but you mustn't worry. I'm putting up at the Bull in Lydmouth. You'll hardly know I'm here.'

Thornhill had the odd sensation that Jordan was playing a part – and that the Sandleighs were responding in kind: but if that were true, the three of them were acting out a playlet solely for his benefit, which was clearly absurd.

'You must come in and have some coffee,' Vera said. 'Bernard and Mr Thornhill have something to do. You'll excuse them, won't you?'

'Of course I will.' Jordan glanced from Sandleigh to Thornhill; he raised eyebrows whose perfection probably owed something to the tweezers. 'Though I'm dying of curiosity to know what's happened.'

No one offered immediately to inform him. Sandleigh nodded with stately civility at Jordan, smiled down at his wife, touched Thornhill's arm and moved off down the drive. Almost immediately, he and Thornhill turned into a gravelled path, partly cleared of snow, which led away from the main buildings of the school.

'Burton's House isn't far from the main gate,' Sandleigh explained. 'But it's a much shorter walk than one would think. The drive goes the long way round.'

They passed a white-painted clapboard construction with a veranda at the front, which looked as if it might have strayed from the set of *Gone With the Wind*.

'Our chapel,' Sandleigh said. 'Unusual building, isn't it?'

Behind it were playing fields where rugby posts stood like pairs of alien duellists; in the distance a shuttered cricket pavilion waited for spring.

Sandleigh coughed. 'Now tell me—'

He broke off, and the frown reappeared. The path had just dived into an overgrown shrubbery. In front of them was a gangling youth walking slowly downhill.

'Boy!' Sandleigh shouted. 'Come here.'

The youth stopped and slowly turned. All skin and bone, he was very tall and looked about sixteen or seventeen. His wrists poked out of the cuffs of his jacket. Despite the cold, he was not wearing a coat. His scarf trailed along the ground behind him.

'Walton,' said Sandleigh. 'I expect you'd like to explain to me what you are doing.'

'Yes, sir,' said Walton, examining his scuffed shoes.

'Look at me, boy, not at the ground.'

'Sorry, sir.'

'Straighten your scarf,' Sandleigh commanded. 'This is not an academy for ragamuffins. And why aren't you in class?'

'Mr Rockfield said—'

'I'm sure Mr Rockfield did not tell you to come out without a coat, Walton. Now, what are you doing?'

Walton's eyes flicked towards Thornhill, perhaps to assess the chances of help coming from that direction. 'I don't feel well, sir. Mr Rockfield told me to go back to the house and see Matron.'

'Indeed. Off you go, then.'

Walton's face glazed over with relief. He turned and walked rapidly down the path. The two men followed more slowly. Sandleigh waited until the boy was out of earshot.

'Some of our boys need firm handling, I'm afraid. Now, I was about to say that the news that Carrick has vanished will be all around the school by the end of morning break. And so will the fact that a police car's in the drive and a plainclothes policeman is on the premises. I wish I had something to tell the boys.'

'I'd say simply that Mr Carrick has died unexpectedly.'

'Yes, but how? Oh, I know you can't answer. But it's bound to cause talk.'

'Perhaps your other visitor will serve as a distraction.'

Sandleigh glanced at Thornhill. 'You'd think an actor would have a better sense of timing. Larry Jordan is an old friend of the family. But I understand you've already met him.'

'Very briefly – yesterday evening.'

'He was in Lydmouth?'

'Yes.'

'His arrival must have caused quite a stir.'

Thornhill noted the fact that Jordan's visit was apparently unexpected. 'I gather that Mr Jordan is travelling incognito.'

'Dear me,' Sandleigh said dryly. 'How very romantic.'

Thornhill almost smiled, caught offguard by the glimpse of

the private man behind the Headmaster's mask. 'You say you saw Mr Carrick last night,' he said abruptly.

'That is correct. As I mentioned, it was at the Classical Society meeting. We have one every three or four weeks in the winter months. Sometimes we have a guest speaker, but last night our senior classics master gave us a most interesting talk on the military strategy of the Emperor Augustus. Very good man – Neville Rockfield. Afterwards we had the normal questions from the floor. A discussion developed, as it so often does on these occasions. I'm glad to say it was a thoroughly well-attended meeting.'

'And Mr Carrick – did he take part in this?'

'Yes, indeed. Mr Carrick read history at university, and he has – had – strong views himself on Augustus's military record, which made for a very stimulating end to the evening. I noticed nothing untoward about him either. He seemed much as usual. Ah – here we are.'

Burton's House was a plain, stone building, of much the same vintage as the school, but trying less hard to convey an impression of antiquity. Sandleigh opened a side door and led the way into a tiled corridor.

'The Burtons' quarters are at the other end of the house. Carrick's rooms are here – up in the gods.'

Sandleigh led the way up a flight of stairs, along a short landing past open doors revealing dormitories on either side, and up another flight of stairs. At the top, two doors faced each other across a tiny landing. Both were closed. Sandleigh tapped on the door on the right. When there was no answer, he turned the handle and pushed. The door opened.

'You don't lock your doors around here?'

'Oh no, Inspector. We trust our boys.'

As they advanced into the room, the first thing that struck Thornhill was the smell of a pungent and unpleasant tobacco. He heard Sandleigh sucking in his breath. He looked back at Thornhill, his eyebrows arching in surprise. Thornhill stepped past him and understood why.

They were in a small, square sitting room with a dormer window set in the sloping ceiling. It was very cold. In a sense, the contents were much as Thornhill would have expected to find in the study of a bachelor schoolmaster. Among them were books, exercise books, a cricket bat, photographs, a gown and a mortar board.

The trouble was that Mervyn Carrick's possessions were not arranged as Thornhill would have expected to find them: someone had been there first; someone had flung everything that was movable onto the floor, until the carpet was almost concealed.

Had someone wanted to express their dislike of Carrick in a way that made words unnecessary? Or did this chaos have a purpose behind it? Had someone been looking for something?

THREE

A Woman's Place

Lady Ruispidge gave a most interesting talk to the Ashbridge Women's Institute about her adventurous life. She spent her early years in India, where her father was in the Indian Political Service. Later she travelled extensively with her husband, who was in the Royal Navy. Since Sir Anthony's retirement, the Ruispidges had come back to Lydmouth for good.

In answer to a question, Lady Ruispidge said that in her opinion a woman's place was in the home – wherever that might be. After all, she continued amidst much hilarity, someone had to look after the men and the children, and in her experience men were quite unfitted for the job.

The *Lydmouth Gazette*, 3rd February

1

News travelled fast in Lydmouth. Jill Francis had gone home for lunch – having a home to go to was still a novelty for her. The phone rang as she was eating a sandwich and skimming through the *London Illustrated News*.

'Jill, dear,' Charlotte Wemyss-Brown announced without preamble, her voice booming down the telephone line like a tidal bore roaring down an estuary, 'one of the masters at Ashbridge School has hanged himself. Frightful, isn't it? Sophie Ruispidge told me – Sir Anthony's a governor, of course. Such a bad example to the boys. Still, at least it wasn't actually in Lydmouth.'

'Do you have any details?'

'A man named Carrick. His brother farms near the school. Quite ordinary sort of people, I believe. But you'll never guess where the man did it – the Hanging Tree. Do you remember? I wrote a little piece about it for the *Gazette* last month. An extraordinary development.'

'That's useful,' Jill said. 'It'll give the story an edge.'

'I know you'll make the most of it. Who's our correspondent in Ashbridge?'

'I'll check. Not usually my province.'

Charlotte rang off, leaving Jill to finish her lunch. She knew the identity of the *Gazette*'s Ashbridge correspondent, but Philip Wemyss-Brown had told Jill in confidence and the secret was not hers to reveal. She wished that he were not up in London. Usually, Philip acted as a buffer between Charlotte and the *Gazette*, a role to which he was eminently suited as both husband of the proprietor and editor of the paper.

After lunch, Jill washed up. She was still new enough to domesticity to find pleasure even in the most routine activities; it was as though she were playing house. Alice had disappeared again, so Jill left a saucer of milk outside the back door.

On her way back to the office, she called at the vicarage. Mary Sutton answered the door.

'Come in. Have you time for some coffee?'

Jill slipped into the hall. 'I won't stay. I just wondered if you'd heard the news from Ashbridge?' She saw the hint of alarm in Mary's face. 'Nothing to do with the boys,' she added quickly. 'It's one of the masters. It seems that he's killed himself.'

Mary took her into the kitchen, warmer than the huge drawing room at the back of the house, where Jill relayed what Charlotte had told her. The Suttons' two boys were at Ashbridge, one in the preparatory department and the other in his first year in the senior school. Alec Sutton believed that boarding was good for a boy's character; Mary did not; so they had compromised on a school which was close to home, where it would be possible, at a pinch, for the boys to continue as day boys should the need arise.

'Carrick? Poor man. I wonder what was on his mind.'

'Perhaps there's a letter.'

'I expect we'll hear soon enough. I've a feeling he taught history. I don't think he'd impinged much on Jim's life.' Jim was the Suttons' elder boy.

'Do you know any of the other masters?'

'Not well. The only one we hear much about is Mr Rockfield, the senior classics master. His main qualification seems to be that he's a Cambridge rugger blue and he won lots of medals during the war. The boys adore him.'

'Yes,' Jill said. 'I think I've heard of him.'

Mary raised her eyebrows but said nothing. Jill sensed that the other woman had recognised the lack of enthusiasm in her voice. Fortunately there was a diversion. Alice appeared, insinuating herself in the gap between the kitchen door and the jamb. She mewed piteously, looking from one woman to the other.

'She was on the kitchen windowsill this morning,' Mary said, a little defensively. 'I knew you were at work and I wasn't sure if you'd be back for lunch. I couldn't *not* let her in.'

Jill smiled, knowing that Alice would do as she pleased whatever the humans around her decided. 'I'll leave you to keep each other company. I must go back to the office.'

The *Gazette* was based in a Victorian house at the southern end of the High Street, no more than a few minutes' walk from Church Cottage. The editorial and advertising offices were in the house and the printing works occupied a range of outbuildings behind. When Jill arrived, there was a caller waiting for her in the front office.

'Wanted Mr Wemyss-Brown,' the advertising clerk murmured over the counter to Jill.

She glanced at the caller, a red-headed woman in her late twenties, apparently engrossed in a copy of *Punch*. Most counter callers were an unmitigated nuisance, motivated by a craving to publicise stories which interested no one but themselves or simply by anger about such burning issues as names, generally their own, which had been misspelled. You couldn't ignore them, though, because very occasionally someone who had wandered into the front office had a real story to tell. On the other hand, until this had been established, you didn't allow them to waste the time of the editor or even the senior reporter who was standing in for him.

'She seems to know Mr Wemyss-Brown personally,' the clerk said apologetically. 'Very put out to find him away.'

'All right. I'll see her.'

Jill went over and introduced herself. The woman stood up. She was slender, quietly dressed and with a pale, lightly freckled complexion.

'Sorry to barge in like this without an appointment. But it's important. My name's Kathleen Rockfield. I don't know if Mr Wemyss-Brown has ever mentioned me?'

'Of course. Come upstairs.'

Talk of the devil, Jill thought as she led the way to Philip's room; she was camping in his office while he was in London. She settled Mrs Rockfield in the visitor's chair where she perched with her hat on her head, her gloves on her lap, looking as if she would bolt for cover at the slightest provocation.

Jill sat down behind the desk. 'I expect we would have been contacting you soon, in any case. So your visit's rather well timed.'

'Because of Mervyn Carrick. You've heard?'

Jill nodded. 'Just the bare facts.'

'I was hoping to see Mr Wemyss-Brown.' Mrs Rockfield glanced round the room, as if wondering if she might find him crouching beside the desk or perched on the filing cabinet. 'I've always talked to him before.'

Jill repressed the irritation she felt. Philip had a talent for making people trust him, seemingly without any effort on his part. It was one of the qualities which made him such a good journalist. But it could also make life difficult for those of his colleagues who lacked his Pied Piper qualifications.

Mrs Rockfield looked at her watch. 'It's getting on, isn't it? Perhaps I should come back another day.'

'Why not tell me? We shall need some background information on Mr Carrick, you know.'

'Well, yes, but—'

'Mr Wemyss-Brown has told me how valuable your work is,' Jill said mendaciously, racking her memory for an example. 'We were particularly impressed by your piece on Saturday about Lady Ruispidge's talk.'

The pale skin flushed. 'That woman made me so cross,' Mrs Rockfield said unexpectedly, a trace of an Irish accent appearing. 'A woman's place is in the home – I thought the war had knocked all that rot on its head.'

'But it hasn't, I'm afraid.'

For the last three months, Mrs Rockfield had been the *Gazette*'s Ashbridge correspondent, feeding the *Gazette* with regular snippets of local information. Such material was the staple of the paper's news coverage and the reason why many of its readers bought it.

'We'll give her a try,' Philip had told Jill when the arrangement started. 'She's keen as mustard. But she doesn't want her husband to know. He's a master at Ashbridge School. Apparently he thinks that a working wife would be undignified. Might harm his career.'

Mrs Rockfield made up her mind. 'I haven't got long. This isn't my normal day for Lydmouth, so I need to get back before the end of afternoon school. That means the bus at twenty past two.'

'You could have phoned.'

'I thought it would be better if I could talk to Mr Wemyss-Brown face to face. It's all rather delicate, you see.'

Jill understood, or thought she did: Mrs Rockfield really wanted the reassurance of Philip's bumbling presence, the touch on the shoulder, the warmth of his smile. A telephone call would not have had the same effect. All this suggested not only that finding Jill must be a sad disappointment but also that Mrs Rockfield was seriously worried.

'When will Mr Wemyss-Brown be back?'

'At the beginning of next week.' Jill knew she would have to be quick or Kathleen Rockfield might gather up her gloves and handbag and leave. 'In the meantime he's left me to hold the fort. I know he would feel that it's vital we make the most of this. Are you finding it very difficult? Torn loyalties?'

Mrs Rockfield sighed. 'It's so strange – the atmosphere at school has changed overnight. It's a very small community. Everyone knows everyone else's business. Or if they don't, they want to find out.'

'How long have you been here?'

'About eighteen months. I wish Neville hadn't decided to come. I wanted him to find a job at one of the London day schools.'

Jill decided that it was time to get to the point. 'Is Mr Carrick's death general knowledge?'

'Mr Sandleigh held an emergency staff meeting before lunch, and then told the boys. But everyone knew already, of course. We're to carry on as normal. How on earth do you do that? In any case, it's all so strange. Mrs Burton told me . . .' Mrs Rockfield hesitated.

Jill smiled encouragingly at her. 'Who's she?'

'The wife of one of the housemasters. Mr Sandleigh told her husband that when he and the police inspector went to look at Mr Carrick's things, they found his rooms had been searched. They were in a frightful mess. But if Mr Carrick committed suicide, that doesn't make any sense at all, does it?'

'He might have been looking for something before he died,' Jill suggested. 'Or someone might have heard he was dead, and taken the opportunity to look for something, something quite separate, I mean.'

For the first time Mrs Rockfield looked directly at Jill. She had small, green eyes, rather like boiled sweets; once you noticed the eyes, they pushed the prettiness and the shyness into second and third place. 'But what could they have been looking for?'

'I don't know,' Jill said, clinging to her patience. 'What was Mr Carrick like? Was there any bad feeling between him and anyone else?'

Again the eyes fixed briefly on hers. This is it, Jill thought suddenly, this is why she's here. The eyes dropped away from hers, down to the hands entwined on Mrs Rockfield's lap.

'There's been gossip. I hardly like to mention it.'

This was familiar ground for Jill. 'If you don't, someone else will. And someone we can't rely on, either.'

The implicit compliment had its effect. 'There was a story going round the Women's Institute before Christmas . . . They say there was bad blood between Mervyn Carrick and his brother.'

'The farmer?'

'You know him?'

'No. But go on. What's the brother's name?'

'Les Carrick. He and Mervyn are twins, but not identical, though they are very similar-looking. Were, I mean. Mervyn was the one who went to grammar school and university. But Les just wanted to stay on the farm. And that's what he did. The story was that they'd quarrelled about the money – about the ownership of the farm. That was a few years ago, but more recently it had all flared up again because of Les Carrick's wife.' The green eyes flicked towards Jill, as though Mrs Rockfield wanted to assess the effect her words were having. 'Dilys Carrick is quite a good-looking woman, and there was a rumour – nothing more than that, mind – that she and Mervyn had become rather *too* friendly. Someone saw them meeting near the farm once. All rather clandestine.'

'But it's hard to see how that could have anything to do with someone searching his rooms.'

'I don't know. I suppose one shouldn't speak ill of the dead, but Mervyn Carrick wasn't very well liked. He didn't fit in with the locals any more, because of going to university and working at the school. But he didn't really fit in at school, either. That was partly his fault, you know. He was always needling people, trying to find their weak point. Trying to get a reaction from them.'

'So he wasn't popular?'

'No – though for some reason as far as the Head was concerned, he could do no wrong. But what worries me is, if the police think it wasn't suicide or accident, they might start asking questions at school, and then they might get quite the wrong idea. About – about people.'

Jill guessed the most likely reason for Mrs Rockfield's rapidly increasing incoherence and decided to go directly for it. 'Had he and your husband quarrelled?'

'Well, not to say *quarrelled*. Not really. But when he's arguing, Neville does tend to express himself rather strongly.'

It sounded as if at least one public slanging match had taken place. 'What was the problem between them?' Jill asked. 'Don't think I'm being nosy, but the more we know the better it will be for everyone.'

'There was that silly business about the tobacco. There's a man called Paxford who lives in the lodge, and he grows his own tobacco, and cures it, and sells it very cheaply. It's horrible stuff. The most ghastly smell. But Mervyn Carrick used to buy it. He was always trying to save pennies, I think. And he'd smoke it everywhere, including the staff room. It really did stink the place out. It's one thing in summer when the windows are open all the time, but it got too much in winter. I think Neville was merely voicing what a lot of people were feeling.'

'Surely there's nothing to worry about there? Just one of those silly little arguments that blow up from time to time.'

'But it wasn't just that.'

'There were other . . . arguments?'

'Oh yes. Several, actually. For example, there was a meeting of the Classical Society last night and Mervyn was there. My husband was giving the talk and Neville said that afterwards Carrick was trying to show him up in front of the boys and the Headmaster by asking these silly questions. Trying to be clever. He was that sort of man.'

'I doubt if the police will try to read much into things like that.'

'There's more. Mr Burton is retiring at the end of term – his wife's not very well. And that means his house will become vacant. It's the smallest of the boarding houses, but awfully nice. Neville is the ideal candidate from inside the school – everyone says so, even though this is only our second year at Ashbridge. He works awfully hard, and the boys like him because of his war record. Everyone likes him. Well, almost. But last weekend Carrick said that Sandleigh had promised him the job. But that would have been absurd. I know I'm prejudiced but Neville is the much stronger candidate. Quite apart from anything else, they prefer married housemasters.'

Kathleen Rockfield looked blankly across the desk at Jill. She was not here from a sense of journalistic duty, Jill realised, but because she wanted comfort and advice. Perhaps she also wanted to recruit an ally.

'Would it be a good idea to tell all this to the police?'

'Oh no. I couldn't do that.'

'Why not?'

'Well, I don't see the point. It would just confuse things. All this can't have anything to do with – with what happened to Mr Carrick.'

'We can't know that. I'm sure the police would be discreet.' Jill picked up one of the many pencils which Philip kept ready sharpened on his desk and examined its point. 'Ask for Inspector Thornhill.'

'I couldn't.' Mrs Rockfield bit her lower lip. 'Neville would be furious if it came out. So would the Head. It would mean . . .'

Her voice drifted into a miserable silence. What exactly would it mean, Jill wondered? Schools like Ashbridge were almost like monastic communities, and they tended to close ranks in a crisis. Talking out of turn might mean the destruction of Rockfield's resuscitated hope of taking over Burton's House or even the sack. Or was Mrs Rockfield's fear more personal?

'You could discuss it with your husband first.'

'He'd never agree. I hate to think what would happen if he even found out I was writing for the *Gazette*. Especially for money.' She frowned. 'As far as Neville is concerned, the school comes first. And I couldn't go without his knowing, could I? He would find out.'

For an instant Jill was shocked at this glimpse of what one person in a marriage could do to the other. 'Very well, then,' she said briskly, but still concentrating on her examination of the pencil. 'Would you like me to do it for you? Without mentioning your name, of course.'

'You'd go and see Inspector Thornhill?'

'Oh yes,' Jill said, sketching a policeman's helmet on the virginal surface of Philip's blotter. 'If that's what you would like.'

2

It would have been so easy to use the telephone. At half-past four that afternoon Jill found herself mounting the steps up to the police station. She felt ridiculously nervous – which was, she decided, the reason why she had come in person. The best thing to do with psychological quirks was to confront them. That way you realised how absurd they were, and in most cases they promptly disappeared.

The sergeant on the desk told her that he would see if Inspector Thornhill was available. In the meantime, he asked her to wait. She could see him telephoning but was unable to hear what he was saying. When he returned to tell her that Thornhill would be with her in a moment, Jill did not know whether to be relieved or disappointed.

The moment stretched to five minutes and then to ten. Jill

became annoyed. Quite apart from anything else, it was bad manners to make people wait. Didn't Thornhill realise that she had a job to do?

She heard quick footsteps on the stairs and looked up, knowing they were his. She noted automatically that he was wearing the same suit as yesterday – a heavy, dark blue, double-breasted one which she thought she had seen in Hepworth's window during their New Year sale.

'I'm sorry to keep you waiting, Miss Francis. We'll go in the Conference Room, I think.' He opened a door near the desk and stood back waiting for her to precede him.

She knew the room well – press briefings were usually held there. It was tall and high-ceilinged, filled with scuffed chairs and a large mahogany dining table, scarred with cigarette burns and the circular stains of cups. A portrait of a Victorian chief constable hung over the fireplace. Thornhill offered Jill a chair. He himself sat down several feet away from her.

'I understand you wanted to talk to me.'

'I have some background information on the Carrick case. Hearsay, I'm afraid.' Jill wished he wouldn't look so disapproving.

'Really?'

'The story is that Carrick wasn't popular with some other members of staff.'

'Who told you?'

'I'm afraid I can't tell you that.'

'Why not?'

'Because the person concerned is connected with the school.'

'Fear of reprisals?'

Jill nodded. 'One way or another.' She looked up and caught him staring at her. 'You know what *this* place is like for gossip and back-stabbing,' she said suddenly. 'If Lydmouth can be bad, then somewhere like Ashbridge School must be even worse.'

For an instant his face changed: the eyes narrowed and the lips turned up at the corner. 'I take your point.' Then the official mask dropped back into place. 'You better tell me what else was said.'

Jill rapidly outlined what she had heard from Kathleen Rockfield. Thornhill listened, his face giving nothing away.

'There's one other thing,' she went on. 'I understand that the body was found on a tree near Moat Farm.'

'Yes.'

'Do you know that locals call it the Hanging Tree?'

'We knew some sort of superstition is attached to it, yes.'

'More than that. We printed a piece about it by Mrs Wemyss-Brown last month.'

'Really?'

'The track used to be the old road between Lydmouth and Ashbridge before they cut the new road through. And when people were hanged, they would leave the bodies hanging in chains from the tree. As a warning.'

'I thought there had been suicides there.'

'That came later. There were two or three in the nineteenth century. One of them was a shepherd – he killed himself because his sweetheart married his best friend.'

Thornhill stood up. 'Thank you, Miss Francis.'

'They say you can still hear him weeping.' She stood up and smiled coldly at him. 'But I mustn't keep you from your work.'

He herded her towards the doorway. 'That was most interesting.'

Jill stopped in the hall, infuriated with him. 'Do you have a time for the inquest?'

'Tomorrow morning at nine-thirty.'

'A formality, I imagine?'

Thornhill inclined his head but did not reply. At that moment, Sergeant Kirby approached them from the back of the building. Jill heard him before she saw him because Thornhill was standing between them. Afterwards she realised that Kirby had not seen her, either; he must have thought that Thornhill was talking to the man on the desk.

'We've got him, sir. All we need now is someone who speaks Italian.'

'I do,' Jill said. 'Or at least I used to be able to before the war.'

Simultaneously Thornhill muttered something under his breath and moved. Kirby glanced from him to Jill and apologised for interrupting them.

'Thank you, Miss Francis. But I don't think we need trouble you any further.'

Jill said goodbye, her voice curt, and left them to their search for an Italian speaker whom Thornhill felt he could trust. But she filed away the information for future reference. An Italian-speaker at Lydmouth Station probably meant either a member of the well-established Italian community around Cardiff or a former prisoner-of-war. In either case, there might be a story there. No doubt something would come out at a press briefing or a magistrates' court.

Kirby walked past her and held open the door for her. They exchanged smiles as she passed him. As the door was closing, Jill heard the desk sergeant saying to Thornhill, 'Doctor Bayswater rang, sir. Asked if you could phone him back.'

Jill walked quickly down the High Street towards the office of the *Gazette*. Thornhill was making her life very difficult. Much as she disliked his superior, Superintendent Williamson, he at least enjoyed cooperating with the press in return for a modest helping of personal publicity. It was true that Kathleen Rockfield's information was little more than gossip and probably quite irrelevant. For an instant she glimpsed the dreary possibility that she had manufactured an excuse to go and pester Thornhill.

'Be your age, girl,' she muttered and pushed the idea away. A small boy who was passing stared at her in amazement, probably because she had called herself a girl.

Whatever happened, however, they would need more information about Carrick if they were to make the most of the story. Jill decided that after the inquest in the morning, she would drive up to Ashbridge and try to get people to talk to her, both at the school and at Moat Farm. Fortunately they already had a photograph of the Hanging Tree on file.

As Jill was passing the Bull Hotel, she heard a frantic tapping on glass. She turned. Larry Jordan was at one of the windows of the hotel lounge. He beckoned to her, making signs that they should meet in the hall. She went into the hotel. Quale watched benignly as Jordan joined her.

'You'll join me in a cup of tea, won't you, Jill? I'm drowning my sorrows. It's much more fun with two.'

She allowed herself to be persuaded. Jordan's reception of her was in such marked contrast to Thornhill's. He ushered her into the huge lounge of the hotel, with its faded but comfortable furniture. A log fire burned in the grate. Over the fireplace hung a tall, damp-spotted mirror. Jill caught sight of herself with Lawrence Jordan, and felt a jolt of unreality like an electric shock. *This can't be happening.*

'You've abandoned the glasses?'

'They didn't seem to make any difference. Everyone kept recognising me.'

The room was not crowded but there were more people than there usually were at this time of day. Jill noticed Mrs Thornhill and a friend having tea in one corner. Jordan led Jill to a chair by the fire, gave her a cigarette and ordered a fresh pot and another cup and saucer from the waitress.

'I must say the service isn't bad here,' he said to Jill.

'I don't think that's everyone's experience, Mr Jordan.'

'*Larry*, please. You remember – we agreed, last night.'

'All right. Larry.'

He grinned at her. 'The service isn't for me, you know. It's for Gervase Charlton.' That was the name of the character he had played in *Broken Night*. 'In some ways that makes it worse than bad service.'

'Why do you need to drown your sorrows?'

'It's my car. Or rather it's not mine, it's the studio's. They lent me one to use while I'm here. I went to see some friends today, and on my way back I parked near the station to get some cigarettes. While I was in the shop, I heard the most almighty bang. A lorry had gone into a skid – went straight into the driver's door. It'll take weeks to repair.'

'Will it affect your plans?'

'Not really. It's a bit tedious, though, I'm going to have to get the station taxi to take me up to Ashbridge this evening.'

'Is that where your friends live?' Jill asked innocently.

He glanced at her and smiled, once again creating that dangerous sense of a shared intimacy. 'I expect you're quite interested in Ashbridge today?'

'Am I that transparent?'

He shook his head. 'It's just that I assumed you would be. It's your job. As a matter of fact, I shall be staying up there for a few days. At the school.'

'Who do you know there?'

'The Sandleighs. He's the Headmaster. Of course they're at sixes and sevens at present. But at least that means I can be useful. I think Bernard's quite relieved to have a distraction in the house. I took Vera out to lunch today while Bernard coped with the police. And I'd like to spend some time with the children. I love kids, you know. Bernard and Vera have got three – Dorothy, June and Peter.' He smiled. 'Dorothy must be a young lady now.'

Jill sipped her tea.

'I was hoping to get there by teatime. The trouble is, Quale hasn't managed to get hold of a taxi for me yet, so heaven knows when I'll get there. You'd think that in this day and age a taxi wouldn't be a problem. But in Lydmouth everything seems to stop at half-past four.'

Jill had an agreeable sense that she was being manoeuvred in a direction she wanted to go; she even wondered if Quale really had failed to find Jordan a taxi. 'I could give you a lift if you like.'

'I couldn't possibly put you out. It must be about ten miles.'

'It's no trouble. I have the use of a car at the *Gazette*. I'm afraid it's not quite what you're used to – a little Ford Anglia.'

'Anything with wheels and a heater would do. But I can't ask you to go out there, Jill – it will be a horrible drive in this weather.'

'I gather the roads are clear.' Jill wondered whether she would be safe alone in a car with Larry Jordan. She and her friends used to categorise men according to whether they were or were not safe in taxis. Jordan, she suspected, might be a borderline case.

'That's awfully kind. I'm going to be terribly selfish and say yes. And the least I can do at the other end is introduce you to the Sandleighs and make them give you a cocktail or something.'

A quarter of an hour later, glowing with tea and compliments, Jill returned to the office to read her messages, leave instructions and collect the car. The Ford Anglia was kept in one of the outbuildings behind the office and served as a maid-of-all-work to those employed by the *Gazette*. Afterwards she drove round to the Bull and parked outside the front door.

Quale and the sad-faced chambermaid carried Jordan's luggage across the pavement. Soon they had filled up the boot and the back of the car and had to strap the remaining pieces onto the roof-rack. The little vehicle sagged on its springs.

While they worked, Jordan, dashing in a cashmere overcoat, chatted with Jill in the hall of the hotel. As the car's centre of gravity sank lower and lower, he began to look concerned.

'I don't want to seem ungrateful, but I hope the car can manage the hill.'

'If it doesn't, you can always come back to us, sir,' Quale said. 'Just turn her nose round, look, and roll down.'

Jordan laughed. He tipped both Quale and the chambermaid – generously to judge by their reactions – and took Jill's arm to guide her across the slippery pavement.

At that moment, Richard Thornhill came out of the newsagent's next to the library with a newspaper under his arm. He looked across the road at the Bull, at the Ford Anglia parked at the kerb, and at Jill Francis walking arm in arm with Lawrence Jordan across the pavement. He raised his newspaper in a half-salute, turned right and walked quickly up the High Street towards police headquarters.

Damn, Jill thought, damn and double damn.

3

Laden with Jordan's luggage, the Ford Anglia took the road to Ashbridge at a stately pace that rarely exceeded twenty-five miles an hour. Jill concentrated on the driving. Jordan kept up a steady flow of conversation.

'I'm looking forward to being back in a private house, you know. The trouble with a hotel is that one feels so vulnerable. One never knows when the press aren't going to pop up. Present company excepted, of course. I don't count you as press, Jill.' He leant over to wipe condensation from the inside of the windscreen. His arm brushed hers.

'Excuse me,' Jill said politely, changing gear unnecessarily in order to reclaim the territory he was invading.

'Having me there may do the Sandleighs some good, too,' Jordan went on. 'At least I hope so. It's a sort of vote of confidence, I suppose. When something like this happens, I imagine you soon find out who your friends are.'

'Have you known them long?'

'Since the year dot, almost. Vera's mama was my godmother. I think my mother and hers were neighbours when they were kids. She was very good to me when I was starting out as an actor. Every now and then she'd give me a bed for the weekend and a few square meals.'

Nevertheless it was odd, Jill thought, that someone as publicity conscious as Larry Jordan should be going to Ashbridge School at a time like this. On the other hand, perhaps it wasn't odd at all and Larry was simply a much nicer man than she had assumed.

The real problem could be her own cynicism: she automatically imputed selfish motives to Jordan's actions because he was rich, famous and charming. Since providence had given him so much in other respects, Jill would have preferred him not to be a decent human being as well. Heroes need flaws or else the gap between them and us is too wide.

'You'll have to give me directions,' she said as they reached the outskirts of Ashbridge.

'Left at the green. Just past the pub.'

A moment later they reached the school gates. Jill slowed and swung into the mouth of the drive. At that moment, Larry Jordan was saying, 'Rum places, schools. They always make me feel so glad to be grown up. I think—'

A roaring noise drowned his words. A single headlight stabbed out of the darkness, coming swiftly towards them. Jill pulled the wheel hard to the right. She prayed that she wasn't turning into a stone wall. She screamed one word, 'No!'

Her mind, however, was quite calm — or perhaps frozen in shock. *What a bloody silly way to die.*

FOUR

Thaw on the Way

Weather forecast: thaw tomorrow, moderate west to north-west winds, showers of hail or sleet, and perhaps snow on high ground; sunny intervals. Slight frost inland night and mornings, and a few fog patches especially in industrial areas . . . Further outlook: probably continuing thaw, with showers becoming less frequent in the south.

The *Lydmouth Gazette*, 8th February

1

At five o'clock Thornhill and Kirby left police headquarters in Thornhill's Austin Seven, which Porter had collected from Victoria Road earlier in the afternoon. Umberto Nerini had been left to consider his position in a cell while the county police force searched for an Italian-speaker who was not Jill Francis.

Once again, they took the road to Ashbridge. In the first half-mile, Kirby made two attempts at conversation. When Thornhill snapped at him for the second time, Kirby gave up and sat smoking in silence, staring out at the rapidly darkening countryside.

Thornhill knew that he should be thinking of the interviews ahead, planning his tactics. Instead he thought of what lay immediately behind him, playing back conversations and scenes in his memory – much as he had picked scabs as a child, but without the same satisfaction.

He knew that he had been less than friendly to Jill Francis — that his behaviour had been boorish. What other option had he had? He had taken her into the Conference Room because it was impersonal and he would not have to sit too close to her. In his office, which was the size of a commodious shoe box, they could not have avoided being physically close to each other. As it was, he remembered every word, every look and every silence.

Then there was Edith, her voice chilly when he had phoned her at lunchtime to tell her that he would be late, that he did not even know when he would be back. All she had wanted to discover was whether he had seen Lawrence Jordan that day. It seemed to Thornhill that his wife was more interested in a celluloid hero than she was in himself.

At least celluloid heroes were not so inconsiderate as to expect anything in return. But they were only so reliably undemanding when confined to films. Lawrence Jordan, here in Lydmouth and very much in the flesh, was a very different prospect. Thornhill doubted that he would ever rid himself of the memory of Jill Francis and Lawrence Jordan tripping arm in arm across the pavement from the Bull Hotel, Jill's face turned up towards Jordan's, Jill laughing at some joke Jordan had made. Hadn't Edith said something which implied that Jordan had a reputation as a womaniser?

The silence in the car had become a prison. Thornhill was desperate to break out. He looked at Kirby.

'I'd better let you know what Bayswater had to say,' he said, knowing from experience that work was the safest common ground for them. 'We won't know for certain until the pathologist gets here tomorrow. But it looks as if a second ligature was used round Carrick's neck.'

Kirby's head snapped up. 'So it may not have been the rope that strangled him?'

'No. And before he died, someone hit him on the right side of his head.'

'Did he even die where we found him?'

'It's anyone's guess. There's another point: Carrick wore glasses. According to Sandleigh, he needed them for everything. They haven't turned up. Of course they may still be somewhere around the tree. All the snow isn't helping.'

'Did Dr Bayswater have any ideas about what actually killed him?' Kirby asked.

'He thinks it's possible that Carrick was strangled with his own collar and tie.'

'It still could have been an accident, sir, or even suicide. Just. Say he banged his head and accidentally throttled himself.' Kirby wrinkled his nose. 'Stranger things have happened.'

Thornhill nodded. 'Then someone moved the body. Say it was at the school: they might have wanted to lessen the scandal by getting it off the premises.'

'But what about the trousers?' Kirby sounded aggrieved, as if reluctant to give up the possibility that Carrick's death had occurred while he was suffocating himself as part of a private sexual ritual, an accidental casualty of the pursuit of pleasure. 'They were round his ankles. You can't argue with that.'

'His braces had come adrift. The buttons had been torn off at the back of the trousers. I suppose the most likely thing is when Carrick was moved after death, someone tried to pull him up by the braces and the buttons couldn't stand the strain.'

'If Carrick had been moved after death, someone would have noticed something,' Kirby argued. 'This isn't London. Everyone wants to know what you're up to.'

'Not on a winter night, they don't. Swayne has already talked to a lot of people in the village: if they weren't round the fire they'd gone to bed. No one wanted to poke their nose outside unless they had to.'

'It must have happened at the school,' Kirby said suddenly. 'Someone searched Carrick's rooms.'

'Not necessarily someone from the school. I don't think they bother much about security up there. I doubt if they lock up at night, or only if they remember.'

'So the brother or the sister-in-law might have done it?'

'Or almost anyone else at Ashbridge.' Thornhill rubbed tired eyes. 'Carrick wasn't a stranger. He'd lived around here almost all his life.'

The car turned left into the road that led to Moat Farm. This was no longer impassable. The surface had been especially gritted and was clearer than that of the main road. The car slowed as it neared the junction with the track from Ashbridge, the old road to Lydmouth. No one was there now. Temporary barriers had been erected around the Hanging Tree and its immediate vicinity.

The branches of the dying tree were black against the grey, evening sky. The smaller ones twitched and swayed in the wind. As the car accelerated onto the lane down to Moat Farm, Thornhill glanced back. It was as if the branches were beckoning him.

2

'Can you wait?' Dilys Carrick said. 'He's only just started his tea.'

'Of course.' Thornhill smiled at her. 'We wanted a word with you as well. Just a few questions, nothing to worry about. Perhaps now would be a good time?'

He watched her eyes widen with alarm. But she stepped back into the hall, allowing them into the house.

'I'll tell Les you're here.'

She left the hall, closing the door behind her. The outside lights were on, so Thornhill and Kirby had come round to the front. The hall smelt of damp. The stairs rose into darkness. Thornhill glanced at the nearest picture and was unsurprised to find himself staring at Landseer's *Stag at Bay*. Kirby tapped the dado rail with gloved fingers as though testing its solidity. The walls were dark brown beneath it, and papered with a faded pattern above. The door opened and Dilys rejoined them.

'Is there any news?' She kept her voice low, and her fingers plucked at the edge of her apron. 'We had the vicar here,' she went on without waiting for an answer. 'And Dr Wintle. Les wouldn't see them, though.' Her eyes were restless. 'You don't know how to feel, do you – when something like this happens. I—'

'That's natural,' Thornhill said. 'Are you and Mr Carrick alone here?'

'At present.'

'Sometimes having a friend around can help.'

She shook her head. 'There's no one. Apart from Bert.' Suddenly Dilys was very still, waiting. 'Has he been found yet?'

'Oh yes – I meant to tell you. We found Mr Nerini at Lydmouth station this afternoon.'

She looked up, her cheeks flushing. 'He wouldn't hurt a fly, that man. He probably thought he'd be suspected of killing Mervyn or something.'

'Any reason why he should be?'

Her eyes dropped down again. 'Of course not. But he might have thought he'd get blamed anyway. Him being a former POW and all that. They get blamed for everything.'

'Only if they've done something wrong,' Thornhill said automatically, though he knew as well as she did that in practice there was truth in what she said.

'So what's going to happen to him? Les will need him up here. You need two men for a farm this size.'

'We'll have to see, Mrs Carrick. We need to talk to him properly. Then we can decide what's going to happen.'

She hesitated, visibly considering alternatives. Then she said brightly, 'Here am I keeping you two gentlemen in the cold. What must you be thinking of me? Why don't we go in the lounge?'

'I wonder if we could see Mr Nerini's room while we're here? I think you said he sleeps over the stables?'

Dilys agreed, which was a relief. Thanks to cinema and detective novels, people sometimes made everyone's lives unnecessarily complicated by insisting on a search warrant. She brushed a switch with her hand and led them through another door into what had once been a stable and now housed a tractor. A steep open staircase – the next best thing to a ladder – led up to an opening above their heads.

'There you are. I'll wait here.'

Thornhill climbed the steps, aware of her eyes on him. He found himself in a loft about twenty feet long, lit by a single, unshaded bulb. It was possible to stand up in the middle, but at the sides the roof sloped down to three feet above floor level. The room was cut in two by an enormous tie beam at waist height. The stone walls had been whitewashed. It was very cold – the fireplace in one of the gable walls had been blocked up.

The stairs creaked as Kirby came up behind him. Thornhill ducked under the beam, into the half of the room which Nerini used as his bedroom – presumably because it butted against the house and was therefore slightly warmer.

It was sparsely furnished – a narrow iron bedstead piled high with army-surplus blankets, a kitchen chair without a back, and an old wardrobe. Another blanket did duty as a bedside rug. There was a bowl and jug at the foot of the bed, and a chamberpot beneath it. A wooden crucifix hung on the wall beside the head of the bed. Everything was very clean. Even the ashtray had been emptied into the empty paint tin that served as a wastepaper basket.

Thornhill opened the wardrobe and picked over the few possessions it contained. He found a pile of books – thrillers, mainly, by Peter Cheyney, Edgar Wallace and James Hadley Chase.

'Odd,' Kirby said. 'Usually they've got a few keepsakes, haven't they? Letters, snaps of the bambinos, that sort of thing.'

'Bert hasn't any family left,' Dilys said. 'Their village was bombed.'

Kirby and Thornhill swung round. She had come a few steps up the stairs, and her head floated just above the level of the floor.

'When was he captured?' Thornhill asked.

'Early on, in Libya – 'forty-one, I think. Lost everything, even his uniform.'

Thornhill held up a copy of *No Orchids for Miss Blandish*. 'He reads this sort of stuff?'

'Why shouldn't he?'

'So his English must be pretty good.'

'It should be, after all the time he's been here.'

'At present he seems to have forgotten most of it. That's why we haven't been able to talk properly to him yet. We need an interpreter.'

Her head ducked below the level of the floor. Kirby looked at Thornhill and pursed his mouth in a silent whistle. A moment later the two men went down to the stable, where Dilys was waiting for them.

'He doesn't trust policemen,' she said.

'Playing dumb?' Kirby suggested, examining her with an interest which was not entirely professional.

She shrugged and turned away to lead them back into the house. Once in the hall, she showed them into the lounge. Here she suddenly began to act as if she was their hostess and they were welcome guests. Apologising for the chill, she switched on the electric fire and bustled around the room, turning on lights, drawing curtains, and plumping up the cushions on the chairs.

The room was a surprise – quite unlike what Thornhill had seen of the rest of Moat Farm. Elsewhere there were few signs of the modern world; time might have trickled to a halt in the 1930s. This room, however, was in direct contrast. The sash window had been replaced with an iron-framed casement. The base of the table lamp was a wide-bellied, straw-wrapped bottle which had once held Chianti. There was an upright piano in a streamlined modern case. The chairs and the sofa perched on spindly wooden legs, self-consciously modern. There was a freestanding television in a handsome French-polished cabinet, a Philips model, which had probably cost eighty or ninety pounds. Despite outward appearances, there was money in this farm – either that, or the Carricks were carrying a load of debt.

'Would you like a cup of tea, gentlemen?'

'No, thank you, Mrs Carrick,' Thornhill said.

'Or a glass of something to——?'

The door, which had been standing partly open, creaked. Dilys broke off. Thornhill looked up as her husband slipped into the room, wiping his mouth with a handkerchief. If anything, he looked thinner and paler than before. Thornhill noticed that his wife moved almost imperceptibly away from him as he came in.

'What is it now? Can't you leave us alone?'

'I'm sorry, sir.' Thornhill stood up. 'In any case of sudden death, we have to tie up all the loose ends.'

'He hanged himself. Isn't that clear enough for you?'

'And I thought you'd like to know that the inquest will be at nine-thirty tomorrow. It will be a formality, of course, because the proceedings will have to be adjourned until we've completed our investigation.'

Les grunted.

'Did Mr Mervyn Carrick live here during the school holidays?'

'He used to,' Dilys said. 'Until their dad died.'

Les glanced at her, his dark eyes unreadable, and she closed her mouth.

'He stayed at the school, did he?'

'Sometimes,' Les said. 'Or he'd go away.'

'Do you have any of his things here?' Kirby asked casually. 'Clothes? Personal possessions? You know the sort of thing.'

Les stared at him. 'Maybe. Why?'

'We'd like to have a look through them, sir,' Thornhill said, slipping back into the conversation. 'In a case like this we have to go into all the details.'

'Don't those boxes in the attic belong to Mervyn, dear?' Dilys suggested.

Without acknowledging her, Les nodded at Thornhill. 'He left a lot behind when he went. Had to put it somewhere.'

'I wonder if you could show Sergeant Kirby.'

'Now?'

'Why not? If it's not too inconvenient, that is. Otherwise we'll have to trouble you again tomorrow.'

Les considered this for a moment. He jerked his head towards the door. Kirby followed him out of the room. Thornhill and Dilys listened to their footsteps on the stairs.

Thornhill waited until the two men had passed the first landing and were on the second flight of stairs. 'I'll shut the door, shall I, Mrs Carrick, to keep the heat in?'

She made a wordless sound of assent and sank into one of the armchairs. Thornhill shut the door and sat on the sofa, at the end nearer her chair. She leant forward, resting her elbows on one of the arms of the chair. Thornhill noticed the swell of her breasts and the plumply rounded curve of her forearm. She looked sideways at him and her dark lashes fluttered, though not from coquetry. Then she stared down at her lap, smoothing the skirt of her dress over her thighs. Thornhill found himself trying to visualise those thighs, wondering if they were as neatly rounded as the forearms.

'Who actually owns the farm?' he said with a harshness which was directed mainly at himself.

'Les, I suppose. Or at least he does now. His dad bought it off the Ruispidge Estate just before the war. When he died a couple of years back, he left it equally between Les and Mervyn.'

'So will Mervyn's share come to Les now?'

She looked up, startled. 'How should I know? But you'd think so, wouldn't you? Mervyn wouldn't have left it outside the family if he'd made a will, and Les is all the family he'd got. Except with Mervyn you never quite knew what he was going to do.'

Thornhill glanced around the room, wanting to lighten the atmosphere. 'You've made this very nice. My wife keeps trying to persuade me to buy a television. Do you and Mr Carrick plan to modernise the whole house eventually?'

'It's not him who's doing it,' she said with sudden venom. 'It's me. When we married, Les said I could have a room to do what I wanted with. My room. And it's not his money, either – you needn't think that. It's mine. My dad gives me an allowance.'

'Your father's a local man?'

She shook her head. 'He lives in Abergavenny. He's an auctioneer – that's how I met Les.'

Thornhill stood up and wandered across to the mantelpiece where he pretended to examine one of the ornaments, a piece of purple glass blown into the shape of a small, fantastic horse. He turned towards her and said, 'What about this story that you and Mervyn Carrick were having an affair?'

She flung her head back against the chair as though he had slapped her on the cheek. 'What do you take me for?'

'I'm sorry – we have to ask these things.' He hesitated. 'So there's no truth in it?'

'Who told you, anyway?'

'Even if you weren't having an affair with him,' Thornhill said quietly, as though talking to himself, 'I suppose it's possible that your husband might have thought you were. Don't you think so?'

He had spoken almost at random, automatically exploring the more obvious possibilities. But he knew at once from her expression that this question was one she did not want to answer. 'It really will make it easier for you in the long run if you're frank with me, Mrs Carrick. I'm not taking notes – my sergeant isn't here, and nor's your husband. If what you tell me isn't important to the investigation, I'll simply forget it.'

'All right, then,' she said slowly. 'I've done nothing wrong, mind. But that doesn't always matter, does it?'

'You mean that people will always say there's no smoke without fire?'

'That's the way of it, isn't it?' She held his gaze. 'Especially if you're a woman.'

'And were they saying just that?'

'How did you hear about it, then?'

He leant forward, his hands on his knees. 'I can't tell you. Anyway, it doesn't really matter, does it?'

'If you say so.' She studied his face for a few seconds. 'Listen, Les started courting me just after his ma died. I reckon he wanted a housekeeper and someone to look after the dairy side of the farm. Oh, let's not forget: he knew I'd have a bit of money from my dad. And I married him because I wanted to get away from home, and I thought I could trust a man who was a bit older, and I knew he had a place of his own.'

She paused and dabbed at her forehead with a handkerchief, though the room was not particularly warm. The movement dislodged the sleeve of her blouse, which slid higher up her arm. There was a row of marks on the skin, old, discoloured bruises the size of small plums; damsons, Thornhill thought, and remembered with sudden clarity the damson tree in his parents' garden. Her hand dropped back to her lap.

'Mervyn liked money, too,' she went on. 'That's why he and Les quarrelled, really. You'll have heard all about that, too, I dare say. Mervyn wanted some money out of the farm, sort of regular, like an income. Les said there wasn't any money to spare. Mervyn said that wasn't fair because me and Les had the house to live in.'

'So this all happened after their father died?'

'Yes.' Her mind was still following another train of thought. 'The thing is, they're twins, Les and Mervyn. It's like they're two halves of the same person. Doesn't mean they *like* each other, mind. But they know each other. And Mervyn knew just what would upset Les.' She stopped and swallowed. 'He used to come up here, Mervyn did, walking along the old track from Ashbridge. It's a public right of way, nothing Les could do about that. And once or twice he'd drop in at the farm while

Les was down in Lydmouth. And people saw him, sometimes, he made sure of that. Not just Bert — people from the village, people who matter round here.'

'But it was natural enough he should visit the farm, surely, even since the quarrel? He owned part of it. It was his home. His things were here.'

'He never came when Les was around. Often it was market day. And it was the way he made it seem, especially if someone else was there. Always very nice to me, of course, just like Les was at first. You wouldn't think it to look at them, but they've got a way with them, those Carricks. If they want to, that is. They can switch it on and off, like I can turn that television on and off. Then, one day last September Mervyn drops in while Les was down in Lydmouth. Just before the beginning of term, it was.' She hesitated again, and when she went on Thornhill had the impression that she was choosing her words with care. 'He said that people up in Ashbridge were talking about us, him and me, and that maybe he should tell Les there was nothing in it, and I said, no, it would be like throwing a match in a barrel of gunpowder.' Unconsciously, she caressed the bruises above her elbow. 'So Mervyn said, OK, not to worry. Oh, and did I think I could lend him a fiver until his next pay day? He got paid a proper salary, you see, once a month, and he was running a bit short.' Her voice faded away and she sat staring miserably at the glowing bars of the electric fire.

'And perhaps he wasn't able to pay it back at the end of the month?'

She nodded.

'He asked for another loan instead?'

Another nod. 'A little bit here, a little bit there. Soon he was getting everything my dad gives me. I had to sell a bit of my jewellery to keep up the payments for this stuff.'

'Hire purchase?'

'The telly and the piano and the suite.'

'It adds up.'

She looked straight at Thornhill, her eyes alert and intelligent. 'I didn't kill him, you know. God knows, he had it coming, but I didn't do it.'

'What do you think happened?'

She shrugged heavy, handsome shoulders. 'How do I know?'

3

When Thornhill and Kirby were leaving, Les Carrick mellowed slightly, perhaps from relief at their departure. He took them into the hall and opened the front door.

'At least it's not snowing,' he said.

Thornhill stared up at the starless sky. 'They say the thaw's on its way.'

'Not before time.'

'Been a long winter,' Kirby said, adjusting the set of his hat in the hall mirror. 'Be nice to see a bit of green grass again.'

Les stared blankly at him. Kirby was a Londoner who, despite his best efforts, had not entirely mastered the art of country conversation. 'It'll have its own problems, look,' said the farmer. 'Round here, a big thaw always means a big flood.'

They walked down a narrow path from which the snow had been cleared and reached the gate. Thornhill's car was parked in the lane. Kirby had a small cardboard box under his arm, containing several of Mervyn's school and university photographs, an old address book, and a handful of letters. Thornhill doubted if there was anything useful there. He could usually tell by Kirby's face when the sergeant had found something.

'You've got all you want, do you reckon?' Les asked Kirby.

'Hard to tell at this stage, Mr Carrick.'

On the other side of the house the dogs barked in the yard. A door opened with a creak, and they heard Dilys snarl at them, sounding like a dog herself; and the collies fell silent.

'Old road always floods, given half a chance,' Les went on. 'That's why they had to cut the new one at the top.'

'That's the Ashbridge to Lydmouth road, Mr Carrick?' Thornhill said.

'Aye.'

'You know about the Hanging Tree, I take it?'

Les turned towards him, his face a pale blur. 'Of course I do. I lived here all my life, haven't I?'

'You know the stories?'

'People have to die somewhere. When all's said and done, it's just a tree.'

'They say there are ghosts.'

'My old dad used to say that one of them was a shepherd who used to work on this farm. Killed himself because of a girl, stupid bugger. There was a piece in the paper about it a few weeks back.'

'And did you see any ghosts last night?'

There was a long pause. 'No. I sleep sound. Besides, there aren't any ghosts at Moat Farm.'

Thornhill said goodbye. He climbed into the Austin and started the engine. Kirby got into the passenger seat. Les leant on the gate, watching them. Thornhill let out the clutch and the car moved slowly up the hill in the direction of the Hanging Tree. Thornhill glanced in the rear-view mirror. Les was still leaning on the gate, a hunched silhouette with all the light behind him.

No children, Thornhill thought, and now no brother either. Only Dilys Carrick, waiting for her husband in the smart, modern parlour, with the bruises like damsons on her arm.

4

'Let me do it,' said Larry Jordan, getting to his feet. He picked up the gin bottle and topped up first Jill's glass and then Vera

Sandleigh's. He held the bottle up to the light of the standard lamp. 'If Bernard doesn't hurry, he'll miss all the fun.'

'There's more,' Vera said, her head swaying on the long neck. 'I'm sure there's more. We buy it by the case, actually. It's for the parents, of course, so we have an allowance. You wouldn't believe what they get through.' Her voice wavered. 'It's all because of Mervyn Carrick. Bernard's got such a lot to do.' She turned to Jill. 'Are you sure you're feeling all right, Miss Francis?' she asked for the third time.

'Perfectly all right, thank you,' Jill answered truthfully.

'It must have been such a shock to the system.'

'Not at all. And that poor man was so apologetic.'

'I expect Bernard will be very cross with him.'

'I hope not.' Jill sipped her gin. 'It really wasn't his fault.'

That was not entirely true. Paxford had been travelling at some speed on his motorbike down the drive. And for a moment, Jill had been terrified: had glimpsed her life ending at this time and place. But when she swung the wheel to avoid the oncoming motorbike, the car had slithered harmlessly onto a grassy verge and come to a halt of its own volition. Neither the car nor its occupants had been damaged.

Of the three of them, Paxford had been the most upset – almost incoherent with remorse. At first when he had loomed up out of the darkness, he had seemed positively sinister – he was wearing a Balaclava helmet and a pair of goggles, which together gave him the appearance of a deep-sea diver on a night mission. He had insisted on following their car up the drive and on unloading Jordan's luggage.

'Such a sad case,' Vera Sandleigh said, sounding more than a little sorrowful herself. 'He didn't let you see his face, did he?'

'No – he kept his goggles on even in the house.'

'I saw his face this morning,' Jordan said. 'Poor chap.'

'He was involved in one of those silly accidents when he was in the army: a hand grenade exploded in his face or something.

89

The plastic surgeons did their best, but he really does look rather frightful.' Vera's face brightened. 'But only on one side. The other side looks quite normal. Still, I'm afraid the boys rather rag him.'

'I think I may have noticed him in Lydmouth,' Jill said, wondering why the boys were allowed to laugh at him.

'Yes, I think he's got a sister there. Bernard says he's a very competent groundsman. It's so hard to get good outdoor staff these days.'

Jill knew that she should be on her way, but the gin and the after-effects of the near-accident combined to make her feel tired. Besides, events had conspired to give her a privileged introduction to the Sandleighs. She could imagine how scornful Philip Wemyss-Brown would be if he discovered she had turned down an opportunity to talk to the Sandleighs on the day after Carrick's death.

The door opened and a girl came in. She was in her early teens, fair and slender-necked like Vera, and was wearing the uniform of the Lydmouth High School for Girls. She hesitated in the doorway.

'Dorothy, darling,' Vera said. 'How are you?'

'Fine, Mother.'

Vera said to the room at large. 'Dorothy was looking a bit peaky this morning.'

'So this is Dorothy.' Jordan came towards her, smiling, his hand outstretched. 'I can see you're your mother's daughter.'

She flushed, and shook hands with him.

'This is Lawrence Jordan,' Vera said. 'An – an old friend of the family.'

He touched the girl's arm. 'Call me Uncle Larry, eh?'

The girl stared at him and said nothing. Jill, who could remember being paralysed with shyness, felt a pang of sympathy.

Vera gave a trill of laughter and introduced the girl to Jill. 'Dorothy's been rehearsing after school, haven't you, dear? They are putting on *Twelfth Night*.'

'Really?' Jordan said, addressing Dorothy. 'And who are you playing?'

'Feste.'

'Ah. In a sense the pivot of the whole play.'

The girl said to her mother, 'I'd better start my homework now.'

'Of course. And would you make sure Peter and June have started theirs?'

After Dorothy left, there was a lull in the conversation. As she sat by the fire, drowsily sipping her gin, Jill wondered whether the Sandleighs had private means. They lived in some style. Their drawing room was on the first floor of their house, a high-ceilinged apartment with a bow window. The furniture was old and good. There was a grand piano in one corner. It could have been the home of any professional family in comfortable circumstances.

'I really must be going,' Jill said as Jordan appeared at her elbow with the gin bottle in one hand and a box of cigarettes in the other.

There were footsteps on the stairs, and a few seconds later the door opened and Sandleigh lumbered into the room, followed by another man. The Headmaster looked first at his wife, and Jill wondered if a message had passed from him to her, a warning even.

The second man was as tall as Sandleigh, but younger and much slimmer. He had fair hair, prominent cheekbones and wide shoulders. The Sandleighs made the introductions. To her interest, Jill discovered that she was shaking hands with Neville Rockfield. It was not hard to see why Kathleen Rockfield had fallen for him; whatever he might be like in private, he was an attractive man.

'We have something to celebrate, my dear,' Sandleigh informed his wife and the company at large. 'I've asked Rockfield to take over Burton's House next term, and I'm glad to say that he's accepted.' Once again, the Sandleighs' eyes met. 'Subject to the governors' ratification, of course, but I don't suppose there'll be any problem there.'

There was a murmur of congratulation. Sandleigh poured more drinks. Jill managed to avoid having her glass refreshed yet again. After they had drunk the health of the new housemaster designate, Sandleigh came to stand near the fire, close to where Jill was sitting.

'So you work for the *Gazette*, I hear,' he said genially. 'Must be a fascinating job.'

Jill agreed that it was.

'If rather gruesome at times, especially for a lady. But I expect your editor leaves the more unpleasant jobs to the chaps.'

Jill forced a smile but said nothing.

'You've probably heard about our tragedy,' Sandleigh went on, lowering his voice. 'Very sad. Such a promising man.'

'Mr Carrick?'

'Yes – I dare say we shall never know what went on in his mind. I understand the police haven't found a note. Not yet, anyway.'

'So it was suicide?'

'It's hardly likely to have been anything else. This is off the record, Miss Francis, but I know for a fact that the chap had serious family problems. A fine teacher, but not perhaps a particularly stable personality.' He smiled at her. 'Off the record, as I say.'

Sandleigh turned away to shovel coal onto the fire. Jill glanced across the room.

Neville Rockfield was saying to Larry Jordan, 'According to Swayne – he's our local bobby – the police have arrested someone in connection with Carrick's death. Or taken him in for questioning, anyway. Chap called Nerini.'

'Foreigner?'

'Yes – former Italian POW – works at Carrick's brother's farm. Swayne says he was acting very suspiciously this morning, tried to run away. They caught him trying to board a train at Lydmouth Station this afternoon.'

'Looks bad.'

Rockfield grunted. 'I never felt very happy about these POWs who choose to stay here. I mean, why don't they want to go back to their homes? To my mind, most of them stay because they know they can get an easier ride in this country. It's our fault for mollycoddling them.'

'I doubt if Nerini killed poor Carrick,' Sandleigh said in a voice that brooked no argument. He dropped the shovel into the coal scuttle, straightened up and addressed the room as if it were a staff meeting. 'He probably tried to run away because he thought he'd be blamed. Low moral fibre, I'm afraid, but that's no crime in itself. I'm pretty sure we'll find that it was suicide. It's the only rational answer.'

'I'm sure you're right, Headmaster.' Rockfield looked at his watch and put down his empty glass. 'I really should be going. Must tell Kathleen the good news. Thanks awfully for the drink, Mrs Sandleigh.'

He made his farewells, insisting that he didn't want to break up the party, that he would let himself out. Sandleigh waited until they heard the bang of the front door downstairs.

'Good man, Rockfield,' he murmured to Jill. 'Keen as mustard. Bit of a hero, actually. MC in North Africa, then a DSO in Normandy. Not that he likes one to mention it. Still, it does him no harm with the boys, as you can imagine. I think he and his wife will make quite a success of Burton's. It needs a strong hand.' He smiled at Jill. 'Forgive me, we schoolmasters have a terrible tendency to talk shop, even when we're relaxing.'

Jill stood up, knowing that it was time for her to go. It wasn't just the gin or the warmth of the fire or the cold outside that made her reluctant to leave. It was the thought of Church Cottage, cold and empty, because Alice would be visiting her friends in the vicarage. There was also the memory of that unpleasant incident late last night when she had thought that someone was watching her from the churchyard over the road.

The Sandleighs let her leave without much of a struggle.

Probably they wanted their dinner and the company of their old friend without the distraction of a stranger.

'I'll find Jill's coat and see her out,' Jordan said to his hosts. 'You stay there.'

In another man, the offer might have sounded rude, but Jordan was too skilful for that. He opened the drawing-room door and waited for Jill to precede him onto the landing. In the doorway she turned round to say a final farewell to her hosts. She caught them, just for an instant, in an unguarded pose. They were both looking not at each other, or even her, their departing guest. They were staring at Larry Jordan.

'Nice-looking girl, isn't she?' Jordan said as he helped Jill on with her coat, his hands lingering on her shoulders for a second too long, and setting off a shiver deep in Jill's stomach. 'Dorothy, I mean.'

5

Before they saw Umberto Nerini, Thornhill and Kirby stopped at the Gardenia, a café which stayed open in the evenings to cater for the patrons of the nearby Rex cinema. They warmed themselves with coffee and poached eggs and then drove on to police headquarters.

Thornhill told Kirby to bring Nerini up from the cells and put him in an interview room. He himself went upstairs and phoned his wife. He apologised for not phoning before and told her that he wasn't sure when he would get back. She contrived to sound both irritable and absent-minded.

'Is there anything wrong?' he asked.

'Sylvia's just phoned. Mother's worse.'

'I'm sorry.' He wished he had remembered to ask about her. 'She's seen a doctor?'

Edith said jerkily, 'He wants her to go into hospital. Just to keep an eye on her.'

'Oh, love. When?'

'This evening. Sylvia's going to phone again later.'

'Listen – I'll get home as soon as I can.'

Edith did not reply. He wondered how often he had used those words to her. A moment later they said goodbye, leaving everything else unsaid.

Thornhill went back downstairs and along to the interview room, which was one of several on the ground floor at the back of the building; its small, barred window overlooked the police car park. Nerini was sitting with a cigarette in the corner of his mouth, hunched over the scarred table. Kirby lolled in a chair against the wall, picking his teeth with a broken match.

Thornhill sat down and nodded at Kirby, which was a signal for him to begin his shorthand record of the proceedings. Nerini stared at the table. He was a large, broad man with a weather-beaten skin and muscular hands. His hair was unbrushed and he needed a shave.

'We've just been up to Moat Farm,' Thornhill said, speaking slowly and distinctly. 'Mrs Carrick tells me that your English is very good, so there's no need for us to wait for an interpreter.'

Nerini looked up. His eyes were dark and large like a cow's, and equally expressionless.

'How long have you worked for the Carricks?'

There was a pause. 'Nineteen forty-seven. Old Mr Carrick took me on.'

For the first few minutes Thornhill asked questions whose answers he already knew, safe questions which had nothing to do with the frozen body of Mervyn Carrick on the Hanging Tree. Nerini's replies were slow and cautious: whether his mind worked slowly as well was another matter.

Thornhill felt sorry for the man. By and large, former prisoners-of-war and displaced persons were not popular. If your son or your husband had been a casualty of war, it was easy to look askance at former enemies, living in the places and doing the jobs that might have belonged to the dead. Many believed that only the worst POWs chose to stay behind in the relative comfort of this country, rather than to return to the political and economic uncertainties of their own.

'So what were you doing up at the crossroads this morning?' Thornhill asked at last.

'I went to see if the lane was clear. Mrs Carrick wanted to go shopping today.' He stubbed out his cigarette in the centre of the ashtray, taking his time. 'I check for her. To see if she can get the Land Rover up to the main road.'

'She asked you to?'

Nerini shook his head. 'I just do it.'

'Then you saw the body?'

Another, slow nod.

'What did you do then?'

'I went away.'

'That's not quite true. You ran away across the fields. Why?'

'I was scared. I see Mr Carrick hanging there, I think that maybe people say I killed him.'

'Why should they do that?'

Nerini shrugged. 'Because if something goes wrong in this country, it is always the foreigner's fault.' He looked steadily at Thornhill. 'I was not running away. I wanted time to think.'

'You were found at the station. That looks as if you're running away.'

'I walked down to Lydmouth. I was cold. I wanted some coffee in the buffet.'

It was true that he had been arrested in the station buffet, and that he had bought only a platform ticket. But he might have intended to confuse the authorities by boarding a train without a ticket. Nevertheless, the story was at least plausible.

Thornhill changed his line of questioning and asked about the previous evening. Nerini insisted that it had been entirely normal. As usual, he had had his evening meal with the Carricks in the kitchen. Afterwards he took the dirty dishes into the scullery and washed them up. At that point the Carricks had been drinking tea at the kitchen table.

'You actually saw them there?'

'Yes, sir. Mrs Carrick call to say there was more tea in the pot, if I wanted. But I didn't.'

On Wednesdays, he had the evening free, and if the weather had not been so threatening, he would have gone up to Ashbridge for a pint and a game of darts. As it was, he had gone to his room, climbed into bed to keep out the cold and read for an hour. He had slept well, hearing nothing in the night. Everything seemed normal, until he had found Carrick's body.

'How is Mrs Carrick, sir? What will she do now Mr Carrick is not there?'

There was a moment of shocked silence. Kirby and Thornhill glanced at each other.

'Has no one told you?' Thornhill said gently. 'The man you saw hanging was Mervyn Carrick, not Les Carrick.' He saw the blank expression on Nerini's face and hastened to explain: 'You must have met him, surely? Mr Carrick's brother.'

'No, no,' Nerini said, his tongue stumbling over the words. 'It can't be him.'

6

When Thornhill reached home, Edith was in bed, but there was a light on in their room. She had left him a sandwich and a flask of tea in the kitchen. He wolfed the sandwich and took the tea upstairs.

She was sitting in bed and brushing her hair, which was thick and fair. When she brushed it, the strands seemed to come alive, like living gold.

'Has Sylvia phoned? How's your mother?'

'She's in hospital. No change, really.'

'At least she's in the right place.'

'Yes . . .' Edith examined a lock of her hair. 'We can go and see her on Sunday, can't we?'

'I hope so. But—'

'What kept you? Was it the man who hanged himself in Ashbridge?'

He nodded. 'How did you know?'

'There was something in the *Gazette*. A couple of lines in the late news. Who was it?'

'A master at Ashbridge School.' He hesitated, knowing that Edith liked to hear things which weren't public knowledge, which he suspected enhanced her position among the other mothers at the school gates. 'We're not sure how he died yet.' No harm in telling her that – it would soon be common knowledge. 'The man's called Carrick. His brother's a local farmer.'

She asked one or two questions, but he could tell that her interest was waning. At last she put down the brush on the bedside table and lay back against the pillows. Thornhill reached for her hand which lay on the eiderdown.

'I've got something to tell you,' she said. Despite her mother she looked cheerful, almost excited.

'What?'

'I saw Lawrence Jordan today.'

'Really?' Instantly his mind filled with the picture of Jordan arm in arm with Jill Francis, emerging from the Bull Hotel. 'Where was that?'

'In the Bull. I had to go into town for something, and I thought I'd have tea in the lounge. And there he was, as large as life.'

'How nice.' Tea in the Bull would have been a luxury for Edith, an appreciable dent in the week's housekeeping.

'He was very pleasant to the waitress. A real gentleman.'

'Was he by himself?'

'At first.' Some of her elation seeped away, like air from a balloon. 'Then he saw Miss Francis outside and brought her in. They were chatting by the fire for quite a long time.' She looked at Thornhill. 'I wonder how they know one another.'

'They probably don't. I expect she was interviewing him for the *Gazette*.'

'They seemed very friendly.'

'It's all part of the act, I dare say,' Thornhill said.

'She's lucky – having a job that lets you meet people like that.'

'I expect there are drawbacks. I saw Jordan myself, in fact.'

'Where?'

'Twice, actually. I had to go to Ashbridge School this morning and he was there. Apparently the Headmaster is an old friend.'

'What did he say?'

'We didn't really talk. And I saw him again, very briefly, this afternoon.' *Jill and Jordan, arm in arm, tripping across the pavement like a bloody honeymoon couple.* The car, the *Gazette*'s Ford Anglia, had been piled with luggage, and Quale and one of the hotel maids had been hovering in the background. 'It looked as if he might be leaving.' *As if they had been leaving together.*

'Why don't you come to bed?' Edith suggested. 'It's late.'

He undressed and went into the bathroom to do his teeth. On his way back he looked in on the children. Both were sound asleep and neither stirred when Thornhill kissed them. Elizabeth was clutching a large teddy bear which had once belonged to Thornhill himself, and which had seen better days. David had lined up three cowboys and two Indians on his bedside table: to guard him as he slept, and to be there as soon as he woke up.

Thornhill went back to the bedroom. Edith had already turned off the light. He took off his dressing-gown and got into bed. He touched her leg. She was lying on her back in the darkness.

'Richard, I wonder if we should send David to Ashbridge School. They take day boys, you know.'

'What's the point?' Thornhill began to stroke the leg. 'There's a perfectly good grammar school here in town.'

'But a school like Ashbridge would give him a much better start in life. And he'd meet people too.'

'He'd meet people at the grammar school.'

'You know what I mean: people who could help him later.'

'But think of the money it would cost. And he'd have to spend half the day on the bus.'

'Perhaps he could board.'

'That would cost even more.'

Thornhill moved his hand a little higher, to the soft flesh between thigh and ribcage. There was no doubt about it, he thought with the part of his mind which never stopped being an observer, Edith was beginning to put on weight. Not that it mattered.

'As for that,' Edith went on, twitching slightly as if a fly had landed on her, 'they do have quite a lot of scholarships at Ashbridge. Mrs Sutton was telling me all about it. She said it's the same foundation as the St John's almshouses. And everyone says that David's a bright boy.'

'But what about Elizabeth?'

'Well, it's less important for her, isn't it? If she's lucky she'll get into the High School. And if she isn't, it doesn't really matter. I mean, ten to one she'll end up getting married.'

'We'll see,' said Thornhill, convinced that Ashbridge School was not the right choice for David, even if they could afford it. *If Edith's mother dies, there might be a little money* . . . Enough for Elizabeth as well as David?

Edith turned away from him. 'You know the Sutton boys go there? It must be a good school.' She sounded drowsy. 'Goodnight, dear.'

Thornhill's hand dropped down onto the sheet, the no-man's-land which lay between them. He listened to the ticking of the alarm clock and the slow, steady breathing of Edith. He thought about the man on the Hanging Tree and about whether they could afford to buy this house on a mortgage; the landlord had told him he wanted to sell, and that he would give the Thornhills first refusal. These were safe subjects, familiar worries.

Every time his mind strayed in other directions, he ruthlessly pulled it back. What was the point of hankering after the moon? And what was the use of feeling jealous of those who already had it?

It seemed to Richard Thornhill that he had nothing left except his willpower, and if he abandoned that he would be defenceless. Much later he drifted into an uneasy sleep, shot through with dreams whose content he could not control.

FIVE

Vandals Attack Public Lavatory

Vandals have been at work at Jubilee Park in Lydmouth. Following representations from the Park Committee, the police have appealed to the public.

'If anyone sees someone behaving suspiciously at the Park,' said Sergeant Fowles at Lydmouth Police Station, 'especially in or around the public conveniences, please let us know.'

Mrs P.Wemyss-Brown, chairman of the Committee, said that it was a great shame when a few selfish individuals damaged amenities designed for everyone. She had every confidence that the police would soon find the culprits and deal with them severely.

The *Lydmouth Gazette*, 8th February

1

'If you ask me,' Dr Bayswater said, 'and of course there's no earthly reason why you should, someone found him dead and then moved him to a more convenient location.'

'Why?' Thornhill was talking to himself as much as to Bayswater. 'To lessen the scandal?'

'That's your problem.' Bayswater opened the door of his car and lowered himself into the driving seat. 'I deal in verifiable facts, thank God, and only in a very limited way.' He started the engine and glared up through bushy eyebrows at Thornhill. 'Good luck.'

He drove away, leaving Thornhill standing in the rain outside the magistrates' court and wondering whether the choice of the Hanging Tree was significant, rather than the fact that the body had been moved. After all, the tree had been the place for felons convicted on a capital charge and, more recently, for suicides. So was somebody telling them that Carrick deserved to die, that his death was an execution? Carrick had certainly had his enemies – his brother, his sister-in-law and, if Jill Francis was to be believed, his colleague and rival, Neville Rockfield.

As he had expected, the inquest had been adjourned. He went back to police headquarters and talked to the chief constable, who as usual wanted results but was uncertain where to find them. Later in the morning Thornhill drove himself up to Ashbridge. Most of the snow had melted since yesterday. The thaw was underway at last. Trees dripped and rain fell lightly but continuously, turning the surface of the road to an unpleasant mixture of grit, dirty snow and icy water. Halfway up the hill a mist came down, reducing visibility to fifty or sixty yards.

The area around Lydmouth was renowned for the local variations in its climate. The landscape was as unpredictable as its weather: woods and fields, hills and valleys, and streams which swelled into rivers in winter and dwindled into trickles in summer.

The mist stayed with Thornhill all the way to Ashbridge. In one way, he was glad of the excuse to drive slowly. There was plenty to think about – not from the inquest, which had been the formality he had expected, but because of the bizarre and contradictory evidence that was beginning to accumulate around the fact of Mervyn Carrick's death.

At present it was impossible to say whether that death had been accident, suicide or murder. At some point, probably near the time of death, Mervyn Carrick had been struck on the left-hand side of his head with a hard object with a rounded edge. According to Dr Bayswater, the preliminary examination had shown that Carrick's neck had been marked by two ligatures. The lower, which had almost certainly killed him, had been his collar and tie, which had been drawn tight against the front of the neck. The pressure had been exerted from behind.

Carrick had been suspended from the tree, however, by a length of cord of the type used in sash windows and the principal marks it had made were on the right-hand side of the neck. The cord was not new – one end was frayed; the other had been cut with a blade, but not recently; and there were rust marks at various points. You could probably find similar scraps of cord in hundreds of sheds and cupboards up and down the county.

He drove through the school gates and part of the way up the main drive. Just before a small garage with a pitched roof, he turned left into a side avenue. A moment later the tyres of the Austin were slithering over the slushy gravel in front of Burton's House. He parked beside the police car which was already there.

When he reached Carrick's rooms, the scene-of-the-crime officers were packing up their equipment. Kirby was standing by the window in the little sitting room, flicking through a folder of papers. The smell of tobacco was less powerful than it had been yesterday morning.

'Any sign of the glasses?' Thornhill asked, picking his way through the mess on the carpet. They had found the spectacle case in the breast pocket of Mervyn's tweed jacket.

'No, sir. There's a spare pair in the bedroom. But no sign of the ones in the photo.'

'Tobacco?' That had been another possible discrepancy: a pipe in Mervyn's pocket but no tobacco.

Kirby nodded towards the desk. 'He was using an old Whisky Flake tin – looks like Paxford's home-grown inside. Smells like it, too.'

'Was he a heavy smoker?'

'Not according to the Burtons.'

So there was no obvious significance in the fact that Mervyn had left the tin behind. Thornhill said, 'And no one saw him on Wednesday night?'

'Not after getting back from the meeting. But there's one thing, sir.' Kirby held up the folder. 'Bank statements. Post Office savings book.'

'Where are the accounts?'

'Lydmouth; current account with Barclays. I phoned them, by the way – no deposit box.' Kirby grinned, suddenly boyish, pleased with himself for anticipating Thornhill's thinking. 'Both have got healthy balances. Nearly a hundred in the bank, and well over a thousand in the Post Office Savings Bank, scattered over three accounts.'

The scene-of-the-crime men said goodbye and clattered down the stairs.

'The Barclays account's pretty straightforward,' Kirby went on. 'I've checked the payments against the cheque stubs. Just about all the deposits are his salary, paid monthly. Forty-three pounds, sixteen shillings, to be precise. Not a big spender. He managed to pay fifteen to twenty pounds a month from that into his Post Office accounts.'

'He must have had other payments to have a balance that big.'

'There were one or two largish deposits about two years back. About the time his father died? Maybe something to do with the estate. Plus the ones from his salary. But well over a third of the total comes from small deposits between five and thirty pounds.'

'When?'

'Mainly in the last five months. So it looks like Dilys was telling the truth.'

And if Mervyn had been blackmailing his sister-in-law, Thornhill thought, he could have been blackmailing some-one else.

He left Kirby to his work and drove back to the centre of the village. Glancing at his watch, he was surprised to discover that it was after half-past twelve. He was hungry so he parked the car by the church and walked along one side of the triangular green to the Beaufort Arms. The landlady drew him a pint of beer and promised him a home-cured ham sandwich. She was an elderly woman, comfortably plump and disposed to chat. He was the only customer in the saloon bar.

'Don't think I've seen you in Ashbridge before, dear.'

'No, I live in Lydmouth.' Thornhill sipped the beer, which was excellent. 'Do you know the Carricks, by the way?'

Her good humour evaporated. 'Why do you want to know? Are you a reporter?'

'A policeman.'

'In that case you'd better have a word with Sergeant Swayne.' Her voice had become tart. 'And I'd better see what's happening to your sandwich.'

Before she left, however, the outside door opened and cold air billowed into the bar, followed by a tall, slim man with unusually broad shoulders.

'Hello, Meg.'

'Mr Rockfield – don't usually see you at lunchtime.' The landlady took down one of the pewter tankards hanging above the bar and began to draw him a pint.

He took off his hat, revealing fair hair slicked back over his long skull. 'Have one yourself, Meg. I'm celebrating.'

Her expression must have alerted him to the fact that they were not alone. Rockfield turned round and looked at Thornhill sitting near the window.

'Good afternoon.'

'Good afternoon, Mr Rockfield.'

He looked momentarily startled. Then Meg murmured something in his ear as she handed him his pint. 'Oh – are you Inspector . . . Thornwell, is it?'

'Thornhill. I think Mr Sandleigh mentioned your name.'

'And yours to me.' Glass in hand, Rockfield strolled towards the window. 'How's the sleuthing going?'

'Early days yet. The inquest was adjourned.'

Rockfield stared down at him, his eyes narrowing. 'Is that normal?'

'It's what we expected, sir. It just means we need a little time to complete our investigation.'

'Oh I see what you mean. Not a very orthodox way to die. But there again, Mervyn Carrick wasn't a very orthodox sort of person.'

'What do you mean by that?'

'Carrick went at his own gait, that's all. A bit of a loner – the original cat who walked by himself.'

The landlady left the bar in search of Thornhill's lunch. Rockfield sat down near Thornhill and lifted his glass.

'Anyway – cheers.' He drank deeply. 'Which is not to say I'm not sorry the poor chap's dead. He must have had a lot on his mind. Sad, really. You see a man every day, week in, week out, and you don't have a clue what's going on in his head.'

'Was he well liked?'

'To be frank, he sometimes got on people's nerves. He used to smoke this absolutely foul tobacco in the staff room. It became so bad that the room would start emptying as soon as he produced that pouch of his. In the end I had to have words with him about it.'

'You weren't the best of friends, then?'

'I wouldn't say that, Inspector. Just a storm in a teacup. It meant nothing.'

Thornhill wondered why Rockfield had mentioned it: to prevent the police hearing the story from someone else? 'But you and he were in competition, I understand?'

Rockfield laughed with what seemed like genuine amusement. 'In a manner of speaking. A housemastership is becoming vacant at the end of term – Burton's House. Carrick and I both wanted the job. He'd been at the school for longer, but I had better qualifications in other ways.'

'In what ways?'

'Academically. And I handle the boys better than he did, though

108

naturally I'm biased in my own favour here. Then there's the fact that I'm married. Always a good thing to have a married housemaster, you know: it reassures the boys' mothers to know there's a woman about the place.'

'So you think you would have got the job even if Carrick hadn't died?'

Rockfield took his time answering. There was something almost wilful in the delay; Thornhill thought the man might be enjoying himself. 'Oh yes, Inspector,' he drawled at last. 'In my experience, when push comes to shove, the best man always wins. I expect it's just the same in your line of business. Which reminds me – what about that fellow Nerini up at the farm? I thought you'd arrested him.'

'Where did you hear that?'

'Someone at school mentioned it last night.'

'No one has been charged in connection with the case.'

'Yet.' Rockfield swallowed more beer. 'I've seen Nerini in here a few times, you know. He's in the darts team.'

'Well liked, is he?'

'I wouldn't say that, not exactly. But he throws a straight dart and buys his round. Give him another year or two, and people will forget he's a foreigner. In a sense you could say he's less of a stranger than someone like Lawrence Jordan.'

'You've met him?'

Rockfield nodded. 'He's staying with the Sandleighs – but you knew that, didn't you? I had a drink with them last night. Jordan struck me as surprisingly normal, considering everything. But he hasn't actually lived here for years. I don't mind telling you, he's shocked by some of the changes. Let's face it, this country's not what it was.'

The landlady brought Thornhill his sandwich. Thornhill thanked her. She nodded curtly and moved away.

'I think she reckons she's on the force herself,' Rockfield murmured. 'Our local sergeant is her nephew.'

'Swayne.'

'That's him.' Rockfield began to fill a pipe. 'Captain of the darts team, as a matter of fact. What with one thing and another, our Mr Swayne is quite a power in the land.'

Thornhill glanced at Rockfield's face, wondering if the schoolmaster was trying to tell him something, and if so what. Rockfield finished the rest of his beer and stood up.

'I must be off. Back to the Gallic Wars with the Lower Fourth.' He put the pipe in his mouth and struck a match. 'Has Swayne passed on what I told him?'

'I've not talked to Sergeant Swayne since yesterday afternoon.'

'He probably hasn't had the opportunity yet. I bumped into him this morning when I came out to post a letter.' Rockfield paused to light his pipe before the flame consumed the match and burned his fingers. 'I told him about seeing the Carrick brothers quarrelling.'

'When was this?'

'Sunday evening. We'd just come out of church. The whole school comes to evensong once a term at the parish church.' He nodded out of the window at the square, grey tower rising beyond a line of elms on the far end of the green. 'Carrick wasn't on duty, but I was. So I had to stay behind helping some wretched child find his purse.' The pipe had gone out, and he struck another match. 'Afterwards, the kid scooted off to school, and I walked back more slowly.' Another pause to light the pipe. 'You see the bus shelter out there? I was walking past it and I heard raised voices. I couldn't hear what they were saying, but it was some sort of argument. They must have heard my footsteps because they shut up. As I passed by I glanced in – there they were: Carrick and his brother. Two peas from the same pod.'

'Wasn't it dark by then?'

'The pub's outside light was on. It was the Carricks – I'd take my oath on it.'

Rockfield picked up his hat and strolled to the door, one hand in his pocket, smoke billowing fragrantly from the pipe. He called goodbye to the landlady. As he was leaving, he turned back and smiled at Thornhill. There was no warmth in the smile, only a suggestion of amusement as if at a private joke that he was not prepared to share.

2

At nine-thirty on Friday morning, Jill Francis went to the inquest on Mervyn Carrick. As everyone had expected, the inquest was adjourned; the purpose of her going was as much to see who was there as to hear what was said.

Afterwards she went back to the editor's room at the *Gazette* office and tried to do Philip's job as well as her own. There would be a piece on Carrick's death in the day's paper. Jill played up the location of the body, partly to please Charlotte, and partly because it was just the sort of twist that lifts a story out of the ordinary. Thanks to the Hanging Tree, Mervyn Carrick's death might be picked up by one of the larger provincial dailies, or even by a national.

As far as she knew, there was little doubt that the eventual verdict would be suicide; despite the adjournment of the inquest, it was unlikely that further developments would be of much interest. She was tempted to mention Lawrence Jordan's peripheral connection with the case, which would certainly make the story more newsworthy. But if she did that, she would destroy the good relationship between herself and both Jordan and the Sandleighs. Unlike national newspapers, local newspapers had to think carefully before they antagonised their readers.

At lunchtime, Jill could have gone out with colleagues to the Gardenia. Instead she went home to Church Cottage and opened the tin of tomato soup from which Jordan had rescued her on Wednesday night. Her relationship with other *Gazette* employees had always been coloured by her friendship with the

Wemyss-Browns; and her temporary promotion had increased her sense of isolation.

The house looked rather cleaner than it had when Jill left it, because Friday was one of the charwoman's mornings. Alice was off on her travels again. Jill put the soup on a tray and took her lunch into the little dining room at the front of the house so that she could sit by the gas fire.

As she ate she looked out of the window at the churchyard. In the daylight it was open, innocent and picturesque – there was still enough snow to make it look as if it had strayed from a Christmas card or the lid of a tin of biscuits. It was difficult to associate the place with anything sinister. She wondered if she had imagined everything on Wednesday night. But even thinking about it – remembering the footsteps and what might have been a shadow moving between the yews – made her shiver. She found herself bolting her lunch, anxious to leave this room with its view.

On her way back to the office, Jill called at police headquarters to check that there had been no further developments in the Carrick case. She could have telephoned, of course, but she knew from experience that a personal call was more likely to get results. Still bruised by her encounter with Thornhill, she asked for Sergeant Kirby. Unfortunately neither he nor anyone else was available for comment.

Her feet carried her towards the *Gazette*, while her mind was occupied with Thornhill's iniquities and the work which lay ahead of her. Then a shout from the other side of the road jolted her out of her absorption.

'Wotcher, Mussolini! Thought you'd been hanged.'

A baker's boy was skimming down the road on his delivery bicycle, his head swivelling towards a large, well-built figure striding along the other pavement in the same direction as Jill but several yards ahead. The man was dark haired, and wore a khaki battledress jacket over heavy navy blue trousers and boots.

'Why don't you piss off home, you bloody Eyetie?' The boy

made a V-sign, then turned across the road and disappeared into Lyd Street.

The man gave no sign that he'd heard. Jill saw him turn left after the library. On impulse, she crossed the road. He had not gone very far – he was standing less than fifty yards away outside the bus station, consulting the timetable. Jill walked briskly after him. Without giving herself time to think, she joined him beside the noticeboard.

'Excuse me.'

He turned to look down at her – he was at least six inches taller than she was. He had a large chin, dark, badly cut hair and brown, watchful eyes. His face was reddened by exposure to the weather.

'Yes?'

'I heard that horrible boy shouting at you,' Jill blurted out. 'I'm so sorry.'

She had spoken without calculation, and was rewarded by the glimmer of a smile. 'Not your fault, miss.'

'My name is Jill Francis,' she said slowly in Italian. 'I work for the newspaper.'

'The *Gazette*?' he replied in English. 'I read about the Hanging Tree in your paper.'

Jill nodded. 'I think your English is better than my Italian.'

Again there was a glimmer of a smile, but Nerini was too polite to agree with her. 'I must catch a bus,' he told her, signifying that as far as he was concerned the conversation was at an end.

'To Ashbridge?'

He nodded. 'You know who I am?'

'Signor Nerini.' Jill ran her eyes down the timetable until she found the Ashbridge service. 'You've got almost an hour to wait. I could drive you up, if you like.'

'And?'

Jill smiled, and half-turned, as if about to leave. 'I'm a reporter. I'd like to talk to you, that's all.'

'Sometimes people write lies in the newspaper,' Nerini

113

said, avoiding any personal accusation. 'I think I wait for the bus.'

The baker's boy came to Jill's assistance, conveniently choosing to ride past the bus station on his way up to the High Street. 'Fascist bastard,' he shouted over his shoulder, once he was a safe distance away from Nerini. One of the mechanics at the bus garage stared curiously. A woman walking down the hill with a library book in her hand glanced across the road at them, her mouth pursed in disapproval; it was impossible to tell whether the disapproval was aimed at the boy or Nerini.

'We needn't talk,' Jill said. 'And if we do, I won't write anything in the paper unless you say I may.'

Then, to her surprise, he smiled. 'I have to say yes. I just remember: I have no money.'

She smiled back. They walked up the hill together. At the *Gazette*, Jill told them in the front office where she was going. Nerini earned a few curious stares but no one said anything.

They talked very little on the way. Nerini asked if he might smoke. Following his directions, Jill turned into the lane leading to Moat Farm. She slowed as the lane dipped down to meet the track. No one was there, but the area immediately around the Hanging Tree was still cordoned off, and the crossroads looked as if an armoured division had recently passed through it. The Ford Anglia inched through the mud, its wheels slipping.

'It was there that you saw him?' Jill said.

'Yes. I did not like to look at his face.'

Neither of them spoke again until they reached Moat Farm. Jill pulled up just outside the gate to the yard. She turned off the engine and opened the door, not giving Nerini a chance to say goodbye. There were footsteps running across the yard.

'Bert — are you all right?'

A woman – Dilys Carrick – appeared on the other side of the gate. She was sturdily built with a grave, old-fashioned face of the type Jill's mother would have labelled sweet. For an instant her expression was unguarded and vulnerable. Then she saw Jill.

'Who are you?'

'She is Miss Francis,' Nerini said. 'She gave me a lift up from Lydmouth. She works for the *Gazette.*'

'I see. Have you had breakfast?'

'Yes, Mrs Carrick.'

She jerked her head down the lane. 'Mr Carrick's patching the roof of the barn in Lower Field. You'd better give him a hand.'

Nerini inclined his head in what was almost a bow. 'Yes, Mrs Carrick.'

Watching them, Jill had the feeling that they were both play-acting, and that under this performance they were putting on for her benefit they were carrying on another conversation, one without words.

'Thank you, Miss Francis.' Nerini inclined his head towards her; he had mastered the difficult art of bowing without servility. 'Goodbye.'

He set off down the lane, walking without haste but with deliberation. For a few seconds, both women followed him with their eyes.

'It was kind of you to bring Bert back,' Dilys said. 'But there's nothing we can tell you.'

Jill thought that perhaps the boot was on the other foot. 'They haven't charged Mr Nerini. I was at the inquest this morning. It's been adjourned.'

'What does that mean? That they think someone killed Mervyn?'

'Not necessarily. Just that they need more time to find out how he died.'

There was a pause. Mist clung to the tree-covered hills

further up the valley. Despite the thaw it was still very cold.

'The kettle's on,' Dilys said at last, her voice still brusque. 'Would you like a cup of tea before you go?'

Jill followed her into the farmhouse. Life on a farm was lonely, and old traditions of hospitality lingered on in this part of the world; Jill did not attribute the invitation to anything more personal than that. In the kitchen, Dilys laid a tray with cups and saucers and made the tea. Jill had expected they would drink it there, but Dilys picked up the tray and said, 'We'll be more comfortable in the lounge.'

There was pride in her voice, like a mother talking of her child and not wanting to brag. When Jill saw the room and its contents, she realised that it was more than a lounge: it was a shrine to her hostess's aspirations. While they sipped tea, Jill made admiring comments.

'We had the detective here last night, Mr Thornhill,' Dilys said suddenly. 'Do you know him?'

'Yes, I do.'

'Apparently his wife wants him to get a television.'

'Yes,' Jill said, because that was all she could think of to say.

'He's a nice man, isn't he? You wouldn't think he's a policeman. Has he got children, do you know?'

'Two, I think — a boy and a girl.' Jill saw a wistfulness on Dilys's face and wondered whether it was mirrored on her own. 'You and Mr Carrick don't have any?'

'No. Not yet. Would you have some more tea?'

'No, thank you.'

'My husband's not what you'd call a family man.'

'Most men aren't before they have children. But I imagine they soon change when they're faced with the inevitable.'

'I wonder.' Dilys stared at the blank screen of the television. 'But you never can tell, can you? Not with men.'

3

At this stage of the investigation, the whole case was a tangle – an unruly gathering of facts and suppositions; no real pattern to them, and no real guarantee that there was one for Thornhill to find.

As he finished his beer, he skimmed through his notebook. Something niggled at the back of his mind: a connection he had failed to make; a question he should have asked; an inference he should have drawn? He thought of the Carricks. *All that suffering.* He remembered the bruises like damsons on Dilys's arm. The worst hells, he thought, are those we make ourselves in our own homes.

He finished his pint and settled up with the silent landlady. Outside, the thaw was well underway. On the triangle of open land in front of the pub, ragged patches of green were steadily widening. The air felt moist and appreciably warmer than a few hours earlier. Thornhill climbed into the Austin and started the engine. Most detective work consisted of doing the obvious: and in this case the obvious course of action was to talk to Les Carrick.

He drove slowly down the hill in the Lydmouth direction. The tarmac gleamed with surface water from the melting snow and ice. The right-hand turning into the Moat Farm lane came sooner than he had expected, reminding him that Moat Farm was not in fact that far from Ashbridge by the main road, and even less by the old track. Even in bad weather, on a dark night, it was not impossible that someone who knew the way well could have made the journey.

The lane dropped down sharply to the muddy crossing with the old track. Thornhill braked and pulled over. Perhaps he was ignoring the obvious. What if the glasses had simply fallen off? True, he had arranged for the area around the Hanging Tree to be searched, but that had been yesterday, with the snow on the ground.

Thornhill opened the door of the car and swung his legs out

of the car. His neat black brogues landed in a muddy puddle. He swore under his breath. Snatching the car keys out of the ignition, he picked his way through the mud to the back of the car, unlocked the boot, and took out his wellingtons. When he changed into them, he discovered that his left sock was already wet.

Searching for the glasses no longer seemed such a good idea; no need to waste too much time on it. His mind filled with the distracting possibility that the Carricks would offer him a cup of tea. He tried to ignore it. First there was a job to do.

He crossed the cordon and began to examine the ground around the Hanging Tree. As the minutes passed, he steadily widened the search. He found nothing except the footprints of investigating officers.

By now the pond on the far side of the tree had lost much of its ice. He discovered that it was fed at one end by a stream running down from Ashbridge; after the pond, the stream hugged the side of the lane leading to Moat Farm, and probably ended up in the River Lyd at the bottom of the valley.

He thought it unlikely that the glasses would be over here – the body had been hanging on the other side of the tree. Still, he examined the ground, which was even muddier than elsewhere because it was so near to running water. Presumably the surface had been covered with ice on Wednesday night so at least they were spared the unpleasant job of dragging the pond. He made a mental note to check the point, however, though it was almost certainly irrelevant. As he was thinking about the ice, he glanced upwards at the web of branches silhouetted against the pale grey sky.

Then he saw them.

The glasses were hooked over a branch just above his head. How the hell had they got there? Had someone thrown them at random into the air? The branch projected over the pond, but if he held on with one hand and leant across as far as he could, he should be able to reach them with the other hand.

Standing like a stork on one foot, Thornhill hung over the pond. Just before his hand closed on the glasses, he realised that he had been fooled. What he had taken to be part of the black frames of Mervyn Carrick's glasses were in fact two interlacing twigs. The discovery hit him just as he was congratulating himself on his cleverness in finding them. A rush of unwanted emotions washed over him in an instant – chiefly shame at his own stupidity, and anger that he was wasting his time. He was glad that there was no one to see him. With a tug he jerked himself back towards the tree.

The jolt dislodged the car keys which were in the right-hand pocket of his overcoat. The keys fell. Thornhill lunged at them. The branch he was holding on to snapped under the sudden increase of strain. He fell forwards.

The keys landed on part of the pond where the ice had not melted. For a moment they sat there, easily within reach of a stick. Then Thornhill's body hit the surface of the pond.

The ice shattered. His body plunged into the pond, the shock driving the air from his lungs. He swallowed a mouthful of filthy, freezing water. He struggled to stand up, his limbs catching on dead branches at the bottom. The pond was not deep but it was treacherous. The sleeve of his overcoat caught on something underwater. As he pulled it free, he heard the cloth tear.

At last he managed to stand up. The water came to just above his waist. Spluttering and swearing, he fought his way towards the bank, stumbling over obstructions beneath the surface. His teeth were chattering. He lifted his hand to wipe water from his eyes and discovered that he had managed to cut himself. Blood dripped into the pond.

Then he remembered the car keys and the full horror of the situation burst upon him. He turned round, telling himself that he could hardly get wetter than he already was, and waded away from the bank. His saturated clothes weighed him down like a suit of icy armour.

He guessed where the keys had fallen and, without giving himself time to think, bent down, immersing himself. He tried opening his eyes but the disturbed mud had made the water

119

opaque, as dark as a starless night. The water stung his bare skin and hurt his eyes. His outstretched fingers touched branches, rotting leaves and silt lying on the bottom. He stumbled against something much harder, perhaps a large stone. He resurfaced, gasping for air. Now he was even colder than before. It was no use, he realised, he would never find the bloody keys; he would have to give up.

He staggered towards the bank, the options running through his mind. He could freeze in the car and hope someone would come and rescue him; he could walk up to the main road and try to hitch a lift, though few motorists would be likely to stop for someone who looked like a sodden mud-stained tramp; or he could go down to Moat Farm and throw himself on the Carricks' mercy. He wondered if they were on the telephone; he thought not. There was an irony here, of course – he had been intending to erupt into their lives like an avenging angel; now he would be completely dependent on their kindness.

For a moment, Thornhill had been aware that mixed with the sounds of his own splashing and cursing was the noise of an engine, which he assumed came from the main road higher up the valley. Then he heard a door slam and realised that the vehicle must be much nearer. Suddenly he was dazzled by hope: rescue was at hand.

'Help!' he called, wrenching the word out through chattering teeth. 'Over here!'

Just as he reached the bank and began to haul himself out, he heard Jill Francis call, 'Hello?'

Part of him wanted to fall back into the water and let it close over his head, and stay there in the chilly darkness until she went away.

She walked round the tree and saw him. 'Mr Thornhill.'

He tried to say something but couldn't.

She ran forward and, holding on to the tree, extended her other hand to him. 'Hold on to me, and I'll pull.'

Thornhill stared at the hand, neatly encased in a soft, brown leather glove. His own hands were filthy. 'I—'

'Hurry *up*.'

He put his hand in hers. The firmness of her grip surprised him. She pulled and he staggered forward. A moment later, he was out of the pond and leaning against the tree.

'Car keys,' Thornhill stammered. 'In the water.'

She took his arm and pulled him towards the crossroads. He nearly fell over the cordon. Her car, the Ford Anglia he had seen her in the previous evening, was parked on the other side of the lane from his, its bonnet pointing up towards the main road. She must have been to see the Carricks at Moat Farm.

'I'll ruin your upholstery,' he mumbled.

'Not if you take off your clothes.'

'But—'

'Coat and shoes off first.' She opened the Anglia's door. 'Come and stand here. There's some rugs in the boot. You mustn't get any colder than you already are.' She went round to the back of the car, leaving him staring dumbly after her. 'Come along,' she ordered. 'You'll only feel worse if you hang around.'

His fingers clumsily picked at the buttons of his overcoat. His brain felt as numb as his hands. *This can't be happening.* Here he was in the middle of the winter countryside, taking off his clothes in front of Jill Francis. Nothing could ever be the same again. He let the coat drop to the ground and began to peel off his jacket. He had trouble with the small buttons on the waistcoat.

'Let me.'

She undid the buttons quickly and then moved on to those of the shirt. Thornhill cowered against the car, his body trembling.

'Do try and stand still,' she said gently. 'I know this is horrible, but the sooner we get it over with the better.'

Once his shirt was unbuttoned, she left him to pull off his braces and remove his shirt and vest. While he was doing that, she held up a tartan woollen blanket to screen his body from the wind and his modesty from her eyes. As soon as the vest was off, she draped the blanket round his shoulders. She hung another blanket over the door of the car and left him to remove his trousers in privacy. Before she went, she picked up the clothes he had already discarded, shook them out and put them in the boot.

'I'll fetch your hat,' she said. 'It was in the pond.'

Thornhill stepped out of his trousers and pulled off his socks. There was a brief battle between commonsense and modesty, which the former won. He stripped off his underpants, wrapped his lower half in the second blanket and collapsed into the front passenger seat of the car. The effort had exhausted him. He was breathing rapidly and shallowly, and his body shivered uncontrollably.

He was aware of Jill shutting the door and coming round to the driver's side of the car.

'You're bleeding.'

He tried to apologise for allowing blood to drip on the blanket.

'Don't be silly.'

She produced an ironed handkerchief from her handbag and told him to hold it over the cut, which was just below the little finger on the right hand. Then she wrapped a third blanket round him, moving his shoulders and his legs this way and that so she could tuck it more securely around him. He tried to protest but his chattering teeth mangled the sense, and in any case she ignored him.

Her movements dislodged the rear-view mirror and he caught sight of his own face: except that now it was the face of a stranger, pale, drawn and mud-stained; the skin grey; the hair plastered close to the skull on either side of an irregular central parting. He looked less than human, he thought.

'That's better,' Jill said.

She picked up a hat from the back seat and crammed it onto Thornhill's head. He saw himself in the mirror. It was too small for him, bright blue and sported a small feather on one side. Thornhill was past words now but he moaned.

'You lose a lot of heat through your head.' Jill started the engine. 'Don't waste energy trying to talk.'

At the junction with the main road, Jill put on the hand brake. Leaving the engine running, she took her handbag off the back seat, and extracted a bar of chocolate. She broke off a piece and put it in Thornhill's mouth. He felt the sweetness seeping into him.

She was a good driver, he discovered – wasting no time but aware that his arms and legs were swathed like a mummy's, which meant that it was necessary to take the bends more slowly than usual. Several vehicles passed them going the other way, but Thornhill had stopped worrying about what other people would think; his energies were concentrated on fighting the cold.

When they reached Lydmouth, Jill drove through the town. Thornhill stared straight ahead.

'I'll take you to Victoria Road. Will Mrs Thornhill be there?'

He grunted; he had not known that she knew where he lived, which was foolish of him, of course – in Lydmouth everyone knew where everyone else lived.

'If she's not there I'll take you up to the RAF Hospital.'

'No need for that,' he mumbled. He could not remember what Edith had planned for this afternoon, or even if she had told him.

'We'll see.'

He closed his eyes as they drove down the High Street. Soon they turned into Victoria Road. Jill pulled up outside his house before Thornhill had managed to tell her which one it was.

'Wait there.' She left the engine running and the heater on. 'I'll go and see if Mrs Thornhill is in.'

He waited – what else could he do, wrapped as he was like a tartan sausage? Staring up the road towards the cast-iron gates of Jubilee Park, he wondered dully if there were any news about Mrs Wemyss-Brown's Peeping Tom. *Not my problem.* A woman went by wheeling a pram. She glanced curiously into the car. Thornhill shut his eyes again and she was no longer there. Everything had been taken out of his hands. There was something unexpectedly comforting in being in a position of total dependence.

He heard footsteps outside the car. Edith's face loomed up on the other side of the window. Jill was immediately behind her. Edith opened the door and to his astonishment knelt down. She pushed his icy feet into his slippers.

Edith helped him out of the car. With a woman supporting him on either side he tottered towards the house. In the hall he glanced into the mirror and saw a gaunt stranger wearing a ridiculous blue hat. He looked up and saw Elizabeth's face, white and strained, staring at him between the banisters.

'I'm all right,' he tried to say, but the words wouldn't come.

Edith and Jill led him along the hall and into the kitchen. They pushed him into the Windsor chair by the boiler.

'Luckily there's tea in the pot,' Edith was saying, in a voice that sounded astonishingly normal, as if this sort of thing had happened every other day of their married life. 'Would you like a cup as well, Miss Francis?'

'No, thanks. Unless I can help, I'll be on my way. You won't want me under your feet.'

He saw the two women exchange smiles. He was not sure if he had ever seen them so close together before. They were much the same age and both good to look at, but there the similarities ended: Edith was large and fair, while Jill was slim and dark; they moved differently, talked differently and thought differently. Why was everything so confusing?

He closed his eyes. Their footsteps sounded in the hall. The front door banged. A moment later, Edith came back with an eiderdown which she dropped over him and tucked around him, just as Jill had done with the blankets.

'Lucky for you a Good Samaritan happened to be passing. Now — some tea first, I think. Then a hot bath and bed.'

'Nonsense.'

'No, it's not. Look at you. If you tried to stand up you'd fall over.'

He stared at her. All the things he wanted to say rushed through his mind and he couldn't find the right words for any of them.

'What have you done to your hand? Let me see.' Edith peeled back Jill's bloodstained handkerchief. The cut was no longer bleeding. 'Nothing to worry about.' She shook out the handkerchief. 'I'll put this to soak. And while you drink your tea, I'll ring Sergeant Kirby and Dr Bayswater.'

'No.'

'*Yes*. You need the doctor — just in case. Miss Francis thought so, too. And Brian Kirby is more than capable of doing your job for a day or two if necessary. No one's indispensable.'

'Listen, I—'

'What about your clothes? Have you seen the state they're in? Will the police pay to have them cleaned?'

Edith wasn't really angry, he guessed, merely adding a comforting gloss of normality to an abnormally uncomfortable situation. Having silenced him with a question he couldn't answer, she went into the back kitchen to fetch him some tea.

Thornhill sat by the boiler, feeling the cold slowly recede. Drowsiness crept over him. He was aware of Edith bustling about, of water running, of voices in the hall. She brought him a cup of sweet, milky tea, and stayed until she was sure he could drink it by himself. She was humming, usually a sign of happy self-absorption. Was this what she really wanted — to be a mother rather than a wife?

Later, he heard Elizabeth's voice raised in complaint in the hall and the banging of the front door. He wondered where David was; school must have finished by now; but Thornhill lacked the energy to ask Edith. His chin sank closer and closer to his chest.

'Time for a bath, Richard.'

He forced his eyes open. Edith was leaning over him. Baths were either first thing in the morning and cold, or late at night and warm. Confused, he frowned at her.

'Now?'

'Of course. I'll help you. Come along – while the water's nice and hot.'

She helped him out of the chair and led him upstairs. It was much colder here; and on the landing the draughts made him shiver. But it didn't matter. He was aware of what was happening but dissociated from it. His relationship with reality was at best semi-detached, like this house in Victoria Road. The analogy made him smile.

Edith glanced at him as she opened the bathroom door. 'What are you grinning about?'

'Nothing.' He knew he would not be able to find the right words; and even if he could, he was afraid that she would not understand.

'You've had a shock,' she told him, drawing him into the steam-filled room. 'You're not yourself.'

'No,' Thornhill agreed. 'I'm not myself.'

She shut the bathroom door behind them, peeled away the eiderdown and the blankets and helped him into the bath. The heat made him gasp. He stared at his pale, hairy body and thought it looked like a stranger's. *It's the shock*. Nothing was amusing now. Edith added more hot water.

'I must phone the station,' he said. 'Get someone to fetch the car.'

'I've already done that. Brian Kirby said he'd deal with it.'

He knew that she liked Kirby. A few years younger than Edith, he allowed her occasionally to mother him. Thornhill's position made the relationship innocent.

He lay full length in the bath. Edith had added soap powder as the water was running, and the surface of the water was covered in a layer of foam. His kneecaps were bony islands in this Arctic landscape. He could see his distorted reflections in the taps at the end of the bath – new taps, which he himself had fitted at Christmas as a way of making up for the fact that they could not afford to buy a new bath.

He had been going to see Les Carrick, Thornhill remembered; there was so much to ask him. In an instant all the things he needed to do piled into Thornhill's mind. He sat up abruptly in the bath.

'Can you phone Kirby again? Whoever brings the car back can pick me up here and take me to the station.'

Edith pushed him back into the bath. 'You need to get warm before you do anything.'

'But I want to get out.'

'I need to wash your hair.'

He was too weak to insist. He lay in the bath for another ten minutes. Edith added more hot water. He felt as though he were slowly simmering in a stew. When Edith had washed his hair, she helped him out and wrapped him in towels warmed on the hot-water tank. She made him sit on the bathroom chair while she dried him. *Just like one of the children.* The skin on his arms and hands had turned pink. A little later, he noticed that she was helping him on with his pyjamas.

'Look at that water,' she was saying, one eye on the water draining away. 'It's almost black under the foam. When did you last wash your hair?'

'I need my clothes.'

She pushed his right arm into the sleeve of his pyjama jacket. 'Tomorrow.'

In the end, it was easier to give up. He allowed himself to be guided into the bedroom.

'Where are the children?'

'Elizabeth's next door, and David's playing in the park.'

'Isn't it rather late for him to be out?'

'Not very. Anyway, he's with friends.' She covered him with two eiderdowns. 'Now try to get some sleep before the doctor comes.'

'Edith?'

'What now?'

'How's your mother?'

She stared at him. 'No better, I'm afraid. Sylvia said she'd ring tonight when she gets back from the hospital.'

'I'm sorry.'

She bent and kissed him. He heard her footsteps leaving the room, the door closing. Thoroughly warm at last, he slipped into a waking dream: he was back in the Ford Anglia, watching Jill's gloved hands on the steering wheel. *Soft brown leather, stained with mud and water from the pond.* Gradually he slid further and further away from consciousness.

The next time he woke, he emerged with an unpleasant jolt from a nightmare – he was back in the pond, swimming with desperate urgency beneath the surface of the black water, searching in vain for the car keys. An invisible monster of the deep seized his shoulder with its mouth, and shook him as a terrier shakes a rat. Soon, he knew, he would open his mouth and scream; then the darkness would flood in, and he would drown.

Fear surged through him. He opened his eyes as well as his mouth. Edith was leaning over him, her hand on his shoulder. The curtains were drawn and the lights were on. His pyjamas were damp with sweat.

'Richard – Dr Bayswater's here.'

Bayswater shambled towards the bed. He wore an ancient tweed jacket with leather patches at the elbows; one patch now dangled from the tweed, attached by only a few stitches.

'The car keys—' Thornhill began.

'Brian collected the spare set ten minutes ago.' Edith straightened up. 'I'll leave you to it, shall I, Doctor?'

Bayswater ignored her; he had the disconcerting habit of ignoring anyone and anything that did not immediately interest him.

'I can only spare you a moment,' he announced, apparently addressing the wardrobe. 'Already late for evening surgery.' His beautifully modulated voice was permanently at odds with his dishevelled appearance. He turned to the bed, picked up Thornhill's wrist and began to check the pulse. 'Had a ducking, eh? Damn silly thing to do. Waste of everyone's time. Up near Ashbridge, I gather?'

Thornhill nodded.

'Just as well that Francis woman pulled you out.'

'She didn't. She—'

'Why were you up there? That business with Carrick?'

'I was looking for his glasses. They still haven't turned up.'

'I doubt if they're in the pond. Must have been covered with ice on Wednesday night.' Bayswater pulled the covers back over Thornhill. 'You'll do. Good night's sleep and you should be as right as rain. But let me know if you're not.' He frowned, knitting together eyebrows like anarchic barbed wire, and peered at Thornhill's face. 'But you probably wouldn't, would you? Awkward customers like you make my job twice as hard as it need be.' He straightened up, tugging at his trousers, whose waistband tended to slide down his hips. 'I'll tell your wife to ring the surgery if she thinks it's necessary. And don't you dare try and stop her.'

Thornhill lay back against his pillows. 'Any news from the pathologist?'

'You don't want to think about that now.'

'I don't want to worry about it, either,' Thornhill said, suddenly cunning.

Bayswater shrugged. 'Murray rang me this afternoon. Don't know why he bothered, really. Nothing much to add to what I told you already: Carrick didn't die where he was found, and it wasn't the rope, or the blow on the head, that killed him but his own collar and tie.'

'Could it have been an accident?'

'Conceivably. At present the only conclusion you chaps can legitimately draw is that someone else was involved – after the death, if not before.'

'Which we already knew.'

'Can't help that.'

'What about the blow on the head?'

'Murray's working on it. Some sort of tool, maybe, or a bit of scrap iron?' Bayswater picked up his bag and wandered towards the door. 'Rest now. Try and sleep. You may not realise it, but your body's had quite a shock.' With his hand on the doorknob, he glanced back to Thornhill. 'Talking of shocks, I imagine your people will be talking to the sister-in-law at Moat Farm?'

'Dilys Carrick. We already have.'

'That's the one.' Bayswater opened the door and said gruffly, 'Go easy with her if you can.'

The door closed behind him. Thornhill listened to the doctor's footsteps on the stairs. Bayswater had been trying to tell him something about Dilys Carrick. But he wouldn't say it openly. There was an obvious, if unexpected, reason which would account for that.

4

After Dr Bayswater had gone, and after she had checked that her husband was still in bed, Edith Thornhill stood in the darkened hall and bit her nails. Nail-biting was a habit she had managed to break in her early twenties, but in times of stress it tended to resurface.

For a moment she weighed possibilities, balancing one fear against another. Would it be safe to leave Richard by himself? Despite Dr Bayswater's visit, she was still worried about him, and alarmed by his uncharacteristic docility; usually he was the most impatient of patients. Suppose he caught pneumonia. Suppose he died. The thought of a future without him, of just herself and the children, caught her unawares, bringing her unexpectedly close to the edge of panic.

Then there was Muriel next door – who had made it quite clear that it would not be convenient for Elizabeth to stay after five o'clock because that was when her husband was due home; Muriel's husband disliked having his own children under his feet and felt even less enthusiastic about other people's. And he was a man who habitually blamed his wife for anything he did not like.

On the other hand . . .

Edith went into the underfurnished icebox they called the dining room, and where they dined perhaps once every six months. The telephone was here, standing at one end of the long bookcase. Richard's raffle prize, the unwanted bowl of crocuses, was beside it. She dialled the number of the house next door.

'Muriel? It's Edith. I—'

'Elizabeth's just ready, aren't you dear?' Muriel's voice was loud and bright, presumably for the benefit of her husband.

'I'll be with you in ten minutes,' Edith said, plucking a number at random from an uncertain future. 'I need to fetch David.'

She put down the phone before Muriel could marshal her objections. Edith told herself that she did not want to drag Elizabeth out at this time of the evening. She shut her mind to the other reasons why she did not at present want Elizabeth's company. It was ridiculous to think that anything could have happened to David. He was often out by himself, even after dark. He was a very sensible little boy, too, for his age. At times like this, Edith wished she were not a policeman's wife.

Stifling her guilt at leaving Richard alone, she went into the hall and put on her outdoor clothes, including wellington boots. She slipped a torch into the pocket of her raincoat.

When she let herself out of the house, her lungs filled with damp, raw air flavoured with the harsh tang of burning coal; at this time of the evening everyone was building up their fires. She tramped through the slush up the gentle slope of Victoria Road towards Jubilee Park. *What if?* The words repeated themselves time and again in her mind. *What if?*

She tried to divert herself by thinking about Richard. She should feel grateful that he was none the worse for his ducking. How fortunate that Jill Francis had been in the vicinity. Jill's face

appeared in Edith's mind and Edith clung to it: a smart woman –
how could she afford to dress like that on whatever she earned
on the *Gazette?* Perhaps she had money of her own. Life was so
unfair. It must be so wonderful, not having to scrimp and save
all the time.

What if, what if . . .

The park's wrought-iron gates, black against the sky, loomed
up before her. She had met no one and seen no one as she
plodded up Victoria Road. She went inside the park and peered
into the gloom.

'David?' she called, at first quietly and then more loudly.
'David?'

She strained to hear an answer which did not come. In front
of her the ground sloped gently down from the gates towards the
children's playground. She could just make out the tall silhouette
of the slide, which in this light looked like a stooping skeleton
of a huge dragon with a long tail. Immediately to her right was
Lydmouth Cemetery, screened from Jubilee Park itself by a row
of oaks and a tall hedgerow. To the left, almost a hundred yards
away, were the public lavatories.

'David? David?'

From the town centre came the distant sound of engines.
Someone was shouting. Up here, however, there was only silence.
Fear squeezed her. David was still such a little boy, not much
more than a baby, really. Before David's birth, Richard had once
told her that sometimes his work forced him to deal with wicked,
perverted people who did terrible things to children. Suddenly it
was hard to breathe.

'David? David?'

*Don't panic. Think sensibly. The naughty boy. He's scared of the
graves, poor darling, scared of the dark even as a baby.*

Edith took the path that led along the boundary of Jubilee
Park towards the public lavatories. On her left were the gardens
of houses in Albert Road, which met Victoria Road at right angles
beside the main gates of the park. She met no one; the children

and the dog walkers who haunted the park even at this time of year had returned to the warmth of their homes.

This can't be happening, not to me, not to us.

The further she moved away from the main gates, the darker it became. She took out her torch and sent its beam zigzagging in front of her along the path.

'David? David?'

He might have gone home with one of his friends. It was unlikely he would do that without asking her permission. Come to that, Edith would have said that it was unlikely he would stay out so late. He must have realised that it was long past time for his supper. The need to find him dwarfed her other responsibilities – Elizabeth, an unwelcome guest at Muriel's house, Richard recovering in bed, jacket potatoes turning to cinders in the oven, her mother dying in a strange hospital. She should have called the police, Edith thought; she should have found someone to stay at home in case David returned before her, in case Sylvia rang with news about their mother. Too late for all that now; much too late.

'David?'

Edith reached the lavatories. She walked round to the men's entrance. To her surprise, the door was shut and locked, though the outside light was on. A moment later, she discovered that the ladies' lavatory was closed as well.

There was a rustling in the bushes which formed a decorous screen between the lavatories and the bus shelter on Albert Road. Automatically Edith flicked the torch beam towards it.

'Who's there?'

Her voice was breathless, and she felt ashamed of her fear. The torchlight danced on dark, gleaming leaves. Edith heard the scuffle of retreating feet. She backed away from the sound. For an instant the light picked out a pair of shoulders: Edith caught a glimpse of light brown wool, of a hood rising up from the shoulders. A duffel coat?

For an instant she saw a shadow framed in the small gateway

on the other side of the bushes. Then there were footsteps running down Albert Road. That was what really alarmed her – the obvious panic, presumably guilty, of the person she had disturbed.

'*David?*' she screamed.

Edith forced herself to move into the bushes and search them methodically. The torchlight slid over the ground, picking out bare earth, jagged islands of snow, dead leaves, cigarette packets, a used condom, a yellowing copy of the *Gazette* and an empty milk bottle.

But no David. No broken body, thank God. But if he wasn't here, where was he? *Such a little boy* – not big for his age; not over-confident; scared of the dark.

The panic threatened to well out of her. David needed her, she told herself, and she would be no use to anyone if she didn't keep a cool head. What would Richard do in this situation? First, he wouldn't panic; that went without saying. Second, he would make a plan and follow it, come hell or high water.

The thought of Richard steadied her. She decided to make a circuit of the park, calling David's name. It took her much longer than expected, partly because the ground was rough, made more treacherous by the snow and the darkness. It occurred to her that if she slipped and broke an ankle or leg, no one might hear her cries. At this time of year windows were closed. She might even die of exposure.

Another possibility slid like a snake into her mind: that the lurker in the duffel coat had returned and was following her silently through the snow.

'David? David?'

The ground dipped unexpectedly. Edith fell to one knee with a jolt that jarred her body. Mud on her coat now, she thought grimly, and probably on her skirt; and heaven alone knew what she had done to her stocking. She concentrated doggedly on these lesser worries.

'David?'

The park formed an irregular quadrilateral, several acres in extent. By now, Edith had reached the last of the four sides – the long hedge which separated the park from the cemetery. Her feet were freezing in the wellington boots. She had been crying for some time, weeping soundlessly in case she should miss David if he called out. The police, Edith thought: she would phone them as soon as she reached home. *Dear God, please God, may he be all right.* The need to scream and scream squirmed within her.

'David?'

'Mummy—'

At first Edith continued walking. An instant later her brain registered what she had heard.

'*David.* Where are you?'

'Here. Here.'

'In the cemetery?'

'Yes . . .' His voice sounded beyond tears, close to the borders of hysteria.

'I'm here, darling. Just wait for Mummy and I'll be with you in a moment.'

That, she knew, was easier said than done. The hedge between the park and the cemetery was old and dense: hawthorn, elder, holly, a formidable barrier even in daylight.

'Just wait there, darling, and call out when you hear me.'

Edith broke into a run. Slipping, sliding and stumbling, she followed the line of oaks towards the main gates. The entrance to the cemetery was just outside the gates, on the other side from the end of Albert Road. A cottage stood in the angle between cemetery and park, but its windows were dark. Edith picked her way among the graves, calling her son's name.

'Here, Mummy, over here.'

She heard him crying. Suddenly, much sooner than she had expected, his school raincoat – navy blue gabardine, caked with mud – appeared in the circle of torchlight. David emerged from the dark and flung his arms around Edith's waist. He was sobbing with relief and trembling, his whole body shaking in spasms as though someone were passing an electric current through him; *on, off, on, off.*

Edith knelt on the ground between two graves and hugged him until the trembling became less violent. Then she led him home. David was not usually a boy who showed his emotions. She thought of the lurker and another fear stirred in her: what could have upset David so much?

At last they reached home. Edith let them into the house and propelled David into the kitchen where she peeled off his coat and boots and settled him into the chair by the boiler. His bare knees were filthy and grazed. One of the blankets which Richard had used was still on the table. Edith tucked it round David. He stared at her, his eyes huge and dark in a white, tear-stained face.

'Warm milk,' she said, knowing that reassurance was needed as well as warmth. 'And I'll fetch you a jersey as well.'

She brought him a piece of chocolate, too, in recognition that this was a special occasion when ordinary rules did not apply. Gradually he became calmer. His first coherent words took her by surprise.

'Where's Lizzie?' he asked.

'Next door.'

'Good.'

Edith realised that he would not want to appear in this state before his sister. Was that a good sign? Perhaps it meant that he couldn't be too badly damaged if his masculine pride was still intact.

'Now – would it be a good idea if you told me what happened?'

He sipped his milk, staring at her over the rim of the mug.

'I thought you were going to play with Bill and Henry.'

'I did.' His face brightened briefly. 'We were commandos in Norway, because of the snow. It was super. Then they went home for tea and . . .'

He swallowed more milk.

'You were playing in the park?' Edith suggested.

He nodded.

'Then how did you get into the cemetery? And why didn't you come home?'

'They made me.' His voice crumpled like a paper bag screwed up by a hand. 'They said if I tried to go home the ghosts would get me.'

It is difficult to remain calm and motherly when your dominant emotion is a powerful urge to find and murder, preferably slowly, the people who scared your child. But Edith managed. Gradually she winkled the story out of David. When Bill and Henry had gone home, David had lingered, looking for a stick they had been using in the game – one which looked, at least to the eyes of the imagination, almost exactly like a Bren gun; Bill had left it leaning against one of the oaks, and it had taken David several minutes to find it. By that time, it had been almost dark. Just as he had found it, he had heard a noise behind him.

Two boys he had never seen before had crept up on him. They were larger than he was – after questioning David, Edith thought they had probably been a year or two older, not much to an adult but a huge gulf of maturity to a small boy. They had taken against David immediately – or perhaps they had been looking for trouble. At first the cause of their hostility was that he went to the wrong school – David had been wearing the scarf of St John's School. The other boys went to a school near the station, on the fringe of the Templefields area, so they had been outside their usual territory.

Nasty rough boys, Edith thought, *but what can you expect if they live in Templefields?*

The two strangers had shown considerable artistry in their cruelty. They had taken off David's tie, and tied his wrists with it. They pushed him painfully through a gap in the hedge and took him into the cemetery, where they lashed him with his own scarf to a stone cross attached to one of the graves.

'If you try and escape,' one of them had told David, 'the ghosts will get you. Your only chance is to stay here. Don't move away from the cross. Otherwise it's curtains.'

They had left him then – at least in theory. But for some time afterwards, David had heard rustling and laughing and strange noises; more than enough to keep him where he was. At last they had left him alone with his fear. After what seemed like hours, he had heard his mother calling him. Only then had he dared to wriggle out of his bonds.

'I knew you'd come if I waited.'

David sounded sleepy. After the storm comes the calm. Edith wondered if now was the time to fetch Elizabeth and make her apologies to Muriel. She also wanted to check that Richard was all right.

'Mummy? They found out that Daddy's a policeman.'

'How?'

'They asked my name and what Daddy did. When I said he's a policeman it made them worse.'

'Never mind, darling. Just silly boys.'

'They called him names.'

'We'll tell Daddy, and he'll see to it that they're found and punished.'

'No. *No.*'

'Why ever not?'

'They said if I told anyone they'd come and get me.' David began to tremble again. 'And now I've told you.'

'I don't count, darling,' Edith said automatically. 'I'm your mother.'

5

Jill worked late that evening. There was a council meeting to attend, a wearisome business which made great demands on her powers of alertness. Afterwards she went back to the *Gazette*.

The building was empty – even the cleaners had departed. The office lost its familiarity at night: it became a place filled with small but inexplicable sounds, clean ashtrays, silent telephones and shrouded typewriters. Jill worked there for an hour and a half, trying to catch up on jobs she had left undone during the day. She missed Philip Wemyss-Brown more than she had expected. She had not previously appreciated how much work he managed to do between trips to the bar of the Bull Hotel and afternoons on the golf course.

While she worked at Philip's desk, the day's events swirled in her mind, the patterns breaking and re-forming as though at the bottom of a kaleidoscope. It was a pity she couldn't use what had happened with Richard Thornhill. She could see the headline: GAZETTE REPORTER RESCUES TOP POLICEMAN.

The memory of his white body slipped into her mind as she tried to make something interesting from her notes about a sluggish debate about the relative merits of traffic lights and zebra crossings. Richard Thornhill was surprisingly well muscled for a man of his build. Edith was almost as tall as he was – and large in all directions. Perhaps Thornhill liked big women. Jill felt warm with embarrassment.

She abandoned the council meeting, the report unfinished. It was a quarter to eleven: time to call it a day. While she locked up, she debated whether to drive back to Church Cottage. The distance was so short that it seemed a criminal waste of petrol. But the car seemed curiously tempting.

A moment later she realised why: she was afraid of being followed. She told herself not to be so stupid and cowardly. The only thing to do with a fear was to face up to it.

She let herself out of the front door and walked briskly up the High Street, forcing herself to act as if it were eleven in the morning instead of eleven at night. It was cool and damp, but milder than it had been; the wind had dropped. Most of the snow had gone in the centre of town, and the street glistened with moisture.

As if expressly to allay Jill's fears, a policeman appeared on his bicycle and wished her goodnight as he passed. She turned into Church Street. There were lights in the vicarage and in Victor Youlgreave's house beyond the church on the other side of the road. She slowed as she approached her own front door, feeling for the key in her handbag, and glanced over her shoulder. The street was empty.

Church Cottage was chilly but welcoming; Jill thought with satisfaction that it was beginning to feel like home. She lit the gas fire in the dining room. She would have a bath, she decided, and then a mug of cocoa and perhaps a small brandy by the fire.

The bathroom was on the ground floor next to the kitchen. Jill switched on the wall heater and left it to warm the room while she took off her outdoor clothes and fetched a hot-water bottle, her night clothes and a book to read by the fire.

On her way upstairs she passed the little window on the landing which looked out over the back of the house. Before she drew the single curtain across it, she stared out, her face close to the glass. At the front of the house you knew you were in a town; but if you looked out of this window at night, you might almost be in the country. On the left was the vicarage and its garden, both invisible. Directly in front of her was the cottage's small garden, separated by a wall from what had once been the vicarage's kitchen garden, now becoming a wilderness. To the right was an empty house. True, the faint radiance of the streetlamps tinged the horizon, but the brightest part of town, the High Street, was blocked by the empty house and the buildings beyond.

For a moment Jill stood there, resting her eyes on the soft darkness. Not that it was all dark. She had left the lights on in the bathroom and the kitchen.

Another light caught her eye – over to her right. For a moment, a tiny speck of red glowed in the darkness. It moved in an arc, and simultaneously its intensity diminished. Suddenly it was no longer there.

Jill stayed at the window in the darkness for several minutes, her eyes trained on the spot where she had seen the glow. It did not reappear. She might have imagined it. After all, why should someone be standing in the darkness at a first-floor window of the empty house next door, smoking a cigarette?

SIX

The Weekend Gardener

Crocuses are one of the most popular families of spring-flowering bulbs. Everyone knows the snowdrop, but when we see the pretty flowers of crocuses appear like brightly-coloured arrow-heads in the garden, we know that spring is truly on its way.

They may be planted in clumps, as edgings to a border, in the lawn, and also in rockeries. The corms should be set at least two inches deep and about three inches apart, or rather more.

There are purple, white, striped and yellow varieties, and it is the last-named kind which sparrows are so prone to pick to pieces when the blossoms open. The wise gardener will take care to protect blossoms by criss-crossing black thread to and fro from wooden pegs.

NB There are miniature crocuses specially raised for rockeries.

The *Lydmouth Gazette*, 10th February

1

'There's only one more thing.' Mrs Weald glanced over her shoulder to make sure there were no eavesdroppers. She lowered her voice to a whisper like air hissing from a tyre. 'I think it was a negro.'

'Not the sort of thing you expect at a respectable hotel,' Mr Weald pointed out. He was a Yorkshireman who had already remarked that he liked to call a spade a spade. 'It's an insult to my wife.' He looked balefully at Mr Frinton, the manager of the Bull. 'We shall expect compensation. Especially in the circumstances. A negro, indeed.'

Brian Kirby opened his notebook. He had just arrived in the manager's office and he had not expected to find the Wealds waiting for him. He directed a conciliatory smile at Mrs Weald. 'Could you describe what happened, madam? From the beginning.'

'She already has,' Mr Weald said. 'She told that lad who came round last night. And that's another thing: if you get a serious complaint like that, do you usually send round a boy in uniform? He were hardly old enough to shave. It's not how we do things in my part of the world.'

'It's standard practice to go over the ground again,' Kirby said, ignoring the second part of the complaint. 'Often people remember things they forgot to mention the first time. Or they have second thoughts.'

'I'll leave you to it, then.' Mr Frinton slipped out of the room.

Kirby wished he could follow. 'You were having a bath, Mrs Weald: what time was this?'

'About seven o'clock. Just before dinner. Not that I felt like eating a thing after what happened. Any sort of upset goes straight to my stomach. Always has, even when I was a little girl.'

Kirby nodded sympathetically. Mrs Weald opened her handbag and took out a handkerchief scented with eau de Cologne. She patted her forehead with it. She was a dark, plump woman, carefully made-up and expensively dressed. Kirby found her not unattractive. After a respectful pause, he began to extract her story.

As Mrs Weald talked, her fingers fiddled with a long loop of pearls, a secular rosary. She and her husband had been staying at the Bull since Tuesday. Mr Weald was something to do with tinned foods, and he had been negotiating a contract with a company near

Abergavenny. She and her husband were in Room 8. They used a bathroom on the other side of the corridor, which faced the back of the hotel. The bathroom had a sash window with frosted glass in the lower half. There were curtains on the window but the rail was slightly twisted, and the curtains would not meet; there was a four-inch gap between them.

'Typical,' interrupted Mr Weald. 'It's details like that that show you what a hotel's really like.'

It had been dark outside. Mrs Weald had stood up in the bath and reached for her towel. (A disturbing mental image of what she must have looked like flashed through Kirby's mind – all that rich flesh, swathed in diaphanous veils of steam.) As she was stretching out her arm, she happened to glance at the window.

'I didn't get a good look. Just a fleeting impression.'

'Disgraceful,' commented Mr Weald. 'And a nigger, too.'

'I'm not sure about that, dear.' Mrs Weald peered anxiously at her husband. 'It's all such a muddle. I *think* he was a darkie.'

Kirby spent another five minutes asking questions but got little further. Mr Weald had been downstairs in the bar, preparing himself in his own way for the rigours of the evening ahead. Having seen the face at the window, Mrs Weald had screamed, clambered out of the bath, tripped over the bathmat and at length wrapped herself in the towel. She thought that the face had vanished as soon as she saw it; but she wasn't sure – she had not wished to look too closely. She had draped her dressing-gown around her and run to her room. By the time the alarm had been raised, there was no sign of an intruder.

As far as Kirby could tell, the Wealds did not know that something very similar had happened to another guest in the hotel on Wednesday evening. Had he known, Mr Weald would scarcely have failed to mention it.

'It's just not good enough, Sergeant,' Weald told him. 'I want that bugger caught. All right? Perverts like that need to be locked up for their own good. And I'm not having them peeping at my wife. She didn't get a wink of sleep last night.'

At last Kirby managed to say goodbye to the Wealds and went to look for Frinton. The manager took him to the back of the hotel and showed him the fire escape that snaked up the building.

'That's room seven, by the way,' Frinton wheezed, pointing to a large sash window as he pulled his bulk up the iron steps. 'Mr Jordan's old room. Don't tell me there's not a connection between the two.'

'And which is the bathroom, sir?'

Frinton pointed to the window beside it. The frame had lost most of its paint and was quietly rotting. There was nothing to see on the fire escape, either. The snow had melted. It had been raining on and off during the night.

What does Frinton expect? A bloody miracle?

'What about the other time?' Kirby asked. 'Does everyone know about it?'

'I damn well hope not. We tried to keep the whole thing quiet, for obvious reasons.'

'People talk.'

'That's what I'm afraid of, Sergeant. Something like this will do the Bull no good at all.'

Kirby looked down at the yard. 'Do you shut those gates at night, sir?'

'No – some of our patrons park their cars in the yard. I don't even know if the gates *will* close.'

The gateway from the yard led into Bull Lane, a side street running down from the High Street.

'If the worst comes to the worst, maybe you should think about shutting them.'

'That's all very well, Sergeant, but—'

Frinton broke off. One of the maids had come out of the door by the kitchens and was standing at the foot of the fire escape, her hands clasped in front of her and her head bowed.

'What is it, Joan? Can't it wait?'

The woman lifted her face. 'It's about last night, sir. I've only just heard.'

Frinton frowned at her. 'Who told you?'

'Mr Quale. He knew I'd been on duty, you see. I think – I think I might have seen something.'

'One of our chambermaids,' Frinton murmured to Kirby. 'Quite a reliable type.'

The two men clattered down the iron stairs. The woman waited. When he reached the ground, Kirby glanced at her face. She was younger than he had thought. From a distance, grey hair and an unsmiling face had put ten years on her age.

'This is Sergeant Kirby, Joan. Let's go inside and you can tell him what's on your mind.'

They went into the hotel. Quale was at reception, apparently absorbed in examining the hotel register. Frinton glanced in his direction to make sure he was out of earshot.

'Well?'

The maid stared up at Frinton. 'Is it true what Mr Quale said? That someone was on the fire escape yesterday evening, trying to look into one of the bathrooms? When Mrs Weald was having a bath?'

'We think that may have been the case, yes.'

'I saw him.' The maid was trembling slightly.

'What time was this?'

'It was about ten past seven, sir. I'd been sorting laundry, you see, and I was running late, and I'd just looked at my watch. I was feeling very hot, so I opened the back door to get a breath of fresh air. There was a man at the bottom of the fire escape.'

'Did you recognise him?' Frinton demanded.

Joan shook her head.

Kirby moved forward a step. 'What did he look like?'

'Small,' Joan said slowly. 'Wearing a grey mac, and a dark hat, a beret, maybe, pulled down low.'

'Was he a nigger?' Frinton burst out. 'Did you see?'

'Was there enough light to see?' Kirby interrupted, irritated that Frinton had asked such a leading question.

Joan's face twitched. 'Yes, sir, the door was open, look, and there was light from the kitchen windows.'

'Would you be able to recognise the man again?'

'I don't know. Perhaps.'

'What did he do? Did he speak to you?'

'No. Just walked away very quickly – out into Bull Lane. I think he turned left up to the High Street, but I can't be sure.'

Frinton's face reddened. 'Why on earth didn't you raise the alarm, Joan?'

'He was near the fire escape, sir, but he wasn't actually on it. I thought he'd just come in to use the gents in the yard.'

Frinton shrugged. 'Fair enough. People do, I'm afraid. God knows why when there's a perfectly good public convenience on the corner.'

Kirby took out his notebook again. 'This is very useful, Mrs——?'

'Davies, sir.'

'I'd better take down your details in case we need to talk to you again. Do you live here?'

'Oh no, sir. Victoria Road. Number sixty-five.'

Kirby was surprised, though he tried not to show it. Victoria Road was one of the more expensive parts of Lydmouth. He would have expected the woman to live in Templefields or near the station.

'Our house is the one near the cemetery. Ernest looks after the graves. It goes with the job.' Her voice was defensive but she spoke mechanically, as if she had said these words often before.

'So it's Mrs Joan Davies. And Ernest is your husband?'

She nodded.

Kirby turned over a page of his notebook. 'Now can you tell me what you saw again – about the man?'

'Oh yes,' she said, and he could have sworn she looked relieved. 'About the nigger.'

2

Jill Francis was not usually an indecisive person but on Friday night she lay awake until the early hours wondering what to do. When she was woken on Saturday morning – by Alice, sitting on her stomach and purring loudly – she found she was still no nearer to a decision.

The problem was that the evidence was so skimpy – indeed, in one sense, there was no evidence at all. How could she prove that she was being watched? She had heard footsteps behind her on Wednesday night when she was returning from dining with Larry Jordan at the Bull. On the same evening, she had thought she saw a shadow in the churchyard. Last night, she had seen – or she had thought she had seen – the glow of a cigarette at one of the windows of the empty house next door. It added up to very little. And the real unpleasantness – her sense that she was the object of the prurient curiosity of an invisible watcher – was something she could hardly mention to the police.

After breakfast she put on her coat and opened the front door. The weather was milder: you could believe in the possibility of spring. She walked along the pavement and stopped outside the empty house next door, which butted against Church Cottage on one side and against an irregular terrace of cottages on the other. The house was larger than its neighbours. Jill stared at the grimy windows and the dingy bricks and wondered whether anyone was watching her now.

This was a kind of violation, she thought, in its way as bad as robbery or rape. Someone was stealing her privacy. It defiled her as surely as poison in a well. *Even if I'm imagining it?*

She walked along to the vicarage and rang the doorbell. Asking favours did not come easily to her. Nor did making friends. It was only as she was waiting for the door to open that it occurred to her that the very fact she felt able to ask must mean that she now thought of Mary Sutton as a friend.

The door opened. There was Mary, to Jill's relief; much as

she liked Alec, Mary's husband, he wouldn't have done at a time like this.

'Jill – what's wrong?'

After that it was relatively easy. Mary took charge, which was reassuring, as was the fact that she believed unquestioningly that Jill was right in her suspicions.

'Of course someone's watching you. You're not the sort of person who would make up something like that. Anyone can see that.'

Mary quite understood the difficulty, however – there was nothing much to tell the police.

'We'd better have a look at the house.'

'We can't just break in.'

'No need to do that. Victor will have a key.'

'Victor Youlgreave?'

'Didn't you know? He owns that house. And several others, too. Our Victor's quite the man of property.'

Mary did not always see eye to eye with Victor Youlgreave, who was one of her husband's churchwardens. 'On his good days,' she had once confided to Jill, 'he's one of the nicest old women in the parish.'

She fetched her coat and the two women walked along to Youlgreave's house, which was at the northwest corner of the churchyard.

'Victor's between tenants,' she told Jill. 'I think the house needs a lot of work done to it and he's bracing himself to open the purse-strings.'

When the housekeeper opened Youlgreave's front door, 'The Ride of the Valkyries' rushed out on a current of warm air. Mr Youlgreave, she explained, was not at home to anyone apart from the doctor. Still in his pyjamas, he was huddled over the fire in the sitting room, nursing a cold and listening to Wagner. Mary explained what they wanted. The housekeeper left the two women in the hall. A moment later she returned with the keys to the house next to Church Cottage.

'Tell him we'll bring them back before lunch,' Mary said, raising her voice to be heard above the music. 'I do hope he feels better soon.'

The housekeeper smiled sardonically. 'He wishes he was well enough to come with you.'

'Never mind. We'll manage. Thank you so much for your help. Goodbye.'

A few minutes later, Mary unlocked the front door of the house next to Church Cottage. She pushed the door open: this time cold, damp air swirled out to meet them. The door stuck on a heap of post, most of it circulars. As they went into the hall, Jill pulled her coat more tightly around her.

'Let's have a look at the back, first,' Mary suggested.

Jill thought Mary's enthusiasm a little indecent but what could you expect of a woman who had a professional interest in private investigation? Mary made more than her husband earned by writing detective stories in her spare time. Jill followed her down the hall to the kitchen. There was a scullery beyond, and here they found what Jill both wanted and dreaded to find. There was a pantry opening off the scullery and its small window had been forced. Smears of mud streaked the dusty marble shelf under the window. On the floor was a small puddle of water.

'Well, that settles that,' Mary said with evident pleasure. 'Shame he didn't leave a footprint or a handprint in the mud. Still, one can't have everything.' She retreated into the scullery and peered through the window, larger than the one in the pantry, into the overgrown garden beyond. 'He probably came over that wall on the right. He could use the tree as a ladder.'

'What's on the other side?' Jill asked.

'That little car park off the High Street. The one by Woolworth's.' Mary hesitated. 'Do you suppose—?'

'That he's still here?' Jill automatically lowered her voice. 'I suppose he might be. It could just be a tramp, couldn't it? Nothing personal at all. Perhaps he wasn't watching me. Perhaps he was just having a quiet smoke before settling down for the night.'

'Shall we find Alec before we go upstairs?'

'So he can lead the way, waving a big stick?'

'Something like that,' Mary said, unembarrassed. 'Men occasionally have their uses. Except if Alec thought it was a tramp, he'd be far more likely to take a cup of tea than a big stick.'

'I think I'd rather go up now.' Jill went into the hall. 'Personally I wouldn't mind having a stick to wave.'

'Take my umbrella, dear.'

Side by side, the two ladies advanced up the uncarpeted stairs. They did not hurry and they made no attempt to walk quietly; Jill had no desire to surprise anyone, and she suspected that Mary felt the same.

The house was a place of dank, empty rooms, flaking plaster, rotting floorboards and peeling wallpaper. They found a wren's nest in what had once been the bathroom, and signs of rats and mice everywhere. At last they came to a room at the back of the house overlooking the walled garden of Church Cottage.

'Blast,' Mary said. 'Damn and blast. But I suppose it's all to the good, really.'

There wasn't much to see: an old, stained blanket, used matches, a couple of cigarette ends, a pile of dottles surrounded by a scattering of ash where a pipe had been knocked out repeatedly on the floor, an empty Pale Ale bottle, and a copy of the *Lydmouth Gazette*.

Jill picked up the newspaper. It was yesterday's edition.

3

'Should you be here, sir?' Brian Kirby asked.

'I'm perfectly all right, thank you.'

Looking unconvinced, Kirby put down the tray of coffee on the desk.

Thornhill waved him to the single visitor's chair. 'By the way, thanks for fetching the car yesterday. Much appreciated.'

Both men sipped their coffee. Kirby lit a cigarette. Embarrassment hung like a fog in the little office: gratitude was a difficult emotion to express and a harder one to receive.

Thornhill drew the Carrick file towards him and tapped the buff-coloured folder. 'Before we get on to this, what's going on at the Bull?'

Kirby told him about the second visit of the Peeping Tom.

'A *negro?*'

'Someone with a dark skin, at least. That's what Mrs Weald thought, and the chambermaid confirmed it. He was only a few feet away from her when he came off the fire escape. I know the light wasn't good but she struck me as observant.'

'And Mrs Weald?'

'Quite attractive in her way,' Kirby said primly.

'No doubt.' Thornhill remembered the well-fleshed woman he had passed on the stairs of the Bull as he was leaving Jordan on Wednesday night. 'But that wasn't what I meant. What sort of a witness is she?'

Kirby stubbed out his cigarette. 'She was in a bit of a state at the time, of course.'

'Had she heard about that business with Jordan?'

'No.'

'So it was independent of the other sighting?' Thornhill sighed. 'So we've either got two Peeping Toms or Jordan's wrong.'

'I don't follow, sir.'

'Jordan assumed that the person at the window was one of his fans. But perhaps it wasn't. Perhaps it was the same man as last night, looking for a woman with no clothes on. Do you know what the Wealds' room number is?'

Kirby flicked back the pages of his notebook. 'Eight.'

'Jordan's first room was number seven. Next door, do you think? So perhaps the man wasn't looking for Jordan, he was looking for Mrs Weald all along. And yesterday he found her. For all we know it's someone working at the hotel.'

Thornhill pushed aside his coffee cup. His immersion yesterday seemed to have cleared his mind; or perhaps he should thank his long sleep. He felt physically weak but his mind was clear.

'My wife was up at Jubilee Park at about half-past five yesterday evening,' he went on. 'There was a man in the bushes between the public lavatories and Albert Road. As soon as she shone a torch towards him, he ran off down the road.'

'You think there's a connection?'

'Could be. Have a word with Mr Jackson, will you?'

Inspector Jackson was in charge of the uniformed branch of the Lydmouth division. The business at Jubilee Park was not yet a CID matter.

Thornhill looked at his watch. 'I want to get up to Ashbridge now. Or rather to Moat Farm.' He stood up, feeling unsteady on his legs but managing to conceal it by leaning unobtrusively on the back of his chair. 'I was reading the pathologist's report while you were at the Bull. I don't much like that, either. All right, the body was moved after death. And Carrick was a small man — just under nine stone. Even so, it's not easy to move a dead body single-handedly.' He lifted his coat off the hook on the back of the door and pushed his arms into the sleeves. 'Let alone trek across the countryside with it and string it up on a tree, and all in the dead of winter.'

'Unless he died where he was found.'

Thornhill picked up his hat and gloves. 'If that were the case, what was Carrick doing there in the first place? The last we know of him he was leaving the Classical Society meeting up at the school.'

'Suppose he had an assignation with the sister-in-law. Suppose—'

'Even if he did, it wouldn't explain how he died.'

At that moment the phone began to ring. Thornhill snatched it from its cradle.

'There's a Mr Sandleigh wanting to speak to you, sir,' said the clerk at the switchboard.

'Put him through.'

'Inspector.' Sandleigh's voice, like Charlotte Wemyss-Brown's, sounded particularly resonant over the phone. 'Good morning.'

'How can we help, sir?'

A chuckle thundered down the line. 'More a question of our helping you this time. I have Mrs Hirdle with me. She's the sister in charge of our school sanatorium. She has one of Burton's sixth formers as a patient. Boy called Walton.'

In Thornhill's mind, a memory clicked into place. 'Have I met him?'

'Briefly, yes, on Thursday morning. He went down with flu – been *hors de combat* for a couple of days. But he's fairly clear-headed now. According to Mrs Hirdle, the boy actually saw Carrick on Wednesday night. *After* the meeting of the Classical Society.'

'We'd better come and talk to him. Is he well enough?'

'Mrs Hirdle thinks he'll be all right – as long as you don't give him the third degree, of course. Ha, ha. I just hope he was all right before.'

'What do you mean?'

'As a witness. According to Mrs Hirdle, he had a temperature of a hundred and three on Thursday morning. That suggests that he may not have been perfectly clear-headed on the evening before.'

Thornhill said goodbye and put down the phone. He looked at Kirby. 'The school first, then the farm.'

The two men left the room. As Thornhill was closing the door, his telephone began to ring. The door shut with a click, muting the sound and he followed Kirby down the stairs.

Let them leave a message.

4

Having screwed herself up to telephone Thornhill, it was annoying to find that neither he nor Brian Kirby was available. Jill explained what she had discovered to a detective constable who effortlessly gave the impression that he thought she was an hysterical woman who needed to be humoured. He promised to pass the details on to Thornhill. Jill hoped that he meant what he said.

By now she was back at Church Cottage. Mary had given her two cups of coffee and a cigarette at the vicarage. Jill had been in two minds about ringing the police, and Mary had given her both moral support and chemical stimulation.

Jill went into the kitchen, where Alice made figures of eight round her ankles and purred loudly in the hope of attracting a mid-morning snack. She stared without enthusiasm at the porridge saucepan waiting for her in the sink. Why on earth had she bothered with porridge this morning? Why did she ever bother with porridge? It simply wasn't worth the trouble. But she could hardly leave the saucepan there until her charwoman's next visit. She stretched out her hand towards the apron draped over the back of a chair. At that moment there was a knocking on the front door.

Jill went into the hall, pausing to check her appearance in the mirror, and opened the door. Edith Thornhill, flanked by her children, was outside. For an instant, the two women stared at each other – one of those awkward moments which are gone in a flash and yet last far too long for comfort.

'Good morning,' Edith began, her face breaking into a smile. 'I hope we're not—'

'Hello,' Jill said simultaneously. She stepped back, opening the door more widely. 'Do come in. How's Mr Thornhill this morning?'

'He seems perfectly all right. He was off to work at nine o'clock.' Edith gave a little laugh. 'You know what men are like. They don't like a fuss.'

The children followed their mother into the house. The boy was carrying an awkwardly wrapped parcel about the size of a football. He glanced up at Jill and then looked down at the floor.

'You'll have some coffee now you're here, won't you?'

'We wouldn't want to put you to any trouble.'

'No trouble at all. I was making some in any case.'

'I wanted to bring back your handkerchief.'

Edith held out a small brown paper bag. Inside, Jill guessed, would be the handkerchief, now washed and ironed.

'And there's also this. Just a little token of thanks. David — give Miss Francis what we've brought.'

The boy held up the parcel. The top was open, revealing a bowl of flowering crocuses, purple smudges which seemed almost luminous in the gloom of the hall. Their colour made Jill think of muted maiden aunts sucking cough lozenges.

'How lovely. I've only just moved in and I need some colour about the place. Let me take your coats.'

She led them into the dining room where she lit the gas fire and wondered why on earth she had invited them in. The sitting room was a much nicer room, but it was too cold for a day like this; Jill had not lit the open fire in there for several days. She put the crocuses on the table beside her typewriter. There were two armchairs by the fire. Edith settled in one with the children hovering close beside her.

Jill left them there and went to the kitchen, where she reheated coffee, poured milk for the children and decanted a packet of Marie biscuits onto a plate. When she returned to the dining room with the tray, the Thornhills were where she had left them, unchanged like a waxwork tableau at Madam Tussaud's. Jill had the feeling that none of them had moved or spoken in her absence.

Alice, scenting the possibility of food and affection, followed her into the room. The children seized upon her as a welcome diversion. With an eye firmly fixed on the main chance, the cat allowed herself to receive their caresses. Edith, placid but watchful, did not interfere.

'I think I saw you the other afternoon,' she said after a sip of coffee. 'In the Bull.'

'Oh yes. I was having tea.'

Edith smiled. 'With a friend?'

'Not exactly.' Jill was disconcerted not only by the line of conversation, but by the glimpse of cunning at work.

'Richard told me Lawrence Jordan was here. I thought he might be a disappointment in the flesh. But he's not, though, is he? Are you going to write something about him in the paper?'

'Eventually.' Jill wondered how much Thornhill had told his wife, how much he habitually told her. 'Mr Jordan's given me an interview, but I've promised not to use it until he's left Lydmouth.'

Edith nodded wisely. 'I can understand him wanting to avoid publicity. He must long for a little peace and quiet – just to be an ordinary person again.'

Jill smiled but did not commit herself to an opinion.

'Is he as amusing as he was in *The Oldest Friend*? It had me in stitches, that film. Not just the words he said, it was the way he said them.'

Lawrence Jordan kept the conversation going for five minutes. David tried to feed Alice with a piece of his biscuit and was reprimanded by his mother. Elizabeth gradually lost her self-consciousness and showed a disposition to squabble with her brother over Alice's affections. Jill offered the children paper and pencils, a suggestion which Edith heartily endorsed. The children sat at the table, drawing and occasionally kicking each other when they thought that their mother wasn't looking. Jill thought David was exactly like a fairer version of his father.

Edith did most of the talking. 'Richard and I enjoy Lydmouth. Of course I come from this part of the world, so when there was a possibility of a job down here I encouraged him to apply for it. It's almost like coming home. The children love it here.'

The children showed no signs of loving anything at present, least of all each other.

'And what about school?' she asked, remembering that this was usually a safe topic with parents.

'So far so good. It's what happens when they are older that's the worry. Richard and I were talking about it only the other

day. A school is such an important choice, isn't it, especially
for a boy. We have been wondering about Ashbridge School.
We've heard very good reports.'

Jill remarked that the Suttons' boys were there. 'Mary Sutton
said that it didn't seem to be doing them too much damage.'

'Personal recommendation is so important. The trouble with
local schools is that they do have some very rough children.' As
Edith was finishing her coffee, St John's clock began to chime
twelve. 'Is that the time already? We really must be off.' She
smiled at her children. 'We need to buy Daddy some ice cream
on the way home, don't we?' She glanced at Jill. 'Richard's very
partial to a little ice cream after his Sunday lunch, even in the
depths of winter. Men are such creatures of habit, aren't they?'

'But we won't be here tomorrow lunchtime,' David pointed
out. 'We're going to Auntie Sylvia's.'

'Yes, dear. Then I expect we'll have the ice cream tonight,
instead. But we mustn't keep Miss Francis any longer, must
we?'

Jill showed the Thornhills out. When prompted, the children
thanked her for their entertainment. Edith sailed serenely down
the hall.

'You're making this house so nice, Miss Francis. Just the right
size for one.'

Jill agreed that it was a perfect size. For one.

She closed the door behind her visitors and went back to
the dining room. She found Alice on the table with her head
in David's glass of milk.

'Get off,' Jill snarled.

Without undue haste, the cat leapt down from the table, jumped
onto the armchair where Edith had sat and began to wash its face
with a paw. Jill looked at the crocuses and wondered what to do
with them. She was not particularly fond of plants in the house
and she didn't like purple crocuses.

She picked up the bowl, intending to move it onto the little
sideboard. Perhaps the glaze was more slippery than she had

expected. Perhaps she wasn't attending to what she was doing. Perhaps her subconscious mind had secretly planned the accident that was about to happen, a sort of Freudian slip.

The bowl fell through her fingers. It turned as it fell. The rim hit the tiled corner of the hearth and the bowl shattered. In a flash it was transformed into a surprisingly large heap of earth, crocuses and shards of pottery. Jill stared down at it for a moment.

'Good,' she said.

At that moment, her telephone began to ring. She picked up the receiver and said 'Yes?' in an unfriendly voice.

'Jill – it's me, Larry. Are you doing anything today? I don't suppose you could do me a favour, could you?'

5

It was raining heavily. Sheltering under a large black umbrella and clutching a pipe, Neville Rockfield came out to meet the two police officers in the drive outside the Headmaster's House.

'The Head's tied up with some prospective parents,' he announced, 'and George Burton is teaching, so would you mind making do with me?'

'Not at all,' Thornhill said. 'While we go to the San, I'd like Sergeant Kirby to have another look at Carrick's rooms.'

'Of course.'

Thornhill turned to Kirby. 'You've got the keys?'

Kirby nodded. They had discussed this in the car on their way up to Ashbridge. Although Mervyn Carrick's rooms had been examined, their surroundings had not. Kirby was also going to check the floorboards and fireplaces. Something must have happened to the missing glasses. And there was a chance that whoever had searched the rooms before Thornhill had arrived on Thursday morning had failed to find what he or she was looking for.

Rockfield sucked vigorously on his pipe and stared after Kirby as he walked down the drive towards Burton's. 'Mr Sandleigh will be free in about ten minutes, if you'd like a word with him after we've been to the San.'

'You're not teaching yourself?' Thornhill asked.

'I've a free period. Though the last thing it tends to be is free. And now of course I've got even less spare time than before – I've taken over Carrick's job as house tutor at—'

He broke off as the door of the Headmaster's House opened behind him. Thornhill expected to see Bernard Sandleigh, perhaps with a brace of parents. Instead Lawrence Jordan emerged with the three Sandleigh children.

'Morning, Mr Thornhill,' he called. 'Morning, Rockfield.'

'Morning, sir.'

The younger children, June and Peter, sidled down the drive, away from the adults. Dorothy stayed beside Jordan. She looked even paler and slighter than usual, dwarfed by her raincoat; her blonde hair was hidden by her broad-brimmed felt hat; both coat and hat were part of the uniform of Lydmouth High School for Girls. Her skin was almost transparent, Thornhill thought, and her eyes large and beautiful despite the smudges of tiredness beneath them.

'Miserable weather.' Jordan bounced up and down on the balls of his feet. He glanced at Dorothy. 'Do you know what? I've forgotten the car keys.'

'I'll ask Mother for them.'

Jordan watched the girl going back into the house. 'Bernard's trusting me with the Hudson. I am honoured, indeed.'

'We must be off ourselves,' Thornhill said.

Rockfield cocked an eyebrow at Thornhill. 'Ready when you are, Inspector.'

They said goodbye to Jordan. Rockfield took Thornhill through a corridor that cut through the main school building from front to back and into the garden beyond. A lawn stretched before them, muddy and bedraggled after winter. They followed a path running between the lawn and line of classrooms.

Thornhill glanced inside one window and saw rows of little boys in grey suits, sitting at wooden desks and scribbling rapidly as if their lives depended on it, while a large, black-gowned figure patrolled up and down the room. He tried to imagine what it would be like if David were one of those boys.

'Hang on,' Rockfield said, taking shelter in a doorway. 'Pipe's gone out.'

'Let me hold the umbrella.'

As the flame from Rockfield's lighter danced over the bowl of the pipe, a memory settled at last into its appointed place in Thornhill's mind: something Rockfield had said when they had met yesterday in the Beaufort Arms under the watchful eyes of Meg Swayne; a tiny discrepancy.

'You mentioned Carrick used to smoke in the staff room,' Thornhill said.

'More like a sort of fumigation.' Rockfield's eyes, wary above the flame, glanced at Thornhill. 'I can't help feeling glad we've seen the end of that.'

'You said he had a tobacco pouch.'

'Ah.' Very deliberately, Rockfield shut the lighter and dropped it in his pocket. He drew hard on the pipe. 'Yes, one of those yellow oilskin ones you roll up. Enormous thing – looked as if you could stuff about half a pound of tobacco into it. Why?'

'We have to check all the details, sir. Shall we go on?'

Rockfield started to say something but thought better of it. The two men began to walk through the rain. The path swung left and moved away from the school.

'The San's in a dip beyond those chestnuts,' Rockfield said, speaking indistinctly because of the pipe between his teeth. 'Very much San Sister's kingdom. The only higher authority she acknowledges is the school medical officer.'

'Who is your MO?'

'Wintle – do you know him?'

'Only by reputation.'

Dr Wintle had a practice in Ashbridge. He and Dr Bayswater

had conducted an acrimonious debate about the National Health Service in the correspondence columns of the *Gazette*.

'I'm told he's very cut up about poor Carrick,' Rockfield went on. 'Perhaps that's the wrong way of putting it. Wintle takes it as a personal slight if any of his patients shuffle off their mortal coil before their allotted biblical span.'

'He's the Carricks' family doctor?'

'Apparently.' The path forked and Rockfield pointed to the right-hand branch, which wound its way between two chestnuts. 'Almost there. I hope this rain stops by this afternoon. The cross-country course is going to be a quagmire.'

The school sanatorium stood on the slope just beyond the trees. It was a modern brick building, on one level. Rockfield propped his umbrella in the porch and held open the door for Thornhill. In a moment they were standing in a lobby that smelled of disinfectant and polish. Rain trickled down their mackintoshes onto gleaming linoleum. As they were taking off their raincoats, a door opened and Sister advanced towards them, rustling as she moved because of her starched apron. She was small and plump, with a face like a currant bun, a royal blue uniform with a gold watch pinned to her bosom.

'Sister – this is Inspector Thornhill.' Rockfield turned to Thornhill. 'And this is Mrs Hirdle, who keeps us all healthy. *Mens sana*, eh, Sister?'

'*In corpore sano*, Mr Rockfield,' she replied without a glimmer of a smile. 'That's my job. You want to see Walton, I understand?'

'If you think he's well enough.'

'As long as you don't tire him. He's already had Mr Sandleigh to see him this morning.' Mrs Hirdle looked at Thornhill, the severity of her expression enhanced by her chaste white cap. 'So just a few minutes, and don't let him get excited. His temperature's beginning to come down but he's not out of the woods yet.'

'Is Walton your only customer at present, Sister?' asked Rockfield.

'So far. But if this flu gets hold, who knows?'

Mrs Hirdle opened a door on the other side of the lobby. The two men followed her into a small, cheerless room with a window overlooking dripping branches and a grey mist concealing the Welsh hills.

'Here are your visitors,' Sister announced.

Walton was sitting in bed, propped up with three pillows. He looked younger than Thornhill remembered – a bony-faced, loose-limbed boy with large, sad eyes, a small chin and a delicate mouth. His face had a transitional look – a temporary arrangement of skin and bone to bridge the gap between the child and the man. He looked anxiously from Thornhill to Rockfield and licked chapped lips. On the eiderdown was a book, face downwards. Thornhill recognised the lurid cover of *Inspector Coleford and the Hand of Death*, one of Mary Sutton's pseudonymous detective stories.

Rockfield moved up to the bed. 'How are you, Walton?'

'Fine, sir. Well, sort of.'

'Soon have you back on your feet. Shame you'll miss the cross-country this afternoon. I know Mr Burton had high hopes of you.'

The boy flushed.

'You'll just have to have another crack at it next year. Still, I mustn't stand here chatting, must I? Here's Inspector Thornhill come to talk to you.'

Rockfield stepped back, allowing Thornhill to take his place. Thornhill wished there were fewer people in the hot little room.

'I'm sorry you're not well,' he said. 'But I gather you may be able to help us.'

Walton looked warily at him. Just like an old lag, Thornhill thought with sudden amusement: an old hand at confronting authority and revealing nothing.

'Can you remember much about Wednesday evening? Just before you were taken ill.'

'Yes, sir. There was a Classical Society meeting after prep. Mr Rockfield was there.'

'That's right,' Rockfield chipped in. 'I saw you there, too. You looked rather pale round the gills, come to think of it.'

'I felt a bit off-colour, sir. I thought it was the heat – I was sitting by a radiator. And when you and Mr Carrick were talking at the end, I had a headache.'

Talking or arguing or even quarrelling? Thornhill said: 'What happened after the meeting?'

'I went back to the house—'

'Burton's?'

'Yes, sir.'

'By yourself?'

'Yes – I'd been sitting with some other fellows, but I left first. I – I wanted some air. Then, on the way back, I started to feel shivery, so I went up to my study and made myself some cocoa. It didn't help much. Then I thought I'd better – better go to bed. That's when I saw Mr Carrick.'

'Can you remember what time that was?'

'Ten-fifteen.' Walton, his face suddenly and inexplicably anxious, darted a glance at Rockfield. 'Perhaps ten-twenty.'

'Did you and Mr Carrick say anything to each other?'

'Just goodnight. Then he went down the stairs. I think I heard the side door closing.'

'Can you remember what he was wearing?'

The boy looked blankly at him. 'The usual things, I suppose.'

'Outdoor clothes? Coat and hat?'

'Yes, I think so.'

'What about his glasses?'

Walton's bewildered face looked five years younger than at the start of the conversation. 'Well, yes, sir. Mr Carrick always wears glasses.'

'Wore, old chap,' Rockfield said. 'Not wears.'

'Sorry, sir.'

As Mrs Hirdle advanced on the bed, there was a rustle like dead leaves underfoot. 'That's enough now, gentlemen. Walton needs a rest.'

Rockfield patted the boy's shoulder. 'See you this afternoon, old man. I'll come and tell you who won the cross-country.'

Thornhill saw Walton's lips move, speaking silently to Rockfield's retreating back. *Sod the cross-country.* Thornhill grinned at Walton and followed Rockfield out. At the door he paused.

'By the way, how did Mr Carrick seem to you? Angry? Tired?'

Walton's eyelids were half-closed. His thin shoulders twitched. 'I don't know. But he must have been in a good mood.'

'Why?'

'Because I was five minutes late for bed, sir. And he didn't punish me.'

6

Thornhill phoned Dr Bayswater from the office at Sergeant Swayne's section house in Ashbridge. He left Swayne and Kirby sitting in silence in the formality of the front room, sipping tea provided by Mrs Swayne. Fred Swayne's face was even redder than usual. Thornhill had just explained to him in simple language why anything germane to the case, such as a report of a recent quarrel between the dead man and his brother, should be referred immediately to divisional CID.

Swayne's office was a cubby-hole filled with unfiled papers and the smells of stale tobacco and stale sweat. Bayswater took a long time to come to the phone. At last there was a clatter at the other end and a muffled curse.

'Thornhill? Now what?'

'I'm ringing from Ashbridge. I tried to talk to one of your colleagues this morning. Dr Wintle.'

'Ha! I don't think I'd call him a colleague exactly.'

'I gather you and he have had your disagreements.'

'Dr Wintle was born in the Victorian age and has remained there ever since. I'm reliably informed he takes the Book of Genesis literally. If he'd had any sense, he would have gone into the Church, not medicine.'

Thornhill said carefully, 'People in Ashbridge seem to give the impression he's rather a benevolent despot.'

'Despot, certainly.'

'I'd like to ask you something—'

'As long as you remember there's a limit to what I can tell you,' Bayswater interrupted. 'I'm a doctor, not an unpaid policeman.'

'I had a case in mind,' Thornhill said. 'An entirely hypothetical one.'

'That's all right, then.'

'Imagine a village rather like Ashbridge. With a GP who is rather old-fashioned – quite prepared to tell his patients if he thought they were doing wrong.'

'Go on.'

'Let's say this GP has been in the village for years and years. He knows everyone. He knows their parents. He knows their difficulties.' Thornhill paused. 'Now, let's say one of his patients had a problem – a medical problem, and she didn't want to take it to this GP because he would treat it as a moral problem, not as a medical one. There might even be a risk he might tell other people about it, despite his oath. Would that person be able to go to another doctor – in a neighbouring town, perhaps?'

'Yes – as long as the patient was ready to pay the fee.'

'But naturally the second doctor couldn't talk about the visit, could he?'

'Of course he couldn't. You know as well as I do he'd be bound by his oath.'

7

When Larry Jordan asked a favour, he could be very persuasive. 'If you don't come, Jill dear,' he said on the telephone, 'it's going to be a nightmare.'

So Jill had agreed, partly to give herself something else to think about after Edith Thornhill's visit. Jordan called for her at Church Cottage half an hour later.

'Dorothy's fine,' he said when Jill opened her front door. 'Practically an adult in some ways. It's the younger two that are the problem. Still, I thought I'd get them out of Bernard and Vera's way for a few hours. Least I could do, really.'

He was driving the Sandleighs' Hudson with the children packed in the back. Jordan took them to Ross-on-Wye. He was not a good driver; and the gearbox gave him particular trouble, perhaps because he was used to an automatic transmission. The younger children, June and Peter, squabbled over who should sit in the middle and one of them threatened to be sick. Dorothy kept aloof from her brother and sister, clinging to a precarious adult dignity. Jill was relieved when they pulled up outside a large hotel on the hill near the church. Before he left the car, Jordan put on his glasses.

'Uncle Larry,' Peter shouted from the back seat. 'Why don't you grow a beard? That'd be a much better disguise.'

'Because they're itchy, old man. And the ladies don't like them.'

Once inside, they went straight to the dining room, where they were shown to a round table beside a window. They had the place almost to themselves. No one appeared to notice their illustrious visitor. For her own peace of mind, Jill took charge of the seating arrangements, putting Peter between herself and Jordan and June between Dorothy and herself. Jordan ordered melon followed by plaice and pommes frites for the younger children. ('Fish and chips!' Peter said. 'Hooray!') Jordan also insisted on ordering a bottle of champagne.

When the wine waiter had gone, he murmured to Jill, 'I know what you're thinking. Rather flashy? A touch of vulgarity, Hollywood style?'

'Of course not,' Jill lied. 'It's lovely to be taken out.'

'I feel like celebrating.'

'Why?'

He stared across the table at her for a moment longer than was comfortable. 'Need you ask?' Then he shifted his gaze and smiled at Dorothy, drawing her into the conversation. 'Two charming women — what more could a fellow need?'

Jill watched the girl begin to blush. To divert attention from Dorothy, she said, 'Champagne, apparently.'

Jordan smiled at her. 'Actually — all this makes me want to celebrate, too.' He moved his hand in a gesture that encompassed the high hotel dining room, the huge Georgian window and the view of green countryside beyond, drifting down to a grey horizon. 'It's so unlike California. It's wonderful.'

'Don't say you're getting homesick.'

'That's nothing new. Home is where the heart is.'

The waiter brought the champagne. Jordan gave a glass to Dorothy. One day, Jill thought, Dorothy might be beautiful, if she retained those delicate features and learnt to hold herself properly. The younger children, June and Peter, were heavier in build and dark haired. They were restless in this formal setting, darting away from the table at the slightest opportunity. Both Jordan and Dorothy tried ineffectually to control them but Jill did not intervene, even when he looked pleadingly at her. If Larry Jordan thought she was going to look after other people's children for him for the price of a lunch, he had another thought coming.

The arrival of food quietened Peter and June for a while. Dorothy made up for her siblings' behaviour. She sat straight-backed, eating small mouthfuls, glancing at Jill when in doubt which knife or glass to use. Occasionally she threw a formal remark into the conversation — 'I wonder if this was once a coaching inn?' — with the air of a diver plunging into cold water.

Jordan tried surprisingly hard to talk to her, though not always successfully. He was uncertain whether to treat her as a child or a grown-up; and, like so many men, he found it difficult to talk to a member of the opposite sex when it was not appropriate to flirt with her.

While they were waiting for coffee, Jill went to the ladies' lavatory. She asked Dorothy if she would like to come. The girl accepted with an alacrity which suggested that either she was bursting to go or she didn't want to be left alone with Larry Jordan.

'Well,' Jill said as she was powdering her nose. 'How do you feel about having a film star in the house?'

'He's not like a film star when he's at home.' The girl was washing her hands with furious concentration. 'Only when he's outside the house. Then either people look at him or he's afraid they will.'

'Or even that they won't.' Jill kept her voice light. 'But it can't be much fun for him. Or for you, I suppose.'

Dorothy dried her hands. 'We looked after someone's Irish wolfhound once,' she said. 'Having Uncle Larry around is rather like that.' Her eyes met Jill's. 'I told him that myself.'

'Of course. And it must be a difficult time for other reasons, too.'

'Because of Mr Carrick?' Dorothy ran a comb through her hair, so fine that it was almost impossible to control. 'The worst thing is, no one will talk about it. Uncle Larry just pretends it never happened.'

'Personally I find it's better to have that sort of thing out in the open.' Jill smiled at the girl. 'You know what they say about a trouble shared.'

Dorothy frowned at her reflection. 'I keep thinking of him. When I'm going to sleep ... Mr Carrick, I mean. It must be frightful to die like that. In the dark, trying to breathe, that bang on the head, not really knowing what was happening – and oh God: do you think he knew he was dying?'

'I don't know,' Jill said. 'But we all have to die. And many people, maybe most, die perfectly natural deaths which are just as painful as that. And often the pain lasts for months. Years even.'

'But *why* does Uncle Larry pretend everything's wonderful, that we're having a super time?'

'He's probably trying to help. Maybe this is *his* way of trying to cope.'

'I wish he'd go away. I wish everything was all right again.' She sniffed. 'I'm sorry. I shouldn't have said that.'

'Better out than in. I won't pass it on.' Jill raised her eyebrows, one adult to another. 'Shall we go back?'

When they returned to the dining room, they found the other children sitting beside Jordan.

'Uncle Larry's got a plan,' Peter announced. 'But he wouldn't tell us what it is until you came back.'

Jordan waited until they were all sitting down. 'Miss Francis and I need to talk business,' he told the children. 'She's writing something about me, you know. So, while we do that, I suggest you three go and explore the town.' He took out his wallet and extracted a five-pound note. 'I'd like you all to buy yourselves a little present.'

Peter and June stared wide-eyed at the note. Jill glanced at Dorothy's face and thought she saw disappointment there.

'All right, kids? Dorothy's in charge. Back in forty minutes, say.'

Peter and June dragged Dorothy away from the table. At the door the elder girl looked back at Jill. Then she was gone.

'Much more fun for them,' Jordan said, opening his cigarette case. 'And much more fun for us.'

'I haven't written up the interview yet.' *Too many distractions.*

'No hurry. What do you think of Dorothy, by the way? Nice child, isn't she?'

'Not a child any more.' Jill absentmindedly took a cigarette.

The champagne had made her feel slightly muzzy, now its initial effect had worn off.

Jordan clicked his lighter under her nose. 'She photographs well. She's going to be in her school play.'

Jill lit her cigarette. 'So I heard.'

'*Twelfth Night*. It's the junior half of the school, and they're doing an abridged version. She's playing Feste.' He paused to light his own cigarette. 'A nice part.'

'The Fool? So she'll have to sing as well.' The words of one of the songs slipped through Jill's mind. *Come away, come away, death*. She shivered.

'Are you cold?'

'No – I'm fine.'

'She's got a nice voice – not much volume, but good pitch. And real stage presence ... She could be good, you know. I could help her.'

'Get her a part in a film? Is she that good?'

'She could be. Given the right training, she could be another Elizabeth Taylor. And she'd need a helping hand, of course. But I could see to all that.'

'And how would she like it?'

'She'd love it. I'm sure she would. No, the problem is Bernard and Vera. I mentioned the idea to them last night. Just as a possibility. They weren't exactly enthusiastic.'

Jill shrugged. 'It's their decision, I suppose.'

'But it's such a waste,' Jordan burst out. 'You don't see many children with that sort of talent. Believe me, I know. And Bernard's going on about hoping Dorothy would go to university as if that was the best thing that could happen to her. That's the trouble with these schoolmasters – they live in their own world. Either you're learning things or you're teaching things – as far as they're concerned, there's nothing else to do in life.'

'If she's really keen on acting, perhaps she'll change their minds.'

Jordan stuck out his lower lip like a sulky little boy. 'But it's best to start early – for all sorts of reasons.' He hesitated. 'Jill – I don't suppose you'd have a word with them?'

'But I hardly know them.'

'Even so, they might take a bit of notice of you. Bernard used to read your column you know. He said it was frightfully good. Most of the time he didn't even realise you were a woman.'

'Thanks,' Jill said.

'Well, it's just a thought.' Jordan sat back to allow the waiter to put the coffee on the table. 'If an opportunity happens to present itself. Would you like a liqueur?'

Jill shook her head. For a moment they drank their coffee in silence. She preferred it when Larry Jordan didn't talk. On the whole he was more attractive that way.

'Jill? May I ask you something?'

She smiled at him. 'Depends what it is.'

'I don't want to pry but – well, I imagine I'm right in thinking there's a chap in the background somewhere?'

'Why should there be?'

He smiled and despite herself she felt a pleasant tremor snaking through her body. 'Being the sort of person you are – looking as you do – damn it, Jill, you know what I mean.'

Jill stubbed out her cigarette. 'It's none of your business.'

'You've no idea how nice it is to meet someone who belongs to a completely different world. It gets so monotonous – people either want to use me or treat me as a holy relic or sometimes both. But you – you're different.'

Again that treacherous little tremor ran through her. Jill said nothing, knowing that if she did she might betray herself. She tried to divert herself from the antics of her body and her emotions by thinking what a corny seduction line this was. Assuming, of course, that seduction was what Larry Jordan had in mind. Perhaps she was indulging in a bout of wishful thinking.

'I've got several weeks before I've got to get back. Do you ever have any time off? We could go and find some sunshine, some good food. What about the Med? Beirut, perhaps. We could fly there. Not unlike the South of France but less crowded. And less risk of people recognising me.'

'It would be hard to get away,' Jill heard herself saying in a voice she despised. She knew that she had two weeks' holiday owed to her.

'I'm sure you could manage something. If you wanted to. Think about it.'

They sipped their coffee. Jill asked a question about American newspapers and the conversation moved to safer subjects. Then, without warning, Jordan returned to a dangerously personal level.

'Tell me, has anyone ever told you what a talent for interviewing you've got? You should specialise in that. In the film world, it's largely a matter of contacts, but that needn't be a problem. It can be quite a lifestyle and a good interviewer carries a lot of clout in the profession.'

He was saying one thing and meaning another.

'Well?'

Jill wondered what on earth she could say. When you are thoroughly confused there are no right answers and no wrong ones either.

Jordan lowered his voice and miraculously made it more husky. 'We could have such fun, you and I.'

'Larry, I—'

The dining-room door opened. Peter ran into the room with June at his heels. 'Uncle Larry, I've got a penknife. It's got a horn handle and a corkscrew and a thing for getting stones out of horses' hooves. And it's really sharp — look, I've cut myself.'

'Later,' Jordan murmured to Jill as they turned to deal with the children. 'Later, Jill, later.'

Soon afterwards they left the hotel and drove back to Ashbridge. When they reached the school drive, they found it was blocked by a slowly moving stream of muddy, red-faced boys dressed in navy blue shorts and rugby shirts. Jordan drew up just inside the gateway, beside Paxford's cottage.

'My God,' he muttered to Jill. 'Looks like a rainy Saturday on the Western Front.'

'It's the cross-country,' Dorothy said from the back of the car. 'They're going up to the finish on Big Side.'

'Poor devils.' Jordan glanced at Jill. 'Shall we go and watch? I always like this sort of thing – reminds me why my school days weren't the best days of my life.'

One of the prefects, a youth who looked about thirty-two, was acting as a marshal of the course at the bottom of the drive. Jordan beckoned him over to the car.

'Can we park this here for the time being? If I try to drive up to the Headmaster's House, I'll mow down half the school.'

'You could leave it over there, sir. Just by the lodge.'

Jordan drove the car onto the grass verge. Mud sprayed up when it left the metalled surface of the drive. 'Do you want to come too, kids? Or would you rather go home?'

The three Sandleighs decided to go home. The younger ones set off up the drive, but Dorothy lingered by the car. Jill wished she'd had the foresight to ask Jordan to return to Ashbridge via Lydmouth. The prefect was hovering outside her window. When Jill showed signs of wanting to leave the car, he opened the door for her with a courtly flourish.

She looked down at the muddy grass. 'I can't walk in this.' She was wearing shoes with heels, suitable for lunch in a country hotel, but most unsuitable for tramping across playing fields in winter.

'Oh damn. Of course you can't.' Jordan, who was already out of the car, ducked down to window level again. 'I'm sure Vera would lend you a pair of gum boots or whatever. Your feet are a bit smaller than hers, I think.'

Jill noted in passing the fact that Larry Jordan was the sort of man who noticed the size of a woman's feet.

'There's some wellies in the boot,' Dorothy said. 'Mine might fit you.'

'Wonderful,' Jordan said. 'A woman with a head on her

shoulders. And if Bernard's are there, I can wear his. Let's have a look.'

'May I help, sir?'

The prefect was speaking to Jordan but his attention was on Dorothy Sandleigh. The girl might be young, Jill thought, but she was already having an effect on the other sex; an effect that was all the more powerful because she was unconscious of it. Dorothy and the prefect eventually produced two pairs of boots.

When Jordan had changed into his, he wandered round to the nearside of the car. 'Oh dear. I didn't realise there was a flowerbed there. I've rather chewed it up, I'm afraid.'

'Nothing to worry about, sir,' the prefect told him. 'It's one of Frankie's. He's a great one for tulips and so on in the spring.'

Jill lifted her head. 'Frankie?'

'Paxford.' The boy looked slightly embarrassed. 'Our groundsman.'

Frankie. Oh, I see.

'If you take that path,' the prefect said to Jordan, pointing out a track that wound round behind Paxford's cottage, 'you come to Burton's, and then there's another path that'll take you past the Head's garage and straight up to Big Side. It's much shorter than going up the drive.'

Jill and Jordan set off, leaving Dorothy with the prefect. The path was muddy in parts and climbed sharply. Jordan offered Jill his arm, and it seemed natural to accept.

The path came out near the school chapel. They walked past it to the windswept expanse of Big Side. Jill saw Kathleen and Neville Rockfield among the small crowd of adults around the finishing line for the cross-country. The stream of running boys had dwindled to a trickle. The leaders had already finished. The rank and file were still staggering across the field.

'Come on, Fontenoy.' Sandleigh's voice boomed across the grass. 'Put some spunk into it.'

One small boy – about the same age as the Suttons' elder son – was crying as he ran onto the field. He must have fallen, for his knee was smeared with fresh blood. Drops of it trailed behind him on the grass as he passed close to Jill and Jordan. He was followed by a pink-faced sixth former, carrying a long flexible stick. Neither of them realised that adults were so close to them. The youth slashed at the smaller boy's calves.

'Faster. We don't like slackers in Burton's.'

'It's barbaric,' Jill said quietly.

'It's the public-school system, my dear,' Jordan murmured. 'It makes men out of boys. Look what it did to me.'

At that moment Jill liked him more than she had ever done before. 'Would you mind – I'd like to go home now?'

'Of course not. I'll run you back.'

They walked together down the path, past Burton's, back to the car by Paxford's cottage.

When they reached the drive, they found Paxford standing beside the Hudson. The groundsman heard them coming and turned towards them. Automatically he angled his face so that the damaged half was concealed. Did he know, Jill wondered, that the boys called him Frankie, and that Frankie was short for Frankenstein's Monster? Almost certainly. Suddenly it seemed to her totally unnecessary that the world should contain such masculine extremes as Paxford and Larry Jordan.

'I'm afraid I made a mess of the verge – and your flowerbed,' Jordan said to Paxford. 'Sorry about that.'

'Can't be helped, sir.'

Talking to Paxford was as disconcerting as talking to someone with a squint because of the way he held his head.

'I'll give the car a clean when you get back, if you want.'

'Thanks.' There was a rustle of paper as Jordan found a ten-shilling note in his pocket and passed it to Paxford. 'Much obliged. In this weather the only way to keep a car clean is to leave it in a garage, eh?'

Paxford nodded. He retreated to a shed behind his cottage. Jordan and Jill changed out of their boots.

Neither of them said much on the drive back to Lydmouth.

Jordan parked the car outside the door of Church Cottage. He came round to the passenger side and opened Jill's door. She wondered if he expected her to invite him in. She wasn't sure whether she wanted to; she wasn't sure what would happen if she did.

She unlocked the door of Church Cottage. 'Thank you for lunch.'

'Jill?'

'What?'

He said nothing but held out his hand.

Confused, she took it.

'I'd like to see you tomorrow.'

'I see.'

'I'll telephone, shall I?'

The suggestion had caught her off balance. 'Yes – I suppose so. I—'

'Good.' He raised her hand to his lips, kissed it and then released it. He turned and went back to the car. He opened the door but before he got in he looked across the roof of the car at her. 'Jill.'

That was all. He said nothing else. He climbed into the car and drove away without so much as a wave. Jill went into the house and sat down in the cold sitting room. She sat down because her legs were trembling. Her mind was in a daze.

There was something familiar about what had just happened. A moment later she remembered. There had been a parallel parting in *Broken Night* when Larry Jordan had said farewell to his American inamorata and gone off to war, never to return. The last thing he had said was the woman's name. He hadn't waved that time either.

8

They heard Les Carrick before they saw him. Thornhill and Kirby walked across the bottom field from the lane to the barn. Les was inside, swearing at the weather, at the tiles, and at Umberto Nerini.

'Mr Carrick?' Thornhill said as he reached the open doorway. 'May we have a word?'

Both Les and Nerini swung round. Nerini sucked in his breath.

'You pick your moments, don't you?' Les said.

He threw down his hammer on the earth floor of the barn. He and Nerini had been trying to patch the roof at one end. A tiling batten had just broken under the impact of the hammer. The barn was dark, and it smelt of damp and manure.

'Outside, perhaps,' Thornhill suggested. 'The rain's eased off.'

Les jerked his head at Nerini. 'Get on with it, Bert.' Rubbing his unshaven chin, he joined the policemen outside the barn. 'Well? Any news about Mervyn?'

'We have a report that you and your brother were having a chat in the village on Sunday night.'

The farmer's hand dropped to his side. 'Let's walk. Get cold standing here.'

The three men set off towards the stile to the lane – the policemen like guards on either side of Les. Thornhill allowed the silence to linger.

'What if we were?' Les said at last. 'There's no law about it. He was my brother, after all.'

'You didn't mention it to us.'

'Why should I?' Les waved his arm up the hill, past the farm towards the Hanging Tree. 'Nothing to do with that, look.'

'Then what was it about?'

'Family matters.'

'Such as?'

'Well – the farm. It was partly his. We often used to talk about it.' He glanced at Thornhill, as if assessing how well he was doing. 'Let's go up to the house. Maybe there's tea in the pot.' Another glance. 'We talked about that barn as a matter of fact.'

'You told him that the roof needed some work?'

'Of course. Bloody obvious it does, isn't it?'

'Why did you meet him there?'

Les climbed onto the stile. 'Because I was going up to the village for a pint at the Beaufort, and I knew Mervyn had been in church with the school.' Sitting on the stile he looked down on Thornhill. 'It was easier to catch him then rather than phone him at Burton's House. Mervyn didn't like being phoned there. Or not by me.'

'According to the account we heard, he didn't like meeting you after church, either.'

'What's that supposed to mean?'

'You were heard arguing with Mr Carrick in the bus shelter. In fact quarrelling might be a better word.'

'Rubbish.'

Thornhill and Kirby followed Les over the stile. The three men began to walk up the lane towards the farm.

'Are you a driver, Mr Carrick?'

'What do you think?'

'I think that means you are. What have you got?'

'Just the tractor and a Land Rover.'

They walked on in silence. A Land Rover could have coped with the weather on Wednesday night. Someone must have brought Mervyn Carrick down from the school to the Hanging Tree, whether dead or alive. Someone must have searched Mervyn's rooms in Burton's House.

'Any news about whether your brother left a will?'

'Not that I've heard. I talked to Mr Shipston yesterday. He didn't know of one.'

'Your brother might have used another solicitor.'

'We always use Shipston.'

'So you think it will all come to you?'

Les shrugged. 'Such as it is. The other half of the farm. Won't make much odds, really. I've run the place since Dad died so what's the difference?' He stared at Thornhill, a tactic, Thornhill noted, which people often employed when they were telling a lie on the assumption that eye contact would be taken as a guarantee of veracity. 'There won't be any money to speak of. Mervyn may have gone to college but all that studying was a waste of time. He was worse off than I am.'

'I think there might be something for you.'

Les stopped and the others stopped too. 'What are you saying?'

'Just that there might be more money than you think. You never know, do you, Mr Carrick?'

'Why don't you bugger off and leave us in peace,' the farmer snapped. 'We've had a death in the family – or didn't you know?'

'You didn't go out on Wednesday night, did you?'

'No I didn't. You know I didn't. I've already told you.' Les's voice was rising in volume. 'Look, Mervyn had problems, he killed himself, all right?' He started walking again. A moment later he added in a quieter voice, 'That's all there is to it. Can't we just bury him and let him rest in peace?'

'We can't release the body for burial yet, Mr Carrick. There are too many unanswered questions.'

'Like what?'

'Like why did he commit suicide if he was perfectly cheerful the last time he was seen on Wednesday evening? Who moved him after death and why? Who put him on the Hanging Tree?'

'You think he was murdered? Is that what you're trying to tell me?'

'I don't know what to think, Mr Carrick. All I know is that there are some questions I'd like answers for.'

They had reached the gate to the farmyard now. The border collies ran out to meet them.

'I want to think about this,' Les said. 'Have you finished?'

'For the time being, Mr Carrick.'

He walked back down the lane, weaving slightly as if tipsy.

'There's one thing more,' Thornhill called after him.

'What is it now?'

'What did your brother keep his tobacco in?'

Les stood there, hands on hips. 'A pouch.'

'What sort of pouch, sir?'

'Why do you want to know?'

'Just answer the question, please.'

'He had our Dad's pouch as a matter of fact. Yellow oilskin.'

'Thank you, Mr Carrick.'

The farmer shrugged and continued walking.

Kirby stared after him. 'Either he's telling the truth or he's a damned good liar.'

The back door to the farmhouse opened and Dilys Carrick came out.

'I thought I heard you. Where's Les?'

'Get in the car,' Thornhill murmured to Kirby. He raised his voice and said to Dilys, 'He went back to the barn.'

She walked across the yard towards him, arms folded underneath the heavy breasts. He leant on the gate and waited until she was only a few paces away from him.

'Tell me, Mrs Carrick,' he said quietly, 'are you pregnant?'

She put her hand to her mouth and stared at him with huge, frightened eyes.

'Will you answer me, please?'

She nodded slowly.

'Who is the father?'

She burst into a torrent of words. 'I didn't kill him, I swear it, I wanted to sometimes, but I didn't. You've got to believe me.'

'Who was the father?'

'Mervyn.' Her lips twisted, revealing her teeth. 'I told you he could be a charmer when he wanted to be. And Les just isn't interested. Never was, not in that.' Unconsciously she stroked her arm, the place where the bruises were under the cardigan. 'How did you guess?'

'Did your husband know that you were having an affair with his brother?'

Her face quivered as though trying to dissolve. 'I – I don't know.' She stared at Thornhill. 'What are you thinking? For God's sake, what are you thinking?'

Thornhill smiled and shrugged.

'You think Les killed him, don't you?' She looked up at his face. 'Why won't you answer me? Why?'

SEVEN

Letters to the Editor

Dear Sir,

How would your readers like it if their children were tied in a sack and thrown into the nearest pond and left to drown? In Ashbridge, two boys were about to murder a litter of kittens in broad daylight when I stopped them. They told me that their parents could not find homes for them, and killing them was the kindest thing to do. They ought to be ashamed of themselves, and so should their parents.

If you do not want your lady cat to have kittens, the kindest thing is to take her to the vet and have her spayed. It is very cruel to kill kittens just because it makes life easier for you. If you can't look after a cat properly, you should not own one in the first place.

Yours faithfully,

M.Swayne (Mrs)

The Beaufort Arms, Ashbridge

The *Lydmouth Gazette*, 11th February

1

Edith Thornhill drifted through the day like a spectator in her own life: neither happy nor unhappy – but at a remove from herself, as though in the audience at the cinema. She did not think a great deal about what might be happening at East Marryott Cottage

Hospital. She thought often of her mother, however – not as she was now but as she had been when Edith and her sister were children. *It's as if she's dead already*.

After they returned from their visit to Jill Francis, the day dragged. The children squabbled incessantly throughout the afternoon. David allowed Elizabeth to get the better of him on several occasions. Edith worried more about him than about her mother. He stayed in the house, which was unlike him on a Saturday afternoon, and was unusually affectionate towards his mother.

Edith had given Richard an edited version about what had happened in the park the previous evening, stressing the lurker by the lavatories rather than what had happened to David. She was afraid that Richard might try to find the boys who had been responsible, which might not be the best way to handle it as far as David was concerned. Alternatively Richard might dismiss the episode as 'character-building' or with one of those masculine formulas which are essentially admissions of indifference. ('The boy has to learn to take the rough with the smooth.')

The fact that her husband was in the middle of a major investigation was another reason for caution. Edith loathed this side of his job – not just the obvious dangers it subjected him too, but also the way that such cases sucked up all his attention.

Edith spent the afternoon waiting for a telephone call, either from Richard or from Sylvia and Len. No one rang. Late in the afternoon she made an effort and dragged the children out to the library. It was raining again and they caught a bus to the centre of town. Only a few sodden shoppers scurried along the pavements of the High Street.

'I hate reading,' Elizabeth announced as they went up the steps to the library.

'Find a book with some nice pictures, then,' Edith said.

Inside the building, disgruntled people in dripping raincoats sheltered from the weather. The place smelt of old paper and wet rubber. Edith left the children in the junior library and drifted into the adult fiction section, where she studied the spines of romantic novels. *If only, if only.*

'Hello. Isn't this weather perfectly foul?'

Edith turned to see the vicar's wife, Mary Sutton, with a shopping basket in one hand and a couple of detective novels in the other.

'Beastly,' she agreed, wishing she had not been found beside the romantic novels.

'How's your mother?' Mrs Sutton was good at remembering other people's problems.

'No news today. The children and I are going to see her tomorrow.'

'Your husband can't get away at present?'

'No. He's too busy.'

'It's a difficult time for you both, isn't it? Good luck.'

Mrs Sutton said goodbye and joined the queue to have her books stamped. Edith postponed their return by taking the children to have high tea at the Gardenia. The treat would blow another hole in the weekly housekeeping budget, already damaged by her visit to the Bull Hotel on Thursday. But she wanted something nice to happen to them today. Besides she was reluctant to go back home. It was as if by staying away she could prevent the telephone from ringing, could prevent bad news.

Like the library, the Gardenia was crowded. They had to wait for a table. Elizabeth spilt her milk and Edith caught David eating sugar with his fingers; it was loose sugar, not lumps. The tables were too close together and the clientèle, Edith thought with a little shudder, was rather too varied for her taste; and the atmosphere was hot and smoky – all very unlike the Bull, with its high-ceilinged rooms and the acres of space between empty armchairs.

From the Bull Hotel, it was but a short mental step to Jill Francis and Lawrence Jordan. There was obviously something going on there, Edith thought, judging by the way they had been looking at each other in the lounge the other day. She allowed her eyes to close. *If only, if only.* Worst of all was the sense the telephone was ringing on and on in the empty house. By the time they were halfway through the meal Edith was desperate to be home.

'Mummy.' Elizabeth had hardly touched her fried egg on toast. She was faddy about food when away from home. 'I feel sick.'

Edith took her to the lavatory, which was almost as crowded as the restaurant. Elizabeth failed to be sick but continued to claim that she might be in the future. When they returned to the table they found that David had eaten Elizabeth's egg and was now investigating the sugar bowl once again.

Shortly afterwards, Edith recognised defeat and took the children home. She made them walk, on the grounds that they would all find this slightly less unpleasant than waiting for an indefinite period at the bus stop.

When they reached Victoria Road, the first thing that Edith noticed was that Richard's car was not parked outside the house. Only then did she realise how much she had hoped that he would be at home. It wasn't just that she wanted another adult to talk to, though that was important. She was worried about him. He might have caught a chill after falling into that pond yesterday.

Edith unlocked the front door and pushed it open. The children rushed past her into the darkened house. David automatically turned on the light in the hall. As if this were a signal, the telephone began to ring.

She dropped the bag of library books on the floor, ran into the dining room and snatched the telephone.

'Edith?' It was her brother-in-law's voice.

'How's Mother?'

'Not too good. We think you'd better come this evening if you can.'

'I'll have to come by train. Richard can't get away. And I'll have to bring the children.'

'Don't worry. We'll manage. Get a taxi from the station. Better go to the house first.'

A moment later Len rang off. Edith followed the children into the kitchen and told them what had happened. Instead of making a day trip to East Marryott, she informed them, they would go now. It would be quite an adventure, wouldn't it? There was a train they could catch at five past seven if they hurried. (Her mind shied away from the thought of the journey – on Saturday evening, in winter, with two tired children, and changes at both Gloucester and Swindon.) The children's enthusiasm surprised her. She realised that in their minds Granny's illness was dwarfed by the prospect of spending the night at their cousins' house.

She phoned for a taxi and then phoned police headquarters. Richard was not back yet. Would his family never come first, Edith wondered? If you took his job away from him, what would be left?

She packed a few clothes for herself and the children in a small suitcase. Rummaging in Richard's desk, she found the cheque book for their joint account, which she slipped into her handbag along with what was left of the housekeeping money. There was no time to make sandwiches, so she packed a loaf of bread, the bread knife, a piece of cheddar, four apples and a slab of chocolate in a basket. The children, meanwhile, had assembled the array of toys which they felt essential for their overnight stay. Edith decimated them. The children protested.

'I've got more important things to think about than your toys at present,' Edith snapped, her voice unusually loud. 'You'll take what I say you can and no more.'

Both children, shocked, stared at her. Edith telephoned police headquarters again, with the same result.

'Would you tell my husband I've had to go to East Marryott?' she asked the switchboard operator.

'East where?'

The doorbell rang. It would be the taxi.

'I have to go now,' Edith said and put the phone down.

2

Thornhill and Kirby reached Lydmouth a little before seven o'clock. They drove over the bridge, past the station and up the hill. Greasy rain fell gently from a dark sky. The wipers slapped the windscreen with an irritating squeak as they changed direction. Thornhill was tired; the thought of his home, with supper on the table and a fire in the grate, was particularly attractive. He decided he might even treat himself to a glass of whisky as a nightcap.

'Are you planning to go out tonight, Brian?'

'Unless something comes up.'

'Anything special on the cards?'

'There's a dance at Edge Hill. Doesn't matter if I miss it. The usual rustic hop, probably.'

Brian Kirby, a Londoner born and bred, affected to despise provincial amusements. But he hated spending Saturday night at home. Unlike Thornhill, he enjoyed parties and his vigorous love life had assumed epic proportions in the minds of the gossips in the police canteen.

Thornhill drove to police headquarters and left the Austin in the car park behind the station. He and Kirby went into the building by the rear entrance.

'Why don't you get off home?' Thornhill suggested.

'Thanks. I'll just fetch my bag.'

Weariness washed over Thornhill as he climbed the stairs to the first floor. The problem was the paperwork: as the years went by, there seemed to be more and more of it; and the amount increased proportionately with the seriousness of the investigation. Thornhill knew that if he managed half an hour at his desk tonight, at a time when the phone was unlikely to start ringing, it would pay dividends later.

At the top of the stairs, they parted – Kirby to the CID office along the corridor, and Thornhill to his own cell-like room. Once inside, Thornhill hung his coat on the door, lit the gas fire and picked up the phone to ring Edith. He thought smugly that she would appreciate knowing when he would be home. And there would be selfish advantages in this, too – it would give her time to get the children through their baths; she would also be able to make sure that supper was ready a few minutes after his arrival.

The phone rang at the other end. There was a tap on the door.

'Come in,' he called.

Kirby, still in his outdoor clothes, put his head in the room. 'Couple of messages, sir. I think you should see them.'

Thornhill held out his hand for the sheets of paper. The first was from Edith, announcing her departure to East Marryott with the children. The second was from Jill Francis. He nodded to Kirby, telling him he could go, and dropped the phone back on its base.

Thornhill dropped the first message into the wastepaper basket and glanced again at the other. He read it through again and then, with mounting anger, looked at the time at the top – the time the message had been received. Just after eleven o'clock – and almost certainly no one had acted on it. He stalked along the corridor to the CID office. Kirby was still there.

'Where's Porter?' Thornhill demanded.

Kirby looked at him and then away. 'Off duty, sir.'

Thornhill resisted the temptation to take out his annoyance on the innocent. 'Is Mr Jackson still here?'

'Left about half an hour ago, sir.'

'Damn.' Thornhill thought for a moment. Inspector Jackson of the Uniformed Branch would have to wait. 'What have we got on that Peeping Tom at Jubilee Park?'

Kirby already had the file on his desk. 'There's a note about the man Mrs Thornhill saw yesterday. The only other thing that's come in today is from the fingerprint department. They've found a couple of smudged prints up in the loft over the toilets. Not perfect, but they reckon they're usable.'

'Have they checked them downstairs?'

Kirby spread wide his hands. 'Yes, sir – no luck.'

The county force had its own criminal records office in the basement of police headquarters. If necessary, they would also check these prints with the CRO at Scotland Yard, the central clearing house for information about criminals, but that would take time.

'What about the hotel? Any prints there?'

'No, sir.'

'He was outside so he probably wore gloves in any case.'

'I thought every bloody criminal wore gloves these days.' Kirby sniffed. 'We had a couple of kids breaking and entering the other day, and even they were wearing gloves.'

'Our man doesn't necessarily think he's a criminal.'

'Just a bloody pervert, eh?'

'He may not even want to do what he does. Who knows?'

Kirby examined his fingernails. 'So if Miss Francis is right, it looks as if he's found another person to watch?'

'Probably been scared away from the Bull and the park. I'll go over to Church Street now.'

'Would you like me to come, sir?'

Thornhill stared at Kirby, whose face was respectful and carefully devoid of hidden meanings, just like his tone of voice and his choice of words.

'No need. If you've finished here, you might as well go home.'

Thornhill returned to his room and dialled the number for Church Cottage, which had been included on the message. The phone was answered on the second ring.

'Miss Francis? This is Inspector Thornhill.' He wondered suddenly whether she was alone. No reason why she should be. 'I'm sorry no one has phoned you earlier. I've only just got back and found your message.'

'That's all right.'

'I think we'd better have a look at this house next door.'

'When?'

'Would now be inconvenient?'

'As far as I'm concerned,' she said tartly, 'the sooner this is sorted out the better.'

'How did you get into the house yourself?'

'I didn't have to break and enter. It belongs to Victor Youlgreave. He lent me the key.'

'You have it now?'

'Yes.'

'Then I'll be with you in about ten minutes.'

It was a wonderful excuse, Thornhill told himself as he walked through the darkened streets, to defer the paperwork. The torch in the pocket of his overcoat banged against his leg at every other pace. The town was preparing to entertain itself. Saturday evening was the busiest of the week. There were queues outside the Rex cinema. A dance had just begun at the old Corn Exchange. Sleek masons were climbing out of sleek motor cars beside the Bull Hotel; for once Superintendent Williamson would not be joining them. The fish and chip shops were packed, and the smell of frying food made Thornhill's mouth water. He passed a pub, and a wave of laughter, tobacco and beer swept out to greet him.

A moment later, he knocked on the door of Church Cottage. While he waited, he glanced to his left at the frontage of the vicarage. Its windows were dark, as were those of the house on the other side of Church Cottage. He heard a bolt shooting back. The door opened.

'Hello.' Jill was wearing a coat and headscarf.

'Are you going out? I hope I'm not keeping you from something.'

'I thought you'd want me to come with you. I can show you where the room is.'

'You wouldn't mind?'

'Why should I?' She picked up a torch that was lying on the hall table. 'Shall we go now?'

'There's just one thing,' Thornhill began. 'Have you considered—'

'That the man may be there? Yes, as a matter of fact I have.'

'And that doesn't worry you?'

'Of course it does. But waiting here would be worse.' She hesitated, licking dry lips. 'Besides, it would be a sort of victory for him.'

'Yes, I can see that. Then shall we go?'

Thornhill waited on the pavement while she locked the door. It took her a few seconds to work the key into the lock and he wondered if her hand were shaking. Being brave was all very admirable but it didn't stop you being afraid. She turned and handed him the key to the house next door.

'Mr Youlgreave is frightfully upset,' Jill said. 'He takes this personally.'

'I dare say you do, too.'

She said nothing. Thornhill unlocked the door of the empty house. He pushed it open and shone his own torch into the hall. A flight of stairs rose up into the gloom above.

'Are those the only stairs?'

'Yes.'

'First, would you show me where you think he came in?'

She took him down the hall, through the kitchen and into the scullery. She ran her torch beam around the frame of the little window to the garden. The broken glass told its own story.

'No one's come in this way since the morning,' she said.

'How do you know?'

'I left a couple of hairs on the window frame. Look – they're still there so it can't have been opened.'

'That was clever.'

'I was with Mrs Sutton. She came up with the idea.'

'It's her field, of course,' Thornhill said, amused. 'I suppose if you write detective stories, you're always having to think of little details like that.'

He shone the torch around the scullery, noticing the smears of mud. There was a possibility of fingerprints, too; a job for the morning.

Jill stood in the doorway, her arms folded. 'There may be footprints outside. The ground looked muddy.'

'You better show me the chap's observation post.'

They went upstairs, their torch beams dancing on the walls, and along to the room at the back of the house which overlooked the garden and rear windows of Church Cottage. Thornhill moved cautiously to the window. The light was on in Jill's kitchen. The curtains were drawn. The silhouette of a cat was visible on the sill.

Jill shivered. 'I'm glad he's not here.'

So am I. Thornhill shone his torch slowly around the room.

Standing in the doorway, Jill provided a running commentary. 'That's yesterday's *Gazette*. An old blanket. An empty beer bottle. There's a lot of ash and one or two cigarette ends.'

'I wish I'd come here in daylight.'

'Why didn't you?'

'I had your message about five minutes before I phoned you this evening. There was a hitch. I'm sorry.'

Thornhill was tempted to take away everything in sight for examination. But that would warn the man if he came back. He compromised by taking a sample of the ash and the beer bottle — the latter too good a chance to miss. They went back downstairs. Once they were outside, Thornhill locked the front door behind them.

'Would you like some coffee?' Jill asked.

'Thank you.' He remembered that it was a long time since he had had anything to eat or drink. 'If you're sure I wouldn't be in your way.'

'I wouldn't have suggested it if that were so.'

Her brusqueness surprised him. He said nothing as she let them in to Church Cottage. Jill put down her torch and scarf on the table. A small tabby cat came down the hall towards them.

'No, Alice,' Jill said, 'you're staying here.' She crouched down and seized the cat by the scruff of its neck as it tried to slip between her and the wall. 'Shut the door, would you?' she asked Thornhill. 'I think the cat's in season and I'm trying to keep her inside.'

He closed the door. 'You're not thinking of having her spayed?'

'I must do it, I suppose. To be honest, I keep putting it off. It seems such a *final* thing.'

'Acting God?'

'That, too.' She opened a door on the left. 'We'll go in the sitting room. There's a fire.'

The room had changed a great deal since Thornhill had last seen it, when it had been filled with the possessions of its previous owner. In those days it had been a parlour kept for best and never used, crowded with overlarge and uncomfortable furniture, with every horizontal surface covered with ornaments. Now there were old rugs on the floor, books on the shelves in the alcoves on either side of the fireplace, a desk at the window, and watercolours on the wall. A fire burned in the grate, throwing out enough heat to warm a room of this size. There were four elderly armchairs, none of them matching. It was a room for relaxing in.

'Do sit down. I'll fetch the coffee – I won't be a moment.'

Thornhill was used to trespassing in other people's lives, and it no longer troubled him. This evening, however, he felt uneasy, almost embarrassed, as he glanced around the room. He wandered to the bookcase. The door opened, sooner than he had expected, and Jill came in with a tray. He hurried to help her.

'It's all right, I can manage, thank you.' She put it down on the low table in front of the fire. 'Oddly enough, your wife was here this morning and we had some coffee.'

'I didn't realise—' Thornhill hesitated. 'I didn't realise that she was coming.'

'She and the children brought the handkerchief back – you remember?'

'Of course I do.' In his agitation, Thornhill ran his fingers through his hair. 'I've not really said thank you for all you did yesterday.' He remembered the hideous embarrassment of being naked in Jill's car, apart from a rug round his shoulders and one of Jill's hats on his head. 'Do the rugs and so on need cleaning? You must let me pay.'

'There's no need.'

'I'm afraid I put you to an awful lot of trouble.'

'Not at all. Mrs Thornhill kindly brought me some crocuses.'

'Some crocuses?' he echoed, his mind filling with the memory of the bowl he had won in Youlgreave's raffle.

'Yes, some purple ones.' Jill sat down in the chair on one side of the fire and waved him into the one on the other side. 'Black or white?'

Alice had followed her into the room. She jumped onto Jill's lap. While Jill poured the coffee, the cat moved with restless affection to and fro across the tops of Jill's legs, occasionally mewing. Jill passed Thornhill a cup of coffee and sat back in the chair.

'She seems very fond of you,' Thornhill said.

'It's because she's in season.'

'Oh — I see.' Thornhill covered his embarrassment with a change of subject. 'In a moment I'd like to use your phone, if I may. We'll have someone watching that house tonight. In the morning, we'll see what sort of evidence we can find there.'

'Where's your man going to be?'

'At the back of the house. Actually inside, I think. You should be able to sleep soundly tonight.'

'Thank you.' She stared at him with large, candid eyes. 'You're taking this very seriously, aren't you?'

He was, partly because it made him furious to think that a man was spying on Jill. 'This may not be an isolated incident.'

'You've had other complaints?'

197

'Yes.' As he watched, the cat climbed up Jill's body and nudged her under the chin with its nose. *Lucky bloody cat.* 'We're not sure they're connected. Not yet.'

'The park – wasn't there something in the paper about the lavatories?'

Thornhill nodded. 'This is between ourselves at present, you understand.'

'Of course.'

'There's a loft over the ladies'. Someone has bored a hole in the ceiling. Several holes in fact.'

Jill shivered.

'I'm sorry – perhaps I shouldn't have—'

'No, I want to know. It's always far better to know. Otherwise it leaves more room for the imagination.'

'That's true. As well as that we have had a couple of incidents reported at the Bull Hotel in the last few days. Someone on the fire escape – looking in at guests.'

She nodded, but showed no special sign of interest or recognition – which might mean that Lawrence Jordan had not told her about the face at the window on Tuesday night. Thornhill found this possibility reassuring: it suggested, perhaps mistakenly, that Jill and Jordan were not quite as close as he had supposed.

'Edith saw someone in the park yesterday evening – just had a glimpse of someone in a duffel coat – hanging around in the bushes by the lavatory. And then he ran off.'

'Have you anything to go on?'

'One or two poor-quality fingerprints at the park.' Thornhill hesitated. 'And witnesses at the Bull seem convinced that the man has got a dark skin. One of them told us he was a negro.'

Jill raised her eyebrows. 'Doesn't that simplify your job?'

The cat jumped down from Jill's lap and onto Thornhill's. Automatically he began to stroke it. 'No,' he said slowly. 'I don't think it does.'

3

On Saturday evening, there was a dinner party at the Headmaster's House. It had been planned several weeks earlier and was one of Bernard Sandleigh's 'mix-and-match' dinners; he was rather proud of this idea.

Since they had come to Ashbridge, he and Vera had held two or three such dinner parties each term. The idea behind them was simple: you mixed together people who did not usually sit at the same table, but all of whom were concerned with the school. The result, in Bernard Sandleigh's view, was universally beneficial to the community as a whole.

Tonight's guest list included one of the governors, Sir Anthony Ruispidge, and his wife; the Reverend Alec and Mrs Sutton, who were parents – and Sutton was also one of the trustees of the charitable foundation which supported the school; Neville Rockfield, representing the staff, and his wife; and of course the wild card, Larry Jordan.

The original guest list had not included the Rockfields – or, of course, Jordan. Only the Sandleighs knew that Mervyn Carrick had originally been invited; in fact Bernard had asked him after the meeting of the Classical Society on Wednesday. Vera felt that his memory hovered over them all, a spectre at the feast.

The Sandleighs had discussed between themselves whether or not it would be appropriate to hold the dinner party in the light of Carrick's death. They had agreed that they must carry on as normal. The life of the school must continue. At Vera's suggestion, Bernard had telephoned Sir Anthony and discreetly sounded him out on this; he, too, thought that the show should go on.

It was not too bad before the meal. Dorothy joined them in the drawing room. On these occasions Vera was especially proud of her, and so was Bernard. Dorothy was a credit to them – everyone said so. Her presence kept the conversation comfortably general. She said the right words to everyone, even Sir Anthony, who was notoriously difficult to please.

Dorothy left them before dinner, however, and from then on the evening grew gradually more difficult. This was partly because of Carrick's death and partly because of Larry Jordan. Larry had nothing to do with the school. *A cuckoo in the nest*, Vera thought, and wished that they had invited a partner for him, the Jill Francis woman perhaps. But it was too late to worry about that now. Another woman had been on the original guest list – the widowed mother of one of the boys in Burton's House; an ideal choice because she was on one of Lady Ruispidge's committees. Unfortunately she had gone down with a bad cold and had cried off at the last moment.

After dinner, they had coffee upstairs in the big drawing room. The curtains masking the bay window swayed in the draught. Despite the fire and the central heating, the room felt chilly and damp.

Conversations flickered and sputtered and died like damp fireworks. Vera suspected that the Rockfields had quarrelled: certainly they took pains not to address a word to each other during the evening. The Suttons, usually reliable guests, seemed tired and abstracted; Mary murmured that Alec was still recovering from a perfect stinker of a cold. Larry drank heavily during dinner and afterwards but said little. His was the sort of silence it was impossible to ignore – stormy and sulky; a silent tantrum. Had the Francis woman rebuffed him, Vera wondered, or was he still upset because she and Bernard would not agree to his absurd suggestion?

The Ruispidges, who tended to be a law unto themselves, contributed little to the evening; they had had their problems recently and both of them had aged several years in as many months. Bernard himself did his best to keep the conversation going all around the room, but Vera could tell that his heart wasn't in it. That, of course, was hardly surprising.

After his first cup of coffee, Sir Anthony stood up and said that they really must be going. Lady Ruispidge's mouth thanked Vera for a wonderful evening while her eyes commiserated with her. Their departure was taken as a general signal by the rest of the guests.

Soon only Larry Jordan was left. While Bernard was showing out the Rockfields, the last to leave, Larry stood up and refilled his glass from the brandy decanter. He turned to face Vera.

'Have you had time to think, Vera?'

'I have. And the answer's still no.'

Bernard came back into the room. 'Are you talking about Dorothy again?'

Larry turned to him. 'It would be for the best.'

'I doubt that. In any case, it's not your decision.'

Jordan lit a cigarette. 'It's early days. Perhaps you'll reconsider. Next time I come—'

'Next time?' Vera said, her calm evaporating. 'I hope to God there won't be a next time.'

'My dear—' Bernard began.

Simultaneously Larry said, 'Listen, you've got to admit—'

At that moment the window shattered.

The sound of breaking glass was deafeningly loud, diminishing rapidly to a tinkle as falling fragments hit the furniture and the floor.

Vera felt as though a huge finger had flicked her back into the chair; the shock was like an actual blow. Larry spilt his brandy. Bernard gasped, his mouth curving into an O, which gave his profile a fleeting resemblance to that of a goldfish.

The thud should have come after the sound of breaking glass. In fact the two sounds were inextricably tangled with each other. A stone thumped onto the leather top of the desk in front of the window, bounced, scraped against the arm of a chair and fell to the carpet with another, lesser thud.

Cold air billowed into the room through the smashed window. It upset the draught in the fireplace. The fire belched a cloud of smoke into the room. The stone must have hit the glass at the spot where the curtains joined. Vera stared at it, scarcely believing that she was really seeing a jagged piece of the pinkish-purple local sandstone, about the size and shape of a man's clenched fist.

'What the devil—'

Bernard moved towards the window. Larry put down his glass and stood up, cigarette still in his hand. The curtains were now flapping in the draught.

Bernard glanced back at Larry, then at Vera. 'Nothing to worry about, I'm sure,' he said in a shaky voice, rather higher pitched than usual. 'My dear, you'd better phone Sergeant Swayne. No, perhaps phone Rockfield and Paxford first. They can get here sooner. Yes, Rockfield, that's who we need.' He turned again and advanced slowly towards the window. He pulled aside one curtain and called out, 'What on earth do you think you're doing down there?'

The only answer was another stone. It smacked onto the same part of the windows as the first, enlarging the hole. Fragments of glass fell on Bernard's head and shoulders, where they gleamed like diamonds on the black of his dinner jacket.

Vera leapt up and ran to him. 'Darling, get back! Are you hurt?' She seized his arm and pulled him away from the window.

'The barbarians.' Trembling, he pulled Vera towards the door. 'Go and telephone, please. Jordan, I want you to come with me.'

'What are you going to do?' Vera asked, panic bubbling inside her.

'Try and find out what's happening, of course. Damn it, there are two of us. And Rockfield and Paxford will soon be here.'

'Murderers! Bloody murderers! You fucking killed him.'

It was a man's voice, hoarse, with a local accent. As they listened the same words were shouted over and over again. It was like one of those scratched records, Vera thought, where after one revolution the needle jumps back and begins the same revolution all over again, and so on and on, for ever and ever, or at least until the gramophone winds down.

'The man's drunk,' Bernard said.

Larry gave a little giggle. 'So am I, actually.'

'Murderer! Bloody murderer!'

'I can't stand any more of this.' Vera left the room and went towards the head of the stairs. 'He'll wake the children in a moment.'

'Mummy. What is it? What's all the shouting about?'

Vera looked upwards. Dorothy was standing in her white nightdress on the landing above them, craning over the banisters. She looked five years younger than she was, delicate as a fairy. Vera wanted to hug her, to protect her from all harm.

'Go back to bed, darling. Just some silly man who's had a bit too much to drink.'

'I'm scared.'

'Nothing for you to worry about. Your father will soon sort it out. Off you go now. I'll be up to see you in a moment.'

She ran down the stairs to the hall as fast as she could, her long skirt rustling. The two men followed her. Glancing back, Vera saw that her husband was holding the poker from the drawing-room fireplace and Larry was carrying his glass of brandy. Somewhere above their heads came the sound of more breaking glass.

'This is ridiculous,' Bernard said. 'Quite ridiculous. In the middle of a civilised country . . . For God's sake, Vera, phone someone.'

Larry staggered across the hall and put his hand on the front door. 'Let me talk to him.'

'No!' shouted both Sandleighs.

It was too late. Larry put the Yale on the catch, twisted the handle and pulled back the front door. The porch light was still on, illuminating golden flecks of rain against the darkness. Outside on the gravel was a thin, slightly stooping figure.

'Oh my God.' Vera clutched at the newel post for support. 'It's – it's—'

'Carrick.' Bernard flung back his head and laughed, and the laughter rose higher and higher in the darkened hall. 'It's his twin. His wretched, bloody twin.'

'Hello, old chap,' said Larry, holding out his glass. 'Have a drink.'

'I hate you,' Carrick shouted. 'Murdering buggers. I hate the lot of you.'

'Let's talk about this man to man.' Larry sipped his brandy and giggled. 'Drunk to Drunk.'

There was the sound of an engine on the drive.

'Thank God,' Bernard muttered.

A Land Rover appeared in the circle of light around the front door. The driver braked sharply, and the gravel made a sound like sandpaper on wood. The passenger door opened first and a tall man emerged. Then the engine cut out and a woman jumped down from the driver's side. The man seized one of Les Carrick's arms and the woman seized the other.

'Hello there,' said Larry, and Vera knew that he was eyeing the woman with interest. 'Come to join the party, eh?'

4

It was a long evening; and as time passed, it seemed to defy the laws of logic and grow even longer.

After Richard Thornhill had gone, Jill went round the house checking doors and windows and drawing curtains. Leaving the spare room in darkness, Jill lingered by the window, looking out over the shadowy churchyard and black bulk of the church. Nothing moved. If she craned her head to either side, she could see lights – the windows of Youlgreave's house on the right and those of the almshouses on the left. But straight ahead, there was nothing but shadows, patchily illuminated by a streetlamp.

Jill went downstairs. Alice was waiting in the hall and

followed her into the sitting room. The fire had burned low and Jill knelt on the hearthrug to add more coals. The chair to the right of the fireplace still showed signs of Richard Thornhill's presence: an indentation in the seat, a crumpled cushion. She put down the shovel and picked up the cushion, intending to puff it up. For a moment she held it in both hands and wondered if there was a trace of warmth still there from Richard Thornhill's body. The humiliating absurdity of what she was doing hit her. With a grunt of disgust, she tossed the cushion onto the chair.

Alice pressed herself against Jill's kneeling legs and mewed. She trod the ground with her back legs. Jill stroked her head and Alice arched her back and purred loudly.

'Must do something about you, old lady,' Jill said aloud. 'You're just a slave to your lusts. Stupid girl.'

She stood up and glanced round the room. Something was missing, she knew. She was not afraid of her own company – indeed, she relished it – but sometimes being alone was not enough.

A dark line between the curtains caught her eye. She went quickly to the windows. The curtains had come from her flat in London, and they were a little too small for this window. They would close; but, as the minutes passed, the weight of the material would pull each one back – not much, only a fraction of an inch; but enough for someone to use as a peephole.

For a moment Jill seriously considered moving to another room – to the dining room with its gas fire, the kitchen with its stove, or even upstairs to bed with a hot-water bottle. Then it occurred to her that there was an obvious solution to the problem.

She went into the dining room and rummaged through her workbox until she found half a dozen safety pins. She took them into the sitting room. She knew that when she came down in the morning and found the curtains pinned together, the precaution would seem silly. Better that, however, than the alternative – allowing herself to be scared out of the room for the rest of the evening.

After that enormous lunch in Ross, she was not very hungry. Having pinned the curtains, she made herself a cheese sandwich, added an apple to the plate, poured herself a small glass of sherry, and carried her tray into the sitting room. She turned on the radio, tuned it to the Home Service and waited for the beginning of 'Saturday Night Theatre'.

Unfortunately, the play turned out to be a ghost story. Jill listened, unable to summon up the strength to turn off the radio. In the real world, the wind was rising, and there were moaning noises in the chimney, sometimes indistinguishable from the sound effects of the play. Jill found herself dwelling on the fact that the Suttons were out for the evening, and that the house next door was empty.

Empty? Surely there should be a policeman there by now. Thornhill had told her that someone would spend the evening in the house, and that the beat constable would pay particular attention to the car park behind Woolworth's and the wall which divided it from the garden of the house next door. At the slightest sign of anything wrong, all she had to do was to pick up the phone.

The trouble was, she had to satisfy herself that something really was wrong before she did that.

She forced herself to listen to the play until the bitter end, even deriving a certain pleasure from the sensations it aroused in her. Afterwards, it was still too early to go to bed, and she felt wide awake, so she put another shovelful of coal on the fire and picked up a novel.

Alice was becoming increasingly restless. She patrolled the room, every now and then stopping to stare reproachfully at Jill and to mew. Jill found it impossible to concentrate on the novel. Her body was tired, she decided, but her mind was still restless. Perhaps routine was the answer.

She put down her book and went into the kitchen. Alice padded silently after her. Jill found the milk saucepan and opened the refrigerator. Alice gave her dirt box a wide berth and howled piteously at the back door. Jill filled the saucepan and put it on the gas to warm. She rinsed out the milk bottle and went through to the hall, intending to leave it outside the front door. She unbolted and unlocked the door and opened it, just a little, just enough for her to put out the milk bottle.

At that moment two things happened. First, she was distracted by the realisation that tomorrow was Sunday, and therefore the milkman would not be delivering any milk. Second, a streak of fur brushed against her hand and insinuated itself through the gap between the edge of the door and the jamb.

'Alice!'

The cat ran straight across the road and jumped onto the wall of the churchyard. She turned and looked back at Church Cottage. The only light came from the streetlamp and from the doorway of the house. For a moment it looked as if Alice was smiling.

The street was deserted. Jill knew that her best chance was low cunning.

'Alice,' she called, and rattled the milk bottle against the doorstep. 'Puss, puss?'

Alice was a greedy cat who usually responded enthusiastically when she heard the chink of a milk bottle. This evening, however, she was in the grip of a more powerful urge than greed and she stayed where she was.

Jill hesitated, uncertain whether to advance slowly across the road making kissing noises with her lips or to give up this attempt at birth control as a bad job. Then, suddenly, they were no longer alone.

A large cat was strolling along the wall of the churchyard, moving steadily towards Alice and coming from the direction of Victor Youlgreave's house. In this light it was impossible to be sure, but Jill thought that it was the heavy-jowled tom who belonged to one of the old ladies in the almshouses facing the churchyard.

The two cats caught sight of each other.

'Go away,' Jill shouted desperately.

The tom ignored Jill completely. It advanced on Alice, who gave an unearthly yowl, leapt off the wall and bolted into the shadows of the churchyard. The tomcat followed her.

'Damn.' Jill ducked back into the hall and seized her torch from the hall table. If she moved quickly there was still a chance that she could prevent Alice doing something that she, Jill, would come to regret. She ran across the road and through the gate to the churchyard.

Here she stopped, suddenly realising what she was doing and how vulnerable she was. She could not see the cats and she definitely wasn't going to comb the churchyard for them. The night air was icy on the bare skin of her face, neck and hands.

Just as Jill was turning to go, she heard a rustle in the yew nearest to the gateway. Automatically she raised her torch and pressed her thumb on the switch. The beam leapt across the grass to the darker green of the yew. There, just to the right of the tree, was a tall figure, cowled like a monk.

Like the cats on the wall, the two humans stared at each other for an instant. One second? Two?

Jill was not sure if she screamed. She fled across the road, back to the security of the house, back to the lock and the bolts, back to the telephone, back to bright lights and solitude.

In one sense she left behind what she had seen. Outside in the darkness, for ever separate. Yet in another sense she brought what she had seen with her, where it would stay for ever.

The man had been wearing a light brown duffel coat with the hood over his head. He wore a black Balaclava, too, with a wide hole for the eyes and a smaller one for the mouth. The coat had been open, the toggles gleaming in the torchlight. Underneath the coat was a confusion of disordered clothing, and in the centre of that was a large, pink, erect penis.

EIGHT

Local Man is New Bishop

The new Bishop of Gambia and Rio Pongas in the Province of West Africa is the Rt Rev. G. B. Wintle, son of Doctor Wintle of Ashbridge and the late Mrs Wintle.

Bishop Wintle was born in Lydmouth and was educated at Ashbridge School, where he was Head Boy and Victor Ludorum. He read theology at Cambridge University and, after ordination, became active in the mission field in West Africa. Before his new appointment he was Assistant Bishop of Niger.

On his last visit to England at the end of last year, Bishop Wintle preached in the chapel of Ashbridge School, taking as his text the famous verse from St John's Gospel: 'He that is without sin among you, let him first cast a stone at her.'

The *Lydmouth Gazette*, 11th February

1

Jill, he thought, still half-asleep, *Jill*.

The telephone was ringing. Thornhill swung his legs out of bed and reached for the light switch. He pushed his feet into slippers, draped his dressing-gown round his shoulders and stumbled towards the door.

His mouth was dry and he had a dull headache which lay inside his head like a hot, rusty nail. He clattered down the stairs. It was still dark outside. He opened the door of the dining room and the ringing grew louder. The clock on the mantelpiece told him it was almost seven o'clock, later than he had thought. He lifted the receiver.

'Richard?'

'Edith.' He rubbed his eyes with his free hand. 'Where are you? How's your mother?'

'She's just fading. I don't think she'll last the day.'

'I'm sorry.' It was a painfully inadequate thing to say. 'Is she conscious?'

'Not really. She recognised me last night, but she's been dozing now for hours. I don't think she's in much pain.'

'And the children?'

'Oh . . .' Edith sounded vague, as if wondering which children he meant. 'They were having the time of their lives when I last saw them. Playing hide-and-seek when they should have been in bed. Heaven knows what they've been up to. Len's looking after them, and you know what he's like with children. Sylvia and I have been at the hospital all night.'

'I wish I could help.'

Edith said nothing.

'Where are you phoning from?'

'Sister's office. I mustn't be long.'

Despite this, another silence descended. Neither suggested ending the call.

'Is she in pain?' Thornhill asked at last.

'I don't think so. But who knows? Richard, she's so changed. She's *shrinking* – she's hardly larger than David.'

'Oh my dear.'

'Anyway,' Edith said brightly. 'Anyway, enough of me. How are you coping? Did you manage to fend for yourself last night?'

'I was fine, thank you.' He had eaten fish and chips, sitting in the chair by the boiler, and washed it down with a glass of whisky. 'Don't worry about me.'

'Did you find the ice cream?'

'No.'

'It's in the shed, wrapped in newspaper. Oh, and there are three ironed shirts in the airing cupboard.'

'Thank you.'

'I suppose I'd better go.'

'Yes. I suppose so.'

'Richard, I wish—'

'So do I,' Thornhill said. 'So do I.'

They said goodbye. Shivering, he went upstairs and ran his cold bath. He put a dash of hot water into it to take off the chill. In the bedroom the alarm clock began to ring.

Without Edith and the children, the house felt cold and empty. The tea he made tasted strange, and he couldn't find the tie he wanted to wear. The kitchen smelt of fish and chips and there was an unwashed whisky glass still in the scullery sink. He could not face the prospect of cooking himself breakfast. He shovelled down a bowl of corn flakes. By eight o'clock he was out of the house.

It was another grey, sad day — the frost carpeting the lawns of the houses in Victoria Road and the mist clinging to the hills on the other side of the river. Thornhill thought of Edith's mother dwindling into oblivion; and he was glad that his job gave him a reason not to be involved. Still shivering, he drove to police headquarters. The only people he saw on the way were a few early churchgoers.

The building was wrapped in its Sunday-morning calm. Two drunks were sleeping off the night's excitements in the cells. Thornhill went upstairs to his office. While he waited for Kirby to appear, he settled down to plough through the paperwork he had neglected last night. He wondered how Jill was after her disturbed night. He had a good reason to see her later in the day, he realised; and the thought filled him with a covert pleasure which he tried to ignore.

The phone rang. The old sergeant on duty in the fingerprint department, galvanised by a late-night call from Thornhill, wanted to report his progress.

'I think we've got a match, sir. Not perfect, but just about good enough to stand up in court.'

'Which fingers?'

'Index finger and middle finger of the right hand. There's a good one on the beer bottle – very close to what we found around the hatch in the loft over the toilets.'

Kirby came in a little later, his hangover evaporating when he heard that an arrest was imminent.

'Do you think that there could be a link, sir?'

'With Carrick?'

'Why not? Say he found out. He wouldn't have been afraid of trying to use his knowledge, would he?'

Thornhill raised his eyebrows. 'It's a long way from an indecent exposure to murder.'

'No harm in hoping, sir. You do desperate things when you're scared. You lose your temper.'

'First things first. I want a couple of men to go over the churchyard and see if they can find any footprints. And also the garden of the house and the car park.'

'If Miss Francis is right, you'll hardly need any extra evidence.'

'I want to tie this one up as tightly as possible.'

Kirby looked at him for a moment longer than was comfortable for either of them. 'Right ho, sir.'

They left Lydmouth at half-past nine in a marked police car with Porter driving them. Thornhill could have gone alone in the Austin, but sometimes a show of official strength had its uses. When they reached the school, they parked just off the drive and walked back a few paces to the lodge cottage. Porter stayed with the car. Kirby knocked on Paxford's front door.

'He saw us come in,' Kirby murmured. 'I saw a curtain moving.'

The groundsman opened the door. He was unshaven, his hair unbrushed. He wore a collarless shirt, stained corduroys, a jersey and a baggy tweed jacket.

'Good morning,' Thornhill said. 'May we come in?'

Paxford was taller than either of them. He stared down at them and said, 'What do you want?'

'We just want a word with you, Mr Paxford. We can talk out here if you prefer.'

His single eye flickered up the drive, in the direction of the police car. 'You'd better come in.'

He led them into a small sitting room with a bay window overlooking the drive. It was very cold but the grate contained only a pile of ashes. A bulb without a shade dangled from the ceiling. Grubby net curtains hung across the window. The place smelt strongly of tobacco, the smell that Thornhill had noticed in Carrick's rooms. There was a single easy chair near the fireplace, linoleum on the floor, a small table by the window with two hard chairs beside it and a bookcase without any books. On the table were unwashed cups and plates, copies of the *Gazette* and a large ashtray. Flecks of ash had settled on most horizontal surfaces. Two empty beer bottles adorned the mantelpiece.

Pale Ale.

The three men remained standing. Paxford looked from Thornhill to Kirby, and back again. Kirby glanced round the room. Thornhill stared out of the window. The net curtain covered only the lower half. He saw a car arriving, and glimpsed smartly dressed people inside.

'Parents, are they? Coming to chapel?'

Paxford ignored this. 'What do you want? I haven't got all day. I'm busy.'

'So are we, Mr Paxford.' Thornhill turned to face him. 'All right, then. Tell me, where were you between nine o'clock and twelve o'clock yesterday evening?'

'Here. I had a drink at the Beaufort after work. Then I came back here about seven-thirty and read the paper. I went to bed early. Like I always do.'

Thornhill nodded. It was a nice tidy answer, delivered without hesitation, without any apparent need for thought. 'And the evening before – Friday?'

'The same.' Paxford lifted his right hand and rubbed the undamaged side of his face. There was a strip of sticking plaster at the base of his little finger. 'You can't stay long. I told you – I've got work to do.'

'Where do you keep your motorbike, Mr Paxford?'

'Round the back.'

Kirby snapped, 'What are your duties, exactly? What do you do with yourself all day?'

'I'm the groundsman.'

'You just look after the pitches and so on? Mow Mr Sandleigh's lawn?'

A sullen shake of the scarred head. 'I do a bit of maintenance when I've time. Odd jobs. It depends. I do what I'm told.'

'And in your spare time you grow tobacco?'

A nod.

'And you sell it, too,' Thornhill suggested gently.

'I give it away as a present, look.'

'And sometimes people give you a little present back, eh? I'm not interested in the legality of growing your own tobacco and selling it, Mr Paxford. It's a very distinctive tobacco, isn't it?'

Paxford said nothing as he watched Thornhill. It was unnerving when you stared full-faced at Paxford. It was like seeing two people at once.

'The smell's characteristic, isn't it? Perhaps because of the way you cure it. You'd recognise it anywhere – I smelled it in Mr Carrick's room, for example.'

'He smoked it. I wasn't there, if that's what you mean. I had nothing to do with him.'

'Who said you did, Mr Paxford? To go back to your tobacco, it doesn't just smell differently, does it? It looks different, too.' Thornhill moved to the table and pointed at the mound of ash and half-smoked tobacco in the ashtray and on the table around it. 'If you found some of that elsewhere, you could probably tell that it was the same tobacco, couldn't you? And if you had access to a laboratory, as we have, I expect you could prove it, too.'

Paxford stared at him. 'I didn't do it.'

'Do what?' Thornhill gave him no chance to reply. 'Then there's fingerprints, Mr Paxford. The courts like fingerprints. We've got them in two places now, and soon we'll match them with the suspect's. That's good news, isn't it?'

Paxford glanced at Kirby, who was staring at his open notebook, pencil in hand.

'And if all that weren't enough, which of course it is, we have independent eye witnesses, too. Reputable members of the community.' Suddenly Thornhill felt his temper slipping away from him. 'One of them was my wife, Mr Paxford. What do you think about that?'

He had been speaking quietly until then, but the last words came out as a shout. This was only partly from policy. As he spoke, Thornhill had been thinking of Jill as well as Edith.

The scene dissolved. Paxford flung a punch at Kirby, catching the sergeant on his shoulder with a fist like a bunch of pink bananas. Kirby dropped his notebook and spun with the force of the blow, which flung him against the wall. Thornhill jumped forward but he was too late. Paxford had launched himself through the doorway.

Thornhill ran after him — across the hall and into a squalid kitchen which also served as a primitive bathroom. Paxford seized a saucepan from the draining board and threw it over his shoulder. Thornhill ducked. The saucepan collided with the jamb of the door and a gout of greasy water splashed over Brian Kirby's overcoat. Paxford pulled open the back door and stumbled outside with Thornhill and Kirby a few yards behind him.

The garden attached to the lodge cottage was as neat as a municipal park, though most of the ground was given over to vegetables rather than flowers. Thornhill had a confused impression of parsnips, sprouts, potatoes, leeks and savoys. Even in his haste, Paxford did not run the shortest way to the gate, for that would have taken him over one of the beds, but took a slightly longer route – down the cinder path and out through the gate at the end. The gate opened onto the path which led steeply up from the drive.

Thornhill and Kirby pounded after Paxford. Their quarry had longer legs and was fitter than either of the policemen. He began to gain on them.

Paxford reached the gravelled sweep in front of Burton's House, milling with boys in white shirts, Sunday suits and dark raincoats, their hair slicked back with grease. Paxford glanced over his shoulder at Thornhill and Kirby panting up the path behind him. With a wordless cry he bolted for the narrower path that led up to the main school.

Thornhill was dimly aware of startled faces, of a hymn book falling to the ground with a thud, of a small boy in glasses saying in a high voice, 'I say!'

He was panting badly now, forced to confront how badly out of condition he was. On the second path, Kirby overtook him. Thornhill knew, too, that in a sense the whole exercise was a waste of time: Paxford couldn't escape. The most he could gain would be a few hours on the run.

The path forked. The one to the right led up to the main school buildings and the Headmaster's House; this was the way Thornhill had come with Sandleigh on Thursday morning when the Headmaster had taken him to see Les Carrick's rooms.

Paxford chose the path on the left. This was muddier, too, and Kirby slipped, almost falling. The three of them ran on. At last the ground levelled out and the bushes on either side fell away. They were on a wide, green plateau. Paxford set off across the grass.

Directly ahead was the white chapel. Beyond it was Big Side and the rest of the school's windswept playing fields. Files of boys – some wearing black raincoats, some carrying umbrellas – were making their way towards the chapel. Gowned masters strode as giants among the grey and black rabble. A few women and girls –

wives, daughters and sisters – provided touches of colour. By the doors of the chapel a group of older boys, also wearing gowns, stood in chilly splendour, surveying the approaching masses.

At the sight of them all, Paxford stopped, his boots skidding on the wet grass. Flinging his arms apart, he threw back his head and howled. He darted to the left, towards the open spaces of the playing fields, with Kirby at his heels like a terrier chasing an enormous rat. Thornhill pursued them, glumly noticing that the distance between himself and Kirby was growing wider and wider.

As he staggered onwards, Thornhill registered the presence of the Sandleigh children, shepherded along by their mother. Behind them were Neville and Kathleen Rockfield, walking in single file on a path wide enough for two or three abreast.

By now everyone was staring across the grass at the three running figures. Suddenly Neville Rockfield broke away from the path. He sprinted towards Paxford, obviously aiming to cut him off before he reached Big Side, the first of the playing fields. Thornhill swore, the words snatched away by the wind.

Rockfield's gown flapped behind him. The gap between him and Paxford was rapidly closing. Paxford seemed not to have noticed this new threat. His head down, he was pounding towards the nearest pair of goal posts as if his life depended on reaching them first. Just before Rockfield caught up with him, Paxford turned round and saw the master. He swerved, but he was too late. Rockfield flung himself at the groundsman's knees in a perfect running tackle. Paxford hit the ground with Rockfield partly on top of him. There was a ragged cheer from the boys.

Paxford thrashed on the grass, moving his legs and body so violently that for a moment he dislodged Rockfield. He managed to get to his knees before the master again threw himself on top of him. The two men grappled.

'All right, then,' Kirby shouted, still a few yards distant from the struggling men. 'Break it up.'

With a stab of anxiety, Thornhill remembered that Rockfield

was meant to be some sort of war hero, and was presumably trained in arcane methods of unarmed combat. He need not have worried. Paxford was larger than Rockfield, and far more desperate. He kneed the master in the crotch and Rockfield jack-knifed in half, retching with pain. Then Kirby flung himself on top of Paxford and twisted the man's right arm up behind his back. A moment later Thornhill reached them. Behind him came the thunder of many feet as the rest of the school came to watch the fun.

'Cuffs,' Thornhill ordered.

All the fight seeped out of Paxford. He allowed Kirby to handcuff him; he stared at the ground, avoiding looking at Rockfield, who was still moaning on the grass. Thornhill tried to get his breath back.

Sandleigh ran up, red-faced and puffing. 'Into chapel, boys, into chapel.' The crowd began slowly to dissolve. '*Now*, I say. Into chapel.'

'Bastard,' Rockfield muttered, managing to sit up. 'Can't you even fight clean?'

'My dear Neville,' Sandleigh said. 'Are you hurt? What on earth is happening?'

'We wanted to talk to Mr Paxford, sir.' Thornhill sucked in air. 'He ran away.'

'What's he done?'

'We'll talk about that later, if you don't mind.' The pain in Thornhill's side was slightly less acute than it had been. 'Perhaps you could go into the chapel and calm the boys. And Mr Rockfield, too, if he's up to it.'

Sandleigh lifted his chin as if proposing to use it as a battering ram. He looked like a heavyweight boxer run to seed but still spoiling for a fight. Thornhill waited. He was used to people in positions of authority who objected to being told what to do.

Rockfield stood up and tried ineffectually to rub the grass stains from the knees of his trousers. Sandleigh glanced at him, perhaps glad of an excuse to change the subject, and then glared at Paxford.

'We were all witnesses, gentlemen,' he said, glancing round. 'This man assaulted one of my masters.'

Thornhill touched Paxford's arm. 'Come along.'

With a policeman on either side of him, Paxford walked unsteadily towards the path which had brought them here. This maimed, shambling giant bore little resemblance to the man who had shown every sign of being able to get the better of Rockfield; but Thornhill knew that it would be unwise to forget that Paxford was a powerful man with a talent for effective violence. Just the sort of qualities you would need to strangle Mervyn Carrick and leave his body dangling from the Hanging Tree.

On the way back, they met more boys coming up from Burton's House, who stood aside to let them pass and stared with wide eyes at the handcuffs on Paxford's wrists.

As they were nearing the drive, Kirby raised his eyebrows and jerked his head in the direction of the car: a silent question, to which Thornhill replied by nodding his own head in the direction of Paxford's cottage. Soon they were back in the cheerless sitting room with its view of the drive.

'Sit down, Mr Paxford,' Thornhill said.

He pointed to the armchair near the empty grate. Paxford, still handcuffed, slumped into it, leaning forwards so his elbows were on his knees and his head was in his hands. He muttered something under his breath. Thornhill asked him what it was.

The groundsman looked up, one side of his face miserable, the other grotesque and unreadable. 'He hates my guts, look.'

'Mr Rockfield?'

A shake of the head. 'Old Sandleigh. Never liked me.'

At a nod from Thornhill, Kirby slipped away to search the cottage.

Paxford stared into space, apparently unaware that he and Thornhill were now alone. 'I didn't do no harm,' he said at last.

Thornhill could hear Kirby moving about overhead. 'Watching women?'

'Yeah.'

'You like watching women?'

Paxford nodded slowly. 'What else can I do?' The hand with the plaster strayed up towards his face, towards the damaged side.

'Where do you watch? Here?'

'Too dangerous. Not many women, anyway, all those bloody boys.'

'Tell me where,' said Thornhill gently.

'Toilets at the park.'

'Up in the loft?'

Another nod.

'Where else?'

There was a long silence.

Thornhill went on, 'It would be better if you tell us. Better for you, as well as for us. Then I can say you cooperated with us.'

'At the Bull. There's a fire escape.'

'And where else?'

'House in Church Street.'

'Who were you watching there?'

'Lady next door.'

For Thornhill, it was like picking a scab. *What did you see, you bastard?* 'How did you know she lived there?'

'Saw her outside the Bull one night. Followed her home.'

'Why?'

Paxford stared at Thornhill with bewildered eyes. 'How do I know? Looked pretty, I suppose.'

There was a silence in the room again. Kirby could be heard opening a drawer.

'What's he doing?'

'Just taking a look around.'

Paxford nodded, as if perfectly satisfied. 'Thought so.'

'Tell me,' Thornhill said. 'Tell me about Mr Carrick now. Mervyn Carrick.'

'What's there to say? He bought my tobacco sometimes. They say he was a nasty bugger but he was all right to me.'

'Did he know about the way you like to look at women?'

Paxford looked up, surprised. 'Him? Why should he?'

'No reason. You usually wear a Balaclava at night and a duffel coat, don't you?'

A nod.

'Where are they?'

'In the cupboard in the hall.' Paxford jerked a thumb in the direction of Kirby who was coming down the stairs. 'He'll find them.'

'You always wear the Balaclava when you go out?' The Balaclava which, seen through steam and glass by a short-sighted woman like Mrs Weald, had made him look dark skinned.

Once again the hand rose up towards the shattered face. 'Keeps the cold out.'

And keeps the prying eyes away, Thornhill thought, and provides night camouflage. 'How did you get that cut on your hand?' If there was blood in the house next to Jill's, it might be an additional way of tying Paxford into the case, if any extra evidence were needed.

'On a bit of glass.' Paxford glanced down at the plaster. 'Had to see San Sister, Mrs Hirdle.' There was a note of pride in his voice. 'Three days, and it's still not healed right.'

'How did you cut it?'

Before Paxford could answer there was a banging on the door. Thornhill heard Kirby open it and Sandleigh saying, 'I want to talk to Inspector Thornhill, Sergeant.'

Thornhill opened the door of the sitting room. 'I won't keep you a moment, Mr Sandleigh.' He beckoned Kirby. 'The duffel coat and Balaclava are in the cupboard here,' he murmured. 'Have you found anything I should know about?'

Kirby shrugged. 'Not really. Just a few saucy pictures.'

'Keep an eye on him.'

Thornhill walked down the hall towards Sandleigh, who was so eager to talk that he laid a hand on Thornhill's sleeve.

'What the devil's going on?'

'Mr Paxford's helping us with some enquiries.'

'Is this about poor Carrick?'

Thornhill shook his head. 'Another matter.'

'I don't mind telling you, I never liked the fellow. What's he been up to?'

Thornhill hesitated. 'I think the charge will be indecent exposure, sir. And perhaps one or two other things.'

'I knew it. I knew he was a wrong 'un. What will he get?'

'In what sense, sir?'

Sandleigh twitched impatiently. 'How long a prison sentence?'

'That's not my province.'

'Come *on*. Suppose he's found guilty. You must have some idea.'

'Exposure is tried summarily, sir, under the Vagrancy Act of 1824. You can be sent to prison for up to three months, or fined up to twenty-five pounds. That's assuming it's a first offence.'

'That's ridiculous. What about assault and battery on Mr Rockfield? The man's clearly a menace. He should be locked up for his own good.'

'Yes, sir. The court will decide.' There was also the little matter of breaking and entering.

'I tell you one thing,' Sandleigh said, almost shouting now, 'he won't have—'

'Bernard!'

Both men turned. Vera Sandleigh was coming down the drive. If she had been a horse, you would have said that she was trotting but on the verge of breaking into a canter. The exercise had brought a flush to her usually pale cheeks. Thornhill felt a pang of admiration, aesthetic rather than sexual. He had thought of her as a delicate woman with little physical stamina; but now she was magnificent in motion, a pocket Boadicea without the chariot.

'My dear. I thought you were in chapel with the children.'

'Bernard.' She was almost shouting. 'What are the police doing with Paxford?'

2

Alice stayed out all night. She was waiting on the back-door step when Jill came down on Sunday morning. There was comfort in that Jill thought – at least she hadn't gone to the vicarage.

Purring vigorously, as well she might, the cat slipped into the kitchen and did her usual figure-of-eight trick around Jill's bare ankles. While waiting for the kettle to boil, Jill prepared Alice's breakfast and served it. The cat ate ravenously. Her nocturnal exercise had obviously given her an appetite.

Jill left the tea to brew and went into the sitting room. She unpinned the curtains and drew them back. Across the road was the churchyard, silvery-green with dew. Alec Sutton, wearing cassock and cloak, hurried through the lychgate towards his church. Jill smiled and went over to the fireplace. There were still glowing coals under the ash she had heaped on at the end of the previous evening. She laid more kindling on them, added pieces of coal and in a few minutes pale flames were streaking up the chimney. After collecting her tea from the kitchen, she crouched on the hearthrug to drink it.

The bell of St John's began to toll, summoning a handful of worshippers to the early Holy Communion service. How would they react if they learnt what had happened in the churchyard last night? Jill supposed that she herself should be shocked by what she had seen. One penis, however, was much the same as another, even when erect; and once you had seen one, in a sense you had seen them all. As for the rest – Paxford's disordered clothes, his Balaclava, and his lurking in the churchyard until disturbed by two courting cats – well, there was something comical about it, or perhaps tragic; but neither shocking nor frightening. Her reaction puzzled Jill. For a moment she toyed with the idea that there was something wrong with her, a moral deficiency. She abandoned the speculation as unprofitable and went to fetch another cup of tea.

The day stretched ahead of her. Now the Peeping Tom question had been settled, Jill felt able to relax in her own home. An unknown voyeur was far more frightening than poor old Paxford relieving himself in a position of extreme physical discomfort. She supposed that Richard Thornhill would telephone at some point during the day to tell her what had happened. For once she was almost looking forward to talking to him.

After breakfast she changed into old clothes and started to prepare the woodwork in the spare bedroom for painting. It was tedious work, but oddly soothing. She worked steadily and by the middle of the morning she was undercoating the window frame. She was just weighing up the attractions of a cup of coffee when there was a knock on the front door.

Jill was annoyed at being disturbed, and irritated that her caller should find her in a paint-spattered headscarf and a boiler suit she had owned since the war. She went downstairs and opened the door. Kathleen Rockfield was standing outside.

'Miss Francis – I'm so sorry to disturb you.' Gloved hands fluttered. 'I know I could have phoned – but it's the sort of thing that needs to be done in person.'

Jill took a step backwards. 'Won't you come in? I was about to have some coffee.'

There was no reason not to make a virtue out of necessity. Jill showed Mrs Rockfield into the sitting room, where Alice was sleeping the sleep of the satiated on the most comfortable armchair. Her guest flicked a glance around the room as though estimating the net worth of the contents.

'How . . . how cosy,' Mrs Rockfield said.

Jill left her trying to make friends with Alice and went to fetch the coffee. When she returned to the room, Alice was waiting by the door to escape and Mrs Rockfield was sitting in a chair by the fire and smoking a cigarette. She looked up as Jill came in. Her pretty face was paler than before, making the freckles more marked. The room smelt of her perfume.

'You must think me awfully pushy, I'm afraid.' Her voice was hesitant and apologetic, but the green eyes stared at Jill, assessing the effect of her words. 'You see there's no one I can turn to.'

'I'm not sure I understand. Would you like milk and sugar?'

It took a moment or two to settle Mrs Rockfield with a cup of coffee and a plate of biscuits. A cigarette in one hand, she used the other hand to eat two of the biscuits in swift succession, explaining that she had been too upset to eat any breakfast.

'You don't mind if I'm frank, do you? It's always best, I find. And if I don't tell someone, I think I shall burst. And you were so kind and helpful the other day.' The eyes narrowed. 'Besides, I need your help.'

'What's happened?'

'It's Neville. He and I have had the most terrible quarrel. We've always had rows, but this was something quite different.'

Jill sipped her coffee. Mrs Rockfield threw her cigarette in the fire and took another from the open packet on the table beside her. As an afterthought, she offered the packet to Jill.

'He's never been an easy man to live with,' she announced in a husky voice, leaning forward to light her cigarette from the spill which Jill held out for her. 'I think it must have been the war. Having to do all those frightful things. He's got a terrible temper – I'm actually scared of him. But it just can't go on. It all seemed to come to a head last night. He wants me to be the perfect housemaster's wife and the perfect mother and I don't want to be either of those things.' She stared broodingly at the contents of her coffee cup. 'I want to be *free*. I want my own career.'

Jill murmured sympathetically, and said she wasn't sure how she could help.

'Oh, but you can. You've done it, haven't you? People accept you for what you are. I think what you've done is *marvellous*.'

'It wasn't easy,' Jill said. She added, before she could stop herself, 'and it's not nearly as marvellous as you seem to think.' For an instant she would have given anything to be able to take those words back, to take them away from Kathleen Rockfield, because they revealed more than Jill wanted to reveal, even to herself.

Fortunately her guest had not been listening. Mrs Rockfield, Jill realised, was the sort of person who, when she asks advice, is in fact asking for an opportunity to explain and justify herself; Jill was an inadequate substitute for an articulate mirror.

'We went to dinner last night at the Sandleighs. It was the most dreary evening you can imagine, and the thought of having to go through that sort of thing for another forty years was more than I can bear. And then when we got home we had a row. Neville ended up— well, practically *assaulting* me.' She turned her gaze on Jill; her eyes were more like boiled sweets than ever. 'I'm not shocking you, I hope. But I just can't pretend it hasn't happened.'

Jill nodded.

'It was the final straw. I'm going to leave him. I've made up my mind. I'm going to London. A friend of mine will put me up while I find my feet.'

'But how will you live?'

'I've a savings account which will keep me going for a few months. After that, I hope to be earning my living.' Mrs Rockfield smiled triumphantly. 'With my trusty typewriter.'

'As a journalist?'

'Why not? Everyone says I have a talent for it. You told me Mr Wemyss-Brown said how valuable my work was. Once I'm established, of course, I might diversify. Write some short stories. A book even.'

'Yes,' Jill said, carefully non-committal, 'I suppose you might. But it may not be easy.'

'Oh, I'm ready for a few ups and downs in the school of hard knocks. And talking of hard knocks, anything would be better than life with Neville.'

'Have you seen a solicitor? If you're planning to leave your husband, it might be useful to find out about the legal implications.'

Mrs Rockfield waved her hand. 'Later. The first thing is to get away.' She pursed her lips and stared over the rim of her coffee cup at Jill. 'I thought perhaps you might be able to give me a couple of names.'

'I'm afraid I'm rather out of touch these days. In any case, there's no one I can recommend who'd be able to give you work.'

'But surely – surely that's how it's done?' Mrs Rockfield looked reprovingly at her, as though at a pupil who had just produced a wilfully inadequate response. 'It's not *what* you know, it's *who* you know.'

'Up to a point.'

'I thought I could start at the ground floor. I wouldn't mind that. Doing book reviews, or something. I often see the ones in the *Sunday Times*, and I'm sure I could do better than a lot of their reviewers.'

Jill leant forward in her chair. 'It really is very difficult to make your living as a journalist when you haven't any experience.'

'But I have. I—'

'If I were you, I'd stay where you are for the time being and try to acquire some. You could write some articles, or short stories, and try and place them. Then you'd begin to build up your own contacts.'

Mrs Rockfield shook her head. 'That won't do, I'm afraid. Out of the question. I want to leave now, you see.'

There was an authentic note of desperation in her voice, which stopped Jill from being as curt as she might. She wondered what lay beneath the woman's urgency to leave her husband. How reliable was she? The word *rape* hung in the silence between them, where Mrs Rockfield had so carefully placed it when she claimed her husband had assaulted her. It was that, true or false, which made Jill say something which she knew she would later regret: 'I'll tell you what I can do. I'll write to the man who used to be my editor. I'll give him your name and say you've worked on our local paper, and you're coming to London and looking for work. And then when you get in touch with him, he'll at least know who you are.'

Kathleen's face brightened. 'I'm sure that will help. And

perhaps there're some other people you could write to as well?'

With an effort, Jill kept the smile on her face. 'I think he's the best. Perhaps Philip Wemyss-Brown might have a few suggestions.' She added, with a touch of mischief, 'You could always write to him and ask, once you're settled in London.'

'That's not a bad idea.'

'When will you go?' Jill asked, to be civil, not because she wanted to know.

'I'm not sure.' Mrs Rockfield giggled. 'Just imagine if I went today. The whole school would be in a ferment. What with Mervyn Carrick dying, and Lawrence Jordan on the premises, and then this business with Paxford . . . Actually, Lawrence Jordan's quite a thought: I could do a feature on him, couldn't I? I bet almost any newspaper would be glad to have that. We had dinner with him last night, you know, and once I'm away from Neville and the school, it won't matter what I write. He was drinking like a fish and hardly said a word. You'd never think he—'

'What was that about Paxford?'

'Oh.' Mrs Rockfield blinked. 'I suppose you won't have heard. There was a terrible fuss this morning. Apparently the inspector and two other policemen turned up at the lodge and tried to arrest him. And he turned violent and knocked one of them out and ran away. The other two chased him up to the playing—'

'Which two?' Jill interrupted. 'Who was knocked out?'

'It must have been the driver, I suppose. It was the inspector and the sergeant who were chasing Paxford. Not that they caught him. Everyone was going into chapel when Paxford reached the top. It was quite dramatic, actually. Paxford made a run for the playing fields but Neville cut him off.' The corners of her mouth turned downwards. 'Neville's good at that sort of thing. And now he's the hero of the hour, which is *just* what he likes.'

'What's Paxford done?'

'Indecent exposure, and *interfering* with people.' Mrs Rockfield shivered. 'It makes my flesh creep. And he kicked Neville in a

very – well, *delicate* place. The Head has already said that whatever
happens Paxford won't be coming back to the school.'

'What will he do?'

'Paxford?' She shrugged. 'How should I know? Go and live
with that sister of his, perhaps. I don't envy *you* if he does. He'll
be practically on your doorstep. But I should think they'll send
him to prison. With any luck they'll throw away the key.'

'Where does his sister live?'

'I don't know – but she works at the Bull.' Mrs Rockfield
looked up at the clock. 'I must get back to Ashbridge. There's
a roast in the oven.'

Jill grappled with this picture of domesticity, trying without
success to equate it with the aspiring careerist in front of her.
Both women stood up.

'Where's your husband now?' Jill asked.

'At Burton's, taking Letter Prep. He's on duty today. Don't
worry, he won't know I've come. I slipped out of chapel early
– I said I wasn't feeling well – and borrowed the car. He won't
come back home till lunchtime.'

Jill nodded and opened the door. Mrs Rockfield paused in the
doorway.

'I wonder if Paxford killed Mervyn Carrick, too?' she said.
'Perfectly possible: he'd be just the type.' Then she shook her
head, disagreeing with herself. 'No – if anyone killed him, I
should think it was the brother because he was carrying on
with the sister-in-law. Did you know they used to meet at that
tree? Mervyn and the sister-in-law, I mean. The tree where the
body was?'

'At the Hanging Tree?'

'Yes – I saw Mervyn there, waiting for her. It was in January
– one of those lovely sunny afternoons we had near the beginning
of the month. I was walking the dog along the old road – and
I actually saw him there in the tree.'

'You mean he was climbing the branches?'

'No. Most of the centre of the tree is dead and there's a sort of platform you can stand on. He was there.' Mrs Rockfield's mouth turned down again, and beneath the prettiness Jill glimpsed the woman she might become in middle and old age. 'Quite disgusting. Almost as bad as Paxford.'

'Was she there?'

'Probably. Either that or he was waiting for her. I didn't stay to find out – it might have been nasty. I just turned round and went back at once. Luckily Cuddles didn't bark.' She saw the look on Jill's face and added, 'My poodle.'

'I see,' said Jill.

After Kathleen Rockfield had gone, Jill opened the window in an attempt to rid the sitting room of her visitor's perfume and washed the coffee cups. Paxford lingered in her mind. It sounded as if her intervention had cost the man his job and his home. She told herself that she had no reason to worry about this. The man richly deserved to be punished for what he had done. But would it help if he lost his job and his home as well? Jill's pleasure in the day had gone. Kathleen Rockfield, she thought bitterly, was that sort of person: she would blight whatever she touched.

A little before two o'clock Jill put on her coat and went out. She walked up to the High Street and into the Bull Hotel. The place had not yet settled into the post-prandial calm of Sunday afternoon; there were still diners in the dining room and drinkers in the bar. Quale was at the reception desk.

'Miss Francis.' The wizened head swung to and fro, and the red-rimmed eyes gleamed with interest. 'And what can we do for you?'

'Do you know a man called Paxford, by any chance? He works at Ashbridge School as a groundsman.'

Quale nodded.

Jill smiled encouragingly at him. 'Someone mentioned that he had a sister who worked here.'

'One of our chambermaids, miss.'

'Is she here at present?'

'No. Doesn't usually work Sundays.'

Jill knew that with Quale it was sometimes best not to be subtle. She put her handbag on the desk and opened it. 'I wonder where I could find her.'

'She lives locally, miss.'

'I could always ask Mr Frinton. He must have a note of her address.'

Quale smiled. 'I'm afraid he's out. Having lunch with friends.'

'I'm not in any great hurry.' Jill took out two half-crowns and laid them on the counter, tapping them absentmindedly with her gloved fingers. 'On the other hand, it would be nice not to have to come back here today.'

'No need to, either.' Quale grinned, exposing yellow false teeth. 'She lives in that cottage up by the gates to Jubilee Park. Her name's Joan Davies. The husband looks after the cemetery. Not that Ernie does a very good job, I'm afraid.'

Jill's fingers glided away from the two half-crowns. Quale's hand scuttled across the counter towards them.

'What's she like – Mrs Davies?'

The hand stopped moving. 'Keeps herself to herself. I dare say she's had her troubles.' The hand began to advance once again.

Jill thanked him and said goodbye. She went out in the street and discovered that in her absence it had filled with watery sunlight. The clouds had rolled back. To the west, almost half the sky was a delicate, washed-out blue. Jill decided to walk to Victoria Road. The exercise would do her good.

She glanced at the Thornhills' house as she turned into the bottom of Victoria Road. The Austin was not outside. Jill wondered whether Richard Thornhill had been trying to phone her. She wasn't sure whether to be relieved or disappointed that she might have missed his call. Alternatively, she thought, mocking herself, if she were at home, she might be irritated that he hadn't called at all. On the whole, as so often in life, it was better not to know. The price of knowledge was often more than one wanted to pay.

She walked slowly up the road towards the gates of Jubilee Park. The Davies' cottage stood between the gates and the entrance to the cemetery, a narrow driveway with grass verges. The cottage was a detached building no more than fifty years old; it had tall gables, like witches' hats, tall windows, and a garden well stocked with funereal evergreens.

Jill rang the bell. She stood back, away from the shadow of the porch roof, to enjoy the thin sunshine on her face. A moment later the door opened. On the threshold was a sturdy woman with a lined and faintly familiar face. She wore a pinafore apron; her cardigan sleeves had been pushed up above the elbows, and her arms and hands were still wet and flecked with soapsuds.

'Yes?'

'My name's Jill Francis.'

'We're not interested, thanks.' The door began to close.

'I've come about your brother.'

'What about him?'

'I think he's been arrested.'

The woman's face did not change but she stretched out an arm and rested it against the jamb of the door. 'When?'

'This morning – up at the school.' *When*, Jill thought, not *why*. 'In a way, it was my fault. I reported him to the police.'

'Not your fault, miss.'

It was odd, Jill thought, that the glow of a pipe or cigarette at a darkened window had been far more worrying than what she'd seen last night. 'I think the school may sack him.'

Mrs Davies glanced back at the interior of the house. 'I can't talk here. Can you wait a moment?'

Jill nodded. A moment later, Mrs Davies, now wrapped in a long, beige raincoat and wearing a woolly hat, joined her outside.

'You don't want to disturb your husband?'

'Ernie's asleep. If he isn't disturbed he'll be dead to the world till teatime. He's not going to like this, and I'd rather choose the best time to tell him. You'd better tell me what my brother's been up to.'

'I think you know some of it.'

'What do you mean?'

'You know what's been happening at the Bull with Mrs Weald and . . . and with the other guest. You told the police you saw the man on the fire escape. You said he was a small man, a negro.'

'Let's go into the cemetery. It'll be quieter there.' Mrs Davies plodded up the driveway towards the graves. 'Well, what could I do? Say yes, it was my brother, up to his old tricks? He'd have been sacked, and most likely I'd have been sacked, too. What would have been the point? I thought if I talked to him, he'd leave off. That's what I've done before.'

'In a way he did leave off. He transferred his attentions to me.'

Mrs Davies glanced up at her. 'You're not angry, miss?'

'Of course I'm angry. But I'm not sure it should cost him his home and his job.'

'Nothing we can do about that. If it happens, it happens.'

After a pause Jill said, 'So he's done this before?'

'Yes.'

'Has he been caught before?'

'Once. He wasn't much more than a lad. It was just after they sent him his call-up papers. Didn't go to court, because of the war. They let him off with a warning.'

A central path divided the cemetery in two. Several people were already there – mainly old women visiting graves. The newer plots were on the right. Mrs Davies veered to the left, among the older graves. The dead would not listen. She said nothing more until they reached the hedge that divided the cemetery from the park.

'What will they do? Lock him up?'

'I'm not sure. Not necessarily. Has he always been like this?'

'It started when he was a boy. My fault, in a way. Hubert and me lived in Mincing Lane then, the two of us and Mam. All in one big room and a sort of kitchen in the corner. Mam worked behind the bar in the Bathurst. I used to stay at home with Hubert. Then Ernie came courting. And sometimes when we thought Hubert was asleep, well, I suppose we got a little bit carried away. A little later Hubert started trying to look at other girls. There was a bathroom we shared with other people in the house. He made a little hole in the door.'

She fell silent, and they paced among the graves.

Jill said, 'Did he ever do more than watch?'

'Oh no. Too scared for that. He was always a shy boy. Needed a nice girl to look after him, to tell him what to do. But he never found one, did he? Instead, there was the war. And when that grenade went up, he had even less chance of finding a girl. That's when it got really bad.' She stopped suddenly and turned to face Jill, her face red. 'All right, miss, it's wrong. I know that, you know that. But they can't say it's all his fault, can they? And how's locking him up going to help him? Or turning him out of his house and his job?'

Jill shook her head. 'I don't know.'

Mrs Davies sighed. When she next spoke her voice was calmer. 'He can't live here, you know. Ernie would half-kill him. They've always fought like cat and dog.'

'It may not come to that.'

'I lied to the police. What do you think they'll do to me?' Mrs Davies' voice rose. 'Send me to jail, too?' The nearest of the old ladies turned to look at them. 'That'd serve me right, wouldn't it? That'd sort it all out. Sweep us all under the carpet. Then everyone else could live happily ever after.'

3

The first Fred Swayne knew about the morning's events at Ashbridge School was when he telephoned Sergeant Fowles at police headquarters to discuss yesterday afternoon's football results. Fowles said that he was surprised Swayne had time to chat, what with all the excitement in his part of the world. Then it all came out.

That bastard Thornhill was strutting about on Swayne's patch and he hadn't even had the courtesy to let Swayne know. To make matters worse, there was sod-all he could do about it. You didn't make an enemy of the head of your divisional CID without very good reason.

According to Fowles, Thornhill was not a good man to cross. 'You'd think he's all meek and mild, the way he looks at you and doesn't say much — but he's a ruthless bugger, Fred, believe you me.'

Paxford was a freak, no better than a bloody animal, no argument on that score: they called him Frankie at the Beaufort as well as up at the school. Fowles thought they'd got him on a sex crime, which seemed more than likely; there seemed to be a lot of it around since the war. Swayne hated perverts. If he had his way, he'd castrate the lot of them. He was not surprised to hear that Paxford was one: the man had never fitted in Ashbridge. It stood to reason that if you kept yourself to yourself like that, you must have something to hide.

No, Paxford almost certainly richly deserved to be arrested: the trouble was, Thornhill should have taken Swayne with him. Paxford had tried to escape, Fowles said, something which would not have happened if Swayne had been there. Swayne suspected that Thornhill didn't have the guts for a rough house; he was a pen-pusher, nothing more; all nerve and no muscle.

There was also the matter of his own reputation in the community to consider. Swayne considered that he had a position to keep up. If there was a crime on his patch, he liked to be the first to know — and the first to tell other people. Swayne felt that he had been put unfairly at a disadvantage, and he wanted someone to suffer for it.

He shouted at the children, banged their heads together when they answered back and sent them scurrying upstairs to their bedroom. He found his wife in the kitchen, spooning the juices over the joint, a shoulder of pork. 'What did you get pork for?' he screamed, noticing with pleasure how she flinched away from him. 'You know it upsets my stomach.'

Having reduced his family to tears, he left the house at two minutes after twelve and stalked across the green towards the Beaufort Arms. Sunday lunchtime was one of the busier times of the week. In the saloon bar, Fred Swayne was undisputed king, partly because of his job and partly because of his relationship with the landlady.

There was already a group of men around the bar. Swayne was mildly surprised to see Les Carrick among them. Les had his vices, but he was a mean old bugger so you didn't often see him drinking in the Beaufort.

Swayne's aunt, standing behind the bar and drawing a pint, was the first to see him. 'Morning, Fred.'

Heads turned and there was a chorus of greeting. Auntie Meg reached for his pewter tankard, hanging above the long counter. The man who kept the village stores clapped him on the shoulder and asked what was he was drinking.

At first the conversation in the bar centred around Paxford's arrest. It was rumoured that Paxford had taken on four policemen and that he had only been pacified when Neville Rockfield led the school rugby XV to the rescue. The other drinkers appealed to Swayne for confirmation and further information. He gave the impression that he could have enlightened them but that duty prevented him.

'It'll all come out soon enough,' he said weightily. 'You'll see.'

A local farmer changed the subject, asking advice about a dispute with a neighbour. Swayne began to relax. This was how it should be. By the time he was ready for his third pint, he felt almost cheerful.

Every now and then he glanced at Les Carrick, who sat by himself in the corner at the far end of the bar counter, furthest away from the fire. For most of the time he stared at the mahogany of the bar top, smoked and drank, especially the latter.

Swayne took his glass up to the bar.

His aunt leant across the bar towards him, her face framed between hand-pumps. 'He's pushing the boat out a bit,' she murmured, nodding towards Les. 'In here last night, too. Last to leave. Had a proper skinful.'

'He'll be upset still. Takes people like that sometimes.'

She pulled Swayne's pint and took the money. She turned away to the till. When she came back with his change, she said, 'A little bird told me that Les went up to the school after he left here last night. Caused a proper rumpus. Smashed one of the Sandleighs' windows.'

'I've heard nothing about that.' Swayne guessed that the little bird was Doris, the sister of one of the girls who worked for Auntie Meg; he remembered hearing that she had a job up at the school. Simultaneously he wondered if this was one more thing Thornhill was keeping from him. 'Mr Sandleigh will be lodging a complaint later in the day, I expect.'

'He might or he might not,' Auntie Meg said. 'Les was shouting out he was a murderer. Then Dilys and the Eyetie turned up in the Land Rover and took him away.' She sniffed. 'Not a nice business, Fred. I know you have to make allowances for him, but even so.'

Swayne tried to make light of it: 'At least it's good for trade.'

The sound of an engine made them both glance up. A Land Rover drew up outside the pub.

'Oh dear,' Meg murmured. 'Dilys. *And* she's got the Eyetie with her.'

A moment later Dilys Carrick and Umberto Nerini came into the bar.

'Morning, Mrs Carrick,' Meg called. 'What can I get you?'

Dilys glanced at her. 'Nothing, thanks, Mrs Swayne. I've just come to collect my husband.'

Fred Swayne stared at her. Her colour was high and she stood in a way that emphasised her full breasts. A damn fine woman, he thought; wouldn't mind an armful of that.

'Then you can bugger off home again,' Les Carrick said, not loudly but in a carrying voice which killed all the conversations around the bar in an instant.

'Now, now.' Meg began to polish a glass. 'Language, please.'

Dilys strode up to Les. 'Come on.'

He looked up at her. 'I'm staying here.'

She lowered her voice. 'Why? This is stupid.'

Suddenly Les's lethargy dissolved. His hand snaked out like the thong of a whip and slapped her on the cheek. The crack of flesh on flesh filled the bar like a gunshot. Dilys staggered to her right in the direction of the blow and stumbled against the edge of a table.

'You know what?' Carrick said to Meg in that quiet but carrying voice. 'That's my wife. She's just a bloody whore.'

NINE

First Aid at Local School

All pupils at Lydmouth High School for Girls now learn First Aid as part of the curriculum, the Headmistress, Dr Margaret Hilly, told Old Girls at the Lent Term Sherry Party.

'It will be an invaluable skill if there is another War,' she told Old Girls in the School Library. 'Our girls will also find it useful in their everyday lives.'

The *Lydmouth Gazette*, 11th February

1

Thornhill had watched men weeping before, but not enough to become used to it. Paxford sat beside his empty fireplace, snivelling into a handkerchief the colour of old parchment which crackled softly when his huge hands screwed it into a ball.

It was not Thornhill that had brought him to this place of utter desolation but the Sandleighs. Husband and wife, judge and jury, they had confronted him outside the lodge, informing him that he no longer had a home or a job.

'For the good of the school,' the Headmaster had said.

Afterwards, when Paxford had run back to his living room, Vera Sandleigh said in her silvery voice, 'Inspector, don't think I'm trying to teach you your job, but I'm sure you're wondering what might have happened if poor Mr Carrick had found out what Paxford was up to.'

241

'I'm sure you're not trying to teach me my job, Mrs Sandleigh,' Thornhill had replied. 'Now, if you would excuse me.'

'He will have to leave today.' Sandleigh stooped over Thornhill and poked out his well-developed chin. 'If you're going to remand him in custody—'

'Unlikely, sir, in a case like this.'

Sandleigh had waved the objection aside. 'There's a sister in Lydmouth, I believe. He can go there. I'm not having him on the school premises for a moment longer than necessary.'

The Sandleighs walked slowly back up the drive, arm in arm, Bernard's head lowered so that Vera could murmur something in his ear. Thornhill had gone back to the wreck of a man waiting for him in the living room of the lodge cottage.

While Kirby searched the sheds with the dogged assistance of P.C. Porter, Thornhill tried to talk to Paxford. From delicacy, he avoided looking directly at the man, wanting to spare his feelings. As a result, it was at least a minute before Thornhill realised that there was a patch of red on the yellowing handkerchief, the colour uncomfortably vivid in these drab surroundings.

'Where's the blood from?'

Paxford did not reply; not that it mattered because as he spoke Thornhill guessed that the old cut on Paxford's hand must have reopened, probably during the struggle near the chapel. He stood up, went over to Paxford and took his hand. He peeled away the handkerchief. Underneath it, the plaster was now trailing from the skin. Blood welled out of a deep, jagged cut. The hand was filthy – partly ingrained dirt, Thornhill thought, and partly fresh mud picked up during the struggle.

'We'd better clean this up,' he said briskly. 'Come along.'

He gave the hand a gentle tug. Paxford got to his feet and allowed himself to be towed from the living room and to the kitchen. Thornhill turned on the tap.

'You don't want that to get infected.'

The big man stared down at Thornhill with puzzled eyes. Slowly he nodded. 'San Sister said that.'

Speech of any kind was progress. Thornhill held the hand under the stream of cold water. Paxford winced at the shock and the muscles in the hand tensed. Then they relaxed. Thornhill tried to brush away some of the dirt.

'Have you any disinfectant?'

'No, sir.'

'We'll have to get you some, then.'

Thornhill turned off the tap and looked around for something to dry the hand on. Both the tea towel and the handtowel looked as if they had not been washed in living memory. Thornhill took the white, crisply ironed handkerchief from the breast pocket of his jacket and unfolded it.

'Shake your hand to get the water off. Then we'll wrap this round the cut. Have you any plaster?'

'No. Ran out, yesterday.'

It was odd, Thornhill thought, what custom could do. The blemished face no longer seemed especially horrifying. Unusual, yes; but who among us was usual?

'Thank you,' said Paxford unexpectedly.

Thornhill smiled at him. 'How did you get that cut? Quite a nasty one.'

'Cleaning the car.'

A memory twisted in his mind like a key turning in a lock. 'You were cleaning Mr Sandleigh's car on Thursday morning when I first came here. Was that when it happened?'

A nod.

'But how could you cut yourself when you were cleaning a car?'

'Bit of broken glass, look. Inside.'

'Where?'

'In the back – on the floor.'

'What was it like, this bit of glass?'

Paxford hesitated, staring at Thornhill's face, as if hoping to find there the answer required. He shrugged. 'About that size.' He held up his hand with the index finger curled up against the

243

inside of the thumb, making an aperture no larger than a farthing. 'Thick glass.' The corner of his mouth lifted on the undamaged side of his face: half a smile. 'Sharp edges.'

Thornhill's hands were balled into fists in the pockets of his overcoat. Keeping his voice low and casual he said, 'What did you do with it? Can you remember?'

Paxford frowned. 'Threw it away.'

'Where?'

There was a long pause. 'Don't know. In the garage, I suppose.'

'In the garage? But when I saw you, you were washing the car outside. In the drive, remember, just out here, by the gates.'

Paxford nodded. 'I cleaned the outside of the car outside, and the inside inside.' Again, there was the half-smile, lopsided and charming. 'In Mr Sandleigh's garage.'

'So if you threw away the glass, it might still be there?'

'Could be.'

'You'd better take me there.'

Paxford hung his head, looking more than ever like an overgrown child. 'But Mr Sandleigh said I had to go right away. If he sees me—'

'I'll deal with Mr Sandleigh. Let's find your coat.'

Thornhill told Kirby where they were going.

'You want me to come too, sir? In case he blows his top again?'

'I don't think he will. And if there are two of us, he'll clam up.'

A moment later Thornhill and Paxford were walking up the path towards Burton's House.

'Faster this way,' Paxford said. 'Twice as long if we go by the main drive.'

'Where is this garage?'

'There.' Paxford waved his arm towards the bushes, further up the slope. 'Not far now.'

There was no one about outside Burton's. Paxford took them

up the path towards the chapel and playing fields; this was the way that Thornhill had come with Sandleigh on the Thursday morning, when Sandleigh had escorted him from the Headmaster's House to Mervyn Carrick's rooms in Burton's. On that occasion, Thornhill had not noticed a smaller path winding into the bushes on the right-hand side. Paxford and he walked along it in single file. A few yards later, they reached the garage.

It was a wooden building with a pitched roof of corrugated iron. The double doors at the front faced the access to the main drive. They were secured with a large padlock.

Paxford glanced over his shoulder to check they were not observed and then reached up to a spot just below the overhang of the roof. When he lowered his hand, it contained a key.

'Who told you to clean the car on Thursday?' Thornhill asked suddenly.

'No one, sir. I got standing orders from the Bursar: if Mr Sandleigh's car needs a clean, I do it. Pronto.'

'But what if Mr Sandleigh wants to use it?'

'I ask his secretary first. In this weather, it needs a lot of cleaning. All that salt and grit on the roads – bad for the paintwork. And a lot of it gets inside the car too. They bring it on their shoes.'

'How often do you have to clean it?'

'Two or three times a week, since we had the snow. He's that particular, Mr Sandleigh. Only had that car for a few months. Used to belong to Sir Anthony Ruispidge. Apple of his eye, look.' Paxford spat on the grass by the door, a neat, glistening globule of phlegm. 'And if it's not sparkling like a new pin, he gives me hell. Like he did the other day. So if it looks a bit dirty, I clean it, sharpish.'

'The other day? Which day?'

'Day I had a bonfire in Mr Sandleigh's garden. She complained about the smuts on her washing. Mrs Sandleigh, that is.'

'But which day of the week?'

Paxford pushed the key into the padlock. 'Must have been Wednesday.'

Paxford lifted the padlock from the staple, flicked back the hasp and hung the padlock on a rusty nail in the lintel of the doors. He tugged open one leaf. Inside was the gleaming grey bulk of the Hudson.

Thornhill moved slowly into the garage. The place smelt of oil and petrol. A workbench ran beneath the single window, its surface clear of dust and debris. A selection of tools, neatly arranged by size, hung on racks beside and beneath the window.

'You keep it well, Mr Paxford.'

'I do my best. But I do wish people wouldn't borrow my things without asking.'

'Do it often, do they?'

'Too often.' He pointed to a gap in the rack under the window. 'My big spanner was there till this week.'

'Really? When did it go?'

'I used it last weekend.'

'This piece of glass, Mr Paxford – where do you think you might have put it?'

The big man looked around. He ran a hand along the workbench, as if feeling for the glass with his fingertips. He gave another grunt and stooped under the workbench. When he straightened up, he was carrying an old paint tin in one hand and a copy of the *Gazette* in the other. He spread out the newspaper on the bench and upturned the tin over it. A shower of cigarette ends, rusty nails, spent matches, washers, and scraps of oily rag tumbled out. He poked his forefinger in the rubbish.

'Ah.'

The fingernail touched the gleam of glass. He picked up the fragment and dropped it on Thornhill's outstretched palm.

Thornhill swallowed. It was a thick piece of glass, an irregular oblong in shape, its plane surfaces slightly curved. He held it up to the light and, closing one eye, squinted with the other through the glass at the branch of a tree just outside the window. The branch rippled and buckled.

Optical glass.

Paxford felt under the workbench and produced a set of car keys. 'Do you want these as well, sir?'

'I'd better take them. And the padlock key, too.'

Paxford stared at him for a moment, his face visually ambivalent as always: part surprised, and part familiarly, monstrously blank. Thornhill took two envelopes from his pocket. He put the glass in one. He opened the other and held it out. Paxford dropped the keys inside.

'How many people would know where to find these?'

Paxford shrugged. 'Don't know. The Sandleighs. The Bursar – he showed me where to hide them. The secretary. Some of the masters probably. It's no secret – except from the boys, of course.'

'There must be other sets of keys for the car,' Thornhill snapped. 'The Sandleighs must have at least one. Anyone else?'

He had spoken sharply, not because he was in any way cross with Paxford – quite the reverse – but because his mind was galloping ahead, in front of his words, towards conclusions he had not quite reached. But Paxford took two steps back as if Thornhill had threatened him and his hand went up to his damaged cheek.

'What does it matter? Be me that gets the blame.' His voice rose in pitch and trembled. He slammed his hand down on the workbench, scattering the rubbish. 'Of course they'll blame me for it. Of course they will.'

'It's all right.' Thornhill held out his free hand towards Paxford. 'Listen. There's nothing for you to—'

The light in the garage suddenly diminished. Thornhill looked at the doorway. Kirby was standing there, panting as if he had run up from the lodge. Thornhill joined him in the doorway.

'Call from Fred Swayne, sir,' Kirby murmured, keeping his voice down so Paxford would not hear. 'There's been trouble up at the pub.' His eyes gleamed. 'I think we might have found ourselves a motive.'

2

When she turned into the driveway of Ashbridge School, the first thing Jill noticed was the police car parked outside the lodge. A young uniformed police officer with a red, familiar face was leaning against the wing, smoking a cigarette. When he saw the Ford Anglia, he straightened up and tried to conceal the cigarette.

Jill glanced at the lodge as she passed. No smoke from the chimney, she noticed, and no sign of Paxford, Thornhill or Kirby. She felt a stab of anger on Paxford's behalf: had they really needed to turn up in force like this, proclaiming his guilt for all the world to see? Hadn't they better things to do, such as catch a murderer?

She drove up the drive and parked outside the Headmaster's House. The school was wrapped in a Sunday afternoon calm. As she climbed out of the Ford, she glanced up at the bay window of the drawing room. There was a large hole like a jagged star in one of the upper panes, covered on the inside by what looked like a sheet of hardboard. She went into the porch and rang the bell.

A moment later, Vera Sandleigh herself opened the door. When she saw who it was, her face lightened.

'Hello, Miss Francis. I thought I was going to find a policeman on the doorstep.' She stood back to allow Jill into the tall, dark hall. 'Larry's upstairs. I'll fetch him.'

'No,' Jill said. 'No, please don't.'

Vera looked puzzled.

'I wondered if I could have a word with Mr Sandleigh. It's about Paxford.'

'Paxford? But – I don't understand. The police have just arrested him.'

'Then you know he's a Peeping Tom?'

'Yes, we—'

'I was one of the people he was watching. It was because of me that he was caught.'

'Oh, my dear – how awful. You must be so relieved.'

'No,' Jill said. 'I mean, yes, of course. It's just that I'm worried about what's going to happen to him.'

Vera laid a hand on Jill's arm. 'You mustn't worry about that. There's no risk of his being able to pester you again. Bernard's going to make sure he gets exactly what he deserves.'

Jill resisted the temptation to point out that, although Bernard might wield the power of both judge and jury over Ashbridge School, this power did not extend to the outside world. 'I'm not making myself clear, I'm afraid.'

'It's the shock, I'm sure. It takes me the same way.'

'I understand that Paxford may lose his job because of this. And his house.'

'Well, naturally. Bernard has no choice. He is responsible to the governors for the welfare of the boys, and their parents, of course. He simply can't allow—' Vera lowered her voice '— a pervert on the school premises. I'm sure you agree – that it would be completely irresponsible of him.'

'But nothing's even been proved, yet.'

'I don't think there's any doubt about it, do you? I thought you said that you yourself—'

'Paxford doesn't need punishment – he needs help.'

'That's not Bernard's concern. Surely you must understand that?'

A door opened on the floor above and there were footsteps on the landing. Both women glanced at the stairs. Bernard Sandleigh descended, his head bowed and his tread heavy. Then he saw Jill and his wife in the hall.

'Miss Francis – this is a surprise. How are you?'

'Very well, thank you.'

'Miss Francis has come about Paxford,' Vera said, her voice cool. 'I was explaining to her why it was necessary for you to make sure he leaves the school immediately.'

Sandleigh had reached the hall by now. He glanced at his wife and then at Jill. 'Yes, I'm afraid so. Still, we must remember that the man has only himself to blame.'

'I think he's had a lot to put up with,' Jill said, her voice trembling slightly. 'I think it would be charitable to give him a second chance.'

'I quite agree, Miss Francis,' said Sandleigh. 'But unfortunately we are not a charitable institution, or not in the sense that you mean. The boys' welfare must come first. Imagine what the parents would say, or even the press.'

'I shall have to talk to my editor,' Jill said, knowing as she spoke that the threat was an empty one, for Philip Wemyss-Brown would never risk alienating his readership and his advertisers.

'Don't think I'm not sorry for the poor fellow, Miss Francis,' Sandleigh went on, perhaps sensing that Jill was beaten. 'But what can one do? It's a question of moral tone. If a school loses that, it loses everything.'

'I'm sorry to have troubled you.'

'Not at all. If I may say so, your concern does you credit.'

'Would you like some tea?' Vera said brightly. 'I'm sure Larry would love to see you.'

'No, thank you. I really should be going.'

Affable in victory, the Sandleighs saw her out to the car. Bernard held open the door of the Ford Anglia. When she was behind the wheel, he bent down and murmured, 'There's another possibility I have to consider, Miss Francis. I'm afraid that Paxford may be guilty of more than – ah – prurient behaviour.'

Startled, she looked up. 'You mean – this other business?'

'We have to bear it in mind, Miss Francis. I think you'll find the police are doing just that.'

He smiled and straightened up. He and Vera waved.

She drove slowly down the drive. As the Ford Anglia emerged from the first bend below the Headmaster's House, a figure darted out from the track that led to the Sandleighs' garage and flagged her down. It was Dorothy, pale and thin-faced, with glittering eyes; more like a waif than a girl on the verge of becoming a young woman.

'Hello,' Jill said. 'Do you want a lift?'

Dorothy shook her head. 'Uncle Larry would like to speak to you.'

'Where is he?'

'Over there. On the path.' Dorothy licked her lips. 'We – we were walking, and he saw you leaving, but he – he didn't want to interrupt while you were talking with my parents.'

It was clear that the child thought she was acting as a romantic go-between. Both irritated and amused, Jill parked the car on the verge of the drive and followed Dorothy into the bushes. She glimpsed the corrugated-iron roof of the Sandleighs' garage a few yards away.

Larry Jordan was waiting in a little clearing sheltered by overhanging branches. The ground was littered with dozens of cigarette ends in varying stages of decay. Half-concealed in the undergrowth was a bench. He smiled at her, and despite herself Jill found it impossible to think of him merely as a demanding male with more than his fair share of charm.

'Thanks for coming, Jill.'

Dorothy, a well-trained Cupid, melted away into the bushes.

'What *is* this?' Jill said.

'A smoking hole. Didn't you have them at your school? We did. All mod cons, including a bench and three exits in case of emergencies. Very nice.'

'What do you want? And why *here*?'

'I don't mean to be so cloak-and-dagger. The thing is I didn't realise you were here until I saw you leaving, and I didn't want to interrupt. It looked as if you and Bernard and Vera were being very earnest together.'

Jill said nothing.

'The thing is, I wonder if you could give me another lift.'

'Where?'

251

'Just down to Lydmouth. I've booked myself back into the Bull.'

'I thought you didn't like it there.'

Jordan arched his eyebrows, and Jill wondered how often he plucked them. 'It won't be for long,' he said. 'To be honest, I don't want to outstay my welcome here. What with this business with Paxford on top of everything else, Bernard and Vera are under an awful lot of strain. The last thing they need is to have to be polite to a guest.' He gave her what could only be described as a quizzical smile; Jill felt as though she were his shaving mirror. 'Let's face it, the fact people know my name makes it worse for them. If the press realise I'm on the premises, there'll be no stopping them. And the news is bound to break sooner or later.'

Jill thought of Kathleen Rockfield, husband-hater and cub reporter. 'When do you want to go?'

'Good girl. I knew I could rely on you. Whenever suits you, really. Half an hour, say? That would give me time to throw my things into a suitcase and say goodbye to Bernard and Vera.'

Jill remembered Jordan's enormous quantity of monogrammed luggage, and suspected that it would take him longer than thirty minutes to pack. 'Shall we make it an hour? There's something I want to do first.'

'Of course. I really don't want to be a bother. It's awfully good of you.' This time the smile wasn't so much quizzical as frankly amorous.

'I have to go now,' Jill said primly.

Larry saw her back to the Ford Anglia. 'I'll give you a job as a chauffeur anytime, my dear,' he murmured just before he closed the door. His eyes raked down her body. 'You'd look very fetching in uniform.'

Jill crashed the gears as she drove away. She glanced in the driving mirror: Larry was standing in the middle of the drive, one hand raised in farewell.

Magnetism, Jill thought: so easy to forget that it can repel as well as attract.

3

The police Wolseley swung smoothly off the main road and into the lane that led to Moat Farm. Porter was driving, and Brian Kirby sat in the front beside him, whistling tunelessly through his teeth.

Thornhill's decision to remain at school had surprised him. Kirby himself would not have delegated an interview as important as this one promised to be. The governor was acting out of character. Why was he being so soft with the pervert, for example?

Kirby wondered if there was a simple explanation for all this: Jill Francis. He had noticed her arriving at the school; perhaps her presence was the reason Thornhill had wanted to stay. Kirby was fairly sure that Thornhill was attracted to Jill Francis; less sure that Thornhill admitted it to himself; and even less sure that Jill Francis was attracted to him. Kirby couldn't find it in himself to blame Thornhill. Jill Francis had more sex appeal in her little finger than Edith Thornhill had in her whole body. Still, it was a little unnerving to think that someone like Richard Thornhill was prey to the vagaries of sexual attraction. After all, the man was a senior police officer. He had children. And he couldn't be much less than forty, either.

The car slowed as it approached the bend before the crossroads and the Hanging Tree. Porter glanced at Kirby.

'My gran says the tree's thirsty for blood, Sarge.' He took one hand from the steering wheel and tapped the side of his head. 'These old folks, I ask you. Still living in the Middle Ages.'

As they approached the farm, Kirby saw that the Land Rover was standing in the yard. The dogs began to bark. Porter parked across the gate.

'Shall I come in with you?' The hope in Porter's voice was unmistakable.

'No.' Kirby prided himself on the subtlety of his interviewing technique. Having Porter breathing heavily at his shoulder would be a fatal distraction. 'You stay here. I want to keep this low key.'

The back door opened and Dilys Carrick came into the yard. She shouted at the dogs who backed away towards the barn.

'May I come in, Mrs Carrick?'

She shrugged heavy shoulders. 'If you must.'

Kirby crossed the yard and followed her into the house, admiring the swing of her bottom as she walked and the way the material of her skirt stretched tightly across her hips.

'It's that copper, again,' Dilys said to someone in the kitchen. 'The young one.'

Les Carrick was sitting at the table, a gin bottle and a tumbler in front of him.

'Good afternoon, sir. Where's Mr Nerini?'

'Search me,' Dilys said. 'It's his afternoon off. We left him up the pub. If it's him you want, you've had a wasted journey.'

'It's all a bloody waste,' Les mumbled, as though through a mouthful of toffee. 'Everything is.'

'Just a few more questions. Mind if I sit down?'

Neither of them objected, so Kirby pulled out a chair. Dilys was at the range making tea.

'I heard there was a bit of trouble at the pub at lunchtime.'

'Fred Swayne – always was a blabbermouth.' Les sipped his gin. 'All piss and wind that one.'

'And you were up at the school last night?'

Dilys sucked in her breath. 'It was nothing.'

'I heard a window was smashed.'

'We'll pay for it. He'd had a bit to drink, that's all. Who told you, anyway?'

Les lifted his head and glared at Kirby. 'I went up there. Not ashamed to admit it. Someone killed our Mervyn, and it must have been one of them up there. Always hated him. Not lah-di-dah enough for them. Besides, buggers were jealous.'

'So you think it was someone at the school. Have you any evidence, sir?'

'Evidence – who needs bloody evidence? That's your job, copper. Who else could it have been? Tell me that.'

'He's not himself, Sergeant,' Dilys said hurriedly. 'Won't you have some tea? And you'll have a cup, too, won't you, Les?'

'I don't want any tea.' Her husband looked wildly around the room. 'I don't want anything.'

'Mr Carrick? Is it true you called your wife a whore in the pub today?'

Les rested his head on his folded arms on the table. 'What if I did? It's no more than the truth.'

'Oh, Les – do stop talking such nonsense.' Dilys looked at Kirby. 'He doesn't know what he's saying. He gets that way sometimes when he has a few drinks.'

'I'm not a fool,' Les snarled, sounding like one of his own dogs. 'I can see what's in front of my eyes. You and Mervyn – makes me sick.'

'It won't make you sick any more,' Dilys retorted. 'It's over.'

'No, it's not over. Not with that thing in your belly.' Les sat up and picked up his glass. 'Here's to you, young one. Here's to the next generation.' He drained his glass, belched and put his head back on his arms.

For a moment no one spoke. Dilys poured three cups of tea. When she put Les's down beside his head he did not stir. She brought Kirby the sugar and sat down beside him. Les was breathing heavily, the next best thing to a snore.

Kirby wasn't sure if the farmer was really asleep or just pretending or in a drunken stupor; perhaps it didn't matter. He spooned sugar into his tea. The spoon chinked on the side of the cup – chipped earthenware; everyday use. Dilys Carrick waited. Kirby thought she was a woman who must have had a lot of practice at that.

'So when's the baby due?'

'August.'

'And Mr Carrick thinks his brother was the father?'

'He *knows*.' She raised her head and he saw the glint of anger in her eyes. 'I told him last night. All right?'

Suddenly the wheezing stopped and the head lifted itself from the table. 'I gave her a bloody good thrashing,' Les said in a conversational tone. 'Playing around with my brother – she was asking for it. But the Eyetie stops me. Says I can't hit a pregnant woman. But we'll see about that, won't we?'

She looked steadily at him. 'It's a little Carrick in there. You can't change that by hitting me. You wouldn't hurt a Carrick, would you? One of your own flesh and blood.'

Les screwed up his eyes, as though the sun had come out and he were staring straight at it. Then he picked up his cup of tepid tea, glanced at its contents, and threw them, cup and tea together, at his wife.

4

Driving down the hill from Ashbridge, Jill met a police car coming the other way. The passenger in the front waved, the hand and face reduced to pale blurs on the other side of the windscreen. Her heart twitched, a temporary interruption in its regular beat. Then she glimpsed Kirby beside the driver. The rear seat was empty. The car flashed past in the direction of Lydmouth.

A few minutes later, Jill turned right towards Moat Farm. By now it was the middle of the afternoon, and the light was already fading from the sky. Rather too soon for her liking, she found herself approaching the junction of the lane with the track up to Ashbridge. The branches of the Hanging Tree were dark against the sky.

Jill parked the car where Richard Thornhill had left the Austin on Friday afternoon. The thought of him, soaking wet and plastered with mud, made her smile despite herself as she got out of the car. He had looked so young, no more than about fourteen.

It was very quiet. She walked diagonally over the crossroads to the tree. The police would have searched the whole area thoroughly, she told herself, trying even now to persuade herself that there was no point in her being here and so she might as well leave. The trouble was, the police had been looking in the wrong places and for the wrong sort of things – for Mervyn Carrick's glasses, for signs of people coming and going.

Jill was glad that she had taken the precaution of wearing a short coat, a thick tweed skirt and sturdy shoes. Nevertheless she thought that, one way or another, she was probably on the verge of making a fool of herself.

In one sense she already had. She was not a superstitious person but she knew that this was not a place where she wanted to linger in the gathering dusk of a winter afternoon. It wasn't the fact that people had died here. People died everywhere. It was more that they had died when they were unhappy, and before their lives had reached their natural term. The Hanging Tree was haunted by dead hopes. It shouldn't have mattered to Jill, but it did; and that in itself was disturbing.

She walked slowly round the tree. On the side away from the road, where the ground rose up sharply, the trunk was pockmarked with holes and studded with protuberances. Jill glimpsed her childhood self and knew it was the sort of tree she would not have been able to resist climbing. She took a deep breath and glanced over her shoulder. No one was there.

She climbed automatically, without conscious thought; her hands reached for branches, her feet found footholds. She had climbed scarcely above her own height when the tree forked into two massive branches. One of them was now no more than a stump with a fractured, blackened end, amputated by lightening;

but the other still arched over the track. The rope from which Carrick had been hanging had been suspended from an offshoot from this second branch.

Here, where they forked, was a broad space; there was even a convenient niche at the base of each of the branches – natural chairs. Panting, Jill sat down on the nearer one. It was a child-size seat, and it brought her knees uncomfortably close to her chin. This was a place made for children and, when the leaves were out, you would be unlucky if you were seen by anyone in the lane or on the path below. Methodically she ran her eyes over the part of her surroundings which was within arm's reach.

The hole was immediately in front of her, waiting to be discovered. It was almost an oval, little more than four inches wide at its narrowest point. The mouth had been filled with twigs and dead leaves – not by bird or a squirrel, Jill thought, but by a human. She pulled the debris out and the leaves and twigs fluttered down to the ground. She put her hand slowly into the hole. Her gloved fingers touched something soft and smooth. She lifted it out of the hole and placed it on her lap.

It was a yellow oilskin tobacco pouch. Jill unrolled it. She drew out two sheets of paper, folded once. One of them was much creased – not just by having been rolled in a cylindrical shape in the tobacco pouch, but crumpled as if at one time it had been crushed into a ball and thrown away. Jill unfolded both sheets, smoothing them out on her skirt. Small black writing marched across the uppermost page – difficult to read, partly because of the fading light and partly because the characters were small and ill-formed, moving like lines of insects across the page, slanting downwards from left to right, with the slant growing more pronounced at the right-hand margin.

What caught Jill's eyes was the letterhead:

The Headmaster's House
Ashbridge School
Lydmouth

Then she heard footsteps.

She crouched motionless in the tree and waited. The footsteps were slow and at times irregular, as though the walker were stumbling. A moment later a pair of broad shoulders came into view beneath her. Jill recognised Umberto Nerini. He had been walking along the old track from Ashbridge. He paused at the crossroads and glanced at the tree. Jill held her breath and ducked back out of sight.

Nerini stood there for perhaps thirty seconds. What was he doing? She guessed that he was staring at her car and wondering why it was there. She heard him walking slowly round the tree. Then he went over to her car. At last she heard his footsteps on the lane, going down the hill towards Moat Farm.

She moved, gradually and quietly, and risked a glance after Nerini. She saw him walking slowly and unsteadily towards the farm. She also saw Dilys Carrick closing the gate to the farmyard. As Jill watched, Dilys waved to Nerini and began to run up the lane towards him.

5

Paxford's hand was bleeding badly, much worse than before. Slapping it against the workbench in the Headmaster's garage had reopened his old wound and made it deeper. He stood in the doorway of the garage, shuffling his feet, while Thornhill examined the damage he'd done to himself.

'You need to have this looked at by someone who knows what they're doing.'

'It'll be all right. Can't we just wash it, like before?' Paxford had automatically angled his face so only the good side was visible to Thornhill. 'Sorry to be such a bother, sir.'

'We'll go and find San Sister.' Thornhill smiled up at Paxford. 'Don't worry – she won't bite.'

The two men walked up the path to the top of the drive. They skirted the Headmaster's House and the main school building and went down to the San behind its screen of trees. They found Mrs Hirdle in her office, dozing in front of the electric fire over the *Sunday Express*: her shoes were off and she was not best pleased to be disturbed.

'Busy, are you?' Thornhill asked her, with a touch of malice.

'In this job I always am,' she replied, with a fine disregard for her surroundings.

'Is Walton still here?'

'He's resting. I don't want him disturbed.' She glared at Paxford. 'Now what have you done to yourself?'

Thornhill left Paxford to her ministrations and went outside. At some point he wanted to check Walton's story about meeting Mervyn Carrick on Wednesday night; but there was no hurry. It was hot and airless inside the San and it was a relief to be outside again.

He strolled slowly round the building, weighing possibilities and calculating chances. Carrick's optician should be able to tell whether the fragment of glass they had found in the garage belonged to his patient's glasses. If it did, there was at least a strong possibility that the Hudson had been used to transport Carrick on Wednesday evening, after the meeting of the Classical Society and before the snow started falling in the night. The car had been cleaned on Wednesday; and by the following morning it had needed cleaning again.

Suppose Carrick had been taken from the school to the Hanging Tree. To lessen the scandal at school? Or because someone had felt that the Hanging Tree was an appropriate location for his body to be found? Whether he had been dead or alive at the time was a separate question; the broken glasses suggested violence.

Unfortunately, even if the glass had come from Carrick's glasses, they weren't much further on. They didn't know why or where Carrick had been killed, nor who had done it. In all probability, half the school had known where the keys of the garage and the car were kept. At the head of the list would be favoured members of staff such as Rockfield and Carrick himself. Carrick might have told his brother – there was no reason why outsiders should not have known. It was doubly unfortunate that Paxford was so quick and efficient at cleaning the car. Almost certainly he would have obliterated any remaining evidence. Still, at least they were a little further on. The next step would be to talk to—

The sweet, rich smell of fresh tobacco came to Thornhill's nostrils, interrupting his train of thought. He paused. He was halfway round the San now, following a path which led round the building to a small sheltered lawn at the back. There were bushes on his left – a dark green mass of rhododendrons and laurels. Suddenly Thornhill darted round the nearest bush. He found himself looking at Walton.

The boy was standing with his hands behind his back. His face was pink, and the eyes looked huge in the gaunt face. He was wearing a raincoat; beneath the hem trailed a tassel attached to the end of a dressing-gown cord.

'Good afternoon,' Thornhill said. 'I'm glad you're feeling a little better.'

Walton opened his mouth, swallowed and shut it. A wisp of smoke emerged from his lips.

'Don't let me interrupt you,' Thornhill said. 'When I used to smoke, it always seemed to taste nicer in the open air.'

The boy produced the cigarette from behind his back. He smoked self-consciously, darting glances at Thornhill.

'Are you – is this something you'll have to mention, sir?'

'Why should I? It's not illegal.'

'It's just that Mr Sandleigh tends to get rather upset about smoking. Unless you're a prefect.'

'They're allowed to smoke at school?'

'Only on Sunday afternoons and if they're not in training. But for the rest of us it's rather different. The first time you're caught, you're beaten, and the second time you're chucked out.'

'That seems a little drastic.'

'Rules are there to be obeyed,' intoned Walton, obviously quoting. 'I've already been beaten, you see. So next time I'm in for the high jump.'

'And yet it's worth it to you?' asked Thornhill, genuinely curious.

Walton let out a plume of smoke. 'My father was a prisoner-of-war, sir. He said that you had to make a stand sometimes – just to show that they hadn't got you beaten.'

'It's not quite the same, is it? At least you know they can't keep you here for ever.'

Walton shrugged. 'Sometimes it doesn't feel like that.' He glanced sideways at Thornhill. 'I nearly got caught on Wednesday evening, you know. I was having a quiet cigarette when old Sandleigh walked by. He couldn't have been more than two or three yards away. It was a miracle he didn't smell the smoke.'

'I thought you were feeling ill on Wednesday evening.'

'I was, sir. Maybe that made me more careless. I went to one of the smoking holes close to the house. I should have gone further.'

'You saw Mr Sandleigh?'

'He came pounding down the path.' Walton was relaxing now, and his voice slid into a drawl. 'Gave me one hell of a shock.'

'How could you see it was him? It must have been dark.'

'He was smoking a pipe. Just for a second I saw his face in the glow. I thought it was going to be Mr Carrick coming back.'

'*Carrick?*' Thornhill took a step closer to the boy, who looked suddenly worried. 'What time was this?'

'I don't know. A quarter to eleven? Ten to? Something like that.'

'Listen,' Thornhill said softly. 'You saw Mr Carrick going out about half-past ten, didn't you? Are you telling me you went out *after* that?'

Walton nodded.

'Why the hell didn't you tell me before?'

'You – you didn't ask.'

'Surely you must have—'

'But sir, I couldn't,' Walton blurted out. 'Mr Rockfield was there. I couldn't admit I was breaking bounds at night, could I? Anyway, they'd know what I went out to do. They'd know I'd been smoking. It would be like putting my head in a noose.' He stopped, flushing.

Putting my head in a noose.

'So you saw Mr Sandleigh – which way was he going?'

'Down the little path to his garage. And I was in the smoking hole by the corner – where the path goes off to the garage from the main path.' Walton drew heavily on his cigarette and then dropped the butt on the ground. He ground it into the earth and covered it neatly with a small mound of dead leaves. 'Sir – this needn't come out, need it?'

'I don't know. But I don't think you'll be expelled, whatever happens. So don't worry. What happened next?'

'Mr Sandleigh must have gone into the garage. I didn't wait to find out – I scarpered down to Burton's and got into bed as soon as I could. I was feeling awful, remember, and the next morning I was sent back to the house and Matron packed me off to the San. It didn't seem very real, you see. I'd almost forgotten about it.'

'Did you see anyone else?'

A shake of the head.

'Any other glowing cigarette ends?' Thornhill demanded with a trace of desperation. 'Is there anything else you're not telling me?'

Walton opened his eyes very wide. 'No, sir. I promise.'

Thornhill was reminded of the impression he had had when he met Walton before: that the boy was an old lag, expert at dealing with angry authority. Still, he might be telling the truth. He had little to lose now.

'Are you meant to be out of bed?'

'Yes, sir – I'm sitting in the armchair by the window reading my book.'

'Well, I'd get back there as soon as you can.'

The boy's eyes filled with alarm. 'San Sister was asleep.'

'Well, she's not now. How did you get outside?'

'There's a fire door over there.' Walton nodded towards the rear of the building. 'I'd better go. You won't let on?'

'I'll do my best not to.' Thornhill turned to go and then paused. 'And Walton?'

'Yes, sir?'

'I shall be coming to see you again – to take a statement. In the meantime, say nothing of what you've been telling me. All right?'

The boy nodded and slipped away. Thornhill walked back to the front of the building. He found Mrs Hirdle engaged in wrapping an enormous bandage round Paxford's right hand.

'It's the only way, Inspector,' she told him. 'If Paxford's not careful, he'll knock it again and it'll start bleeding. You're a clumsy oaf, eh, Paxford? And next time you'll probably manage to get it infected, too. You're your own worst enemy, aren't you?'

6

One was not supposed to read other people's letters.

Jill had been brought up to believe this; and it was one of those beliefs which had survived intact during the transition from childhood to adulthood. She scrambled inelegantly down from the Hanging Tree, glad that there was no one to watch her, for Dilys and Nerini were out of sight in the lee of a hedge near the farm. Once in the car, she put the tobacco pouch on the seat beside her and started the engine. She drove up to the main road and turned left towards Ashbridge.

The letters did not belong to her. She had seen enough to know that there were two. She had also glanced at the signatures and knew that they could be returned to their owners. Alternatively, if she thought their contents might be germane to the police investigation, would it not be her duty to hand them to Richard Thornhill? The problem here, of course, was that the only way to discover whether the police should see their contents was by reading them.

She was driving very slowly, at less than thirty miles an hour, her speed steadily dropping as she wrestled with the pros and cons, trying to arrange them in such a way that the decision would be the one she wanted. There was a loud hooting behind her. A bus was coming up the hill. She pulled over into the mouth of a track which went up into the Forest.

Jill looked at the pouch and decided that if nothing else she should be honest with herself. She was going to read those letters not because it was her duty to do so but because she wanted to; and damn the consequences, moral and otherwise. She unrolled the pouch, catching a whiff of Paxford's home-grown. Both letters were dated.

The first, according to the letterhead, had been written at the Plaza Hotel in New York. The writing was large and full of flourishes. The letter was dated the third of December.

My dear Vera,

I know I promised not to write, but don't chuck this on the fire straight away, please. We owe each other that, at least. First I want to say Happy Christmas to you and Bernard and the children.

It's hard to know where to begin. Such a lot of water under the bridge in the last fourteen years. I often think of those weekends in Roth. It seems like another lifetime. Sometimes I think I made the wrong decision. Certainly I worry about all the pain and grief I must have caused you. Thank God Bernard came along.

I want to try to make it up to you, if I can. Since The Dark Sea, *I don't have money problems any more! Sometimes I almost wish I did — easier to cope with than the other kind. But enough of me. How are you? I saw Bernard's appointment for the headship of Ashbridge School in* The Times. *You must be awfully proud of him. Of course you have children now, more children, I mean.*

I know you'll think me foolish but I keep thinking of Dorothy. Isn't that strange? Thinking of a person one has never seen. I always wanted children, you know, they help to make sense of life somehow. Something to pass on to the next generation, I suppose. Unfortunately, I've not had much luck in that department. I sometimes wish I'd never come to America. Everything has gone wrong since then. I miss England and I miss my friends.

I'm afraid I'm rambling. You always said I was bad at getting to the point. Here goes. I plan to spend a few weeks in England in the New Year before starting the next film, probably in late January and February. Do you think I could invite myself down for a few days? Just as an old friend of the family. You've no idea what it would mean to me — to be part of an ordinary family again, just like the old days in Roth.

There's another favour I want to ask. Perhaps I should wait until I see you, but if I put if off until then I might put it off for ever. It's about Dorothy. Is there any way you and Bernard would let me help her? There's so much I could do, so much I want to do for her.

I shall be in New York until the third of January. Please write — or cable or telephone.

Give my best wishes to Bernard, and my love to you and the family.

Larry

The name Roth was familiar. Jill put down the letter. There was an AA book in the car. She consulted the Gazetteer. There it was — a village fringed by commuter suburbs in the Thames valley west of London.

She picked up the second letter, the one that at some stage had been crumpled into a ball and then retrieved and smoothed out. The handwriting of this letter was harder to decipher.

First Aid at Local School

Dear Larry,

I don't know how you had the nerve to write that letter, let alone send it. How dare you? My mother used to treat you like a son. You abused her hospitality. You walked away from me when I needed you. You ruined my life and left me to pick up the pieces. God knows what would have happened if Bernard hadn't come along, if he hadn't been so understanding.

So now you suddenly want a family. You always did want the fun without the responsibility. Well in this case you are fourteen years too late. Bernard thinks of Dorothy as his own daughter, and so do I. I don't want you turning up and spoiling her, turning her head, just because you've got some stupid, selfish dream about how nice it would be to have a daughter. The trouble with you is that you never—

The letter broke off here. Jill imagined how it might have been. She saw Vera Sandleigh writing at her desk in the bay window of the big drawing room upstairs in the Headmaster's House. Dissatisfied with what she had written, Vera would have screwed up the sheet of paper and thrown it into the wastepaper basket. And then Mervyn Carrick would have called. Left alone for a moment in the drawing room, he would have needed little temptation to snoop. Having found and read the second letter, he would have lost no time in searching for the first, the one from Larry Jordan. It would not have been far away – under the blotter, perhaps, or in a drawer, where Vera had slipped it when the maid announced Mervyn's arrival.

Given that Mervyn had been unscrupulous – and no one seemed to have any doubt about that – the next stage was obvious. He must have used his new-found knowledge to blackmail the Sandleighs. This, surely, was the explanation for Sandleigh's otherwise barely defensible decision to promote Mervyn to a housemastership.

It followed that Bernard must have known of the letters. He was a big man, too, with the physique of a rugby forward. He had a car. It would have been easy for him to have called Mervyn aside after the meeting of the Classical Society. Or, more probably, it could have happened the other way round: that Mervyn had buttonholed Sandleigh and made a further demand; and that Bernard Sandleigh's patience had snapped.

Jill stared at the letters on her lap. It was growing colder and colder in the car. All right, Sandleigh had both a motive for killing Mervyn and the opportunity to do so. But it was only circumstantial evidence. It didn't follow that he had done. In any case, even if he had, it was a long step between premeditated murder and an impulsive action by a man goaded beyond his powers of endurance.

Mervyn had clearly been a blackmailer. To hand these letters to the police would almost certainly lead to the Sandleighs' ruin. What would be the effect on the children? Even if it were never proved that Sandleigh had killed Mervyn, the circumstantial evidence was strong enough to throw a lasting blight on his career and on the lives of his family.

Now it was up to her, Jill knew. She couldn't walk away from this. Even by doing nothing, she was making a decision which would affect other people's lives, for good or for ill.

The responsibility scared her. It was difficult enough to be responsible for oneself, let alone for others. The fingernails on her right hand plucked at the wool of her skirt like sparrows pecking at the earth. She wished very much that there was a way to put the letters back in the pouch, and the pouch in the Hanging Tree.

She rummaged in her handbag for a cigarette. For a few minutes she sat in the car, smoking, trying to will herself into the belief that when the cigarette was over she would have made a decision or that the decision would have somehow been made for her. The trick didn't work. She threw the cigarette end out of the window and started the engine.

You couldn't let a man get away with murder: that's what it came down to. At once the objections rushed back into her mind: what about the wife, what about the children?

She drove up to Ashbridge and into the school, where she

parked outside the Headmaster's House, just behind the police car. The afternoon had slipped away and now it was evening. As she walked towards the house, a large shape detached itself from the shadows in the porch and held up a hand the size of a table-tennis racket.

'Good afternoon, miss,' P.C. Porter said.

'Hello. I'm looking for Inspector Thornhill?'

'He's talking to Mr Sandleigh.'

'Where?'

'Mr Sandleigh's study.'

Jill took a step towards the porch. Porter did not move aside.

'I'd like to see him, please,' she said.

'I'm afraid you can't, miss. When he's finished, I'll tell him—'

'But it's important.'

Porter shook his head. Jill thought suddenly that she had never seen a head that so resembled a leg of mutton. He shifted his weight from one foot to another and one of his boots creaked plaintively.

'Mr Thornhill gave strict orders that he wasn't to be disturbed.'

'What about Sergeant Kirby? Is he here?'

'He's with Mr Thornhill.'

Jill toyed with the idea of insisting, of pushing past Porter, who would surely be too shocked to lay a hand on her, and finding her way to Sandleigh's study. But was it that urgent? Her news could wait a few minutes; in any case it wouldn't do to rush in with the letters when Sandleigh was there. Alternatively, she could interpret the presence of Porter as an omen: as a sign that the letters should not go to the police after all.

As she stood hesitating in the porch, with Porter's dark blue bulk blocking the way, she saw the handle revolving on the door behind him. The door opened and there on the threshold was Dorothy Sandleigh.

'Miss Francis — hello. I saw the car. Won't you come in?'

Here was another omen. But how should it be interpreted?

Jill glanced at Porter. Then she smiled at Dorothy. 'Yes please.'

TEN

Cut Down Fatal Tree, Demands GP

A well-known local doctor has written to both the Ashbridge
Parish Council and the Rural District Council calling for the
removal of the historic oak known as the Hanging Tree. The
tree, which stands two miles outside the village on the verge
of a public footpath, has tragically lived up to its name in
recent months.

'The tree will now draw unhappy young people like a magnet,'
writes Dr G.B.Wintle, who has lived in Ashbridge for many years.
'Many pernicious superstitions have grown up around it over the
centuries. It is no more than our Christian duty to destroy it,
root and branch.'

The *Lydmouth Gazette*, 13th February

1

The Headmaster sat behind the big, polished desk with his feet
planted firmly on the carpet. He was still in the suit he had
worn for chapel. Around him were the trappings of his position:
photographs, books, silver, and an umbrella stand containing one
umbrella, one shooting stick and three canes. The big window
framed a view over rolling lawns under a weeping sky; and
beyond the lawns were trees and misty hills. Bernard Sandleigh
was on home ground.

'But this is most unsettling for the whole school,' he was

271

saying. 'We need to draw a line under this whole affair, not prolong it. It creates an unhealthy atmosphere.'

'I'm afraid that's one of the side-effects of this type of death,' Thornhill said. 'But you—'

'What sort of death?' Sandleigh interrupted. 'There seems to be a good deal of doubt even about that.'

What sort of death? Thornhill thought of Edith. He wondered how she and the children were coping, and how his mother-in-law was. *Another way of dying.*

He glanced at Kirby, who was sitting with his notebook on his knee, waiting for someone to say something which was worth noting down. 'I wonder if we might try to reconstruct your movements on Tuesday and Wednesday? You have an appointments diary, I imagine?'

'Of course I have. And you can see it if you want. But I don't understand the necessity. And why Tuesday? What on earth is the relevance of that?'

'If we might see your diary, sir, it would give us a useful framework. The timetable must be very important for you in a school. So it is for us in an enquiry. It gives a shape to everything.'

Sandleigh stared at Thornhill for a moment. Then he pushed back his chair and went into the anteroom. Through the open door, Thornhill saw him open one of the drawers of his secretary's desk. A moment later he returned with a leather-bound diary. He handed it to Thornhill.

'It's not complete. Mrs Johnson only puts down school engagements, naturally, and she concentrates on those during the day. On Tuesday morning, I spend third period with Upper Sixth – that would be from a quarter to eleven to half-past. In the afternoon, I was on Big Side – the First and Second Fifteens were playing a scratch game.'

While he was talking, Sandleigh picked up a pipe, which he turned round and round in his hands. Suddenly he rapped it on the ashtray. He blew through it and pulled his tobacco jar towards him.

'And afterwards, sir?'

'A quiet evening at home, if I remember correctly. We had dinner by ourselves, and then I worked until bedtime.'

'And where would you have worked, sir?'

'Here, of course.'

Thornhill turned the pages of the appointments diary. There was a page a day. Thornhill ran his eye down the appointments for Tuesday.

'I see you saw Mr Carrick at four forty-five on Tuesday afternoon. What was that about?'

'His forthcoming promotion. In fact, Mr Burton had asked me if I could arrange for Mr Carrick to take over some of his duties at once, because of Mrs Burton's ill-health.'

'Such as answering the telephone if it rang in the evening or during the night?'

Sandleigh nodded. He stuck the pipe in his mouth and lit it with a match.

'And on Wednesday, sir?'

'Inspector, what is all this about? I must say I find it rather disturbing. Are you implying that you suspect me of having something to do with poor Carrick's death?'

'I'm just asking questions, sir. It's my job.'

'Lunch in school. In the morning I dictated letters to Mrs Johnson, and then saw a couple of prospective parents. In the afternoon – let me see.' He glanced up at the ceiling. 'I went down to Lydmouth after lunch. I had an appointment with Shipston – do you know him?'

Thornhill nodded. 'The solicitor?'

'Just so. He acts for the school. We're thinking of buying a small parcel of land between the school and the village, and he's handling the legal side for us. After seeing him, I went to Butter's for a fitting. I've ordered a suit from them.' Sandleigh's eyes gleamed angrily through the haze of smoke. 'You know Butter's, don't you? The men's outfitters in the High Street?'

'Yes, sir, I do.'

'No doubt they can confirm all this. When I left Butter's, I went to the High School and picked up the girls. I drove them home and we – that is, the whole family – had tea. Afterwards I came back here and worked until it was time for dinner. We ate early, because of the Classical Society meeting.'

'And where was that held?'

'In the main building. We use the school library. You may see it if you wish.'

For a moment the only sound in the room was the almost inaudible scratching of Kirby's pencil. A pity, Thornhill thought: if Sandleigh had driven the Hudson down to Lydmouth on Wednesday afternoon, when the roads had been thick with slush and grit, it was no wonder that the car had needed cleaning on Thursday morning.

'And after the meeting – what happened then?'

'We've been through all this before, Inspector. The meeting finished at about ten, I came back here, wrote a couple of letters, then went back to the house and had a cup of tea with my wife. We went to bed at about half-past eleven, I think.'

'Let me see if I've got this straight, sir. After the meeting of the Classical Society, you came back to your study and then you went through the connecting door into the house?'

Sandleigh shrugged heavy shoulders. 'I've just told you.'

'And you didn't go out again that night?'

'No.'

Thornhill left another silence in the conversation. Sandleigh turned in his chair and made a great play of raising his arm, shooting back his cuff and examining his wristwatch.

'Did you or Mrs Sandleigh use your car on Wednesday evening?' Thornhill asked.

'The car? Of course not.'

'Do you always keep it locked?'

'Yes – even when it's in the garage. What's my car got to do with all this?'

'If it's in the garage, is the garage locked too?'

'Yes.'

'And who has keys for the car and the garage?'

'I have, and my wife. My secretary has a set of spares. And there's also a set which Paxford keeps hidden at the garage itself – he needs them when he cleans the car. Why do you want to know?'

'Because Paxford says there's a spanner missing from the tools in the garage.'

'What's a spanner got to do with it? Carrick was hanged.'

'There's one piece of information we haven't released yet. Carrick was also hit on the head with a blunt instrument.'

Sandleigh sucked hard on his pipe. 'Why should Carrick's attacker have taken all the trouble to go into my garage and find a spanner? It simply doesn't make sense.'

'Doesn't it, sir?' Thornhill smiled, and tightened the screw a little more. 'Not if Mr Carrick was attacked and perhaps killed there.'

'What makes you think he was? Or that he might have been?'

'And there's another point. We have a witness who saw you near the garage on Wednesday evening at about a quarter to eleven. But according to what you told us just now, you were either writing letters here or having tea with your wife. Would you like to explain?'

2

In the hall, Dorothy helped Jill take off her coat. The girl hung it on the row of hooks in the side passage leading to the annexe with the Headmaster's study. As she did so, she dislodged a cap hanging on a neighbouring peg. Jill bent down to pick it up.

It was just a navy blue cap with the Ashbridge School badge at the front. Jill turned it over, and saw the name tape: P.J.B. SANDLEIGH. She also noticed a long fair hair clinging to the lining.

'It's Peter's.' Dorothy took it from her and hung it on a hook further down the hall. 'Typical – the silly boy never puts it in the right place. Mummy's upstairs. I don't think Uncle Larry's ready yet.'

In the drawing room, the curtains had been drawn across the big bay window, hiding the shattered pane of glass. Vera Sandleigh sat knitting in a high-backed armchair beside the fire. The needles danced, catching the glow from the fire. Grey wool flowed over her lap.

Dorothy said, 'It's Miss Francis.'

The heavy head swayed on the slender neck, turning towards Jill in the doorway. Large eyes peered across the room, and the high forehead wrinkled into a frown. Vera gave the impression that she had caught sight of a puzzling phenomenon shrouded in fog.

In that instant Jill realised that the younger children were in the room too. A glance told her that Peter was lying on his stomach on the carpet and June was sitting near the window. In front of Peter, about two feet away, was a line of toy soldiers, guardsmen in red tunics and busbies, marching nowhere with their rifles on their shoulders. He was firing matchsticks at them, using for the purpose a small green field gun with a spring-loaded mechanism. Judging by the litter on the carpet, he had already used most of a box of matches. Despite the closeness of the range, he had not yet caused any casualties. June was more peaceably engaged, doing a jigsaw puzzle on a card table. It was three-quarters complete and showed a coaching inn in Merry England.

Jill's arrival broke up the scene as effectively as a hammer breaks a sheet of toffee. June blushed and bent her head over the jigsaw, her hair hanging down and masking her face. Peter imitated the sound of an exploding bomb and swept his arm round in an arc, knocking over all the soldiers; he then rolled over onto his back.

Vera stood up. A ball of grey wool escaped from her fingers, rolled down her skirt and fell to the hearthrug. Her smile was professionally welcoming, the mechanical response of a person whose life involved a good deal of smiling at near strangers.

'You've come for Larry?' she asked. 'So kind of you to offer him a lift.'

All this happened in a couple of seconds – the door opening, Dorothy's announcement, the reactions of the three people already in the room. Jill was looking at Vera, and this was what led to her downfall, all too literally.

The carpet, large though it was, did not fill the room. Linoleum had been laid between it and the walls. Jill's foot hooked itself under the carpet's edge, which had been a little rucked up by the door. She pitched forward. The floor rose to meet her with terrifying speed.

Jill released the grip on her handbag and flung out her hands in the hope of breaking her fall. Her leg collided painfully with the wooden arm of a sofa. Around her was a blur of movement, the thud of feet, as the Sandleighs rushed to her assistance. The bag hit the floor and burst open. The intimacies of her life tumbled out: a powder compact, cigarettes, a small enamel box containing a book of matches, a well-used handkerchief, a diary, letters, a propelling pencil, scraps of paper in various stages of decay, a purse – which itself opened, disgorging change – and a shameful quantity of fluff.

Jill had a second to feel relief: the yellow tobacco pouch was not there. It must still be in the bag, wedged in place by its bulk. But only a second. The bag was lying on its side, still open.

Vera, who had been coming to Jill's assistance, suddenly stooped and snatched up the bag, holding it by the base so that the tobacco pouch slid out into her other hand. Her eyes met Jill's.

Dorothy rushed into the room and seized Jill by the arm. With more enthusiasm than efficiency, she tried to pull Jill to her feet. Jill held onto the sofa and scrambled up.

'Gosh, Miss Francis – are you hurt?'

'No, not really.'

277

She glanced down at her left leg, the one which had collided with the sofa. It is hard to feel poised when one's stocking has acquired a conspicuous ladder in someone else's house. Dorothy gave her the handbag. June and Peter were watching, wide-eyed.

'Come and sit by the fire,' Vera said to Jill. 'Children, pick up Miss Francis's things.' Vera handed the bag to Jill and guided her towards an armchair; she kept the pouch in her hand. 'How clever of you to find this, Miss Francis. Bernard's been looking for it everywhere.'

'I thought perhaps Inspector Thornhill should see it,' Jill said, choosing her words with care because of the children. She sat down because her legs were trembling.

Vera nodded, smiling, as though this were the most natural thing in the world for Jill to suggest. 'My husband's talking to him at present. Perhaps we should wait until they're finished. One wouldn't want to interrupt something important.'

The children were a distraction, bringing Jill's possessions to her, dropping them one by one in the handbag, hovering close to her.

'Actually, I think I should look after it, Mrs Sandleigh.' She held out her hand and noticed that it trembled slightly. 'May I have it, please?'

'Peter.' Vera wheeled round and glared down at her son. 'You *still* haven't tidied your room. I want you to go and do it now, and take those soldiers with you.'

'But Mum—'

'Now.'

The boy knelt down and swept together his soldiers and crammed them into the pockets of his grey shorts.

'And you girls haven't finished your homework, have you? Go and do it in the dining room.'

The girls' eyes had taken on a life of their own, acting independently of their pale, unmoving faces. The eyes flicked from their mother to Jill to the floor. Peter, seemingly unaffected by what was going on, strolled to the door, muttering that *his* room was tidy, unlike some he could mention, or at least not as untidy as it had been; and that in any case he didn't see why it had to be tidy. June ran after him. Dorothy lingered.

Vera frowned at her. 'You too, dear.'

'Mother, I—'

The door opened once more. Vera's lips tightened.

Larry Jordan came into the room.

'Hello, girls. Sorry to keep you waiting, Jill.'

'It – it doesn't matter. I—'

'Shan't be long. Scout's honour.'

He gave a wave – an impartial one, directed equally at the two women and the girl – and sauntered out, leaving the door ajar.

'Off you go, Dorothy,' Vera commanded. She ushered her daughter out of the room and closed the door behind her.

'Give me the pouch,' Jill said.

Vera sat down in her armchair with the pouch on her lap. She unrolled it, took out the two letters and held them up. 'You've read these, of course?'

Jill nodded. She stared at a spot of red on the carpet: one of Peter's guardsmen had been left behind, still marching nowhere.

'Then you will have realised that that hideous man Carrick was blackmailing us. And why.'

Again, Jill nodded. Her mind was a blank, like a white wall in a white room in a white house.

'Carrick planned to publicise the whole business. You can imagine what the gutter press would do with a story like that. Can I rely on your discretion?'

Jill stared at Vera, uncertain what she was asking. 'You can rely on me not to use the story as a journalist,' she said at last. 'But you must realise how the police might interpret those letters.'

Vera wrinkled her nose. 'They are paid to think evil of people.'

'They're paid to solve murders.'

'Be that as it may.' She leant forward and picked up the poker

with her right hand. 'In any case, the question won't arise.' She
threw the two letters into the fire. She looked up at Jill and
raised the poker – not in a threatening way but defensively;
like a sword ready to parry a blow which might or might not
fall. 'Will it, Miss Francis?'

The flames licked along the edges of the letters. The paper
burst into crackling flames which spread rapidly over the paper.
White turned to grey. The ink faded. Pale yellow flames leapt
up the chimney. The paper dried and crumbled. Suddenly Vera
swung the poker into the grate and ground the ashes into the
glowing coals. When at last she stopped, her face was glowing
from the heat of the fire and the exertion. She rested the tip of
the poker on the hearth and stared at Jill.

'You see? It's all over.'

'Is it? There's other evidence – if one knew where to look
and what to look for. There's the timing of your wedding and
Dorothy's birth, for example. And do you really think Larry
would keep his mouth shut if the police put pressure on him?'

'Why not? He's not stupid – or not where his own comfort
is concerned. They couldn't prove anything.'

'Even if they went back to the village where you used to live?
You shouldn't rely on Larry, Mrs Sandleigh. You did that once
before and look where it got you.'

Vera's head snapped up. 'That was very different.'

Jill looked at the poker. The armchair she was sitting in was
a low one. It would be hard to get out of it quickly. Vera, on the
other hand, was on a chair with a higher seat and she was already
leaning forward, with her feet firmly planted on the ground. If
Jill leapt up she might meet the poker coming down.

Fear crawled over her, incongruous in this homely setting. She
had only to raise her voice, she told herself, and people would
come running. Or would they? This was a large Victorian house,
with solid partition walls.

'It will be best if you don't mention this,' Vera said. 'Not
to a soul.'

The poker swung lazily from her hands, like a pendulum in a clock. It was as though Vera had suddenly revealed her true self, the full force of her will. Unwanted metaphors crowded into Jill's mind. The snake had crawled from beneath the stone. The ugly duckling had turned not into a swan but a bird of prey.

'It's not as if this has anything to do with what happened to Mervyn Carrick, is it?'

'No,' Jill said.

Somewhere in the house a telephone began to ring.

Vera sighed. 'A school like this is like a big family, Miss Francis. I was brought up to believe that one must put the family first. I expect you were, too.'

3

'So much has happened since Wednesday evening. I can't be expected to remember every little thing.' Bernard Sandleigh sat back in his chair and scowled across his desk at Thornhill, as though the very idea that he might be able to remember anything at all was entirely unreasonable. 'But you say you have a witness. Dear me. May I ask whom?' When Thornhill did not reply, he went on, 'Are you sure you can trust this person? It seems a strange time for someone to be lurking in the bushes.'

'So you deny that you went out after the Classical Society meeting? You're sure?'

'Now you come to mention it, I suppose it is *possible* that I had a stroll before bed on Wednesday. I sometimes do. It helps me unwind.'

Thornhill thought that only a masochist would have chosen to stroll through the gloaming on Wednesday evening. 'But on two occasions since then, you've told us that after you and Mrs Sandleigh had tea on Wednesday evening, you both went straight to bed.'

'I may have been mistaken, Inspector. I admit it freely. In a school, one day is much like another.'

'Even yesterday?'

'I beg your pardon?'

'When I talked to you on Thursday morning, sir, you made no mention of going out for a walk on the Wednesday evening. That was only a few hours before our conversation.'

'My dear Inspector – my mind was on other things. You'd just brought me some appalling news, the worst I have ever had to cope with in my entire career as a schoolmaster.' Sandleigh lifted his eyes to the ceiling. 'One of my members of staff – a colleague, a friend, even – had apparently hanged himself. I wasn't thinking clearly. Indeed, it would have been strange if I had been.'

There was a moment's silence. Kirby's pencil travelled rapidly across the page of his notebook.

Thornhill said, 'It's looking increasingly likely that your car was used to transport Mr Carrick's body. He may have been killed in your garage. Or even in the car itself.'

'Terrible. You shock me.' Sandleigh shook his head, apparently unsurprised by the line the interview was taking; his self-possession was formidable. 'But, as I've already told you, many people knew of the spare keys.'

'There's also the question of why you were going to promote Mr Carrick. Several people have made it clear that they think your decision to give him Mr Burton's house was most unusual.'

'This is my school, Mr Thornhill, and I—'

There was a heavy double knock on the door. Both Sandleigh and Thornhill called, 'Come in.' Thornhill almost welcomed the interruption. The case against Sandleigh was persuasive but not strong enough to convince a jury. Not that it would ever get to court on present evidence – the Director of Public Prosecutions wouldn't touch it, or not as it stood. Sandleigh was too determined, too strong a personality, to crack easily under pressure. The impasse was both infuriating and familiar: the gap between knowledge and proof which perpetually bedevilled the work of the CID.

P.C. Porter put his head into the room. 'Excuse me, sir,' he whispered hoarsely. 'Could I have a word?'

'Carry on, Sergeant,' Thornhill said, and left the room without looking at Sandleigh. Perhaps Kirby would find a chink in the defences where he had failed.

'Sorry to interrupt, sir,' Porter whispered when the door was closed. 'I know you didn't want to be disturbed. But there was a phone call. Sergeant Fowles ringing up from the station.' He shifted his weight from one foot to another; rubbing his hands together, he glanced towards the door which led from the annexe to the Headmaster's House. The general impression was that he was desperate to empty his bladder. 'Bad news, I'm afraid.'

'What is it?'

'Mrs Thornhill left a message to say that her mother passed away.'

Is that all?

'When did it happen?'

'Well, sir, I suppose Mrs Thornhill must have only just phoned, because Sergeant Fowles would have got on the blower right away, and—'

'When did my mother-in-law *die?*'

'This afternoon.' One of Porter's boots emitted a mournful squeak. 'She – I mean, Mrs Thornhill – said to say that she'd try to ring you at home this evening, sir, but if she doesn't reach you, she'll ring the station in the morning.'

So Edith and the children would be staying at East Marryott, with Sylvia and Len. There would be decisions to be taken, arrangements to be made. The children could hardly come back to Lydmouth to an empty house, to a father who was working. Thornhill nodded curtly at Porter and turned to go. His hand touched the door handle.

Porter cleared his throat. 'Maybe I should mention, sir . . .'

Thornhill turned round and allowed his irritation to emerge as sarcasm: 'Only you can know that, Porter.'

'Miss Francis is here, sir. She wants to see you.'

Thornhill suddenly saw *her* – a vivid image of her face appeared in his mind. 'Did she say what she wanted?'

'No, sir.'

It was almost certainly important, he thought; she would not interrupt him at a time like this over something trivial.

'I told her you were seeing Mr Sandleigh, and that you weren't to be disturbed.' There was more than a hint of smugness in Porter's voice. 'Took her quite a while to understand that.'

'Where is she now?'

'One of Mr Sandleigh's daughters asked her in.' Porter's voice was now defensive. 'Well, I could hardly stop her, could I? They went upstairs together.' Porter stared anxiously at Thornhill. Then his face brightened. 'I expect she's having a cup of tea with Mrs Sandleigh.'

'Mrs Sandleigh,' Thornhill said slowly. 'Yes, of course. I was forgetting Mrs Sandleigh.'

4

As he crossed the farmyard, the dogs ran out of the barn and sniffed at his hands. He patted their heads and they whined softly, puzzled by the change in routine.

He opened the gate and slipped into the lane, closing the gate behind him for the last time. In the gloom, he could just make out the dogs' heads. He knew that they would be staring at him, waiting for instructions, hoping for praise or, better still, for food. He swung the coil of rope onto his shoulder and moved slowly and quietly up the lane.

When he was within twenty yards of the crossroads with the old road to Ashbridge, he stopped and felt in his pockets for cigarettes. He turned back the way he had come, out of the wind, to light one. He cupped his hands round the flame of the match.

Below him he saw the lighted windows of the farm. A wisp of smoke trailed from the kitchen chimney. The sky was cloudy so there were no stars, and the mist concealed the distant lights of cottages in the valley below. That suited him very well. He was glad it was not a clear day, when you could see mile after mile of green hills stretching out into the blue distance. He did not want to be reminded of the possibilities that other places offered.

He threw away the match. From the farm came the familiar creak of an opening door which had warped in its frame; the sound was softened by distance, a tiny blemish on the surrounding silence.

'Les?' He could even see Dilys in the doorway, a doll-sized silhouette against the light from the room behind her. 'Les? Your tea's on the table.'

She stood there for a moment, then turned and shut the door.

He smoked half the cigarette as though competing in a race. It brought him no comfort so he tossed the rest of it into the hedgerow and continued on his way.

5

Heavy footsteps pounded up the stairs like rapid hammer blows. Behind them came other, lighter footsteps.

Vera Sandleigh sighed. She dropped the heavy poker into the hexagonal brass and copper container which held the fire irons. Her delicate face was as unreadable as a doll's. The door opened and the Headmaster thundered into the room, his head low between his shoulders.

'Vera, I'm afraid I have to go down to town with these – with these gentlemen.'

Thornhill and Kirby appeared behind him in the doorway. Jill felt a rush of relief surging through her.

Spots of pink flowered in Vera's cheeks. 'But why?'

'God knows.' Bernard swung his head from side to side. His hot little eyes glared at Thornhill. Then he saw Jill; she had been half-concealed by the back of the wing armchair she was sitting in. 'Miss Francis. I'm so sorry—'

Jill stood up, saying to the room at large, 'I promised I'd give Larry a lift down to Lydmouth. Perhaps I should wait downstairs.'

'Thank you, Miss Francis.'

Thornhill glanced at her and then at Vera. He moved into the room and stood beside the sofa, his hand resting on the table behind it. His attention was now focused on the Sandleighs. Jill was aware that Vera, still huddled in her armchair, was staring up at her with large, cold eyes. She bent down and made an unnecessarily time-consuming performance of picking up her handbag. Richard Thornhill was looking at her. She was not sure why.

'It's quite ridiculous,' Bernard went on, speaking to Vera. 'I thought the police concentrated on finding evidence, motives and so on.' He swung back to Thornhill, towering over the younger man, his very size making him a figure of menace. 'Is there really any need to waste my time and—'

'Bernard, you're in the way,' Vera interrupted. 'Miss Francis is trying to reach the door.'

'It's not ridiculous,' Jill said to Thornhill. She wanted very badly to reach out and touch his hand. 'I wish it was but it's not.' A sob burst out of her throat. She bit it back, furious with herself. 'I found a yellow tobacco pouch in the Hanging Tree this afternoon.' She put her hand on the back of the armchair to steady herself. 'There were two letters inside.'

For a moment no one moved. Only five pairs of eyes were active. From the fireplace came a soft, scraping sound as a lump of coal slipped an inch deeper into the embers.

'The pouch?' Thornhill said to Jill. 'The letters? Where are they?'

'Mrs Sandleigh put the letters on the fire.'

Thornhill glanced at the glowing coals in the grate. Vera let out her breath, half hiss, half soft whistle, and her lips fluttered. To Jill, the nearest person to Vera, the sound might have stood for three words: *You cruel bitch.*

Thornhill hitched up his trousers and knelt on the hearthrug. Jill knew that there was nothing left for him to find. The flames had transformed the letters to grey, meaningless flakes and then Vera had pounded the flakes to ashy dust. Still on his knees, he looked round at Jill.

'Where's the pouch?'

'I think Mrs Sandleigh is sitting on it.'

'Mrs Sandleigh? Is this true?'

Vera said nothing. She stared at her small hands, folded on her lap.

Bernard coughed. 'Listen, Inspector, I—'

Thornhill said to Vera, 'I must ask you to stand up.'

She gathered up her knitting and got to her feet. Once again a ball of wool escaped; it fell to the floor and rolled across the hearthrug, leaving a squiggle of grey behind it. This time no one picked it up.

There was nothing in the armchair.

Sandleigh snorted. 'No doubt it's flown up the chimney. Quite absurd.'

Thornhill lifted up the seat cushion. The pouch was jammed against the arm; Vera had pushed it down between the side of the chair and the cushion. Thornhill took out the pouch and dropped the cushion back. He turned to face the room. Slowly he unrolled the oilskin. He sniffed the inside. Jill thought that she, too, could smell the ghostly aroma of Paxford's home-cured, home-grown tobacco.

Bernard cleared his throat in a long rumble. 'This really has gone far enough.' His voice quavered, and before he went on he cleared his throat again. 'I want to telephone my solicitor. Immediately.'

'By all means, sir.' There was a rare hint of Thornhill's East Anglian background in his voice. 'You may use the telephone on the desk. I'd like a word with Miss Francis. Sergeant Kirby will stay here with you and Mrs Sandleigh. I'd rather you didn't leave the room. We shan't be a moment.'

Vera gave a dry sob, and sank back into her chair. Bernard went to her. As Jill was leaving the room, she looked back and saw that he was kneeling by her chair, holding her tiny hands in his enormous ones.

Thornhill followed Jill onto the landing. He glanced up at the staircase, at the floors in the gloom above them.

'We'd better go outside. You'll need your coat.'

She shook her head. She didn't need her coat. At times like this, you didn't bother about coats.

She led the way down the stairs, wondering who might be listening: children, servants, members of the teaching staff. In the dark, narrow hall, P.C. Porter was standing with his back to a large mirror and his helmet under his arm. Jill wondered if he had been admiring his reflection until he had heard the door opening above; even P.C. Porter might be vain.

It was dark outside, and cold, but Jill barely noticed. Thornhill suggested they sit in the police car. He held the door open for her. Jill stared ahead at the windscreen.

'How did you find the letters?' Thornhill asked.

She told him quickly about Kathleen Rockfield's remark, and her own exploration of the Hanging Tree, and her discovery of the pouch. To her surprise he did not reprove her for her failure to pass on Kathleen's information to the police. This had the perverse effect of throwing her on the defensive.

'I tried to bring the letters to you straight away, but—'

'I know. I'm sorry about that. I should have allowed for Porter to be literal-minded.' He hesitated. 'Did you read the letters?'

'I'm afraid I did.'

'In the circumstances it's just as well. What was in them?'

'One of them was from Larry Jordan to Mrs Sandleigh.' It was

Jill's turn to hesitate. It is one thing to accept the principle that members of the public should help the police; it is quite another to put it so cruelly in practice. 'The letter had been written just before Christmas. It made it clear that they had once had an affair – before she met her husband – and that Dorothy is really Jordan's daughter.'

'And the other letter?'

'Part of a draft reply from Mrs Sandleigh. Jordan wanted to come and see them, and to take an interest in Dorothy. But Mrs Sandleigh wanted nothing more to do with him.'

'Nevertheless he came.'

'Yes. It's a possible motive, isn't it?'

He nodded, a grey blur against the shiny black glass of the window.

Jill described what she could remember of the letters' contents. She told him how she thought Carrick might have stumbled on them when he was poking about in the Sandleighs' drawing room; how Vera's draft was crumpled, as though it had been discarded, perhaps left in a wastepaper basket, a windfall for a nosy visitor.

'Carrick's rooms had been searched before we got there on Thursday morning,' Thornhill said. 'Before the news of his death had reached the school.'

The darkness had made them both anonymous. It was possible to say things that would not have been said in the light. Jill remembered another occasion when she and Thornhill had talked in the darkness, when he had used her Christian name and then apologised.

'You mean whoever searched his rooms was almost certainly the killer?'

'Or an accessory.'

'He might have been blackmailing someone else,' Jill suggested. 'Something that hasn't come to light.'

'It's possible.' Thornhill paused. 'But between ourselves, there's other evidence. What happened after Porter said you couldn't see me?'

'Dorothy was in the hall – she thought I'd come to collect Larry Jordan and take him down to the Bull. She took me upstairs, where her mother was. And when I went into the drawing room, I tripped – so stupid.' She felt herself blushing. She explained what Vera had done to the letters. 'She swore they had nothing to do with the murder.'

'I think we should go back inside now.'

'This other evidence. Does it point towards Bernard Sandleigh?'

'I can't tell you that.' He opened the car door and turned back to her, lowering his voice: 'But Carrick was hit on the head and then strangled. It's not the sort of thing a weakling does.'

'Hit on the head? I didn't know that. What with?'

'It may have been a spanner.' He climbed out of the car, turned back and went on in a soft, urgent voice, as if trying to convince himself as much as her: 'Moving corpses about is more difficult again, even if they are as light as Carrick was. Harder work than the actual killing. Think about it. To string someone up on the Hanging Tree, you'd need a good deal of physical strength.'

Jill opened the car door. *No, no, no,* she thought.

6

Richard Thornhill felt like the rope in a tug of war: under great strain at both ends; at any moment liable to go one way or another; and, if the pressure increased, in danger of snapping in two.

Jill Francis passed very close to him in the doorway between the porch and the Headmaster's House. He would have known she was near him even with his eyes blindfolded. He knew the eau de Cologne she used and the way it mingled with the faint but far more troubling smells of her body. He could not begin to understand why he had been so foolish: to talk so frankly about a murder investigation to a journalist – to a journalist who had shown in the past that the rules she followed were very different from his.

Balanced against this was another excitement, that of the hunter. He knew on a level that was only marginally rational that the case had cracked wide open. The excitement he felt was almost sexual in its intensity. As they went into the dimly lit hall, he glanced at Jill Francis's dark head and realised with uncomfortable clarity that the two excitements were so similar to each other that they were almost identical.

P.C. Porter was still standing under the big mirror with the helmet under his arm. As they came in, he snapped to attention. Thornhill was unable to resist looking at Jill's face. *How could I be so stupid?* She gave him the ghost of a smile.

There was sudden movement on the landing above them. 'I say!' Jordan's neat head appeared above the banisters. The landing light behind him conferred a wholly undeserved halo on him. 'Anyone there? I don't suppose someone could help me with my bags?'

'The car's open,' Jill called up. 'Would you like to put them in?'

'Surely there's someone that can help?'

'Could I have a word, sir?' Thornhill said.

'Hello, Inspector. I suppose so. Where?'

'Down here will do.'

Jordan clattered down the stairs, carrying two of his monogrammed suitcases. 'This won't take long, will it?'

'I'll go and say goodbye to Dorothy,' Jill said, glancing at Thornhill. 'Larry, which is her room?'

Why did she have to call him Larry?

'Second-floor landing. First on the left.'

Jordan dropped his bags at the foot of the stairs. Thornhill beckoned him over to the door of the annexe, as far away as possible from the stolid bulk of P.C. Porter.

'I don't want to cause unnecessary embarrassment, sir.'

'Glad to hear it, Inspector.'

What if she actually cares for him?

'It has been alleged that you and Mrs Sandleigh had an affair before she was married. I wonder if you'd care to comment.'

'It's an absolute bloody slander. Who told you?'

'It was also alleged that Dorothy Sandleigh is in fact your daughter.'

Jordan turned away so Thornhill could not see his face. He took his time over lighting a cigarette. 'Look, Inspector. Someone in my position inevitably attracts a lot of scurrilous rumours. This is just another example of it.'

'I think it may be rather more than that, sir.'

'Rubbish.'

'I understand that Mrs Sandleigh's mother was your godmother. She lived in a village called Roth – in Middlesex, on the outskirts of London. If there is any substance to this story, I don't think it would be too difficult for us to come up with supporting evidence.' Thornhill left a pause. 'But that would inevitably involve rather a lot of publicity.'

Jordan blew smoke into the air. 'If I could answer your question, and I stress *if*, could you guarantee no publicity?'

'No, sir. You know I couldn't do that. But I could guarantee that I would do my best to minimise the risk of it coming out.'

Jordan smoked a quarter of his cigarette in silence. Ash floated down to the parquet floor.

'For God's sake,' he said at last. 'All right, yes, we did have a fling. We were young, and very much in love. Can you understand that?'

Thornhill said nothing, knowing that silence was the best reply. It was one of the penalties of being a professional actor, he supposed, that everything you said in real life inevitably tended to sound false.

'And yes – Dorothy is my daughter,' Jordan whispered. 'But can't we prevent this coming out? Think of the effect it would have on Bernard and Vera. On Dorothy. My God, she's only a child. They'd all be ruined.' He flicked more ash from his cigarette. 'And to be perfectly frank it wouldn't do me much good, either.' He raised his head. 'Not that that matters a jot, of course.'

'So you can confirm the allegation?'

'Well, yes – between you, me and the doorpost. But—'

'Where are you going now?'

'Back to the Bull for a night or two.'

'We may need to be in touch with you later, sir. I'd be grateful if you didn't leave Lydmouth without telling us where you're going.'

'What is this? We're talking about something which happened years ago. I don't see how it can have any bearing on what's happening now.'

Thornhill nodded politely and moved away, knowing that Jordan was staring after him. He went briskly up the stairs and into the drawing room.

Bernard and Vera Sandleigh were now sitting side by side on the sofa, holding hands. They looked more like father and daughter than husband and wife: was that how they made their marriage work? They stared mutely up at him. All the bluster, all the fight, all the pride, had drained away. All that was left were two defeated people, and Thornhill hated what he was going to have to do to them.

'I'm afraid I shall have to ask you to accompany me down to police headquarters.'

Bernard raised his great head. 'Shipston will meet us there. Are you arresting us?'

'I want to ask you some further questions, sir.'

'What about the children?' asked Vera. 'We can't just leave them.'

For a moment Thornhill was reminded of Edith, of her fierce determination to protect her children and to do what was best for them at all costs. 'Someone must come and stay with them for the time being, Mrs Sandleigh. Who would you like us to contact? Mrs Rockfield, perhaps? Or Mrs Hirdle?'

Vera stared up at him. Her eyes filled with tears. Her mouth opened, an ugly pink gash in the pale face. Her hair hung wispily around her head. In her hands she twisted her handkerchief. It was as if she were dissolving before Thornhill's very eyes.

'Leave Bernard behind,' she said. 'He had nothing to do with it, I swear.' Her voice rose and rose. 'You can have a full confession. It was me, don't you understand? It was me, all me.'

7

Jill tapped on the door and waited. She heard scuffling and the creak of bedsprings in the room beyond. A moment later the door opened.

Dorothy was breathing heavily and the lids of her eyes were red and swollen. Her hair was a tangle of pale spikes, as if she had been running damp fingers through it over and over again; she looked like a bedraggled hedgehog.

'May I come in?' Jill asked.

Dorothy nodded and held open the door. Jill went inside. It was a large, bare room, in sharp contrast with the comfortably furnished drawing room. The wind had risen. The curtains flapped like swaying skirts and the two halves of the sash window rattled in their frame. It was very cold.

There were few signs of impending adulthood. A teddy bear squatted on the pillow of the bed. Jill noticed the spines of books by Enid Blyton and Richmal Crompton among the brightly coloured dust jackets on the bookshelves.

Dorothy closed the door and followed Jill into the middle of the room. She looked so young and vulnerable that Jill wanted to hug her. She wore nothing but a thin cardigan over her dress and there were goose pimples on her bare skin. She was shivering.

'What's happening?' she burst out. 'What are the policemen doing down there? I heard shouting.'

'They are talking to your parents in the drawing room.'

'But why?'

'May I sit down?'

Without waiting for an answer, Jill sat at one end of the bed and patted the mattress beside her as an invitation to Dorothy to join her.

'I wish the police would go.' Still standing, Dorothy stared at the empty fireplace. 'They've been here for ages.'

'I think that when they go they may take your parents with them.'

'What do you mean?'

Jill reached up and took Dorothy's hand, which lay cold and lifeless in hers. 'I'm afraid that they think that your mother and father were concerned with the killing of Mr Carrick.'

'They weren't,' Dorothy burst out. 'It's not fair. It's all a terrible mistake.'

'I know they weren't.'

'What?'

'Sit down, Dorothy.'

Frowning, the girl allowed Jill to draw her towards the bed. As she sat down, she whispered, '*What do you mean?*'

'I know your parents had nothing to do with the actual killing of Mervyn Carrick.'

Neither of them said anything for a long time. The window trembled noisily behind the curtains. The wind sighed in the cold chimney. Dorothy's fingers tightened on Jill's hand.

'What will happen to them?'

'Now? Mr Thornhill will probably ask them to come down to Lydmouth for more questions. And if he thinks he has enough evidence, he may arrest them this evening.'

'And they'll go to court?'

'Eventually.' Jill hesitated. 'But Mr Thornhill won't arrest your parents unless he feels there's a strong case against them.'

'What will happen?'

'If they're found guilty? That depends on the court. One or both of them might be hanged.'

Dorothy whispered, 'No.'

295

'Cases involving a husband and wife are always hard. It's very difficult to find out whether one is guiltier than the other. You can't rely on what they—'

'*Hanging*,' the girl interrupted, having apparently failed to hear the rest of Jill's reply. 'They might be hanged?'

Jill chose her words with care. 'It's the penalty for murder – for an adult.'

'But they didn't do it. They're innocent. They can't be hanged for something they didn't do.'

'I'm afraid it happens. Not often, but it has done. And it may do in this case, Dorothy, unless you tell the truth.'

The girl raised her head. Light from the single overhead bulb glinted on her fair hair. Long fair hair, like a strand found in the schoolboy's cap. She squeezed Jill's hand. 'How did you know? How could you know?'

'It was something you said yesterday that gave it away. When we were at the hotel – do you remember, we went to the lavatory together? I didn't notice it at the time. In fact I only realised what it meant a few minutes ago. You said that you'd had nightmares about Mervyn Carrick dying. *It must be frightful to die like that*, that's what you said.'

Dorothy took a handkerchief from the pocket of her cardigan and blew her nose. She glanced at Jill and then began to chew the corner of her handkerchief, quite unconscious of what she was doing.

'You knew it was dark when he died.'

'But it was night time – of course it was dark.'

'And you knew he was hit on the head, as well as strangled,' Jill went on. 'Only the police knew that. The police and the killer.'

'But it was dark, dark, dark.' The hysteria was building up. 'I *thought* it was. That's all I meant—'

'Where was it dark?'

'In the garage. And I just imagined he'd banged his head when – when he fell—'

'But you *knew* it was dark, you *knew* it happened in the garage, you *knew* he had a bang on the head.' Jill reached out and took Dorothy's other hand in hers. *Only a child.* 'Don't try to lie. It'll just make things worse.'

There was fear in the girl's face. There are few things as terrible as a child's fear when you know that the fear is entirely justified.

'What will happen? What will happen to us all?'

'It depends. If you tell the truth to the police, you'll—'

'They'll hang me.' Dorothy's hands bucked and twisted like fish on dry land. 'The judge will put on his black cap and—'

'Don't be so foolish,' Jill said, consciously aping the firm voice of a schoolmistress remembered from childhood. 'They will do nothing of the kind. We don't hang children in this country, thank God.' If she had her way, no one would be hanged at all. 'If the court decides you're guilty, you'll probably go to a sort of special prison school for children for a few years. When you're grown up, and if they think you won't hurt anybody else, I expect they'll let you out.' The parents were another matter Jill thought. Almost certainly both of them were accessories after the fact, and they would pay the price for that.

'I heard them talking,' Dorothy said hurriedly. 'Mummy and Mr Carrick. He was saying horrible things about her, and about Daddy, and about me.' Her voice wavered. 'I don't want my father to be Larry Jordan. I've got a father and I *hate* Uncle Larry.'

Jill tightened her grip on the girl's hands. 'Calm down.'

The words tumbled out of the girl. Carrick had visited her mother on Wednesday afternoon, and Dorothy had heard enough of their conversation to realise what was going on.

'It was my fault,' Dorothy kept saying. Once she added, 'If I hadn't been born, this wouldn't have happened. It's all my fault.' The logic might be warped, but to a child it made a bitter sense.

'But how did you come to meet him in the garage?'

'It was my idea. I thought perhaps if I saw him, if I made

him see how upset he was making everyone, if I made him *understand . . .*'

Late that evening, after the meeting of the Classical Society, Dorothy had phoned Burton's House. She knew from what her parents had said that at night the phone line was now switched through to Carrick, to avoid the risk of disturbing Mrs Burton. When he answered, she said that she wanted to speak to him about her parents. Dorothy had suggested that they meet in the garage. It was private, and it was roughly halfway between Burton's and the Headmaster's House. She slipped downstairs and took Peter's school cap and coat from the pegs in the hall.

'Why?' Jill asked.

'Because it was cold.'

'I mean, why not your own coat and hat?'

Dorothy fiddled with her sodden handkerchief. 'I thought, if I was seen by someone, I could run off and they'd think it was a boy.'

She had reached the garage first. She did not turn on the light for fear of someone coming to investigate. When Carrick came, he had been in a good mood, smiling and joking. He listened to what she had to say. Then he laughed at her.

'He wouldn't stop. He just kept laughing at me, and then he started touching me. *Come on, you laugh, too*, he said. *I'm going to tickle you till you start laughing*. I tried to get away, but he wouldn't let me. We were standing by this sort of table thing under the window. He was pushing me up against it. And I put my hands out and I felt a spanner or something. So I picked it up and hit him. And he fell back against the side of the car and sort of slithered down and rolled onto his face.'

Dorothy's teeth were chattering as if she had a fever. Jill picked up the top of the eiderdown and draped it over the girl's shoulders. She had to do this with one hand, because Dorothy did not want to let go of her.

'I thought he was dead. But he wasn't. He was breathing. And I thought when he woke up, he'd tell the police I'd hit him, and it would all be even worse than before. So I thought it would be better for everyone if he didn't wake up so – so . . .'

'How did you do it?' Jill asked briskly, as though asking nothing more important than how a dish was cooked.

'I remembered what we'd learnt at school in First Aid. We did tourniquets last week. He – he was wearing a soft collar, so I just pushed it up and put the spanner through the gap between the tie and the collar. Then I twisted the spanner round and round. His glasses fell off and I trod on them. And he jerked about a bit and then he stopped – he stopped – stopped moving. It didn't take long. I don't think it can have hurt him much.'

'And then you told your parents?'

'Oh no. I didn't want to do that. I wanted to save them any trouble. That was the whole point of it. At first I thought I'd pull Mr Carrick outside and leave him just outside the garage. And everyone would think he'd disturbed a tramp or something and the tramp had killed him. But he was too heavy to move so I had to leave him where he was. I hoped that would be all right – that people would think the tramp had found the spare key of the garage or Paxford had forgotten to lock up. No, I wasn't going to tell my parents at all. The trouble was, they were up in my bedroom. My mother had just found out I wasn't there.' Dorothy stared at Jill. 'I had to tell them. What else could I do?'

There was little more to say. Dorothy did not know what had happened next – there had been no need for her to know. Vera had given Dorothy a sleeping pill and put her to bed. And while she slept, her parents had done their best to minimise the damage caused by what she had done.

Jill thought of Vera's words: *I was brought up to believe that one must put the family first.*

The Sandleighs must have bundled Carrick into the car and driven him to the Hanging Tree in order to get him away from the school, in order to make murder look like suicide, and in order to tilt the thrust of the coming investigation towards Moat Farm and Carrick's family and away from the school.

'By the way, do you know what happened to the spanner?'

'Do you want it? It's downstairs.' Dorothy sounded as though she were talking in her sleep. 'I brought it home. I didn't know what to do with it. It's in the umbrella stand in the hall.'

8

Thornhill wanted to speak to her before they left the school but could not find an opportunity or invent a plausible excuse. He needed to talk to her alone. In any case, there were too many other things to do.

He was aware, however, that she was still on the premises. Larry Jordan had mislaid a piece of luggage and would not leave without it, so nor could Jill. Thornhill suspected that Jordan did not yet know what had happened to the Sandleighs. Jordan was not a stupid man but, as with so many self-centred people, egoism obscured his view as effectively as a pair of blinkers.

Thornhill had summoned reinforcements in the shape of an extra police car and three scene-of-the-crime officers. These men would remain at the school, making a minute survey of the Sandleighs' garage and the Sandleighs' car. He had told Kirby to drive down to Lydmouth with the Headmaster. He himself would ride in the second car with Vera Sandleigh and Dorothy.

He wished it were not necessary to talk to the Sandleighs or even to look at them. Stripped of both their dignity and their secrets, both of them had wept, Vera naturally and easily, Bernard in awkward, ugly bewilderment. The fault was theirs and yet, as so often, the guilt had rubbed off to some extent on everyone.

After the first car, with Kirby and Sandleigh in the back, moved slowly down the drive, Thornhill glanced up at the main school building. Boys were watching from uncurtained windows, their faces pressed eagerly against the glass, many of them with their mouths open. Thornhill thought of crowds at public executions, of the crowds that must have gathered round the Hanging Tree.

'Wait,' he told his driver. 'I shan't be a moment.'

He went back into the hall of the Headmaster's House. Jill was sitting on an oak chair near the foot of the stairs, smoking a cigarette. To his relief she was alone. She looked up at him as he approached but did not speak.

He had no idea what to say to her, what excuse to give. Awkward as an adolescent, he blurted out, 'Not gone yet?'

'I'll give him three minutes more, then I'm leaving without him.'

'We need to talk. You and I.'

'Yes.'

His eyes met hers and he added, stumbling over the words, 'About the case, I mean. I need to ask you about what exactly Dorothy told you.'

'Of course.'

'The trouble is, I'm not sure how long I'll be.' He gestured behind him, through the door and the porch to the parked car in the drive. 'All that may take time.'

'It doesn't matter. If you like you could drop in at Church Cottage afterwards. I'll be in all evening.' She turned away to tap her cigarette in an ashtray, and he could no longer see her face. 'But you'll want to get home, I imagine. If you prefer, we could meet tomorrow morning.'

'No, this evening would be quite convenient for me – if you're sure it's all right for you.'

'But won't your wife—'

'She and the children are away.'

Still she did not look at him. 'Very well, then. I'll expect you when I see you.'

9

An investigation did not end with an arrest. If only it did. There were questions to be asked, reports to write, evidence to gather, courts to attend. In a sense the slow process of retribution had only just begun. Yet after the arrest, Brian Kirby found, the excitement was over.

By the time he and Thornhill had finished for the evening it was after half-past ten. He knew he would not sleep that night: too much adrenaline in the bloodstream. It was too late to go out for a drink – all the pubs would be shut. Even those with elastic licensing hours tended to close early on Sunday nights. He did not want to go home to his lodgings. He could do nothing there except stare at the wallpaper.

'I'll cut along now,' Thornhill said. 'You might as well push off yourself.'

'I'll stay for a while. Might as well get some of the paperwork out of the way.'

'As you like.' Thornhill paused at the door of the CID office. 'I'll be at home if you need me. Oh, I might drop in at Church Cottage on my way back. There's a few points to clear up with Miss Francis.'

'Yes, sir. Goodnight.'

'Goodnight, Brian.'

The door closed behind Thornhill and Kirby was alone in the long room. Because the CID office was so busy and noisy by day, its emptiness by night had a ghostly quality. *Going to Church Cottage, eh?*

Kirby pushed aside the report he had been writing and felt for his keyring. He unlocked the drawer of his desk and took out a bottle of whisky and a glass. Technically he was off duty. And in any case, there was no one to see him. He poured himself a generous measure, drank it quickly, and poured himself another. He sat back in his chair and watched, a passive spectator, as the events of the day moved restlessly round and round his mind.

He knew this was a stage that he needed to get through: he needed to relive what had happened in order to exorcise it. *Poor bloody kid. Poor bloody parents.*

Time passed. The clock on the wall ticked. The level of whisky in the bottle sank lower. After a while he laid his arms on his desk and his head on his arms. He tried closing his eyes but it didn't work. The images were still there. Suddenly the phone rang, the bell astonishingly loud in the empty room. He picked it up. 'Kirby.'

'Brian, it's Jim.' Jim Fowles was on the graveyard shift tonight. 'Are you sitting comfortably, lad? We've got another body. Suicide.'

'Bloody hell. I don't want to know. I'm off duty.'

'It's the Eyetie up at Moat Farm. Remember? The one who did a bunk, who we had in for questioning. I've got Mrs Carrick down here. Yes *here*. She drove down from Ashbridge.'

'Oh God.' Kirby pushed the cork into the neck of the whisky bottle. 'Holy Mother of.'

'In one hell of a state. Says she needs to talk to you or Mr Thornhill.'

'All right. I'll be down.'

Kirby slammed the receiver on its rest, drained the remainder of the whisky in his glass and locked up both bottle and glass in the drawer. He went out of the door and along the corridor, noticing that his walk had developed a slight stagger. He knew his breath must stink of spirits. *What the hell? Who's there to notice?* Supporting himself carefully on the banister, he walked down to the ground floor. Dilys Carrick was sitting in the reception area. She was crying silently into a handkerchief.

'Ring Swayne up at Ashbridge,' Kirby muttered to Fowles. 'Tell him to check the story. You better warn Bayswater too. Not just about the body – Mrs C's one of his patients.'

'And Mr Thornhill?'

'I'll deal with that. I want to talk to Mrs Carrick first.'

Kirby went over to her. She looked up at him but said nothing.

303

He took her to the nearest interview room, sat her down and offered her a cigarette.

'Now tell me what's happened, Mrs Carrick. In your own time.'

She was shaking uncontrollably. The cigarette fell from her fingers. Kirby picked it up, lit it and handed it to her.

'It's Bert. I found him.'

'Were you looking for him?'

She nodded. 'He wasn't there for milking this evening. And he didn't come in for tea or supper. Les was furious at first but then he fell asleep. Drunken pig . . . So at least I could go to Bert's room. But he wasn't there. Just *this*.'

She took a sheet of paper, grubby and folded, from the pocket of her coat, and put it on the table. Kirby unfolded it. It looked as if it had been torn from an exercise book. The message was written in pencil in a careful continental hand.

Dear Mr and Mrs Carrick,
  It is best I leave you now. With good wishes to all of your family for the future.
                                    Umberto Nerini.

'And what happened then?'

She stared at Kirby, her face amazed, as though he had said something stupid. 'I knew he'd killed himself, of course.'

'Why? It only says he's leaving.'

'All his things were still there. Anyway, he had nowhere to go.' A sob tore its way out of her again. 'He wanted me to come away with him. Me and the baby. And I'd said no. I was staying with Les and the farm. I had to think of the baby, didn't I? We have to live. Need to eat, don't we, have a roof over our heads. Bert had nothing. Less than nothing.'

'How did Mr Nerini take it, then? When you said you wouldn't go away with him?'

'Well, he was upset.'

'Let me get this right. You're saying that Nerini was the baby's father?'

'Of course he was. Who else?'

'Does Mr Carrick know?'

Dilys shook her head so violently that her headscarf came loose. 'And he mustn't. Ever. He thinks it's Mervyn's. And Mervyn's bad enough but at least he's a Carrick. Bloody Carricks.' Her face puckered, the skin red and shiny. 'He shouldn't have killed himself. I can't – I wish – Oh God—'

'Where? And how?' asked Kirby, already knowing the answer.

'At the Hanging Tree. I found him there. Cold as ice. Still there, look. I want him brought down. I want him to have a proper burial.'

'He will have.'

'Don't you understand?' She hammered her clenched fists against the table, making the ashtray jump. 'It's my fault. I killed him. He did it for love of me.'

Kirby allowed her to talk, until she had told him the same story all over again.

'I had to come here. Didn't want to see Fred Swayne. That bastard. He always hated Bert.'

When she was calmer, Kirby took her back to Sergeant Fowles and arranged for him to summon Ma Lincoln, the motherly wife of a recently retired police constable whom they called on in cases like this.

His drunkenness seemed to have left him. He felt clear-headed if a little unreal. He set the preliminaries of the investigation in motion and went upstairs to the CID office to telephone Thornhill.

He dialled the Victoria Road number and let it ring at the other end. There was no answer and he hung up. He glanced at his watch. It was a quarter to midnight. He picked up the telephone again, intending to ask Directory Enquiries for the number of the newly installed line at Church Cottage. Then he dropped the handset on its rest.

There was no hurry, he told himself. Thornhill was off duty. No reason why Kirby should know where he was.

10

Jill carried the coffee, with whisky, a soda siphon and glasses alongside it on the tray, into the hall. Through the open door she glimpsed Richard Thornhill, still sitting beside the fire. For an instant she saw him without his defences: pale, exhausted and sad.

The tray rattled. He looked up, saw her approaching and scrambled up to help her with the tray. She poured him coffee and asked him to pour himself a drink.

Alice miaowed outside the sitting-room door until Jill let her in. Always willing to exploit the kindness of strangers, she jumped onto Thornhill's lap and graciously allowed him to stroke her. She had been calmer since her excursion to the churchyard, and seemed even more self-satisfied than usual.

Jill knelt on the hearthrug, squeezing her coffee cup between her hands. 'Do the Sandleighs realise what's going to happen?'

'Not really. They're still in a state of shock. Maybe that's as well. But it'll be a difficult case for everyone. I mean, *we* know the girl did it. *She* knows it, and so do her parents. But proving it in court's another matter. How will they divide up the responsibility? All three of them were involved. It's a legal nightmare.'

Jill nodded. 'But it's their nightmare, I suppose. Not ours.'

'No. You're right.' He drank his coffee and stared at the fire. 'Ah – what about Jordan, by the way? Did he ever reach the Bull?'

'Yes.' She looked directly at him. 'He made a pass at me in the car. And I slapped his face. Hard. In some ways he's worse than Paxford.'

'He's richer than Paxford. And he doesn't look like a freak.'

'He's got a choice. Paxford hasn't, not really. What will happen to him?'

'Paxford? Not much more than a fine, I should imagine. But that's the least of his problems. He's got nowhere to live and no income.'

'I'll talk to Lady Ruispidge if you like,' Jill offered. 'They might be able to find him something on Home Farm.'

'Would they help?'

'I think so. At least the Ruispidges have been brought up to believe that you don't have privilege without responsibility. It's one of the advantages of the type.'

He nodded. For a moment they sat in silence. *I wish*, Jill thought. *I wish I could stop him looking so sad.*

She said, in too bright a voice, 'And where are Edith and the children? You don't mind if I call her Edith, do you? And – and you must really call me Jill. You nearly did once before, do you remember?' She was running on, she knew, too far and too fast. 'And perhaps I might call you Richard. It seems foolish to be so formal, these days.'

He looked down at her. 'Yes. I'd like that.'

Oh God, Jill thought, *I do wish this wasn't happening. Or not like this.*

'Edith and the children are in Wiltshire,' he said. 'I don't know whether she told you, but her mother has been very ill. Edith phoned this evening to say that she's died.'

'I'm so sorry. I had no idea—'

'There's no need to be sorry – for anyone's sake, really. She was in a great deal of pain, I understand. And Edith and her sister probably feel relieved as much as anything. It sounds callous, I know, but it's not.'

Jill nodded. 'Weren't you going to ask me something? About the Sandleighs, or something?'

'Well, yes – but I suppose there's no hurry. I'd almost forgotten, in fact.' He smiled at her. 'This is so much nicer than going back to a cold, empty house.'

'Would you like some more coffee?'

'Please.'

Simultaneously they stretched out their hands towards the coffee cup on the tray. They missed the cup and touched each other. Jill watched, astonished, as her fingers twined round Richard Thornhill's. They seemed to have a life of their own.

She felt the pressure as his fingers squeezed hers and felt herself return the pressure with an answering squeeze. She looked up at his face and saw that he was staring at her.

'Jill?'

'Yes, Richard.'

BIRTHS

CARRICK – On August 1st, to Leslie and Dilys Carrick of Moat Farm, Ashbridge, a son, Robert Leslie.

The Lydmouth Gazette, 4th August

F
TAY   Taylor, Andrew

           The lover of the
           grave